BURNING BRIGHT

BURNING BRIGHT

NICK PETRIE

G. P. PUTNAM'S SONS | NEW YORK

PUTNAM

G. P. PUTNAM'S SONS
Publishers Since 1838
An imprint of Penguin Random House LLC
375 Hudson Street
New York, New York 10014

Copyright © 2017 by Nicholas Petrie
Penguin supports copyright. Copyright fuels creativity,
encourages diverse voices, promotes free speech, and creates
a vibrant culture. Thank you for buying an authorized edition
of this book and for complying with copyright laws by not
reproducing, scanning, or distributing any part of it in any form
without permission. You are supporting writers and allowing
Penguin to continue to publish books for every reader.

Library of Congress Cataloging-in-Publication Data

Names: Petrie, Nick, author
Title: Burning bright / Nick Petrie.
Description: New York : G. P. Putnam's Sons, [2017]
Identifiers: LCCN 2016011425 | ISBN 9780399174575 (hardcover) |
ISBN 9780698194144 (epub)
Subjects: LCSH: Veterans—Fiction. | Women journalists—Fiction. |
GSAFD: Suspense fiction. | Mystery fiction.
Classification: LCC PS3616.E86645 B87 2017 | DDC 813/.6—dc23
LC record available at https://lccn.loc.gov/2016011425
p.   cm.

Printed in the United States of America
10 9 8 7 6 5 4 3 2 1

BOOK DESIGN BY MEIGHAN CAVANAUGH

For Margret and Duncan,
my heroes and role models

In what distant deeps or skies
Burnt the fire of thine eyes?
On what wings dare he aspire?
What the hand, dare seize the fire?

. . .

Tyger Tyger, burning bright,
In the forests of the night;
What immortal hand or eye,
Dare frame thy fearful symmetry?

—William Blake

PROLOGUE

Don't get in the car.

June Cassidy had heard this many times. From her mom, from her self-defense instructors, from her friends, the same thing, over and over.

No matter what, don't get in the car.

Because then they have you.

It was good advice, she thought.

But it did her no good now that they'd gotten her in the fucking car.

She had her back against the locked door of a big SUV, plastic handcuffs on her wrists, and a witless slab of pseudogovernment beef leering at her from the next seat over.

Her options were limited.

JUNE WAS HAVING a particularly bad week in a challenging few years.

Her newspaper got bought out, just like practically every other big-city paper, and the new owners loaded it up with debt to pay themselves for their investment. When the classifieds plummeted like a rock—

thanks, Craig, for your free fucking List—the paper began to lay off reporters, especially investigative reporters, who might take weeks or months to research a story for publication. June was young, cheap labor, and she was good at her job, so she lasted longer than most. But the economics were brutal and getting more unforgiving by the minute.

Then the ax finally fell and June was just another freelancer with a degree in journalism. In this age of technology, it was almost as useful as a degree in Klingon, or, God forbid, English.

For a woman on her own and pushing thirty, freelancing was no substitute for an actual job.

Somehow, after a year of scrounging for scraps and trying to learn how to drive traffic to her blog, she'd gotten invited to join Public Investigations, a nonprofit group of investigative journalists funded by a Kickstarter-like model, dedicated to doing the kind of work that many papers could no longer afford to pay for.

Public Investigations did awesome work. Their financial reporters broke the in-depth story about the attempted bank bombing in Milwaukee and the flash-crash that went with it. But the budget was small and June was still essentially a freelancer with editorial backup, which was not the same thing as health insurance and a byline in the *Chicago Tribune*.

Still, she was making real progress, splitting time between her garage apartment in Seattle and her mom's little house in Palo Alto, which gave her an inexpensive platform to cover the West Coast. Her specialty was issues of privacy in the electronic age. After Manning and Snowden and the NSA revelations, privacy seemed permanently in the headlines, and her professional life was finally taking off again.

Then her mom, a yoga fanatic and vegetarian who also swam a half mile every day, was killed by a hit-and-run driver and died. A week ago today.

June's mother, Hazel Cassidy, tenured professor at Stanford University, MacArthur "Genius" Grant winner, and renowned pain in the ass, killed by a plumber's truck at sixty.

Like a lot of women, June had a complicated relationship with her mother. June's career choices, her boyfriends, her hair—all were candidates for improvement, although her mother never made a direct assault.

Hazel's trademark was a certain kind of passive-aggressive backhanded compliment. "That outfit wouldn't work on me, but it looks very nice on you." When June's investigative series on data breaches in medical technology was nominated for the Pulitzer, Hazel threw her daughter a fabulous party, but also invited June's ex-boyfriend, because June's current flame didn't meet Hazel's high standards.

The worst of it, of course, was that she was usually right. She was right about the outfit, and she was right about the fucking boyfriend, too. About all the boyfriends, actually. June tried, sometimes successfully, not to be so stubborn that she couldn't recognize how well her mother knew her, and how much she cared.

It was easier now that her mother was dead.

What June wouldn't give for another snarky comment about her goddamn hair.

Her mom had been gone a week, and it already felt like forever.

JUNE HAD SPENT the first few days planning and surviving the memorial service, and the days after in her mother's house, going through her things, crying and remembering and trying to figure things out.

Not least of which was the fact that her mother had apparently been working on some kind of classified software project for the Department of Defense. And she'd never even hinted at it to June.

Unable to sleep, June had planned to use her mother's key card and code to let herself into the cluttered lab at Stanford. She told herself she was there to collect family pictures and the few plants her mother had managed not to kill, but mostly she just wanted to sit with the memory of her mom in the place she'd most fully inhabited, her computer lab.

Instead, June found a broken lock, the door held open by a chair, and a pair of thick, humorless men in dark suits with Defense Department IDs packing Tyg3r, her mother's experimental bench-made mini-supercomputer, into a cardboard box with all the spare drives they could find. They'd already stacked their hand truck with banker's boxes, apparently filled with the contents of her mother's secure, fireproof file cabinet, which now stood open like a corpse for the medical examiner.

Although the G-men didn't show their IDs long enough for her to get their names, they made sure June could see the guns on their hips. The pale one did the talking, while his eyes wandered up and down her body. The dark one didn't say a word. They left her standing in the doorway with a warning that even this incident was classified, and if she even spoke of it she would face federal prosecution.

June watched them trundle the hand truck down the hall, thinking that her mother had always hated the government.

So why would she work for the Department of Defense?

Put another way, why would they show up at three a.m.?

And why would they take Tyg3r, the temperamental mini-super, but leave the big blazing-fast liquid-cooled Cray her mother had been so proud of?

So June had a lot on her mind. And when she finally dragged her ass out of bed the next day, she realized there was no coffee in the house. How the hell had that happened?

When she recognized the emergency conditions, she pulled on yesterday's clothes, slung her messenger bag over her shoulder, got on her mother's ancient but highly tuned single-speed Schwinn, and headed for Philz Coffee.

On Middlefield Road, a giant black SUV with tinted windows pulled up beside her, crowding her toward the parking lane. Red and blue lights flashed on the dash. When the passenger window hummed down, the same pale humorless G-man from the night before pretended to smile at her now.

He wasn't looking at her face, of course. He was watching the way the cross-strap from her messenger bag defined her breasts. Definitely not cool, she thought. Some woman needs to rewrite the DoD training manual.

"Please pull over, Ms. Cassidy. We'd like to speak with you for a few moments."

"Not right now," June said crossly, still pedaling. She was dangerously undercaffeinated, with a headache that would kill a rhino, and hadn't done shit for exercise in several days. The bike ride was just beginning to unknot her muscles when this moron showed up. "I need some coffee."

The big SUV kept pace with her. "This will just take a moment," he said. "We can drive through Starbucks if you'd like."

The G-man clearly failed to comprehend. Plus she would never go to Starbucks unless she was taken hostage, and even then she would fight it. "Hey," she said. "I'm busy. Send me an email. Call my cell. I'm sure you can figure out the number."

The G-man looked at the driver, who was definitely less pale but appeared no less humorless. Why did they have such horrible suits? The driver nodded.

"Ma'am," said the pale G-man, "I'm with the United States government. Are you refusing my lawful request?"

"Jesus Christ, no." Although she was starting to wonder if it was a lawful request. This wasn't her area, but she could make some calls and find out. "After lunch, okay? I have a meeting. Send me a text."

The G-man raised his hand and the driver slanted the black SUV into her path, leaving June no option but to slam on the brakes or be forced into a parked car.

"Hey listen, motherfucker," she began, but the G-man stepped out of the SUV, jammed a crackling electric stun gun into her side, and pulled the trigger.

It felt like being punched by a gorilla. June's legs stopped working, and she collapsed over her mom's bike.

The man captured her wrists in a pair of plastic riot handcuffs, disentangled her from the Schwinn, picked her up like a rag doll, and threw her into the back seat.

The driver scanned his mirrors. "What about the bike?"

"Leave it," said the first man, picking up June's fallen bag and getting in beside her. He took a phone from his pocket, touched a button. "We have her," he said.

The SUV roared back into mid-morning traffic, red and blue lights still flashing, conveying the impression of importance and urgency, with only a faint crunching sound as the left rear wheel rolled over her mother's beautiful old bicycle.

The next car slowed as he detoured around the twisted frame of the fallen Schwinn, but he was the only person to wonder what had happened.

By then, the black SUV was long gone.

JUNE'S SKIN FELT HOT under the T-shirt where the stun gun hit her. She didn't feel damaged, thankfully, just sore, like a long day at the climbing gym. She was more banged up from falling across her mom's bike. Mostly she was scared at finding herself thrown into a strange car with strange men. But that fear was rapidly converting to anger.

She was sure now that these men were not with the government, despite the badges and flashing lights. They wouldn't have used a stun gun on her. They'd simply have had the local cops knock on her door and bring her in.

But why did they want her to begin with?

The only thing that made sense was that it had something to do with her mother's lab.

She took careful inventory of her surroundings. The back doors were locked, and the driver watched his mirrors and the road ahead. The negligent way her seatmate kept an eye on her told her that he didn't consider her a threat, just a girl like any other. Until he began to leer at her a little, checking her out in her handcuffs, like he might ask her out for dinner when the whole thing was over.

As if he didn't quite get that he'd fucking zapped her with a stun gun and abducted her.

She recognized this particular look from the guy who got her staggering drunk on Everclear-laced "punch" early in her freshman year, so that he could rape her in the coatroom of a fraternity. The kind of guy who told himself that the girl came to the party to get drunk and laid and he was just helping her out, and that No really meant Yes because dude he was so damn handsome that a girl couldn't really be turning him down on purpose.

She reported the rape to the campus cops, but his asshole buddies rallied with bullshit stories of how she'd gotten drunk and came on to him, and the investigator couldn't do much. She didn't even know if he believed her.

So, with no other option available but to allow the whole thing to eat her alive, June decided to consider the incident a powerful lesson in poor judgment and a strong incentive to take full responsibility for herself. She stopped going to big parties, started self-defense classes, and never drank anything she hadn't poured herself.

She never thought of herself as a violent person, or someone easily angered. The self-defense training was just that, a means to protect herself. But she had been known to harbor a grudge, and now she took long, deep breaths, oxygenating her blood and stoking her anger to a pure white heat while she waited for a red light.

When the driver stayed in the lane for Old Middlefield, she knew she was running out of time. Once they hit the freeway, she was fucked. There would be no red lights. She saw the sign for Las Mucha-chas, tightened her abs, locked her left hand on the back of the driver's headrest, and pivoted on her seat to kick the man she now thought of as the date rapist directly in the face.

She was wearing her favorite heavy hiking boots, and her legs were very strong from running and biking, so the kick had substantial force. He rocked back and tried to block her, but she kept kicking him as hard as she could in the face and neck and forearms.

When he finally went on the offensive, reaching out for her with thick hands, she leaned in with a wrist lock, grabbed his vulnerable little finger and bent it back, not an easy thing to do with her wrists cuffed but very effective. The date rapist's meaty blood-streaked face twisted up and he shouted in pain, the driver was yelling and trying to pull over, and she really should have thought this through first but she was in it now and not giving up because the alternative was entirely unacceptable.

"Give me the fucking stun gun," she growled. His finger was at the edge of breaking. His face was torn up from her all-terrain soles, but he was clearly furious and she didn't want to get close to him. He was much bigger and stronger than she was, and the enclosed space was not to her advantage. She didn't know how long he'd give a shit about his finger. If he zapped her again or pulled her into a clinch or even hit her once in the face with a closed fist, she'd be finished. She shouted it again, loud and hard, "Give me the fucking stun gun!"

"Okay, okay," he said, and fumbled in his pocket. But she could read his intentions in his piggy little eyes and as the stun gun came out, she broke his finger. She could feel the crunch as the bone broke, a small weak bone despite the meatiness of his hand. He howled, but he'd already reached the same calculus she did, so despite the broken finger he pushed the stun gun toward her, trigger down and contacts crackling bright.

She hadn't let go of his finger. Now she pulled hard on it, twisting, grinding the bone. The date rapist yelped and dropped the stun gun. She had to let go of his finger to scoop up the stun gun, but that was an exchange she made gladly, because the SUV was veering to the curb and soon she'd have the driver to deal with.

The date rapist clutched his injured hand to his chest but dropped his leg. She lifted herself on one knee and drove a kick hard to his unprotected groin. She felt the softness there and knew she'd made contact when he cried out wetly and curled himself up into a ball on his seat.

She pivoted on the knee and jammed the stun gun into the back of the driver's neck and held the trigger down for a long time. The smell of burning meat filled the air.

The SUV was already slowing fast. The resultant electrical spasm made the driver stab the brake hard. The wheels locked and the tires grabbed at the asphalt.

June was on her knees on the back seat and the change in inertia pitched her over the center console and into the dashboard, which did not feel good on her shoulder and arm. The cuffs were a problem but she kept her grip on the stun gun, managed to get her feet under her, and zapped the driver again, holding the contacts against his shirt until he went limp. When the truck finished lurching, she threw the gearshift into park, then reached over the back seat and zapped the curled-up date rapist hard through the shiny seat of his shitty suit. He jerked and cried out but he was jammed against the door and she held the arcing stun gun until he stopped struggling and the fabric started to blacken at the contact point. His bowels released and the smell made her gag.

She popped the door and fell out of the car onto the empty sidewalk like waking from a nightmare, but forced herself to open the back door and reach into the date rapist's pockets. It wasn't easy with her hands bound, but that was the whole point after all. When she found the ugly little knife with a wicked-looking serrated blade, she immediately cut the plastic cuffs, then dropped the knife into her own pocket. He carried a gun in a shoulder holster, which she didn't touch, and a wallet and ID folder in his suit coat pocket, which she took.

The driver was moaning so she climbed back in the front and zapped him again in the chest. She left his gun, too, but his wallet was in his back pocket, and much harder to get to. She had to unbuckle his seat belt and open his door and spill him halfway into the street to take it.

She wanted their wallets and IDs because she was an investigative journalist and she had experience with the power of knowledge. And she didn't want these assholes to have the power of their fake IDs when the cops showed up. Leaving the guns would only make the situation more difficult for them to explain.

By now there was considerable attention being paid to the big SUV, which had come to a screeching halt across two lanes of traffic onto the sidewalk, narrowly missing a low brick wall sheltering a parking lot. Cars were backed up and blocked by the part of the SUV still in the street, and people peered from their half-open doors.

Through the dark abyss of receding adrenaline, June somehow retained the presence of mind to retrieve her bag. She dumped the wallets and stun gun inside, took out her Cubs hat, and pulled it down low over her eyes with shaking hands before choosing the fastest route off the street and walking away, wondering if she'd killed the date rapist and how many security cameras had captured her face.

What the holy hell was going on?

She ran down the service drive beside a car shop, threaded through the ragged plantings that bordered the parking lots, then across Independence to a sheltered mini-mall before allowing herself to walk shuddering into a little boutique called Glad Rags. She beelined to the restrooms in the back, collapsed into a stall with her bag on her lap, and allowed herself to dissolve into silent, convulsive tears.

She only gave herself a few minutes, but it was all she needed. By the time she'd wiped her eyes on the backs of her wrists, rinsed her face, and reapplied her lip balm, her brain was fully engaged, her professional paranoia in high gear, and her anger like a cold iron bar.

She was *pissed*.

They had broken into her mother's lab. They'd assaulted June on the street. She wasn't sure if it was safe to talk to the police, or even where she might go after leaving the relative safety of the ladies' room. Her mother's house? Probably not. Her own place, all the way up in Seattle?

If not there, where?

She assembled a mental list of places to go, people to call. Then wondered if she'd be putting them in danger, too. Jesus Christ.

Gathering her self-possession around her like a cloak, she walked back through the store, where she selected a sleek reversible fleece hoodie and a floppy straw gardening hat. If they were watching the security cameras, she could now make herself look like three or four different people.

June's crying jag had left her eyes red and puffy. The matronly saleswoman looked at her kindly as she approached the counter. "Dear, are you all right?"

June had prepared herself for this question with several variations on the truth. "I just broke up with the most awful man," she said. "He made it so *difficult*. I practically had to jump out of his car to get away."

"Oh, honey," said the older woman, with such profound sympathy that June knew she had chosen the right way to tell the story. "Men are such complete fuckers, aren't they?"

"I'm done with them," June said, pulling out her credit card. "Completely done."

"Like a fish needs a bicycle," said the saleswoman with a secret smile as she rang up June's purchases. "Honey, what kind of bag would you like?"

"You know, I think I'll just wear them," said June. "Can I ask a favor? To tell you the truth, I'm a little afraid he's outside right now. I *really* don't want to run into him. Would it be all right if I went out the back?"

She found an old mountain bike leaning unlocked against a railing, a gift fallen into her lap. She told herself she'd somehow get the bike back to the owner, knowing even then that it was a lie, and rode off just managing not to look over her shoulder.

At her mother's house, another official-looking black SUV squatted at the curb. June just kept pedaling. Luckily, her mom's car had blocked the driveway, June had never found the keys, and she'd had to park her old Subaru wagon around the corner.

She checked to see if her own keys were still in her bag, along with the rest of her professional existence. Notebook computer in a padded sleeve, phone, notepad, pens. She never left home without them.

She leaned the bike against a low fence, got in her car, and drove quietly away.

Where she was going, she had no idea.

PART 1

1

When he rounded the curve on the narrow trail and saw the bear, Peter Ash was thinking about robbing a liquor store. Or a gas station, he was weighing his options.

On foot with a pack on his back, he was as deep into old-growth redwood country as he could get. Although most of the original giants had been logged off decades before, there were still a few decent-sized protected areas along the California coast, with enough steep, tangled acreage to get truly lost. In the deep, damp drainage bottoms thick with underbrush, redwood trunks fifteen feet in diameter shot up into the mist like gnarled columns holding up the sky.

But Peter hadn't counted on the coastal fog. It had been constant for days. He couldn't see more than a hundred feet in any direction, and it made the white static crackle and spark in the back of his head.

It was the static that made him want to rob a liquor store.

The closest one was at least a few days' walk ahead of him, so the plan was still purely theoretical. But he was putting the pieces together in his mind.

He didn't want to use a weapon, because he was pretty sure armed robbery carried a longer sentence than he was willing to take. He didn't want to go to actual prison, just the local jail, and only for a few days. He'd settle for overnight. Although how he'd try to rob a liquor store without a visible weapon was a problem he hadn't yet solved.

He could put his hand inside a paper bag and pretend to be holding a gun. He'd probably have to hold something, to make it more realistic. Maybe a banana?

Hell, now he was just embarrassing himself.

Any respectable liquor store employee would just laugh at him. Hopefully they'd still call the cops, who would put him in the back of a squad car, then at least a holding cell. Maybe overnight, maybe for a few days. It was a calculated risk.

The problem was these woods. They were so dense and dark, and the coastal cloud cover so thick and low, that he hadn't seen the sky for weeks. The white static wouldn't leave him alone, even out here, miles from so-called civilization. It pissed him off. He'd wanted to walk in this ancient forest for years. Now he was here in this green paradise and he couldn't enjoy it.

Peter Ash was tall and rangy, muscle and bone, nothing extra. His long face was angular, the tips of his ears slightly pointed, his dark hair an unruly shag. He had wide, knuckly hands and the thoughtful eyes of a werewolf a week before the change. Some part of him was always in motion—even now, hiking in the woods, his fingertips twitched in time to some interior metronome that never ceased.

He'd been a Marine lieutenant in Iraq and Afghanistan, eight years and more deployments than he cared to remember. Boots on the ground, tip of the spear. He'd finished with his war two years before, but the war still wasn't finished with him. It had left him with a souvenir. He called it the white static, an oddball form of post-traumatic stress that showed up as claustrophobia, an intense reaction to enclosed spaces.

It hadn't appeared until he was back home, just days from mustering out.

At first, going inside a building was merely uncomfortable. He'd feel a fine-grained sensation at the back of his neck, like electric foam, a small battery stuck under the skin. If he stayed inside, it would intensify. The foam would turn to sparks, a crackling unease in his brainstem, a profound dissonance just at the edge of hearing. His neck would tense, and his shoulders would begin to rise as his muscles tightened. He'd look for the exits as his chest clamped up, and he'd begin to have trouble catching his breath. After twenty minutes, he'd be in a full-blown panic attack, hyperventilating, the fight-or-flight mechanism cranked up all the way.

Mostly, he'd chosen flight.

He'd spent over a year backpacking all over the West, trying to let himself get back to normal. But it hadn't worked. He'd finally forced himself outside his comfort zone to help some friends the year before, and it had gotten a little better. He'd thought he was making progress. But they'd gone back to their lives and Peter had gone off on his own again, and something had happened. Somehow he'd lost the ground he'd gained.

Lost so much ground that even walking through the foggy redwoods in the spring was enough to get the static sparking in his head.

Which is why he was contemplating the best way to get himself locked up. Get this shit out of his system once and for all.

He wasn't thinking it was a *good* idea.

Then he saw the bear.

IT WAS ABOUT THIRTY YARDS ahead of him, just downslope from the narrow trail that wound along the flank of the mountain.

At first all he could see was a mottled brown form roughly the size and shape of a Volkswagen Beetle, covered with fur, attempting to roll a half-rotted log down the side of the mountain.

It took Peter a few more steps to figure out that he was seeing a bear.

The trail ran through a deep pocket of old-growth trees in an area too steep for commercial logging. It was mid-March, and Peter assumed the bear was looking for food. There would be grubs under the log, which would provide much-needed protein in that still-lean time of the year. The bear grumbled to itself as it dug into the dirt, sounding a little like Peter's dad when he cleaned out the back of his truck. The bear was focused on its task, and hadn't yet noticed the human.

Peter stopped walking.

Black bears were plentiful in the wilder pockets of the West, but they were smaller, usually three or four hundred pounds when fully grown. Black bears could do a lot of damage if they felt threatened, but they usually avoided confrontation with humans. Peter had chased black bears out of his campsite by clapping his hands and shouting.

This was not a black bear.

This bear was a rich reddish-brown, with a pronounced hump, and very big. A grizzly. At the top of the food chain, grizzlies could be very aggressive, and were known to kill hikers. Clapping his hands wouldn't discourage the bear. It would be more like a dinner bell, alerting the bear to the possibility of a good meal.

The most dangerous time to meet a grizzly was in the fall, when they were desperately packing on fat to make it through the winter.

The second-most dangerous time was spring, with the bear right out of hibernation and extremely hungry. Like now.

Peter was lean and strong from weeks of backcountry hiking. His clothes were worn thin by rock and brush, the pack cinched tight on his back to make it easier to scramble through the heavy undergrowth.

His leather boots had been resoled twice, the padded leather collars patched where mice had nibbled them for the salt while he slept wrapped in his ground cloth.

He'd walked a lot of miles in those mountains.

Now he wondered how fast he could run.

He took a slow step back, trying to be as quiet as possible, then another. Maybe he could disappear in the fog.

Peter had once met an old-timer who'd called the bears Mr. Griz, as a term of respect. The old man had recited the facts like a litany. Mr. Griz can grow to a thousand pounds or more. Mr. Griz can run forty miles an hour in short bursts. His jaws are strong enough to crush a bowling ball. Mr. Griz eats everything. He will attack a human being if he feels threatened or hungry. Mr. Griz has no natural enemies.

The bear was still focused on the rotting log. Peter took a third step back, then a fourth. A little faster now.

Call it a retreat in the face of overwhelming force. No dishonor in that, right? Even for a United States Marine.

The California grizzly was supposed to be extinct. But this bear looked big, and big males were known to travel long distances in search of mates. He was only sixty miles south of the Oregon border, and in this dark primeval forest, anything seemed possible.

Five steps, now six. Peter didn't care how much this particular grizzly weighed, or what he felt like eating. He didn't want to find out. He was almost back to the bend in the trail. This would be a good story to tell someday.

Then he felt a slight breeze move the hairs on the back of his neck. The wind, which had been in his face, had shifted.

He was in trouble.

Grizzlies have fair eyesight and good hearing, but their sense of smell is superb. And the mountain breeze carried Peter's weeks-long hiking stink, along with the smell of his supplies, directly to the bear's brain. The supplies included a delicious trail mix made of cashews and almonds and peanuts and raisins and chocolate chips.

Much better than grubs under a log.

The bear's head popped up with a snort.

Peter stepped backward a bit faster, feeling the adrenaline sing in his blood, reminding himself of the old-timer's advice on meeting Mr. Griz.

You don't want to appear to be a threat, or to look like food. Running away is a bad idea, because bears can run faster than people. And running away is prey behavior.

What you were supposed to do, said the old-timer, was drop your pack to give the bear something to investigate, then retreat backward. If the bear charged, curl up into a ball, protecting your head, neck, and face with your arms. You might get mauled, but you'd be less likely to be killed.

Peter was not exactly the curl-into-a-ball type.

The bear stood upright on its hind legs, now a good eight or nine feet tall, swung its enormous head toward Peter, and sniffed the air like a Silicon Valley sommelier.

Mmmm. Trail mix.

Peter took another step back. Then another.

The bear dropped to all fours and charged.

Peter shucked his pack and ran like hell.

HE'D GROWN UP WITH ANIMALS. Dogs in the yard, horses in the barn, chickens and cats wherever they felt like going. He'd kind of inherited a big dog the year before, or maybe the dog had inherited him, it wasn't entirely clear. In the end the dog had found a better home than Peter could provide.

But he liked animals. Hell, he liked grizzly bears, at least in theory.

He certainly liked how it felt to know a big predator was out there. It made him feel more alive.

The backpack distracted the bear for only a few seconds, barely long enough for Peter to round the corner, find a climbable sapling, and jump up. The bear was right at his heels at the end. Mr. Griz chomped a chunk of rubber from the sole of Peter's boot. Peter was glad he got to keep the foot.

He scrambled higher, finding handholds in the crevices of the soft, deep bark. This was a redwood sapling, tall and straight as a flagpole. He hugged the trunk with his arms and legs while the bear roared and thumped the sapling with his forepaws, apparently uninterested in climbing up after him. The young tree rocked back and forth and Peter's heart thumped in his chest.

Alive, alive, I am alive.

Would you rather be here, or stuck behind a desk somewhere?

"Bad bear," he called down. "You are a very bad bear."

After a few minutes, Mr. Griz gave up and wandered back toward the smell of trail mix. Peter had to climb another ten feet before he found a branch that would hold his weight. He was wondering how long to wait when the bear returned, dragging Peter's backpack. It settled itself at the base of the tree and began to enthusiastically disembowel the pack.

After an hour, Peter's two-week food supply was working its way through the entrepreneurial bear's digestive system, along with his emergency phone, long underwear, and fifty feet of climbing rope.

"Mr. Griz, you give the word 'omnivore' a whole new meaning," Peter said from the safety of his high perch.

The bear then proceeded to entertain itself by shredding Peter's sleeping bag, rain gear, and spare clothing. Peter said a few bad words about the bear's mother.

Mr. Griz was tearing up Peter's new featherweight tent when it began to rain again. Big, pelting drops.

Peter sighed. He'd really liked that tent.

For one thing, it kept the rain off.

HE'D SLEPT IN many strange places in his thirty-some years. His first six months, he was told, he slept in a dresser drawer. As a teenager in fairly constant and general disagreement with his father, he often preferred to sleep in the barn with the horses, even during the severe winter weather common in northern Wisconsin. He'd slept in tents, on boats, under the stars, and in the cab of his 1968 Chevy pickup. In Iraq and Afghanistan, he'd slept in a bombed-out cigarette factory, in a looted palace, in combat outposts and Humvees and MRAPs and anyplace else he could manage to catch a few Z's.

He'd never slept in a tree before.

It wasn't easy. The rain fell steadily, and soaked through his clothes. As the adrenaline faded, the static returned to fizz and spark at the back of his brain, which added to the challenge of sleep. His eyes would flutter shut and he would drift off, arms wrapped around the trunk of the sapling, serenaded by the snores of Mr. Griz below. Then he'd abruptly jerk awake to the sensation of falling and find himself scrabbling for a handhold, shivering in the cold and wet.

The night seemed to last a long time.

He spent the time awake remembering the previous winter, spent camping alone in the Utah desert. But the arid emptiness had left him with a longing for tall trees, so he made his way through the beautiful emptiness of Nevada to California's thirsty, fertile central valley and the overdeveloped mess of the northern Bay Area. It made him think, as he often did, that the world would be better off without so many people in it.

He'd parked his pickup in the driveway of a fellow Marine in Clearlake, California, and walked through housing tracts and mini-malls and vineyards and cow pastures to the southern end of the Mendocino National Forest, where he headed north. Sometimes he hiked on established routes, sometimes on game trails, sometimes wayfinding the forested ridges, trying to get above the rain and the fog and into the sun. He'd come too early in the year for summer's blue skies, but he didn't want the woods all cluttered up with people.

Instead he'd found a very large bear.

When it became light enough to see the ground, he looked down and considered his options. His gear was wrecked, his food supplies gone. Mr. Griz still down there, bigger than ever. Still snoring.

A cup of coffee would be nice, he thought. But not likely.

He was pretty sure his coffee supply was bear food, too.

He looked up. He was astride a sapling in a mature redwood forest. Although he couldn't see far in the fog, he thought the sapling went up another forty or fifty feet. The mature trees probably went up two or three hundred feet after that.

The rain had stopped sometime in the night, and although the fog was still thick, some quality of the mist had changed. It glowed faintly, green with growth and heady with the oxygen exhaled by giants. He thought maybe the sun had come out, somewhere up there. It turned the forest into something like an ancient cathedral.

He looked down. Mr. Griz, still sleeping. The contents of Peter's pack destroyed or eaten. The static fizzing and popping in his head. Peter himself cold and wet and tired.

He looked up again. The promise of sunlight, and warmth, and a view.

What, you want to live forever?

He smiled, and began to climb.

2

t was easy work at first, the sapling's trunk slender enough to put his arms around, branches appearing at regular intervals. Like climbing any tree, only taller.

The grizzly's bite out of his boot heel didn't seem to make much difference. The exercise warmed him, and soon he found the trunk narrowing. After a few minutes, he could hold himself in place with one arm, then the crook of his elbow. When he reached the highest place he felt he could stand without damaging the tree, he could encircle the trunk with one hand. The wind blew more strongly at this height. He felt himself swinging slowly from side to side, as if at the top of an inverted pendulum.

His mother had encouraged Peter to memorize poems as a boy. She liked Robert Frost, and Peter learned "Birches" by heart when he was ten. Then he went out into the woods and taught himself to do what the poet had written about, climbing a birch sapling until he could throw his body into the air as the tree bent beneath his weight, swinging him gently to the ground.

A redwood wasn't a birch. And he was a good sixty or seventy feet in the air. It wouldn't swing him to the ground.

But there was a branch from another tree not far from this one. A small branch, but a big tree. The trunk was nine or ten feet in diameter, even at this height. And beyond it were other trunks, a cluster of them.

Maybe he could swing himself over. And keep climbing upward.

Out of the static.

Into the sun.

So he rode the inverted pendulum, throwing his weight out at the end of each swing, trying to improve the distance he moved through the sky. It was exhilarating, and he made progress. The arc of his travel got bigger with each swing of the pendulum.

Would the sapling flex enough to get him to a branch on the next tree? If it wouldn't, was he crazy enough to jump?

He swung back and forth across that arc of sky, a trapeze in a cathedral, his heart outsized in his chest. If the whole thing wasn't so gorgeous, it would be ridiculous.

He wanted to jump. He wanted to get up into the sunshine. He calculated the distances, how far he could leap, how much farther the momentum of his swing would carry him. How fast he might fall. What would happen if he missed.

But he never found out if he was crazy enough to jump.

Because as he got closer to the big tree, he saw something hanging down from it.

A rope.

A thick green rope, a rock-climber's rope.

What the hell was that doing here? The bottom end hung down ten feet below him, with a big loop tied in the end. Its upper end vanished into the dim light of the high branches.

. . .

HE KEPT THROWING HIS BODY outward at the end of each arc of the reverse pendulum. The arc grew, but not quite enough for him to reach out and grab the green rope.

Now he didn't want to jump. He didn't know if the green rope was even attached to anything. It looked older, faded, with patches of lichen growing on it. It might have rotted up there in the sun and rain. Maybe nothing but inertia held it there.

What he wanted was another length of line, something weighted. Something he could throw out to capture the climber's rope and pull it back to him. If Mr. Griz hadn't chewed up Peter's rope, it would have worked nicely. But without Mr. Griz, Peter would be miles farther down the trail.

His pockets were empty. He thought about his shirt, but it was short-sleeved, probably not long enough. He could take off his boots and use the laces. That seemed like a bad idea.

He swung back and forth, finding the end of the arc, thinking. Searching for an idea better than the one that had come to mind. But he never found one.

It was hard to take off his pants while swinging atop a redwood sapling.

But not impossible.

And as it turned out, they were just long enough.

They were still wet from the rain, which made them heavier.

His pantleg wrapped around the rope on the third try.

He reeled them back in, towing the rope as the reverse pendulum yanked him in the opposite direction. The rope was just long enough that it traversed the arc without shortening enough to steal his pants.

Peter was glad of that.

He didn't want to climb back down the tree in his underwear.

Once he had the rope in his hand, he gave it a tug. It felt solid. Close up, it didn't look more than a few years old. The lichen would grow fast in this cloud forest.

He put some weight on it. He felt no real give, just the normal spring of a fixed rope. From the thickness of it, Peter guessed it was designed to hold considerably more than he weighed. Which meant Peter had some margin of error.

The rope was so long that he couldn't see where it ended. Once he had it in his hand, it was hard to resist. The push of the static, the pull of the sun. Just one thing to do first.

He tied the loop loosely over a branch and put his pants back on.

UP HE WENT, hand over hand, swinging at the bottom of a new pendulum, wrapping his legs to help his stability. His arms were strong from bouldering. The good news was that he was warm, his clothes were drying in the mountain breeze, and the endorphins from the exercise damped down the static.

The bad news was that the rope went up for a very long way. He couldn't see the end. Its green color combined with the dim filtered light to make the rope seem to hover in space above him, then disappear.

After thirty or forty feet of climbing, the rope rose past a small branch, just big enough to support his weight, and he could rest. If he'd had a harness and ascenders, this would have been easier. But he didn't, so he just shook out his arms and flexed his hands and looked around in silent awe at the sheer abundance of life. He could see other trees around him, rising close enough that their branches caught all available light, only glimmers of sun peeking through. Their bark was rust-red, thick and striated, sometimes spiraled, with crevices deep enough to use as climbing holds if needed.

The rope kept threading higher.

Then up again, hand over hand through the mist to the next limb, and the next. It was hard work. His arms ached. Without the rest stops, he almost certainly would have fallen.

As he climbed, he thought about who might have put this rope here, and why. The rope would be nearly invisible from the ground, even if you knew to look for it.

At two hundred feet up, the ground had vanished in the fog. The wind whispered through the soft needles, the evergreen smell grew stronger, and the light grew brighter. The sense of something opening above him was powerful. His arms complained loudly, and his hands were sore. But the branches were more numerous now. He could make his way without the rope if he had to. Still he kept following the slim green line, up and up. He wanted to know why someone had been in this tree. Research? Some tree hugger's dream house? If so, it was a lot of work to get the groceries home.

He was expecting the end of the rope before he came to it, tied off above a stout branch in a beautiful bowline, the first knot Peter had learned as a boy. The branches were closer together now. Peter could monkey up easily from here. Up to the sunlight.

He looked to plan his route and saw a short piece of red rope tied loosely around a limb a dozen yards away. Beyond that, another. Someone had already marked the path. Peter followed. Where the next branch was too far for an easy reach, the tree explorer had thoughtfully provided a green rope to ease the way.

Peter was starting to like this guy.

Whoever the hell he was.

HE CAME TO A PLACE where the thick main trunk ended in a wide blackened stub. It looked like the tree had been struck by lightning, probably many years ago. Around the splintered stub, a half-dozen mini-trunks had sprouted and grown upward seeking the sun, the largest of them two feet in diameter and rising another forty or fifty feet. Each mini-trunk would be a giant in the third-growth Wisconsin forest where Peter grew up. He was having trouble wrapping his mind around the scale of the redwoods.

Another red rope marker, and another. Green travel ropes hung in the difficult places. Sunlight now came through in larger patches, but it was hard to find a logic to the trunks and limbs. There were entire suburbs in this giant tree, each a different tangle, bower, or thicket. It would be easy to get lost. Then he realized that he was seeing more than one tree, that he was in a ring of trees whose main trunks were no more than ten or twelve feet apart.

Peter climbed toward the sun.

It occurred to him to announce himself. "Hello," he called out. "Is anyone here?" If the tree explorer was any kind of a nutcase, Peter didn't want to surprise him. "Hello? Anyone?"

There was no answer but the wind in the branches.

The red rope markers led him in a circuitous path. Around another blackened area, through several dense tangles where branches grew in every direction, but always upward, toward the sun.

The tree canopy opened as he climbed. He could smell the heat of the sun on the redwood bark. The sky was a high brilliant blue, and the peaks and valleys of the Coast Ranges stretched out around him, wearing their undulating pelt of trees.

Finally he saw above him a slender triangular platform. As he got closer he saw it was some kind of netting stretched between the tops of several trees, maybe twenty feet on a side. Irregular shapes showed through the netting at one end, maybe tools or supplies left behind. Above the netting hung a triangular sun cover, larger than the platform, turning the sun strange dappled shades. It would keep the rain off, too. Redwoods grew in rain forest, after all.

This was not just some tree hugger's weekend nest.

It was too well-designed, too organized.

"Ahoy the platform," he called out. "Anyone up there?"

He counted to twenty. No response. The platform cover rattled softly in the breeze. The sun was warm on his back. Through the branches he could see trees without end, or so it seemed.

"Okay," he called out. "I'm coming up."

A broad horizontal branch stretched toward the platform, with safety ropes strung at waist height, making an easy path. He noted where the platform was tied off, checking each rope and knot before he trusted the netting with his weight.

When he stepped onto it, the netting gave slightly beneath his weight, like a trampoline. He heard a faint twanging sound behind him. Then a voice.

A female voice.

"Hands up, asshole. That's far enough."

3

P eter turned and saw a woman with a bow and arrow standing on the broad horizontal branch, ten feet away. The bow was stretched taut, the arrow set to the string and pointed at his chest.

She wore a faded pink Riot Grrrl T-shirt, patched hiking pants, and a daypack on her back. Behind the bow, he saw red hair cut short over a freckled face, intense eyes, and a long narrow nose that came to a point like a rapier. She had serious climber's arms, and held the bow steady. The branch she stood on might have been a city sidewalk for all the attention she paid to it. She was entirely focused on Peter. It was not a comfortable feeling. He was an ant under a magnifying glass, and her gaze was the sun.

Peter put his hands up. The movement made him bounce slightly on the netting, which was probably why she'd waited until he made it to the platform. He'd have trouble moving quickly on the spongy surface. She had good tactics, whoever she was. Better than some infantrymen Peter had known.

"Hi," he said, trying for cheerful and harmless. "Nice place you got here. I'm Peter. What's your name?"

Riot Grrrl looked at him with those blazing eyes, but didn't answer. She had the edge of her lower lip between her teeth, thinking. Her arms did not shake with the tension of the bow. She projected utter confidence and capability, but Peter thought he saw a muscle twitch at the edge of her eye.

It was a compound bow, the kind with pulleys to maximize the force of the projectile and minimize the arm strength required. The business end of the arrow had a broad head, designed to cut its way in and do some damage. Although Peter had given up killing animals for food or sport after the war, he'd been a bow-hunter in high school, and knew that the arrow, at this range, would probably go all the way through his body and a fair distance into the tree limb behind him. Unless it hit bone, in which case it might well become a permanent part of his anatomy, for whatever short time remained to him as he bled to death on a trampoline at the top of a giant redwood.

The bow had a quiver holding three more arrows, so she had several opportunities to put a hole in him.

Peter had led a Marine infantry platoon for eight years in two war zones. Many professional soldiers had pointed their weapons at him, and it was never something he'd enjoyed. But it was the amateurs who really made him nervous. Again he saw the flutter at the edge of her eye. A stress reaction.

"I'm going to sit," he said calmly. "Maybe you'd like to tell me what's on your mind."

With his fingers laced on the back of his head, Peter crossed his ankles and lowered himself to a sitting position as the netting gave gently beneath him. It felt like he was floating. It would have been pretty cool if it weren't for Riot Grrrl pointing a medieval weapon at his center of mass.

She didn't say anything. She was still thinking. The branch she was standing on creaked and swayed in the breeze, but it had no effect on her.

"You could rest your arms," he said. "You look pretty strong, but I'd rather not get shot by accident."

She didn't relax her arms. Finally, she spoke again. "How did you find me?"

"I wasn't looking for you," he said. "I was hiking north and a grizzly bear chased me up a tree. I kept climbing. I saw your rope." He shrugged. "I got curious."

"You're a bad liar. California grizzlies are extinct."

"He might have been on vacation from Montana," Peter admitted. "But he was brown and very big and he took a bite out of my boot. Here, I'll show you." Peter slowly unfolded his legs and held up his boot so she could see the bite mark in the sole. It was fairly dramatic.

She glanced at the boot, then looked Peter up and down with a critical eye.

He wore fast-drying hiking pants thinned down by the trackless miles, and a high-tech T-shirt that was supposed to keep him warm wet or dry, but after several months of almost continuous wear it had begun to smell like a goat's ass. Washing his clothes in a stream helped with the dirt, but not the stink. He figured it was some kind of chemical reaction with the technology of the fabric. He'd carried cleaner clothes in his pack that he usually wore after he stopped hiking for the day, but they were probably shredded and covered with grizzly drool now.

"Well," she said. "You don't look like one of them."

Her voice was rough and scratchy for her years, which he put at late twenties to early thirties. Around Peter's own age. She didn't look like a chain-smoker. From her T-shirt logo, he figured it was from screaming at punk rock shows. Or maybe smoking Humboldt County's finest. Northern California was filled with strange characters gone a few extra steps around the bend. Like a Riot Grrrl in a tree with a bow and arrow.

"What do they look like?" he asked.

She just shook her head. "Better you don't know."

"Give me a hint," said Peter. "Bikers? Dopers? Cops? Aliens?"

The corners of her mouth quirked up in the hint of a smile. She let the tension out of the bow, but still held the arrow nocked to the string. Her shoulders sagged, and for the first time he saw how tired she was.

"Can I put my hands down?"

"No," she said. "You're leaving, back the way you came. The only question is, are you going slow, or the express route?"

"I'd prefer slow," he admitted. "What are you doing up here, anyway?"

"I don't know you well enough to have this conversation," she said.

"I'll tell you anything you'd like to know," Peter said. "I was born outside of Bayfield, Wisconsin. My dad's a builder. My mom's an artist and a teacher. I was a lieutenant in the Marine Corps, honorably discharged. My hobbies are backpacking, carpentry, and current events." He smiled winningly.

Her mouth quirked again, just slightly. Maybe she wouldn't put an arrow into him.

"Not many people could free-climb it up here," she said grudgingly. Then, "Not many people would be that stupid."

"I prefer the term 'eccentric,'" said Peter. "How did you get up here?"

She turned the bow slightly. "See the fishing reel?"

It was bolted to the composite above the grip. Peter had known guys who went fishing with a bow with the same kind of setup, although this seemed like an odd place to do it.

"You shoot a weighted arrow through the bottom loop in that green rope, which pulls the fishing line through the loop. Use the fishing line to pull a leader rope, then another rope large enough to climb. Clip on your ascenders and up you go. The only challenge is when you have to jump the knot. Then untie the first rope and pull it up behind you. Keeps the local idiots from climbing up and killing themselves on our gear."

Peter was clearly the local idiot in this scenario.

Something caught his eye, a kind of golden glint in the sky. He looked out over the undulating land. A half-dozen turkey vultures rode the thermals with their broad square wings, using their superb sense of smell to search for carrion to eat. But they weren't the source of the flash. It was something high above them. He shaded his eye but couldn't make it out. Maybe a small plane?

"Am I boring you?"

He looked back to Riot Grrrl, still holding the bow. "Sorry, I was watching the birds. You have an excellent view."

From far below, over the sound of the breeze through the branches, Peter heard a hard staccato sound. *Takatak. Takatak.*

He'd heard the sound before. Automatic rifles in disciplined bursts. *Takatak. Takatak.* Then sustained, magazine-emptying fire, multiple weapons. *Takatakatakatakatakataka.*

He didn't hear the distant roar of Mr. Griz. If Mr. Griz hadn't woken up and wandered off, Peter figured the last California grizzly was dead or dying by now. He hadn't thought it would make him so sad.

He looked at Riot Grrrl. "You hear that?"

From the way her eyes had gone wide, she'd heard it. Scared but trying to play it cool.

She sighed. "They're not fucking aliens, all right?"

Peter figured she should be gearing up to get herself out of there. But she wasn't moving. The bow hung from her hand, her feet seemed glued to her branch. He knew the look. She was paralyzed.

Peter kept talking. "So who are they?"

She looked past him at the reaching limbs. She sounded tired. "I don't know. I've seen them three times. My mom's lab, on the street, and at my mom's house two days ago." She put her hand to her face. "I didn't think they'd find me here. I'm running out of places to go."

"How many?"

"Four so far. Men in dark suits. Two black Chevy SUVs."

"Sounds like government."

"Their IDs say they're from the Department of Defense. But I don't believe them."

"Why not?"

"I'm pretty sure DoD employees don't use stun guns to try to kidnap journalists in broad daylight."

"That happened to you?"

Her eyes jumped back to him. "Yes."

He saw the anger blazing there, and heard it in the hard edge of her voice. Anger was good. Anger was action. He could work with that.

"Why would they try to kidnap a journalist?"

"I don't know," she said. "I haven't had a chance to do much digging yet." But there was something there, something she wasn't telling him.

"What do you write about?"

"Technology. Big data. Information privacy in the modern age. Investigative stuff." She shook her head. "But I don't think that's why it happened."

"Okay," said Peter. "We should go take a peek. See who's down there."

"We?" She stared at him, and he felt that focus again, like the heat of the sun.

He looked right back at her. "Hey, I'm your prisoner," he said. "Under the Geneva Convention, that means my health and safety are your responsibility. First, I'd like a large cup of strong coffee and a breakfast burrito. Then you need to protect me from those mean men with guns."

She didn't look away. He saw something change inside her, some decision made. "You really want to go down there?"

"Not all the way," he said. "Just far enough to get a look. I don't suppose you have any binoculars in that bag, do you?"

4

JUNE

He sure looked different, June thought. Not some overfed goon in a suit, like those fake G-men. Definitely not the deliberately casual costume she saw so often in the tech industry, hoodies and expensive jeans on the technical types and golf shirts on the money men.

She fucking hated golf shirts.

This guy Peter looked kind of *raggedy*, although that wasn't quite right. Definitely not the golf shirt type. Hair all shaggy, his rough beard not a hipster fashion statement. You'd never describe him as fashion-forward. Too lean and ropy, but with a kind of lightness to him, like one of those uncluttered man-shaped sculptures made of scrap steel.

His clothes were worn to threads, but good stuff, not cheap. So he wasn't broke. And he was fairly clean, especially if you took into account that he'd been in the woods for a while. So he had decent hygiene, again in contrast to many in the tech industry.

No, she thought. Not raggedy.

Lived-in. The man looked lived-in.

Like that pair of old Levi's she'd had since college. Frayed but comfortable, washed a thousand times, and fit her hips like they were custom-made.

She caught herself and sighed.

That's fucking great, June.

You meet some guy in a tree and now you're thinking about your hips.

I know you're approaching your sexual peak, honey, but really? Don't you have more important things to focus on right now?

Like those assholes still chasing you?

She found herself feeling self-conscious, with the bow and arrow. Maybe even a little silly.

She snapped the arrow back into its quiver and jumped from her branch to the platform netting. Her landing made him bounce on the trampoline material. She liked that he didn't look startled.

He seemed like the steady type.

She went directly to the dry bags she'd insisted Bryce buy and dug through them for the gear she needed. Everything was still clean and dry. Rotten rope was a bad thing if you were three hundred feet up a tree.

She found Bryce's old narrow climber's pack, four coils of 9-mil rope, and the heavy clanking bags from Mountain Rescue. "Hey," she said to make sure she had Peter's attention, and tossed him a knot of webbing. "That's a climbing harness. You ever wear one before?"

"Yes," he said.

"Put it on," she said. "I'll check you. How about Jumars, figure eights? Ascenders and descenders?"

"Most of my rope work involved jumping out of helicopters," he said. "But I know the gear."

She dumped out her own pack and sorted her belongings. She laid out rope and gear, divided it up, and made a pile for him with Bryce's old bombproof pack. "Here, take this. You're going to need it."

She collected her gear, made sure the compound bow was tightly lashed to the back of her pack, and pointed him back the way he'd come. The bow would make it more difficult for her to travel through the tree, but she wasn't going to leave it behind.

She liked that he was packed and ready when she was.

They followed the path of red marking ropes past the burnt stub of the original lightning-struck spire, and down through the lower crown. He moved lightly in the tree, found branches that would support his weight without cracking or breaking, and didn't use his boots to kick footholds into the bark. He moved, in other words, like a real climber, even on this easy path.

The next routes wouldn't be so easy.

But if he'd really free-climbed a 9-mil rope twenty stories after climbing sixty feet up a redwood sapling, he was plenty capable.

Now they could hear fragments of voices from below, although the wind in the branches drowned out the words. How many men were there?

She wondered if they were the same men from the SUV, and how badly she'd hurt them. Part of her felt remorse about hitting them with the stun gun. A small part, but still. She didn't want them dead, just unable to ever threaten her again. She hoped these were different men.

Conscious of sound now, she used simple hand gestures to direct him to the Perch. It was a massive limb, six feet in diameter, and horizontal for ten feet before it angled upward toward the sun.

This was the lowest point of decent lateral structure in the tree. She'd run strong webbing from the main trunk to the vertical leg of the Perch, so they had a drop point well above their footing. On their research trips, she'd clipped ropes and pulleys on the webbing for hauling gear up and down in a system she'd privately called the freight elevator. When you had four academic biologists three hundred plus feet up in a tree for two weeks at a time, you hauled a lot of freight. Not just camping gear and sample cases, but all supplies in and all garbage out, including their poop in plastic bags, triple-wrapped.

June wasn't a biologist, wasn't part of that team, but it had been a way to spend time with Bryce. She'd started free-climbing boulders and trees during her lonely tomboy childhood in rural Washington. When she moved to California to live with her mom, she'd joined a climbing club and turned into a serious rock monkey. Ascending tall trees with Bryce was just another way to feed the rat.

As it turned out, she'd also written some of her best articles up there in the high canopy. Surprisingly, her laptop's cell modem caught a signal just fine up there. The trick was getting enough sunlight in the temperate rain forest for the solar chargers to keep her gear powered up.

The green rope hung down into the mist, and voices filtered up, louder now but still indecipherable. Three of them? Four? The wind had dropped. It smelled like rain.

He spoke in a soft voice. "We need to get closer."

June shook her head. She wasn't going down there. She could still see the date rapist's leer, his piggy little eyes. And now there were more of them.

"Don't worry," he said. "I'll go." He seemed so calm. How could he be calm?

"They have guns," she hissed.

"And I don't," he said. "So I'll be very quiet."

Her mouth opened, but she didn't know what to say. Why was he doing this for her?

So she said it. "Why are you doing this?"

He gave her a toothy grin. "Why not?" he said softly. "Maybe we'll learn something."

"I don't know if I trust you yet."

"Tell you what," he said. "If you decide you don't trust me, you can always cut the rope."

What the fuck was she supposed to say to that?

He was already wearing his harness, but he tucked one of her Jumar ascenders into each of his cargo pockets, she assumed so they wouldn't clink together on the harness. Then he pulled a bight from the big rope into a figure 8 descender, ran it around the bottom, and clipped it into a locking carabiner on his harness. From the way he screwed down the lock and checked it, she could tell he'd definitely done this before.

He smiled, held a finger to his lips, took the bottom rope and wrapped it around the small of his back. He was left-handed, she noticed. Then he stepped backward off the Perch and down toward the ground, slowed only by the friction of the rope through the descender and the pressure of the rope around his body.

June watched him slide down the rope, thinking he'd missed something, skipped some step. Then she realized he hadn't attached the ascenders' safety lines to his harness.

Their locking carabiners lay on the wide branch at her feet.

5

PETER

Where the hell is this chick? Is she some kind of ninja or what?"
One of the men held an electronic device in one hand. He
turned in a slow circle, looking from the device to the rugged
landscape and back to the device.

Another stood with his foot on the bloody corpse of Mr. Griz. "Hey,
somebody take my picture." He held the unmistakable form of a compact
semiautomatic rifle, maybe a Steyr or a Heckler & Koch. Either one a
very good weapon, and expensive.

"Yo, shut up," said a third man, a similar rifle slung across his chest,
studying the remains of Peter's gear spread around the base of the sapling
he'd climbed. "I'm telling you, I think this goddamn bear ate her."

The man with the device kept turning, kept looking. His rifle was
slung across his back. "What, it swallowed her whole? Where's the
bones? Where's the remains?"

A fourth man stepped deliberately around the perimeter, eyes out. He
had a different weapon, with a fat barrel and minimal magazine, something out of a sci-fi movie. Like the other three men, he was dressed in
hiking clothes so crisp and new he might have stepped out of REI and

onto the trail. Four big internal-frame backpacks lay against a fallen trunk, out of the way. They were new, too.

Peter hung at the bottom of the rope, one foot in the loop, sixty or seventy feet up, at the edge of the fog. The wind didn't penetrate the lower canopy, and their voices were soft but clear in the hush. Peter couldn't see their faces, just the tops of their heads.

He didn't want to see their faces.

If he could see their faces, they could see him.

Peter was mostly worried about the guy at the perimeter. He was the one most actively searching the landscape. It might occur to him to actually look up.

Peter reached into his left pocket for an ascender. It was a simple device, basically an aluminum handgrip with a channel for the rope. The channel had a locking mechanism so the rope would only move in one direction. Push it up the rope, and the grip would hold while you pulled yourself up. Much easier than shinnying up hand over hand like he'd done earlier that day.

He held the lock open and set it on the line. Closed the lock with his hand fully engaged to dampen any sound. These men would definitely notice a metallic click in this environment.

They were hunters. Serious people.

Hunting Riot Grrrl.

Four on one. Not exactly fair.

What had she done to attract their attention?

They weren't trying to pass for government, like she'd said they'd done before. They were trying to look like backpackers, although with all that new gear they might pass as tourists. The assault rifles gave a different kind of impression. But that's what the backpacks were for. To hide the weapons until they were deep in the forest.

And the handheld device. Some sort of locator.

So they had funding, and technical support.

They were definitely pros.

Riot Grrrl was in serious trouble. And now Peter was, too. But it wasn't his first time.

Peter got the second ascender locked in place. He looked up. Did he see Riot Grrrl's pale freckled face looking down at him?

He should have the ascenders' safety lines clipped to his climbing harness, in case one of them slipped. They would have let him rest, too, on the way back up. But he'd left them behind. He was afraid they'd jingle on his harness.

He started climbing, slowly. The ascenders made a faint sound as the rope slipped through the mechanism. *Zizz, zizz, zizz, zizz.* Making his way back up, a foot at a time. His arms were already tired. Suck it up, Marine.

"C'mon, take my picture."

"Don't be stupid. You want photographic evidence that you were here?"

"Shut up," said a fourth voice. "All of you, shut up."

Peter stopped. He hung by his hands, maybe ninety feet off the ground. Not quite hidden in the fog.

It would have been nice to be able to hang from his harness, and rest. Falling would be bad.

The men had gone silent. He looked down. They were scanning the tangled underbrush, guns at the ready position. The fourth man with the odd, thick-barreled weapon stood motionless. Then, as if he could somehow feel Peter's eyes on him, he slowly tilted his head, peering up into the dim green light.

"Look up," he called. "Look up."

Zizz, zizz, zizz, zizz. Peter climbed the rope as fast as his arms would carry him. Distance and motion meant a more difficult target, and the farther up he went, the harder it would be to see him in that filtered twilight.

"Hey, you up there. Stop or I'll shoot."

They'd shoot eventually whether he stopped or not, thought Peter as he did his best to move faster yet. His arms burned. *Zizz zizz zizz zizz, zizz zizz zizz zizz.*

Then they fired. The shots came, as he knew they would, in those same disciplined three-round bursts, *takatak, takatak.* But they didn't hit him or even seem to come close. These would be warning shots. They didn't know who he was, or what he was doing there. Or even whether he had any relationship with the woman they were hunting.

Peter didn't have any breath left to respond. His arms were slowing down already. *Zizz, zizz, zizz, zizz.* How far had he come? How far left to go until he disappeared into the fog?

"Get back down here. Or we'll drop you hard."

His arms, fuck. The muscles on fire. Keep going, no safety lines, no choice. Think of it as motivation.

His sphincter clenched tight as he waited for the searching rounds to find him.

Then he felt himself rising through the air. The rope trembled slightly. He looked up and saw that big branch, getting closer. Even though he was just hanging by his hands.

"Hold on, you fucking idiot." Her voice came down from above, thin but clear.

He held on, and kept rising. She was pulling him up.

He heard the rifles again. *Takatak. Takatak.* They had a crisp, Germanic sound, a muscular purr that reminded him of a big BMW starting up. Not like the cheap metallic rattle of an AK-47, or the cheerful round pop of his old M4. The high-velocity NATO rounds parted the air around him with staccato whispers. He waited for the punch of hot pain, but it didn't come.

Rising, he was getting harder to see from the ground.

Then a feeling of impact in the sole of his right boot, but not hard, and no pain, not yet. He looked down. No hole in his boot, no spreading red bloom. He looked up, saw the big branch closer still, and a long spool of rope coming down the other side.

As he neared the branch he saw her sitting on a burl twenty feet away, feet braced, hauling away on the rope. She'd rigged a pulley block to the top of his rope and used the ratio to lift him. He could hear the faint tick of the cam lock as the rope spooled through the mechanism.

Then he was up, holding the webbing with both hands and stepping onto the thick rough bark with his left foot, careful of the right, still unsure if he'd been hit. She was red-faced and sweating as she reversed the cam and started pulling up the unspooled rope and coaxing it into a coil. The ratio was four to one, making his two hundred pounds into fifty. Which she'd hauled up at least a hundred feet.

Way to go, Riot Grrrl. "Thank you," he said.

Then her red face turned white. "Don't move." She pointed at his foot.

He looked down. A thin tube with a puffy red tail stuck out of the bottom of his boot. He reached down and pulled it out of the dense sole. Held it up.

It was a dart. A tranquilizer dart? They'd tried to shoot him with a tranquilizer dart? What was he, a rhino?

Peter looked at her. "Who the hell are these people?"

"I have no idea," she said.

"Well, they seem to want you alive," he said, displaying the dart. "Me, they don't seem to care about one way or the other."

He thought about the four deadly men waiting at the bottom of the tree. About the device the man had held, turning in a slow circle. Some kind of locator.

He said, "Did you have that backpack when those men tried to grab you?"

"No," she said. "I had my messenger bag."

"Did they have access to the bag? Could they have put anything into it?"

She shook her head. "They just dropped it on the floor."

"Did anything from that bag go into this backpack?"

"A few things," she said. "My wallet, interview notes for three stories, my notebook, chargers, my phone."

Her phone.

She'd said she got great reception up there.

She saw it in his face. "What?" she asked.

He watched as realization dawned. It only took a second. She was plenty smart.

She shucked her pack and dug into the top pouch. The phone was in a Ziploc bag.

"It's turned off," she said. "Can they still—"

"Someone can," he said. "Unless you take out the battery. They had some kind of locator down there. Your phone's the most likely source of the signal."

She turned the phone in her hands. "I can't take the back off this thing." She raised her arm to hurl it into the air.

"Wait," he said. "Don't throw it."

"Why not?" Her voice was a little louder than it needed to be. "I just want to get it as far away as possible. And get the fuck out of here in the complete opposite direction."

"We could do that," Peter said calmly. "But they would know that we know. And it would be harder for us to predict their actions."

"I don't want to predict their actions," she said, as if talking to a profoundly stupid person. "I want to get away from them."

"We will," said Peter. "But right now we're on the defensive. This knowledge gives us a tactical advantage. Do you want to run forever?"

She gave him a look, and he felt it again, the heat of her focused attention. "You better know what the fuck you're doing, mister."

"This is my first time on the lam in a redwood," he said, "but I'm pretty sure you should leave your phone here."

She made a face, and tucked the smooth aluminum rectangle into a crevice in the bark. "Good-bye, phone. You served me well until you got hacked." Then she went back to coiling rope.

"Is there a way to move laterally?" asked Peter. "From one tree to the next?"

"Way ahead of you," she said, stuffing the rope and pulleys into her pack. "My ex-boyfriend studied the biology of tall tree crowns. This was his lab."

"Ex-boyfriend?" asked Peter.

"Don't even think about it," she said. "Anyway, we used to have lines out to neighboring trees, for a larger sampling area. You and I are going to find out if any of those are still in place."

"Your ex sounds like a cool guy."

She strapped the bow along her pack again, put her arms through the shoulder straps, then looked up into the branches, searching for something. "His other girlfriend thought so, too. But I helped set this place up, so I gave myself visitation rights." She pointed. "There. You see it?"

Peter looked. "The yellow rope?"

"Yep. We marked our paths with colored rope. My idea, by the way. You came up the red path."

The red ropes, thought Peter. "So the yellow path takes us to the next tree?"

"That's the idea. If it's still there." She set off along a wide horizontal branch.

"The tree or the rope?"

"The tree's been there since the Roman Empire," she said over her shoulder. "But these ropes can rot pretty quickly in this damp environment. I used to replace them every year. They're not cheap. But then, I used to write his grant proposals, too." She flashed a grin. "I'm not sure how much funding he's got these days."

Peter wondered if the ex-boyfriend knew what he'd lost. Peter was pretty sure the guy had no clue. If he did, he wouldn't have lost her to begin with.

Riot Grrrl led, Peter followed.

It was more technical than the scramble up along the red path. They had to use the ascenders again and again. The path was not direct. Down to go over, then up again, ropes strung where the climbing was difficult, always following the trail marked by bright yellow ropes. It was hard work, but they were cooled by the damp breeze filled with the astringent tang of evergreen needles and the pungency of bark, while the infinitely blue California sky peeked through the fog.

This time, Peter clipped the safety lines to his harness, and spent most of his attention watching Riot Grrrl. Climbing with anyone was an exercise in trust. Any fall, even on a ten-foot rock face, might mean a significant injury or death. Three hundred feet up in a giant redwood, she could have killed him a dozen times. But she hadn't.

Every climber had their own style, and it didn't take long for Peter to get a pretty good idea who he was climbing with. Riot Grrrl wasn't flashy, she didn't take unnecessary risks. She knew her gear and how to use it. But she didn't rope off for every step, either, and seemed perfectly comfortable free-climbing through the branches as if it were a fifteen-foot apple tree in her backyard.

She stayed ahead of him without any trouble. Peter knew how she'd gotten those serious arms.

After less than half an hour, they stood on a wide limb looking out at the wrinkled tree-covered mountains spread out ahead of them. Thick nylon webbing around the limb held a beefy locking carabiner attached to a gleaming cable, impossibly thin, stretched high above their little pocket valley, barely clearing an impossibly steep rocky ridge and slanting down to the next drainage, where it disappeared into the canopy of another redwood.

Climbing around inside this enormous tree, it was hard to judge or even imagine the whole architecture of it. But from a distance, Peter could see clearly the shape of the next tree, a gnarled asymmetrical giant that certainly looked as if it had lasted two thousand years, and might last a thousand more. He could see other ancient behemoths, standing like sentinels in the rugged rain-collecting pocket valleys and drainages inaccessible to the first loggers who had cut down almost all the old growth on the West Coast. Around these sentinel trees grew their much-younger cousins, the smaller second- and third-growth trees sprouting up since the days of clear-cutting, hundred-foot trees considered tall by any measure but their ancestors.

It was a long way across a very thin cable.

Peter peered into the depths of the valley below. It was a long way down, too.

He kept his voice quiet, thinking about the men below. "How far is it?"

"About nine hundred feet," she said. "That's aircraft cable, stainless steel. It would hold ten of us."

He thought about the logistics of getting the cable in place. The bow and arrow to get the high-test fishing line across. Then the feeder rope, and after that the cable. Hours of dangerous work, high in these giant trees.

"This is your idea of fun?"

She shrugged, a little embarrassed. "I like to keep busy."

"I bet you're a hell of a journalist," he said. "So what happens next? We clip on our harnesses and pull ourselves across?"

"You can do it that way if you want," Riot Grrrl said, rooting through her pack. She extracted a small metal contraption and held it up for Peter to see. Her eyes gleamed with fun, the hunters below forgotten for a moment. "But it's a lot faster to ride."

Peter saw the harness clip, and the handles, and the wheels.

It was a trolley for a zip line. He raised his eyebrows.

"I liked you better when I thought you were worried about aliens."

"Oh, the aliens are real, too," she said, putting the trolley in his hand and taking another from her pack and mounting it to the line. "Their mind-control beams are totally gnarly. If we ever get out of this, I'll make you a tinfoil hat." Her smile was brilliant. "You want to go first, or me?"

"What's the landing like?"

"You can see from here that the cable isn't strung tight. If it was, the movement of the trees in big storms would snap it like twine. So there's a dip on the far end, and the rise should slow you some. The attachment point on the far end is twenty or thirty feet inside the outermost branches. When you get close you'll see a small landing stage like our work platform, with rope railings to keep you from overshooting. But be ready, 'cause you'll be moving fast."

He was heavier than she was, thought Peter. If the cable attachment broke under his weight, better that she was already on the other side of that ridge, away from the men below.

"You go," said Peter. "Show me how it's done."

She clipped her harness into the trolley and checked the locks. "Usually I scream my head off when I do this," she said, then pointed toward the men on the ground. "But I'll try to stay quiet so they don't hear."

Flashing him a last toothy grin, she gripped the trolley handle with both hands and took a running jump off the limb of the tree. The harness caught her hips, and she leaned back and stretched her legs out in front of her like a human projectile. Gravity pulled her faster and faster, down, down and away with a high bubbling laugh that echoed over the trees and rocks and ridges like the call of a wild animal.

Peter saw her disappear into the outer fringe of the next tree. Then he saw the rope go slightly slack, which would be the Riot Grrrl setting her feet on the platform and unclipping her harness from the trolley. Then the cable rose in a series of small waves that traveled up toward him. She'd bumped the cable to signal that she was clear. It was Peter's turn.

He set the trolley on the rope and locked the wheels into place. He clipped the carabiner on his harness to the eye on the trolley body and checked that lock. Nine hundred feet across. Three hundred feet up. He tasted copper in his mouth and felt the smile spreading across his face as the wild exhilaration rose within him.

Alive, alive, I am alive.

He backed to the end of his tether, gripped the trolley hard, took two long strides and jumped off the branch and into the air.

The harness caught him snug and solid. He raised his legs and leaned back as she had done, and he wasn't falling but flying like an arrow over thickly crowded treetops with the ground only an idea below. The valley wall with its rocky ridge rose to meet him, higher and higher, finally so close below that he could see every crevice and stone and spot of lichen before it was gone behind him. The tree ahead grew larger with each moment, the massive canopy becoming a wall of branches that resolved into individual limbs with a narrow slot threaded through by the cable. It began to rise again and Peter felt himself decelerate as he entered the dark notch in the crown of the tree. He went blind for a half second as his eyes adjusted to the dim arboreal light, but his vision returned and he saw the netting platform and ropes strung and he dropped his legs to step lightly down on the mesh and bring himself to a stop, his head ringing like a gong and the wind blowing clear through him like he was transparent to the world.

That was a cure for the static if there ever was one.

Riot Grrrl stood on a large limb just off the landing platform. She watched him closely as he turned to her, grinning like an idiot after a rush of emotion so outsized that it felt like a religious experience.

"Let's do it again," he said.

She looked him full in the face, and he felt like he'd passed some test.

"Another time," she said. "Right now we're running away from the bad people, remember?"

"Tell me one thing," he said. "What's your name?"

"June," she said. "June Cassidy. Now can we go?"

6

Another path marked by red ropes led them down through the new tree in a spiral.

The path ended at a branch six feet across, the lowest substantial branch on the tree. Below was green-tinted air and mist and a few little twigs that looked like they wouldn't hold a sparrow.

Riot Grrrl—June, Peter reminded himself, her name was June, although Riot Grrrl fit her like a glove—opened her pack and pulled out a long coil of rope and another shorter loop of thick webbing. She swung the webbing around the base of a protruding branch hard enough for it to come around the other side, where she caught it, clipped the open ends together with a locking carabiner, and screwed down the lock.

"How far down?" asked Peter.

"About a hundred fifty feet." Fifteen stories. "We don't have enough rope for you to belay me. Or me you." She sat on the wide limb and made one end of the rope fast to the locking carabiner, then checked the lock again.

"No problem," he said. It would be better to have a second line for backup, but they hadn't had one the last time, either. It wasn't the safest way to climb, but when there were men with automatic weapons after you, escape was more important. Nobody had belayed Peter in his fifty-foot helicopter drops, either. It was you and your figure 8, friction, and the strength of your hands. Basic physics.

She began to pay out the rope, making sure there were no tangles.

"What's the terrain like when we get down?" he asked.

"It's a scramble down the drainage, no trail to speak of. The creek runs to the river, which parallels the road out. That ridge we crossed stays between us and where we came up. It's not easy, but it's a much more direct route than the trail they'll be following. Even if they know we're coming down, we should be able to beat them back to the car."

"And if they've disabled your car?"

"It's hidden."

"What if they found it?"

She looked at him, and he saw again how terrified she was. She was handling it very well, using her climbing skills and knowledge of the tree to feel like she had control over the situation, and her sense of humor helped keep things light. But these men had pursued her before, had almost captured her. Once she was back on the ground all her tenuous advantages would be gone, and she was feeling it.

"I'm not trying to scare you," Peter said, keeping his voice deliberately calm. "It's a planning tool. Human nature is to see the outcome we prefer. The 'what if' game helps us to see other possible scenarios, and plan accordingly."

"If they found my car," she said, "I'm fucked."

"Maybe, maybe not. The point is to think ahead. Make contingency plans. What are our options?"

She took a deep breath and let it out. "Okay. We could stay in the woods. Make our way down to the highway. Catch a ride there."

"What if they come after us in the woods? What are our strengths?"

She thought for a moment. "We use the climbing gear. Go back up, hide and wait. Or go down some rock face where they can't follow."

Or the bow and arrows, thought Peter. But he wasn't going to mention that just yet.

"There you go," he said. "You're thinking tactically already."

She gave him a look. "Yeah," she said. "I am so tactical."

She'd seen right through him, of course.

"Regardless," he said. "We need to keep moving, right?"

"Right," she said. "I'll go first."

She ran a bight through her figure 8, passed it under the harness point, then clipped the 8 onto her harness. She double-checked the carabiner lock and wrapped the rope past the small of her back, under the bow where it was strapped to her pack. She turned to face him, her freckled face intent and focused. "See you on the ground," she said, and flashed that grin. "If you fall, try not to land on me."

Then she walked backward off the branch and into the air.

Peter lay down across the branch and poked his head around its curve to keep her in sight. The rope went down and down, but he'd already lost her in the mist and shadow. He couldn't even see the ground from here.

He waited until the rope went slack, just a minute or two. Then a wave ran up the line, and he knew she'd flipped it to let him know she was off. He ran the rope through his own figure 8, clipped on, checked the lock.

He turned away from the drop and bent his knees slightly, enjoying the green glow of the tree and the solidity of the branch beneath his boots for one last moment. Then took a deep breath, wrapped the rope into the small of his back with his left hand, and jumped into the darkness.

A giant grin on his face.

This was turning out to be a pretty interesting day.

7

They moved as quickly as they could through the trackless tangle of rocks and underbrush. But some of the deadfall jumbles were twenty feet tall, and a single misstep could mean a twisted ankle or worse.

Peter didn't know what the hunters would do. But it was a reasonable possibility that they might split their forces. Keep two men at the tree and send two men back down to the trailhead to look for her car. If they hadn't found it already.

If they could track June's phone in real time, they probably also knew where she'd been.

He was hoping they'd lost the signal in the mountains and only picked it up again when she climbed the tree.

Maybe there were eight of them. Maybe they had reinforcements already at the trailhead. Maybe they really *were* government. Maybe June was an escaped mental patient. Speculation was useless without more information. Peter had a distinct lack of information. So he'd work with his instinct, which had proved useful in the past.

As they slogged down the steep slope through the endless brush, each step taking twice as long as it should, Peter's instinct told him it was very possible that at least some of the hunters would get to the trailhead ahead of them. A map and compass would come in handy about now.

He felt better when they reached the creek. They could move much faster and in a more direct line, although they were sometimes up to their knees in frigid water. June was pretty sure this creek eventually ran through a culvert under the logging road below the trailhead, so they could come up behind any watchers. She said she'd hidden her car up an overgrown spur and around a curve that would shield it from view.

The road announced itself as a patch of light ahead of them. Now Peter thought they might be ahead of the hunters, although probably not by much. The creek made a pool at the culvert, which was partly blocked by sticks and brush. He could hear the sound of a river on the other side. He took the lead and belly-crawled his way up the muddy verge, feet soaked and cold. He stopped when his head came level with the gravel. Nobody there. The road just an unsightly scrape in an otherwise beautiful wilderness.

She crawled up beside him. She tilted her head uphill. "The trailhead is another few miles that way. Room for maybe ten cars." She tilted her head downhill. "My Subaru is that way. Past the next curve there's an old logging spur on the right, you'll see the gate. It's unlocked."

Peter wanted to see if the hunters had left anyone up at the trailhead. If so, maybe ask a few questions. But they were likely to be heavily armed. And if something happened to him, June was alone and screwed.

He looked up the road, and down. There were no signs of human life but the damp gravel road and the woman beside him. Her face was flushed. He could see her pulse fluttering in her throat.

"You ready?"

She took a deep breath, let it out. "You bet," she said.

"Okay," he said. "Let's get out of here."

They came up to the road with nobody else in sight, down through the graveled tunnel of trees and around the turn with no sound but their own boots on the gravel. The gate was welded tube steel, rusty but strong. It opened with the soft scream of distressed metal.

Then up the old track, which looked like it hadn't seen a road grader for a decade or more. Bushes grew out of the middle of the road, and runoff had washed out small sections. But her little white Subaru wagon was right where she'd left it, an old four-wheel-drive at least thirty years old. There were a lot of them on the road in the West, where underbody rust was only a distant ugly rumor. A good car. Durable, well made. A classic.

Peter did wish it was a few years younger.

"You maintain this car?" he asked. The tires looked pretty good. He was very happy about the sunroof.

"Of course I do." She sounded a little indignant. "She's my girl." She popped the hatch and dropped her pack inside.

"Shocks?" he asked. He retrieved her pack and propped it on the back seat beside his own. Better access from the front. "When did you change those?" He undid the straps holding the compound bow to the tie panel, then returned to the rear hatch and surveyed her neatly organized gear.

"Last year." She was stretching her legs. "I had to do the whaddaya-callits, too, ball joints and tie rods, the whole front end. It cost me, like, three grand. Why?"

Peter took out a dozen energy bars, some powdered lemonade, and four big bottles of water. He also found a nice wooden box with a lid, about eight by eight inches by three feet long.

He opened it up. More arrows.

"Bad road," he said. "And you're going to be driving fast."

He hoped like hell she was a good driver.

. . .

WHILE JUNE TURNED the car around, Peter jogged back to the gate.

She rolled down her window as he walked the gate closed behind her. She had her seat belt on and snugged up tight. "How do we know they're coming?"

Because they know every place you've been since they hacked your phone, Peter thought, but he didn't say it.

"They're pros. They already found you at least twice." He jogged around to the passenger side and slid in. "They're coming."

"I can't outrun them," she said, revving the engine. It sounded pretty good. "Not in this old girl."

"Don't worry about the car," he said. "Drive it like you stole it."

She flashed that same fierce wild grin he'd seen in the tree. "I can do that."

He patted her shoulder, then reached up and pushed the sunroof back. Got the bow where he could reach it. Put one end of the long box of arrows down by his feet, the other end propped up by the emergency brake. He looked up the road toward the trailhead parking lot. He thought he heard the rumble of a big engine starting up, but it might have been his imagination. "Better get moving," he said.

June wore hiking pants that converted to shorts by unzipping the pantlegs at mid-thigh. At some point she'd removed the lower sections. Her legs were tan and sleek. She popped the clutch and cranked the car around the corner, spitting gravel from all four tires, shifting into second while they were still sliding.

Yeah, Riot Grrrl could drive. But he should have expected that from the way she attacked that zip line.

He turned in his seat to look out the back window, holding on to the lip of the sunroof for leverage. It was too wet for another car to raise a dust cloud, so he wouldn't have much notice. Just the nose of the vehicle coming around the curve behind him.

He was assuming that the hunters would have a big American SUV, something like a Chevy Suburban or a GMC Denali, because that was what a lot of federal law enforcement people drove. Something big and powerful, great for eating up the highway, but also kind of a boat. Not particularly suited to a narrow twisting lumpy gravel road barely wide enough for two cars to pass at a crawl. He was hoping the little Subaru's scrappy off-road handling would force the hunters to make a mistake. Lose it on a curve, maybe even end up in the ditch. That was best case. A hope, really.

If they came to a long paved straightaway, they were screwed.

Peter hoped it didn't come to plan B.

He looked over at the speedometer. She was going about forty, both hands on the wheel. Already too fast for the road, but not fast enough. "How far to pavement?"

"About ten or fifteen miles," she said. "Along the river the whole way. But the road gets better before that, maybe six or seven miles."

Then he saw it, the big black vehicle coming around the curve behind them, the tires chunking up into the wheel wells with each bump, the red Chevy logo on the radiator grille getting larger by the second. It looked like a Tahoe, the short-frame version of the Suburban. Better turning radius, less likely to bottom out. A big engine.

"Here they are," he said. "Punch it."

June's eyes angled up to the rearview for just a moment, and the Subaru's little power plant wound up as the old car responded. She still had it in third, which wasn't the worst way to go, especially if you didn't care much about the engine. She could brake just by letting off on the gas, and the torque would let her build up speed again quickly. He looked out the back again and saw a man lean out the passenger-side window with a rifle.

Before Peter could say anything the man fired, three-shot bursts, *takatak, takatak*. He missed more than he hit, but still Peter heard the familiar unwelcome thunk of a bullet puncturing sheet metal. Then the passenger-side mirror exploded.

"Mother*fuckers*," said June, and she rammed the shifter into fourth, powering ahead. She was using the whole road now, taking the curves on the inside, slaloming around the worst of the ruts, hammering the car on the washboard sections. At higher speed they almost floated above the washboard. Not a lot of traction there.

The hunters weren't losing any ground. The Tahoe's beefy suspension ate up the road. The driver clearly had some training, and thirty years of automotive advances made a difference. The shooter fired low, going for tires, Peter figured, if they wanted to capture her alive. Although at this speed on this road, losing a tire might be fatal.

Fuck this, he thought. Plan B. He picked up the compound bow in one hand, took the lip of the sunroof in the other, and stood on his seat.

Peter and his dad had set up a practice range in the barn for his four-teenth birthday. He'd no shortage of practice in high school, but he hadn't pulled a bow in ten years. He told himself it was like riding a bike.

The man with the rifle looked a little startled to see Peter pop up through the sunroof. Clearly the man hadn't grown up on *Dukes of Haz-zard* reruns, although the little Subaru was nothing like that hopped-up orange Dodge Charger. Peter had changed out some of the arrows on the snap-in quiver, and he now had one broadhead and three of the ball-headed shafts June had used to get a line up into the trees. He notched one of the ball-heads. It would hurt like hell if he hit anyone. He'd be lucky just to spiderweb the windshield with this crappy road and the madwoman behind the wheel. Hell, he'd be lucky to hit anything at all.

He drew the bowstring back to his cheek and aimed, waiting for a moment of calm, the tension still familiar on his two fingers. The ride smoothed out for just a moment, and he released.

The arrow left the bow very fast, but the heavy ball-head dropped faster than he'd thought, skittering off the hood of the trailing Tahoe and skating up the windshield with barely a scratch. The shooter smirked behind his sunglasses and raised his gun.

Peter had another arrow notched and drawn before the shooter could get himself stabilized in the window. The road was forgiving for just that moment as he aimed and released.

The ball dropped again, but this time Peter had corrected. It punched right through the center of the hunters' windshield with such velocity that it made a relatively clean hole, albeit one the size of a baseball.

The Tahoe lurched and dropped back, swerving. Peter imagined the confusion inside as the arrow came through, shards of glass everywhere. Maybe he'd even hit someone. It would be like getting hit with a hammer.

Peter smiled back at the shooter, who was now holding on to his ride for dear life, trailing his rifle outside the window by its strap. The Waylon Jennings song from *The Dukes of Hazzard* stuck in his head. "Just a good ol' boy, never meanin' no harm . . ."

They came to a long turn and the black truck came up again. This time the shooter stuck his rifle out of the hole in the windshield. Peter didn't know if that would help the man's aim or not. He notched another ball-headed arrow.

The rifle purred again, now on full auto, still aiming for tires but firing wild. The bumps would be exaggerated from inside the truck, making it harder for the man to steady his aim.

If it were me with the gun, thought Peter, I'd have shot at the guy with the bow and arrow. They must want her bad, trying not to fire into the car by accident. Or maybe they were figuring two for the price of one, as any loss of control could be fatal for Peter, standing halfway out of the sunroof. If he was thrown clear at fifty or sixty miles an hour, the impact would turn him into jelly.

So why was he having so much fun?

He pulled the bowstring back to his cheek, feeling the pressure on his bare fingers. Aimed at the muzzle of the gun this time, waited again for a moment of calm, then released. The arrow made another hole to the left of the first, and now spiderwebs appeared in the glass. The muzzle of the gun jerked wildly for a moment, then pointed upward. Peter felt the blast of joy, reminded himself to take a deep breath, then watched as the muzzle steadied back down to point directly at his chest.

He already had his last arrow from the quiver notched and ready. It was the broadhead, the hunting point designed to slice into flesh. He aimed for where he thought the driver's center of mass would be. Standing on the seat gave him a high vantage, so he figured the steering wheel wouldn't interfere much with his shot.

He aimed and released.

The broadhead smashed through the windshield high and to the left of where he'd been aiming, although he still could have hit the man. The black Tahoe fell back again. Peter had more arrows below him in the long box, but he wasn't about to ask June to hand him more. The road curved sharply ahead, the mountain on the left, the wide rocky bed of a drought-lowered river on the right.

As he bent his knees to drop back into the car, he heard the blast of an air horn. *Blaat blaaaaaat.*

He turned as he dropped to see the dirty red nose of a giant logging truck coming around the curve, hogging the road and growing fast.

"Omigod omigod omigod." June's voice rose up in a losing battle with the truck's air horn.

The logging truck was two hundred feet away.

At their combined speeds, Peter figured they had about two seconds.

The world slowed. June's knuckles white on the wheel, braking to buy time as she steered them toward the nonexistent right lane. No air bags in this old car.

Peter planted himself in his seat, precious fragments of a second lost as he maneuvered the awkward bow over his shoulder into the back, then jammed his feet to the floor, hoping the box of arrows would be trapped under his legs. Loose arrows could kill them as easily as the crash.

A hundred feet.

Blaaaaaaaat blat blaaaaaaaaat.

The wandering gravel road was not designed for two vehicles to pass at speed. Definitely not when one of them was a giant semi-tractor. Reaching for his seat belt with his right hand, Peter remembered the time in Oregon he had driven in reverse for twenty minutes to find a spot wide enough for a fully loaded logging truck to get past.

Fifty feet.

The Subaru was halfway onto the shoulder, a weedy slope that dropped unpredictably toward the rocky riverbed. The truck's front grille was enormous, taller than the car. Peter could see giant bugs crushed on the glass of the headlamps.

Blaaaaaaaaaaaaaaaaaaaaaaaaaaaaaaaaaaaaaaat.

Peter's hand found the buckle, pulled it down and across, and snapped it into the latch as the car left the road. He planted his feet hard and threw out his left arm to keep June's head from banging into the steering wheel. The front passenger wheel dipped. He reached for the dashboard with his right hand, locked on tight.

Gravity changed.

The landscape whirled around, the sky beneath them, weeds overhead. Then sky above and dirt below. Now clouds beneath and rocks above. Crap floated through the air as the car rolled, energy bars and water bottles and lemonade packets everywhere. Peter banged around in his seat like a toy shaken by an angry toddler, banged in the chest and legs and back over and over for what seemed like forever, until the car finally came to rest.

Peter looked out his window. The glass had disappeared completely.

The sky was up and the ground was down. They were on the dry section of the riverbed.

He looked over at June. "Are you okay? June. June!"

She looked back at him, blinking. "Oh, man," she said sadly. "I really loved this car."

"Are you hurt? Is anything broken? Look at me. Look at me!" All the while taking an inventory of his own injuries, the aching shoulders, the pain in his ribs that hurt when he breathed in, the left leg on fire.

She had a bruised lip that would get nice and fat, and a bloody elbow, maybe from all the glass in her lap. No compound fractures that he could see. Her window was mostly gone, but the windshield was intact.

The hunters. The black Tahoe.

He tried to open the door, but it was stuck. He looked for the bow, couldn't find it. He looked down at June's feet and saw a black short-barreled revolver on the floor. "What the hell?"

He forgot he was belted in when he bent over to get it, and his ribs howled in protest. He gasped and straightened enough to unbelt himself, then bent again. His cheek brushed against her thigh as he reached for the gun, pressed against fine blond hairs and warm tanned skin. Her legs smelled like sunshine and lotion and he wanted to fall asleep right there. His hands were shaking with the aftermath of the crash and it took him a few fumbling seconds to come back up with the gun.

"Hey," she said, "I always wondered where that went."

She was dazed but oddly lucid. Peter figured she was in shock.

"My dad gave it to me. I was fourteen. Kind of a weird birthday present if you ask me. My mom kept telling me to get rid of it, but then I couldn't find it. That was years ago. I haven't cleaned out this car in forever."

It was a Colt .38, the walnut grips worn but solid, the finish starting to go, maybe an old police model long out of service. It looked clean enough except for the gum wrappers and dust from where she'd lost it under the seat. He found the cylinder release and flipped it open. Five beautiful brass rounds, nothing under the hammer, a lovely circle of daylight through the barrel. He'd been a little worried he'd find a crayon jammed in there. He snapped the cylinder shut with a flick of his wrist.

"Stay here a minute," he said. He'd check her more fully when he came back. "Don't go anywhere. Okay?" Without waiting for an answer, he stood on the seat to climb painfully out through the sunroof.

The Tahoe lay on its side like a beached whale about thirty yards away.

8

He climbed down to the dry riverbed, hurting all over but more or less functional. His forehead felt warm and wet. He put his hand up, felt the slickness of blood, and wiped it away, reminding himself that head wounds always bleed like crazy.

He knew too much about damage to human bodies.

He also knew that he would succeed at this next task only if he was the first to act.

The Tahoe's partially crushed roof was facing Peter, blocking his view of the inside. He was expecting someone to pop up with a rifle any second.

Between the two vehicles, one of the hunters lay on the rocks like a thrown doll, all wrong angles. A black man. Was this the man who'd shot at them, or the driver? He saw no weapon. The man's eyes were open, his neck bent strangely, and the side of his head had a softball-sized dent that Peter figured would match up nicely with the profile of some nearby rock. Blood had only just begun to seep from the wound before the man's heart had stopped pumping.

One down. Three to go.

He limped on toward the ruined truck, left leg strangely sore down by his ankle, the .38 in his left hand. Tall trees to each side, the clouds dark with threatening rain.

The Tahoe was bashed and bent like a soda can some kid had kicked down the block. It had obviously rolled a few times, too. He approached it from the back, where anyone inside would be least likely to see him. The glass was tinted and opaque from hundreds of tiny fractures and he couldn't see inside.

There was no sound other than the ticking of the cooling metal, the uneven scuff of his boots, and the sound of his own breathing.

Fuck it. He limped behind the undercarriage, through the chemical stink of leaking fluids and the ruptured fuel tank. Peter wasn't worried about gas. He knew it only exploded in the movies. If it caught fire, he'd have some notice. He was worried about his leg, and the men he could neither see nor hear. He wanted them all to be dead so he wouldn't have to kill them. He wanted at least one to be alive so he could ask some questions.

On its side, the Tahoe was too tall for him to see through the broken-out windows. He didn't want to climb it, not with this leg, although he would if that was his best option. He stepped back for a better view, and that's when he saw the arm. It stuck out from under the truck like it had grown from the ground, the flannel shirt and big black wristwatch as clean and unmarked as an REI mannequin.

If the arm's owner was still alive, he wouldn't be for long.

That was two.

Peter limped forward, feeling more confident. His leg wasn't getting worse, and he thought he'd worked out what had happened. When the Tahoe had rolled, it had thrown the front passenger clear and crushed the driver. Probably weren't wearing seat belts.

He rounded the accordioned front end. The windshield was an irregular mat of cracks and holes, pushed in by the accident to lie loose against the pale pillows of the deflating air bags.

Now he heard a low moaning.

He needed to get in there. He needed to know who was left, and what they knew. But he didn't like the idea of going in headfirst to face someone who'd been trying to kill him just a few minutes before. Especially not a group of pros, like these. He glanced around for a long stick.

"Hey, buddy, y'all okay?" It was the driver of the logging truck, working his way down the riverbank. "Lemme help you out. That was one helluva accident."

He wore blue Dickies work pants and a plain white T-shirt with red suspenders that bowed around his hard round belly. His hair was a gray fringe around a new Crimson Tide cap, his round red face creased with worry.

"Stay up there," Peter called to him. "Don't come any closer."

"No way, buddy," the truck driver said, stumping over the rocks. He had arms like Popeye. "I was a EMT for ten years. I seen more wrecks than you seen cars."

The moaning got louder.

"These guys tried to kill us," said Peter. "They're armed."

"Well, hell," the truck driver said, patting what Peter now realized was a holster at his belt. "I'm armed, too. What are they, dopers?"

Just what we need, thought Peter. A good Samaritan with a gun.

A string of mumbled curses came from the Tahoe. A grunt, a cry of pain.

"Shit, you can't just stand there, somebody's hurt," said the truck driver. He walked to the undercarriage and saw the arm. "Sweet mother of God," he said, his face turned pale. But it only spurred him on. He swarmed up the steaming chassis like a circus performer. "I'm coming," he called out. "Hold on, buddy, we gonna get you outta there and all fixed up. You want to be healthy when you meet the judge."

He was kneeling on the passenger-side door, looking down through the window, when Peter heard the gunshots. *Takatak, takatak.* The truck driver's body jerked and his knees slipped and the weight of his legs pulled him to the ground.

Peter limped quickly to where the engine would provide the most cover and fired the .38 through the windshield opening five times, the gun bucking in his hand until it was empty. Then he limped back to where the truck driver lay on the rocks, his white T-shirt now bright red in growing patches.

"The Lord is mah shepherd," he said. "The Lord is mah shepherd." His voice sounded wet. His shirt was saturated with blood. He coughed once, and was gone.

"I'm sorry," Peter said quietly, closed the man's eyes with his hand, then unsnapped the holster on the man's belt.

The pistol was a big Colt Python .357 Magnum with a six-inch barrel. Not exactly a concealed carry weapon, but perfect for shooting buffalo or small elephants. Still, it was clean and, more important, loaded, with one behind the hammer. So he had six rounds.

Peter limped around to the back of the truck, trying to be quiet. It wouldn't be easy for the man inside to reorient a long gun in that enclosed space, especially with the seats. He hoped his shots from the front had hit the fucker.

He kicked in the back door's shattered glass, stuck the barrel of his pistol through the hole, and fired quickly into the back seat, four shots in a decent grouping. If he'd had a grenade, he'd have used that.

Then he climbed through the window.

Two men lay in a rumpled heap in the back seat, one with an arrow through his chest. Both were spotted with gore from multiple gunshot wounds, and the smell of blood and spent powder was thick in the enclosed space. The man with the arrow didn't seem to be breathing. The other man clutched a Heckler & Koch assault rifle with a grimace on his face, lying halfway into the front seat. It looked like he'd anticipated Peter's maneuver and had turned to face the rear, but Peter had fired first. He reached up and tore the rifle from the man's hands.

"Why?" said Peter. "Why did you do this?"

The man's lips worked for a moment as if his mouth were dry. He took a breath and a soft sucking noise came from his chest, at least one lung punctured. When he spoke, it was just a whisper. "Killed me," he said.

"No," Peter lied, "the ambulance is coming. You're going to be fine. But you have to tell me. Who sent you? Why?"

The man shook his head, and his grimace turned to a look of surprise. "Killed," he said. "Me." His voice the sound of dry leaves in an autumn wind, carried softly away. "Me," he said again.

Then he died.

The white static rose up hard and Peter scrambled out of that tumbled tomb, the broken glass sharp under his palms and his knees, from the dense cloying stink of blood and death into the clean, resinous pine-scented air.

He struggled to his feet on the dry riverbed. He put his face up to the gray sky and felt the first drops of rain. He saw a big gray bird up in the lowest layer of clouds, circling.

He sucked in one breath, then another, and yet another.

9

JUNE

June sat in the car and watched as Peter walked to the body of the man who lay on the dirt. He stood looking down at the corpse for a long moment, then stooped to slide a phone from the dead man's shirt pocket. He had to get down on one knee and roll the body to extract the wallet from his pants.

Man, she hoped he wasn't just robbing the dead.

When the car left the road, she'd felt an immense rush of gratitude at the pressure of his arm against her chest, holding her body in the seat as the world rolled and rolled around her, the strength and safety of him beside her in that tumbling universe. He'd saved her life.

But that thing with the bow? The look on his face as he climbed out the sunroof, that pure distilled joy like riding the zip-line express, only he was singing a goddamn Waylon Jennings song and firing fucking arrows at that huge SUV while the bad guys tried to kill them with all their guns?

He'd saved her life, but she was afraid he might be crazy.

He'd helped her in the tree, protected her in the crash, and checked on her afterward, each time taking pains to make sure she was okay. But he'd also climbed out of her ruined car with utter calm and walked to the wrecked SUV with her dad's gun in his hand and fired through the windows like he was shooting tin ducks at a carnival.

Only they weren't tin ducks. They were people, and he'd killed them.

Maybe he was right to kill them, she thought. Hadn't they tried to kill her, on the road? They'd shot that truck driver who was just trying to help. Those weren't stun guns, not anymore.

She was glad Peter was there. He made her feel safe and protected. He was funny and capable and he seemed to *get* her in a way that nobody else ever really had.

But he'd killed them.

He was a war veteran. Maybe damaged by that in some way, she didn't know, and it didn't feel fair to even think it. But there it was.

She wanted him to come back.

She wanted him to help her.

She also wanted him to walk away so she could stay in her ruined car, her whole ruined *life*, and let herself shudder and cry until she was empty.

She didn't trust her judgment in men. Her therapist had said it was because women often found themselves with men like their fathers. June's dad hadn't exactly set the standard for datable guys. She'd had some bad experiences.

Stevie the tattooed barista with the fine art degree wanted to move in with her and quit his job so he'd have more time to paint his tiny incomprehensible landscapes. The worst thing was that she actually considered it. Paul the app developer wanted her to marry him and quit her job and go to church every day and squeeze out babies for the rest of her life. She'd actually considered that, too, because it turned out that grown-up life in the modern age was so much more complicated than anyone had let on.

Robert the investment banker was the scariest of them. He had a great job and wore good suits and drank good wine. He was smart and polite until he suddenly got very weird, popping Viagra and wanting to tie her up. He became increasingly insistent until one night he got really rough and she had visions of being handcuffed naked to a radiator for the rest of a short miserable life. So she'd kicked him in the balls, scooped up her clothes, snapped a picture of his naked body with her phone for insurance, then climbed out the window.

Even Bryce. An assistant professor, a biologist. She'd loved the trees, but she'd ended up writing his grant proposals and doing his goddamn laundry, all while he fucked that thick-legged slut Cindy from the English department.

What was the matter with her? She'd had enough therapy to know it was all about her crazy overprotective dad. So she swore off relationships, limiting herself to hookups with cute stoner ski instructors and kind-eyed backpacker bums who would never begin to qualify as long-term material.

So this Peter guy. She didn't know. She could tell he liked her, and he hadn't yet tried to tell her what to do. She liked *him*, goddamn it. But that was the biggest strike against him. That and the fact that he'd killed at least one man before her eyes. And she was still actively considering him for dating potential? There was something seriously wrong with her.

Clearly she needed more therapy.

She watched as he limped back to the wrecked SUV and stood staring at it for a minute, as if the dead men might climb out through the shattered openings, or it might somehow right itself on its own. She watched his chest rise and fall like he was breathing hard. What was he thinking? She thought she should get away from him. She should get away from anyone who could do the things she'd seen him do in the last thirty minutes.

Then he bent and crawled back into the wreck.

She found herself shuddering for a long moment and had to grab the wheel hard with both hands to force herself to stop.

Get a grip, girl. Get moving now or you might never leave the car.

Her door was jammed shut. She gathered her legs under her and stood on the seat. Her upper arm was bloody, her lip on fire, her whole body sore as if she'd done three hours of kickboxing then thrown herself off a cliff. The climb through the sunroof was hard. She slid down the windshield on her ass, then scrambled off the hood to put the car between her and Peter. He was still inside that SUV, doing God knows what.

But she couldn't bring herself to walk away.

Finally he emerged with an armload of things he'd taken from the truck, and laid them out on the rocks. He walked around the back side of the SUV with a hatchet and a couple of big water bottles and did something noisy. A thin greasy smoke began to spiral up into the clouds despite the light rain that had begun to fall. He emerged with the water bottles, shook two of them into the Suburban until they were empty, then tossed them in, too. With a lighter, he ignited a long strip of cloth stuffed into a third smaller bottle and lobbed it through the hole where the windshield used to be. He followed it with what looked like the old gun her dad had given her, and maybe the phones he'd taken from the bodies.

Faint flames began to flicker through the broken window openings.

He watched the fire grow for a moment, then bent to the rocks for the remaining things he'd gathered. A black cloth sack in one hand and a new pistol in the other. Black greasy smoke rising up behind him, getting more substantial by the minute.

She didn't know what she would do, but she had to do something.

10

PETER

He limped back from the Suburban, the truck driver's pistol hanging heavy from one hand, the small black cloth drawstring sack in the other.

June stood behind the shield of her car, her face pale and bleak, as if she'd peered through a window into another world, a world far different from the one she'd previously known to exist. She held something in her hand.

"Are you okay?" he asked as he shoved the pistol into the back of his pants. His ribs were sore, his left lower leg a strong dull ache. The rain came in hard little drops, few in number but driven by the rising wind. "Where are you hurt?"

She took a step away from the car, raised the compound bow and drew the string back. She'd found four broadhead arrows for the snap-in quiver. A fifth was nocked in place, pointed right at his chest. Her arms were steady.

"Take it easy." He put his hands up, the black drawstring sack hanging from one finger. "What's going on?" He thought there was a real possibility that she would put a hole in him.

"You killed those men."

"I did." He was very tired, and his head hurt. "It seemed better than the alternative."

"Which was?"

"Them killing me and taking you somewhere."

Her face softened a little at that. She said, "What's in the bag?"

Peter set the black sack down carefully on the half-crushed roof of the car. "Their wallets, the car registration, whatever I could find. If you want to figure out what's going on, you need a place to start, right?"

He didn't tell her what the sack itself was. He'd seen them before. It was a hood. The kind of thing the CIA put over your head when they took you away. He'd found it in the glove compartment along with a gag and multiple sets of plastic restraints. Whatever she was into, it was serious.

"Why did you set their car on fire?"

"To get rid of their phones, anything that might have your name on it. Any DNA and fingerprints I left behind." He could feel the heat on his back as the burn began to really take off. The gas was just the igniter. It was all the plastic padding and upholstery and insulation that would cook the Tahoe down to a skeleton. "Also to send a message."

"What's the message?"

He smiled gently. "Don't fuck with June Cassidy."

Her arms drooped a little, and Peter began to feel better about his chances.

"Listen," he said. "I know what you're going through. This is hard stuff to process. But we need to keep moving. The ammunition in that car is going to start to cook off any minute. And there are probably more of those guys out there somewhere. Maybe you could do me a favor and shoot me later?"

She didn't answer, but she let the tension off the bow. The faint out-line of a smile ghosted across her face.

He put his hands down, took the gun from his waistband, and dropped it and the black drawstring sack through his broken window onto the passenger seat. "I'm hoping your car will get us out of here. Can you drive?"

She looked at the gun and the black sack, then back to Peter. "Yeah." She pushed the bow through the broken back window, climbed up to the sunroof, and swung her legs through.

Unbelievably, the Subaru started on the fourth try. Steam plumed from under the hood and a loud clattering sound came from somewhere in the engine compartment. There was nothing Peter could do about it, so he didn't waste time trying to figure it out.

It was a far better outcome than trying to get that logging truck turned around.

So he limped ahead of the battered little car, scouting down the dry section of the riverbed for a way back up to the road, while June drove slowly behind, piloting around the larger rocks.

The Subaru was rapidly approaching the end of its life, and they were still a long way from anywhere.

Finally they came to a broad oxbow where the river had deposited sand and gravel on the inside bank, leaving a broad shelving path. The Subaru labored up the final steep shoulder, tires slipping on the soft vegetation, Peter pushing from behind with his leg on fire until they hit the packed gravel of the road.

When the tires finally caught, he thought June might keep driving without him, but she stopped and waited without a word.

Peter climbed into the passenger seat. She put the car in gear and pointed it downhill toward so-called civilization and the beginnings of some answers.

. . .

THE RAIN NEVER MATERIALIZED, and the clouds thinned and rose as they drove. June wasn't talking, so Peter opened the black drawstring sack in his lap. Three wallets and the registration. The phones were all password-protected, plus they could be tracked, so he'd thrown them into the fire. He never found the handheld locator device they'd used to track June. There were only so many seconds he could spend inside that slaughterhouse.

The wallets were clean and new and anonymous, although each had a driver's license, a corporate credit card in the name SafeSecure, and federal IDs under different names, one from the Department of Defense and another from Homeland Security. They looked pretty good, but Peter was willing to bet that none of them were real. Each wallet also had four or five hundred dollars in mixed bills.

So they had money for food and gas for the next few days, and a few ways to start looking into the hunters. As an investigative reporter, June would have better resources than Peter for that.

The car was a problem. When the road changed from rutted gravel to uneven asphalt, June put it in third and the clattering got louder. A new noise came from under the car, the unnerving grind of nuts and bolts in an industrial blender. The plume of steam rising from under the hood seemed thinner, and Peter was pretty sure that wasn't good news. June kept both hands on the wheel because the steering was unreliable at speeds over fifteen miles per hour. Something else wrong in the front end, maybe a tie rod, maybe the frame was bent, or both. The list was getting longer by the minute.

But that little car kept running, either out of pure habit or just plain mechanical stubbornness, all the way to a narrow two-lane county highway and the tiny town of Bantam.

It was just a few businesses grouped together like herd animals around a watering hole, more of a populated intersection than a town. June pulled behind a rambling single-story building with a wraparound porch that looked like it belonged on the set of an old Western movie. A large wooden sign announced PIZZA! BEER! LIVE MUSIC ON WEEKENDS!

She drove to the far edge of the wide dirt parking lot to where the scrub growth began. They shared the lot with a Dumpster and a rusted-out Ford Econoline on cement blocks. When she turned off the ignition, the engine stopped with a definitive metallic *clunk*. Peter thought it unlikely that the little car would ever start again.

The rear roof of the car had been partially crushed in the crash, and Peter had to pull open the rear hatch by force. He'd never get it closed. The pain in his lower left leg ranged from a dull ache to a sharp stab depending on how much weight he put on it. A walking stick would be helpful. They emptied the car of anything useful that would fit into their packs. They left the neat coils of climbing rope, but took her tent, stove, and sleeping bag, and all the water and energy bars they could carry. He put the pistol and the black drawstring sack in the pack she'd loaned him.

She found a set of clothes in a duffel, wrinkled but clean. When she stepped into the scrub to change, Peter turned away to give her more privacy.

He wasn't sure if she would come back or just keep walking.

She hadn't said much of anything since they'd gotten back in the car. She was functional but distant, maybe a little disconnected. He hoped it was just shock. He hoped she'd come back. But she'd been through a long nightmare of unpleasant experiences. An abduction and escape, a car chase and wreck. She'd been shot at. She'd seen people killed.

Peter was part of those experiences.

Most people didn't have much practice handling what she'd just been through.

Those who had the practice? Well, he thought. We have our own problems.

For example, he was out of the mountains and back at the edge of the man-made world again, even just this tiny little town, and he could already feel the static prickling at his spine.

To push it away, he thought of what they would have to do next. Finding transportation was at the top of the list.

He was fairly sure that the four men in the Tahoe were not the only people involved.

And if there were more men and more black SUVs out there, they'd be coming.

But to find another car, he needed to look less like an accident victim and more like a normal person. He took a dirty sock and a water bottle and started to wipe the dried blood off his face.

He was relieved to hear June's careful footsteps coming back through the scrub. When she came up beside him, he continued wiping at his face, keeping his movements slow and predictable. She took the water bottle from his hand, soaked her dirty Riot Grrrl T-shirt, and scrubbed at his bloody head with clinical force and precision until he looked presentable.

"Can I help with your arm?" He pointed at her bloody elbow.

"No." She took the T-shirt and rinsed it out again, but wouldn't meet his eye. She was staring at the back of the pizza place.

"Okay," he said. "I'm going to look for a car. Do you want to come with me?"

She shook her head. He saw the clench in her jaw, the muscles knotted just beneath her freckled skin.

He turned to follow her gaze.

She wasn't staring at the back of the pizza place.

She was watching the intersection, a section of which was visible through a gap in the trees.

Looking for the next group of men.

"Will you wait here for me?" he asked. "I'm looking for your new car. I'll try to find a good one. I'll come back, I promise. Then you can tell me what you want to do next."

She didn't answer, or take her eyes off the road. But she nodded.

Peter figured she was trying to make a decision. About him.

11

He limped out into the little town. There wasn't much to it. The commercial buildings were all clustered close to the intersection of the two-lane county highway and the secondary road they'd taken out of the mountains.

Across from the pizza place was a modest hip-roofed shop with cheerful green paint and an elaborate multicolored sign for Esmerelda's Grocery. A nameless beat-down bar with neon in the windows took up one corner of the intersection, two motorcycles and a dusty pickup out front. On the opposite corner stood a sagging frame building with wide overhangs, unpainted redwood siding, and a neatly lettered plank sign over the big front porch: HAPPY HIKE AND BIKE, in the same green as the grocery store. A few long driveways led to houses of various vintages, set back in the trees.

He was hoping to see a car parked on the street with a FOR SALE sign stuck under the wiper. He didn't want to start knocking on doors, although maybe he'd have to. It would make him far too memorable for any hunters.

He looked up at the sky. The cloud cover was higher now, although the air was still thick and damp and he thought the rain would come back soon. They'd need a car quickly.

Then he saw another big bird, or maybe the same bird he'd seen over the riverbed, just the shape of it in the lowest level of the clouds. It was some kind of raptor or vulture he didn't recognize, floating silently in the mist. It looked bigger than it should. He wondered if he was within the range of the reintroduced California condor. Then the clouds shifted and the bird turned and he saw the golden glint again. Maybe a condor, he thought. With some kind of metallic tracking device on its wing or leg.

He kept walking through town. The last building was an old cinderblock structure with a simple façade, a rusty steel roll-up door, and a tin roof. Another crisp hand-painted sign in the same green: ALBERTO'S REPAIR AND REBUILD. As Peter limped closer, he saw a small gravel parking lot with a half-dozen cars in a neat row with prices written on notecards taped to the inside of their windshields.

Inventory ran to Detroit steel from the sixties and seventies. He saw a '71 Plymouth Barracuda with an aggressive green flake paint job parked beside a beautiful red '68 Mustang that looked like a hundred miles an hour standing still. A GTO, a Charger, a Galaxie 500, all of them classic muscle cars and together probably worth half a million dollars if they were mostly original and fully restored. He ran his hand over the silky flank of a sky-blue Chevelle SS with a white hood stripe. Peter was generally more of a truck guy, but for a moment, he wanted them all.

This was what you could do with a few million dollars, he thought. Buy a lot of cool cars.

Then you'd need a garage to hold them. And someone to maintain them. And a lawyer to handle your speeding tickets. Before you knew it, your cars had employees, which didn't sound like much fun. Not at all the same as finding an old car in a barn and restoring it yourself.

And none of these muscle machines were what he needed, anyway. He needed something less sexy, something invisible and reliable. He limped past the cars to another roll-up door set into the cinder-block side of the shop, this one open. Whitewashed walls, a raft of good bright lighting overhead, six repair bays with lifts, three of them occupied. Celia Cruz's distinctive contralto purred from speakers in the back corner. He stood in the doorway but didn't see anyone.

The white static crackled up his brainstem. He didn't want to go inside. "Anybody home?"

"Gimme a minute," a voice called out. Then a brown-skinned man with a long black and gray ponytail walked out, peeling thin blue gloves from his hands. Somewhere in his fifties, he had thick, hairy arms and a few days of stubble. He wore mechanic's blues and steel-toed welder's boots and wire-rimmed glasses with full-round earpieces hooked around big ears. "If you're in a hurry, I prob'ly can't help. I got about twenty good repairs ahead of you."

"I don't need a repair, I need a car."

The mechanic's face opened up in a broad smile. "Now you're talking," he said. "Those are my babies." He put out his hand. "I'm Al. What do you like?"

He had the long fingers of a piano player, but the strong raspy grip of a plumber. The word "HERMANOS" was spelled out with crude blue tattoos on his knuckles, one faded letter each. *Hermanos* was Spanish for *brothers*. It was a word Peter had heard a lot in the Marines.

"I'm Peter, and I like all of them. They're truly gorgeous. But I need something different."

The mechanic looked startled at this radical thought. Who'd want to drive anything but a vintage muscle car?

Then he looked past Peter. "Hi, I'm Al," he said, and put out his hand. "Are you with this guy?"

June had come up behind Peter so quietly he hadn't heard her. But she didn't shake his hand, and she didn't say anything.

"This is June," said Peter, before it could get completely awkward.

"We had an accident." Her fat lip had swollen further, and looked painful. She'd cleaned the blood off her elbow, but the many small cuts were vivid and pink at their edges. Her freckles stood out like reverse constellations in her pale face.

Al looked from June to Peter, and back to June. She was half turned toward the highway, waiting like Peter for the next black SUV. Then Peter felt a tickle at his hairline. His head was starting to bleed again. Al looked back as the first warm drop trickled down Peter's forehead.

"Hell, you people look like shit," he said. "Let me get EMS on the horn. We got a volunteer outfit in Redway, only take them a half hour or so."

"No," said Peter. "Please don't. We're fine. We just need a car."

"Seriously?" Then the implications caught up to him, and he put his hand on the door. "Listen, go bleed on somebody else. I don't need your trouble. Get out of here before I call the cops."

"We won't be any trouble," Peter said, thinking of the Python .357 at the top of his pack. "We just want to buy a car. We can pay you. Cash."

Al turned to June. She cleared her throat. She looked at the highway, then back to Al. "Please," she said quietly. Just one word, but it held a lot.

The mechanic looked back at Peter. There was something substantial there behind the wire rims of his glasses. He was a serious man. Then he shook his head and sighed.

"I have one rule," he said. "I learned it from my *abuelito*. Be honest, that was his rule. Always honest. And I expect the same from the people I do business with. Or I don't do business. So tell me the truth. Who are you and what are you doing here?"

June was staring at the highway now. Peter looked, too, and saw a pair of black Ford Explorers, shiny and new and driving in close formation, turn off the two-lane to the secondary road, heading into the mountains.

Peter said, "Can we go inside? I'll tell you whatever you want to know."

"You first, then her." Al stepped back to hold the door as they passed, and closed it behind them. The shop was bright and open, but Peter's chest tightened anyway. As the static began to rise, his muscles would begin to cramp up. Then he'd start to sweat.

"My office is there." The mechanic pointed to a partitioned corner area. He stood five or six feet behind them and gestured for his guests to walk ahead. He'd scooped up an old-school tire iron and held it low and ready. Al was definitely a serious man.

The office was four steps up, with frame walls and big plate-glass windows looking down onto the shop. One end of the room held an old oak desk with a laptop computer, printer, and neat stacks of paperwork. Behind it stood a tall green steel file cabinet and floor-to-ceiling bookshelves loaded with diagnostic manuals and old Chilton guides. At the other end of the room was a faded brown leather couch, two wooden chairs, and a low table made of a truck rim and a big rough slab of redwood. It looked homey. Comfortable.

The static still didn't like it. Neither did Peter.

His neck felt like it was caught in a vise.

Al walked behind the old desk, placed the jack handle gently atop the old file cabinet, and dropped himself into a modern office chair that looked like it was made for a space station. Before Peter registered the movement, the mechanic had taken a black automatic handgun out of a side drawer and set it on the desktop with a thump. His eyes were hidden behind the reflecting rounds of his glasses. "So," he said. "Let's hear it."

Peter carefully unslung his pack and laid it on the scarred oak desk, then took several steps back. June stood a step back and to one side, closer to the door.

"Open it," he said. "There's a Colt Python .357 on the top. You're in no danger from us. We need help."

Al tapped his pistol with two fingers. Glanced at the pack, at June, and back to Peter. "So why the fuck are you sweating like you just ran a four-minute mile?"

"I have a thing," said Peter. Embarrassed, still. It felt like weakness, although he knew it was biochemical, his brain miswired by the war. But it still felt like weakness. "I can't be inside," he said. "I'm claustrophobic."

"Or what, you sweat to death?"

Peter didn't want to explain this, but he needed a car. No, he needed a favor. The man had a right to ask. He could feel June beside him, watching. She might as well know, too.

"I sweat, my muscles tense up, I start to hyperventilate. It's called a panic attack."

Al gave Peter a long thoughtful look, drumming his fingers on the gun. Finally he said, "I got a nephew with the opposite problem, he doesn't like to go outside. He was in the war. Overpasses, rooftops, high windows, all the places snipers used to shoot from. They freak him out. He's a programmer now."

"Is he getting better?"

The mechanic shrugged. "I think so. He bought a motorcycle. You can't ride that in your living room." He watched the sweat bead on Peter's neck and face. "You were over there, too."

Peter nodded. "Marines."

Al sighed again. Then he pushed Peter's pack back across the desk without opening it. "Bring those chairs over, would you?"

By the time Peter came back with the chairs, the black automatic had disappeared. He held a chair for June, then sat. June was looking at Al's hands with their faded blue tattoos.

"Some people tried to pull June into their car a few days ago. We don't know who or why. They told her they were government, but she didn't believe them. She's an investigative reporter, writes about technology. She went to hide at a university research station, but they found her again. We just met this morning. I helped her get away, but we totaled her car, rolled it a few times, which is how we got so beat up. She needs a new one. Something very reliable, something that won't stand out. A small SUV would be good, or a minivan. Something she could sleep in if she had to."

Al raised his eyebrows, his voice deadpan. He looked at June, at Peter. "You expect me to believe that story."

"You can believe it or not," said Peter. "It's the truth."

Al shook his head. "How do you plan to pay? You can understand that I'm reluctant to take a personal check. You carry that kind of cash around?"

"I don't carry cash, but if I can borrow your phone, I can wire money directly into your account. You can check with your bank before you give her the keys."

"This would be the young lady's car, then."

"Yes," said Peter. He glanced at June. She was looking directly at him now. Peter was aware of the sweat running down his face. His heart like a hammer in his chest. Soon he'd have trouble catching his breath. "I don't know what she wants to do next. It's her show. If she wants my help, she's got it. But no paperwork, no records of any kind. We think they were tracking her phone."

"But I could give her the keys and you'd watch her drive away."

"Yes," said Peter. "If that was what she wanted."

June watched him intently. Al leaned back in his chair with his fingers steepled on his chest, invisible calculations going on behind the wire-rimmed glasses.

"My mom owns the grocery store," he finally said. "She loves that red Mustang out there. Always borrowing it, racing around. Seventy years old, thinks she's Danica Patrick driving the Indy 500." He shook his head. "Anyway, she's got a Honda minivan, forty thousand miles. Maybe that would work?" He was looking at June as he said it. She nodded. He looked back at Peter. "You buy my mom that pony car, we'll call it an even trade. I'll give you two weeks before I call it in stolen."

Peter did the math in his head. The number on the Mustang's FOR SALE sign was double or triple the value of the Honda. He'd expected to pay a premium, but this was a little steep. He thought about the black Explorers pulling off the two-lane. They definitely needed the wheels.

"For that kind of money, June gets legal title," he said. "How about your mom signs it over, dates it two weeks ago, and we register it next week in another state. That protects her and you."

"Done," Al said, and stood to shake hands. From the speed of his agreement, Peter could have done better on the price, but he didn't care. It was only money, and not even his. At least not originally.

Peter pointed to the phone on the desk. "May I?"

Al shook his head. "Use this one." He fished around in his desk again, came out with a basic flip phone. "It's a prepaid," he said apologetically. "I got some old friends who are a little paranoid. They still worry about the Man listening in."

A smile ghosted across June's face.

Peter went to the window and keyed in a phone number he'd memorized. It helped a little to look outside. He could see the highway, too. No more Explorers out there yet.

"Who the hell is this?" The voice was like heating oil, slippery and dark and latent with combustion.

"How are Dinah and the boys?" asked Peter. "That dog chew your ass up yet?"

"Holy shit, it's the jarhead." Peter could hear the tilted grin. "Let me call you back from another number."

Al's friends weren't the only ones who were paranoid.

The phone rang thirty seconds later. Peter flipped it open. "Who the hell is this?"

"Motherfucker," said Lewis. "Where you been, Jarhead?"

"Jarhead" was a term of pride, if you were a Marine. From anyone else it was an insult. Except for Lewis, who'd earned the right.

"Working out a few things," said Peter. "I need some money."

"No money here," said Lewis. "Sad story. All gone. Blew it at the track."

"Uh-huh." Lewis was a career criminal who had put his profits into real estate and the stock market. If Lewis had grown up in Palo Alto instead of a rust belt ghetto, Peter figured he'd be piloting some venture capital firm in Silicon Valley. He'd helped Peter with a problem in Milwaukee the year before. The way it had turned out, there was quite a bit of cash in the end. In an uncharacteristic move, Lewis had refused to take most of his share. He'd gotten a windfall of other intangible benefits: reconnecting with Dinah, his childhood sweetheart, and her two boys.

"Listen," said Peter, "I can't talk right now. Let me give you an account number." He read the number that Al had written on a piece of notepaper, then told him the amount he'd agreed on for the Mustang.

"Gimme a sec," said Lewis. Peter could hear the clicking of a keyboard. He imagined Lewis sitting at the long walnut table in his office, laptop at one end, 10-gauge shotgun broken down for cleaning at the other. "Done. Where the hell are you? You need a hand with anything?"

"Not yet. I'll let you know. Everybody okay on your end?"

"We're good. Boys are growin' like weeds. I'm over there every day, bein' all domestic, but Dinah don't want me to move in just yet."

"She's doing the right thing, you're a bad influence. Hey, I need some walking-around money, too. Can you set up an account for me, put a few bucks in?"

"Jarhead." Lewis said it the way someone else might say *dumbass* or *dipshit*. "We got more than twenty accounts. Switzerland, Caymans, Bank of fuckin' America. You just need to log on."

"A bear ate my ATM card."

"Excuses, hell. Don't be embarrassed, just say you lost it. Where are you?"

"North of San Francisco."

"Let me know where you go to ground. Any half-ass city will do. I'll hook you up."

They said their good-byes and Peter turned away from the window. June was staring at him like he'd stepped out of a flying saucer.

Al had turned on his computer and was peering at the screen through his glasses, occasionally hitting a key or clicking the mouse. "Okay," he said. "Money's there." He picked up his office phone and punched in a number. "Ma? Do me a favor and drive your van over here. I got a surprise for you. Ma, c'mon. You're gonna like it, I promise."

"Tell her to meet us in the back," Peter said, still mindful of the black Ford Explorers and capable men with expensive guns.

In the back, they'd be out of sight from the road.

PETER LIMPED OUT of the shop's rear door into low gray clouds like a ceiling overhead. It wasn't standing on a mountaintop under clear blue skies, but it was better than being inside. The rain had started again, soft and cool, and his chest started to open up a little.

Although June had stopped looking at him.

Al's mom was a round, smiling woman in a designer tracksuit with purple eye shadow and glossy black hair under an orange paisley scarf. When Al handed her the keys to the Mustang, she jumped up and down, smiling so wide they could see the lipstick on her teeth.

The Honda van was pale green and showroom-clean, with a pine-tree air freshener hung over the rearview mirror. "She'll do a hundred," said Al's mom. She stood on the gravel talking to June, who'd climbed into the driver's seat. "Rock solid at speed on a good road. And she's like invisible to radar, the cops don't even see her. Either that or they think you got screaming kids inside and they don't want to deal with it."

June revved the quiet engine, nodding to Al's mom. Definitely not a muscle car, thought Peter. When Al's mom hurried off to her new ride, Peter stepped over to the van's open window. Was he waiting for an invitation? Maybe he was.

"So," he said. "What do you think?"

She looked in the rearview mirror, at her hands on the wheel, anyplace but at Peter's face. Her voice was ragged. "I don't know who you are."

He resisted the urge to touch her. "I'm just a guy," he said. "I went to war and came home. Like a lot of people."

"You're not like other people."

"Maybe not," he admitted.

"I don't know if I can trust you."

"I was a lieutenant in the Marines. Of course you can trust me. I'm like a Boy Scout, with muscles."

She turned to look him full in the face. "No," she said. "You aren't."

God, she was tough. "June, you don't owe me anything," he said. "But I can protect you. Keep you safe."

"Give me the gun," she said.

Peter shifted to let the daypack slide from his shoulder, then held it by the strap while he opened the flap to the main compartment. The .357 sat in easy reach atop the black drawstring sack. She put out a hand and touched the weapon with her splayed hand, laid her fingers across the walnut grip. He thought she'd pick up the gun, but she didn't. She turned from the waist and grabbed the whole heavy pack with both hands and took it from him, laid it beside her on the passenger seat.

Then she stomped on the gas, gravel spitting from her tires as she slewed the van around in a tight half circle and out to the road.

Peter guessed she'd made her decision.

He stood in the softly falling rain, watching her go.

Al walked up beside him, shaking his head. "Man, you are something stupid. It was me, I'd be hanging on to that bumper with my teeth."

Peter nodded. "I sure thought about it."

But he knew it wouldn't have worked if he'd pushed it. She'd seen something in him that scared her. And rightly so. Some days he scared himself. It had to be her choice.

He felt something in his stomach, or just above it. An emptiness there, a dark pit. It made no sense. They'd only met that morning. He knew almost nothing about her. But he also felt like he'd known her forever.

He hadn't thought you could be so attached to someone in so short a time.

They'd packed an awful lot into that day.

He had to admit that it wasn't all about her. Yes, she needed help. But it felt so good, using all those parts of himself that had gone sour and rusty. That Marine inside him, who wanted—who needed—to be useful.

Without that, he was just a guy with a bear bite out of his boot and blood in his hair.

Sore leg, sore ribs, and still cramped up and sweating from ten minutes inside.

No change of clothes, not a nickel in his pocket, and his truck a few hundred miles away.

Not that he was feeling sorry for himself.

He turned to the mechanic. "How much would you give me for a totaled Subaru, maybe thirty years old?"

Al snorted. He was cleaning his glasses with the tail of his shirt. "Not much. Where is it?"

"Behind that pizza place."

"Let's go take a look."

They headed out toward the blacktop, Al moving slowly to accommodate Peter's limp.

The leg was going to be a problem. He didn't know if it was the ankle or something more serious. He should probably give it some rest, ice it. The ribs would take time, too.

He scanned the two-lane and saw no sign of traffic, coming or going. Nothing on the secondary road. They passed long driveways to hidden houses. He peered through the trees, looking for signs of life.

For signs of June, or her pursuers.

It was still possible he might be of use to her.

THE SUBARU LOOKED like a discarded toy, crimped and crumpled, half-hidden in the scrub with the rear hatch stuck open. Peter couldn't believe it had gotten them here. Al walked around the car, scrutinizing the damage, making small sad sounds with each new discovery. When he got to the bullet holes, the sounds got louder.

"You rolled it, what, a couple of times? And drove away?"

Peter nodded.

"Man, I'm gonna buy my mom one of these. You guys should be dead. You know that, right?"

Peter nodded again.

"Don't be that way," said Al. "She'll be okay. That girl looked pretty fierce to me."

"How much for the car? I'm not promising it'll start. And the front end is shot."

"Parts only? I'll give you three hundred. And that's only because you overpaid me for that Mustang."

"I overpaid by a lot more than three hundred," said Peter.

"Yeah you did." Al grinned. "Okay, five hundred. Lemme see what I got in petty cash."

Peter heard the sound of an approaching car. He turned to look through the gap in the trees and saw one of the black Explorers turn from the secondary road onto the two-lane, heading back the way it had come.

"Shit," he said. "I might need to buy another car. And that gun."

"Maybe not," Al said, and nodded at his mom's grocery store across the two-lane. A green Honda minivan rocketed from hiding behind Esmerelda's grocery, across the road, then into the dirt parking lot at speed. It came to a sliding stop snug behind the building. The driver's window hummed down.

"Did you mean it, back there?" asked June. "You'll protect me?"

Her face was tight, her eyes deep wells.

"Yes," said Peter.

"But I'm the boss," she said. "That's the deal. I don't like people trying to run my life, men especially. So I make the goddamn decisions. Not you. Me."

"Yes."

"You promise me."

"I promise," he said. "Cross my heart."

"Then I want to hire you," she said. "Whoever they are, I don't think they're going to stop. So I need someone." A tear streamed down each cheek. "To watch out for me, while I work, while I find out who's behind this. What's really happening."

The shrunken thing in his chest began to enlarge again.

"I can do that," he said. "You don't need to hire me."

"Yeah, I do," she said. She scrubbed at the tears with the heels of her hands. "How much do you charge?"

"Ten dollars a week. Satisfaction guaranteed or your money back."

"And I'm in charge." She looked fiercely at him, her face red. It was important to her.

"Yes, ma'am," he said. "But I don't salute. Or wear a funny hat."

She lifted her head. Her eyes were puffy but he could see the blaze in them again. The slight twitch of her lips that meant the start of a smile.

"Well," she said. "We may have to renegotiate later." She jerked her thumb at the Subaru. "Grab the rest of my stuff and get in the car. You're driving."

Peter turned back to Al, who'd heard everything. The mechanic walked over with his wallet out, a sheaf of bills in his hand. "This is everything I got on me," he said, and jammed it into Peter's hands. It was mostly hundreds and fifties, and at a glance Peter could tell it was almost two thousand bucks.

"Al."

The older man shrugged. The pale sky reflected off his glasses, hiding his eyes. "You really overpaid for that Mustang."

12

SHEPARD

The phone vibrated in Shepard's pocket. He'd ignored it twice in the last hour, but this time he carefully peeled off a latex glove and fished the phone from under the white Tyvek suit. The caller ID was blank, but this information was irrelevant. The phone was a throwaway, dedicated to a single client. He had several phones just like it.

"I'm in the middle of something," said Shepard. "I'll call you later."

"Buddy, listen, something's broken loose and it's serious. I need you and your special skills up here ASAP."

Shepard had spent a lot of time in hotels, waiting. First overseas, now here. As always, the caller's voice reminded him of a television news anchor. Calm and cool on the surface, but unable to entirely conceal his excitement at the prospect of mayhem. And always working hard to sell the audience on his own credibility and authority.

The caller was a gifted salesman who had convinced many people to believe unlikely things. Shepard had seen it happen many times. Even now, the salesman was attempting to manipulate Shepard, appealing to his friendship and pride. Shepard remained unmoved.

Intellectually, he could recognize the emotional cues and perceive their intent. But the deep encoded signals were not received by his own inner equipment. He'd known this from a very young age. It had made him a lifelong observer of human nature, attempting to parse the hidden realities of others. He was still formulating his observations, but it was clear that the salesman's skills were formidable. The man could sell ice cubes to Eskimos.

But not to Shepard.

"I'm working. I need to finish." Shepard stood in a four-car garage beside an idling vintage Mercedes. The walls were clean and white. The garage doors were closed.

"You're freelancing? I thought we talked about this."

"We did. You weren't willing to make up the income stream."

"Well, wrap it up," said the salesman. "This is important."

Shepard looked through the window glass at the man slumped in the driver's seat. The face was slack, the eyes shut. The chest rose and fell in a shallow, ragged rhythm, but the body was otherwise still.

"It's almost done," said Shepard.

The Mercedes was a long rectangular sedan, older than Shepard and recently restored to an impractical degree. The hose for a high-end German shop vacuum was secured in the car window by the simple expedient of running the window up far enough to clamp the hose in place, but not so far as to restrict the flow. A garden hose was more traditional for this use, but the vacuum's hose had a larger diameter and would more effectively transfer the gases. The hose ran along the side of the car to the rear end, then curved several feet into the exhaust pipe for maximum efficiency.

"How are you doing it?"

The salesman was often interested in these details, but this was not his area. The salesman took care of clients and employees, the business aspects. Shepard did what he did.

But not only for the salesman. Shepard had other clients.

"You don't need to know," he said. "Something's broken loose?"

He watched the man in the Mercedes as he spoke into the phone. He could see the slight bulge of the man's eyeballs moving under his closed lids, as if he were having a particularly bad dream.

The man's fingerprints were on the smooth flange at one end of the hose, on the utility knife used to cut the hose to length, and on the button that controlled the window. Shepard knew this because he had put the man's fingerprints there.

It wasn't difficult when the man was unconscious. There were several readily available short-term sedatives which, when taken in quantity, would achieve the desired effect without triggering the attention of a pathologist. Autopsies were rare due to their expense, but Shepard was meticulous in both planning and execution.

"I had Smitty's team take point on something while you were gone." The salesman talked quickly, as he almost always did. He appeared to think it conveyed a sense of urgency. "Our client was in a hurry, and it went south. I need you to clean it up."

"Details?"

"Smitty's out of contact, which has never happened before. Bert's team is on the way. I want you to work alongside."

Shepard did not like working with a team. Or cleaning up mistakes, for that matter.

"We've had this conversation," he said. "I work alone."

"This is different. This could be the big one. Would you please, for once, just do what I tell you?"

"I'm not your employee," Shepard pointed out. "I'm your partner."

"Technically, you're a part-time consultant with a profit-sharing agreement. And you can't see the whole board. Let me do my job. You do yours."

In the Mercedes, the man's head moved slightly to one side. His eyelids fluttered.

"I need to go," said Shepard. "I'll check the drop and call you later."

"What time?"

"Later," said Shepard. "I'm consulting." He turned off the phone and tucked it back in his pocket under the Tyvek suit. When the glove was back on his hand, he compressed the hose to free it from the window, then opened the door of the big black sedan. The smell of exhaust was powerful. The man's eyes were mostly open now and he looked at Shepard stupidly, his lips trying to form words.

The car interior had been restored quite extravagantly. Polished chrome and creamy leather. It had cost a great deal of money, Shepard was sure, but he didn't see the point of luxury at such cost. It was an inefficient use of resources, and appeared to be largely an attempt to convince others of one's worth in the world. If you knew your worth, the expense was unnecessary.

As a place to die, however, there were worse locations. Shepard had seen many.

His plan for this particular death had been for the sedative to fade as the carbon monoxide took over. Clearly the man's metabolism was more active than Shepard had anticipated. He did not like people with vigorous fitness regimes. They complicated his planning. And it never mattered in the end, when it counted.

He climbed into the spacious front seat and straddled the man's lap, blocking the arms with his knees. He felt again the electric thrill of being in physical contact with another person. The intimacy of it. It struck him, as it always did, how odd it was for his most intimate relationship to be with the person whose life he was taking.

But it was an intimate thing, wasn't it? To end a life?

The man struggled weakly beneath him. Shepard maneuvered the end of the vacuum hose past the man's teeth with one gloved hand, and gently clamped off the nostrils with the other. There might be some slight bruising, but it couldn't be helped.

The man didn't fight very hard.

They rarely did.

Soon enough he stopped breathing entirely.

Shepard returned the hose to the window gap, smoothed the wrinkles from the man's clothes, closed the car door, did a quick check for anything out of place, then let himself out the back.

The dead man had complex ties to a certain informal organization that took information security quite seriously. Members of this organization were displeased to discover that the man in the Mercedes had been subverting their resources for his own ends, and were understandably anxious to sever the relationship. There would likely be more work to follow, but Shepard had not yet received those instructions.

He wondered what the man had thought as he sat dying in his unnecessary car. Had the man used diverted funds to restore the Mercedes in which he had died?

Had he thought it was strange? Or funny? Or sad?

Shepard would never know.

On the bluestone patio by the pool, Shepard removed his Tyvek suit, gloves, booties, and surgical cap. He rolled them into a ball and placed them into his tool bag. The back garden was quite lovely, with many flowers in bloom. The smell of plant growth was intoxicating.

He tilted his face to the sun, savoring the heat on his skin, the fresh air in his lungs, the blood flowing through his veins.

Completing an assignment, even one this simple, always made him feel acutely alive.

None of them were difficult, not for Shepard. He liked putting together the puzzle, making events unfold in a certain way. Nor did he mind the actual work, ending the lives of others. Killing people. He was certainly good at it. Years ago, he'd once overheard his instructors saying that Shepard was a natural, the best they'd ever seen. He took pride in this knowledge.

Still, it was important to keep himself focused and fit and prepared. A simple job could become difficult at any moment. And he was approaching a significant milestone.

In years past, the anniversary of his birth had always been simply one more day, the same as any other. So it came as a surprise, this idea that turning forty might be important somehow.

He found himself thinking about this milestone at odd moments, the fact that the years had accumulated to this particular number. It was disturbing, but he also found it encouraging.

He felt it was another signal of some kind, this time from deep inside his strange and meticulous mind. That the time might be nearing to end this current life and begin a different life.

Although what that life might be and how he would progress to it, he had no idea.

He had no intention of dying in federal prison or at the hands of some city cop.

He did like the idea of gardening. Perhaps growing tomatoes. For reasons unclear to him, he thought he might enjoy that.

As he walked through the side yard to the circular driveway and the pool maintenance van he'd borrowed for the occasion, he thought about the kinds of tomatoes he might grow. And maybe other edible plants. There was no need to limit himself.

But first, he would clean up the salesman's mess.

He didn't think that would be much of a challenge.

PART 2

13

PETER

The first time Peter saw the black Explorer was not long after they left the little town of Bantam, coming up behind them fast on the winding local two-lane.

"Get down now," he said. June folded herself into the footwell and pulled her jacket over her head. The driver passed them without looking. He must have been going ninety.

"Maybe I should get into the back," June said when the Explorer had disappeared around a corner.

"Sure," said Peter. "Get some sleep if you can."

She reclined the seats, pulled her sleeping bag over her, and tugged a baseball hat down over her face. Before long he could hear her snoring.

A half hour later he saw another Explorer, or maybe the same one, coming toward him at a much slower pace. This time Peter could see the driver.

He was a clean-shaven white guy wearing a blue dress shirt and a black baseball hat, and he looked at Peter as the cars approached each other. It was just for a few seconds, and the man wore sunglasses, but somehow Peter could feel his eyes, evaluating. Peter also thought he might have seen the white spiral wire of a comms earpiece coming up the side of the man's neck. But it happened so quickly that he couldn't be sure.

Peter was glad that June was asleep. He didn't want her to worry.

He also liked that she wasn't visible to oncoming traffic. To any casual observers, Peter was just a guy in a minivan, maybe a dad going to pick up his kids.

Not some kind of maniac who'd killed two men and set their SUV on fire. He wasn't counting the two who'd died in the accident. That was on them.

Just a guy, he'd told June. A guy who'd come home from eight years at war. But changed.

His plan, if he could call it that, was to drive north as far as possible without attracting attention. Every mile and intersection crossed added to the complexity of the search. The mountains limited the number of major roads in that part of California, so putting distance between them and their last known location was the best way to stay missing. The miles rolling away beneath the tires were a kind of comfort. Eventually they'd end up in Seattle, where June had an apartment. She'd told Peter it was a sublet, not in her name, not even the utilities. She thought they'd be safe there.

Despite the Explorer sightings, the farther Peter drove from the last point of real contact, the less he worried about being hunted. There were too many possible pathways, too many alternate routes for the bad guys to monitor all the possibilities. There were a zillion surveillance cameras out there, but most of them weren't linked into a single system, and most of them were too low-res for search software. So unless the bad guys had the manpower to track down all those surveillance systems and the trained eyes to manually search all that crappy footage—in other words, unless they really were from the government—they weren't going to find Peter and June until they did something to attract attention.

But he didn't want to take the most direct route, either, so he crossed 101 and stuck to local roads for a while, eventually making his way to Highway 36 winding through Shasta-Trinity National Forest. The clouds were low and thick, and rain fell in gauzy curtains. A river was visible on his left for long stretches, silver and white and fast with runoff from the winter snowpack. Mountain slopes rose on both sides, punctuated by small cascades and rockfalls and the occasional small landholding tucked deep into the woods like a discount hermitage. When he crested the pass, he could see the Pacific Range lying on the land like the body of a sleeping dragon wearing evergreen trees for scales.

His leg was still sore when he got out of the car to pump gas at Weaverville. The white static didn't flare in the minivan with its wide windshield and panoramic views, but it rose up hard when he limped into the mini-mart to pay. He didn't know if it was the fluorescent lights or the plastic windowless interior or maybe just the caustic smell of burnt coffee, but his shoulders clamped up immediately. In the time it took him to grab a few bags of trail mix, a case of bottled water, and a good road atlas, he was sweating hard and beginning to hyperventilate. The wide-eyed attendant stepped back from the counter as if Peter were a meth monkey looking to rob the place.

Peter held up Al's money, noting the slight tremor in his hand as he sorted through the bills, then pushed through the door to the open air, where he could begin to catch his breath.

I'm going to have to figure this out, he thought as he limped back to the minivan.

The white static. My war souvenir.

If I'm going to be of any use to her at all, I'm going to have to figure this out.

14

_____

North of Ashland it began to get dark. June yawned and stretched, then clambered forward between the seats to sit beside him, combing her hair with her fingers and checking her fat lip in the rearview mirror. When she saw a mile marker, she announced that they would stop for Mexican food in Medford, one of her favorite stops on her regular drives between the Bay Area and Seattle.

She lobbied hard to eat inside, and Peter gave in. He had to try. But after watching Peter's face turn pale across the table, she sent him limping back out to the car and told the waiter to make their order to go. They ate at a picnic shelter at Bear Creek Park while the rain streamed down around them.

"You've really got it bad," she said.

"I thought it was getting better." Peter shivered in the cold. He still had only the clothes on his back, and his T-shirt wasn't quite up to the Oregon weather. "But now I'm not so sure."

"I noticed your leg is getting worse, too," she said. "It looks like it's swelling."

"I don't know about worse," he said. "But not better, not yet."

June looked at him thoughtfully and took another bite of her enormous steak burrito.

"Tell me about your mom," he said, changing the subject to something useful. "You said someone broke into her office and took some computers. Do you know what she was working on that someone would want to steal?"

"Not specifically," June said through a mouthful of burrito. "She was very secretive. Especially with me, because I'm a journalist. But in general her work had a great deal of potential value. She was on the bleeding edge of research into neural networks, machine learning."

"I don't know what any of that means," said Peter. "Remember, strong back, weak mind."

"I'll use small words," she said with a freckled smirk. "Neural networks are large arrays of computer processors, each working on separate facets of a complicated problem. The idea is to simulate the node structure of the human brain. Object recognition, for example, where you might take a real-world photo of an object, then use that photo to identify the object, is immensely complicated. The most successful solutions use neural networks. Speech recognition, too."

"So what's machine learning?"

"Conventional neural networks need to be taught to do their job. With facial recognition, for example, programmers design the problem-solving pathways. But for really large problems, it's too big a task for people to program line by line. Machine learning, especially a sub-area called unsupervised learning, looks at ways for software to teach itself how to best solve the problem."

"That doesn't sound like a good idea," said Peter. "Isn't that how we ended up with the Terminator?"

She raised her eyebrows. "If you'll recall," she said, "that was a movie."

"That was a documentary from the future," said Peter. "I'm extremely concerned about the robot uprising. Those little self-directed vacuum cleaners are only the first wave."

"You're worse than my crazy dad."

She'd mentioned him before. "Where does he live?"

June looked away. "Up in the mountains," she said. "He's kind of a hermit."

"So he's not in the picture, with your mom."

"God no," she said. "I haven't seen him in years." She looked at her half-eaten burrito. "This is really good, but it's cold already."

She was clearly uncomfortable with the topic of her dad. Although why did she keep bringing him up? Peter let it go for the moment.

"Me too," he said. "I'm freezing my ass off."

"So here's the plan," said June. "We need some clothes, and we need a hotel room."

"We should keep moving," said Peter. "More distance is better."

"I thought I was the boss," she said.

"You most definitely are the boss," he said. "But I'm your highly paid security consultant."

"Hmph," she said. "I stink. I need a shower. And so do you, mountain man. I can smell you from here. Consult on that."

Peter sighed. She wasn't wrong. "Yes, ma'am. But cash only. They might follow a credit card trail."

She gave him a look. How dumb did he think she was?

She directed him to a big store that sold outdoor equipment and clothes, asked for his sizes, and peeled off a wad of bills from their supply. With the mechanic's money and the cash from the dead men's wallets, they had about thirty-two hundred dollars to work with. After basic necessities, it was enough for a few days, but no more. While June shopped for clothes, Peter went looking for a pair of prepaid phones and a cheap tablet with a prepaid data plan. When he picked her up again an hour later, she carried four large shopping bags and wore a stylish new rain shell.

She did a little twirl in the rain when she saw him roll up.

He laughed and reached across to open the door. "Did you buy everything they had?"

"It was all on sale," she said mildly. "Or most of it. Take this left up ahead. There are motels by the highway."

The place that suited Peter best was a long low building with a mossy cedar roof and deep overhangs, just a single line of rooms connected at the front by a wide cement walkway that faced the parking area. Definitely not a chain motel. There was a cheap vinyl bench to sit on while you enjoyed the view of your car and the row of scraggly mongrel bushes that concealed the parking area from the commercial strip. Perfect for the claustrophobe on the run.

The plaster walls were patched many times, and the furniture was so old it was made of actual wood. "Gosh," June said, stepping into the room. "You really know how to treat a girl. I can't wait to see the spa." But it was clean, didn't smell of mildew or bleach, and when June turned on the light, nothing scurried into the shadows.

"Is there Wi-Fi?"

"Listen," said Peter. He stood in the doorway to feel the open air on the back of his neck. His ribs and leg ached. "We need to set some ground rules. Okay?" She nodded. "The people hunting you managed to track your phone, right? They might be able to get into your bank records. So we spend cash only. No credit or debit cards. They might also be tracking your friends and family, so don't call anyone you know unless we talk about it first."

"What about email and social media?" she asked. "I have work to do and friends who will start to worry about me."

She was clearly one of those hyperconnected people. It wasn't a help, not now. "I don't know," he said. "We'll figure something out. Maybe we'll find you an Internet café, someplace anonymous. But don't use your laptop. Not now, not here."

She made a face. "I wish I thought you were paranoid."

"Even the paranoid have enemies," he said. "Are we okay on this, boss?"

"Yeah yeah. I'll stay offline. Shut up and go." She waved him toward the bathroom. "Take your time in there," she called through the closed door.

He turned on the shower and undressed, the walls closing in around him. His lower leg and ankle were swollen up like a grapefruit, the skin white from the internal pressure. He told himself the shower would make a difference. The hot water sluicing down his body helped counteract the claustrophobia, but he could feel his heartbeat accelerate anyway. He told himself it was just the enclosed space.

That June on the other side of the door had nothing to do with it.

He closed his eyes and soaped himself twice, scrubbing at the blood in his hair, wincing when the shampoo found the cut on his scalp. The water ran red for a time.

When he turned off the water and slid open the shower curtain, his old clothes were gone, and new clothes were folded neatly on the vanity, along with a tube of toothpaste and a backpacker's compact toothbrush. He hadn't even heard her come in. She'd bought him a pair of high-tech pants and a cool plaid button-down shirt with a performance T-shirt to wear underneath. New boxers and socks. An oddly intimate moment, dressing in clothes a woman had bought for him, the supple new cloth soft on his clean bare skin, then looking at himself in the mirror. He'd never been so fashionable in his life. He opened the door.

"Everything fit?" she asked, scooping up an armload of her own new clothes. He nodded, and she slipped shyly past him into the bathroom. She'd laid out the rest of his new clothes on the bed. A plastic bag held the clothes he'd been wearing, for fumigation or disposal. He liked that she hadn't just thrown them out. He laced up his new boots, grabbed his new fleece and his half-charged phone, and limped outside to watch the rain, trying not to imagine June in the shower.

And failing miserably.

HE DISTRACTED HIMSELF by calling Lewis again. They were burning through money at a ridiculous rate, and he needed to replenish.

Lewis sounded a little lonely.

"You sure you don't need me out there? Only take me a day and a half to drive."

Peter smiled. "Domestic life a little slow?"

"Domestic life fine, motherfucker. But I gave up working, that was my deal with Dinah. You know we don't need the scratch." Lewis sighed. "I got to say, I miss it, you know? Packing lunches and minding your money ain't the same fun as hustling for a living."

"Trust me, I'll let you know if I need you. We're headed to Seattle. You had a contact for me?"

Lewis gave him a name and a phone number. "It's a big law firm, got branches in twenty-two cities. We their clients now, gives us confidentiality and access to services."

"We? Who's this 'we'?"

"You don't call, you don't write." Peter could hear that tilted grin again, could practically see the elaborate shrug. "I mighta signed your name a couple times."

"Lewis. What the hell am I into now?"

"Can't let your money sleep, Jarhead. Got to put it to work. But first you got to run it through the wash. We got some apartment complexes, we bought into some IPOs, we doing a little venture capital. We got all kinda shit, and we just getting started."

Peter said, "Tell me again how you learned all this?"

"Gotta do something. 'Sides, I don't like to get bored. You know the most dangerous man in America? Black man with a library card."

Peter laughed at the Malcolm X quote. "I'm pretty sure you know more about money than most people working on Wall Street."

"Gone bust a cap in yo' ass, muthafucka. Talk like that gone get you killed." Lewis really had the street in his voice now. He could also sound like a Pakistani cabdriver, a Nigerian prince, or an English professor. Or, as far as Peter could tell, anyone else he wanted to. Lewis was, more than anyone Peter had ever met, the product of his own creation.

"You want to shoot me, you're gonna have to wait in line," said Peter. He told Lewis a shortened version of the story. June's mother. The men who had tried to take June, then followed her to the redwoods, and the car chase and wreck afterward.

"Man, I'm coming out there. I can fly into Frisco and drive your truck up north. Find a gun show on the way, grab some supplies."

"What I really need is intel. Can you find out more about June's mother? Her name is Hazel Cassidy. Business partners, employees, so-called friends. There's an ex-husband out there somewhere, too. Anyone who might have a reason to make her dead."

"You said she was killed in a hit-and-run. But now you're thinking her death might be connected to the rest of it?"

"Wouldn't you?"

June opened the door behind him and stepped outside carrying the depleted shopping bags.

"Listen, I gotta go," said Peter. He didn't want June to know what he'd asked Lewis to do. If it turned into something, they'd have the conversation. If not, there was no need to rock the boat. "How do I get some hard money on the road?"

"I'll set that up tonight," said Lewis. "One of those cash-advance places, I can just wire it in. You got about a zillion to choose from. They can do straight cash, although there are limits to how much they'll give you. They can also do prepaid credit cards, which might come in handy."

"That sounds fine." Peter consulted the map he carried in his head. "How about Eugene? Call me when you know where."

"If I came out there I could just hand you a stack of hundreds."

"Maybe later. Good-bye, Lewis." Peter hung up.

June said, "Your friend?"

Peter nodded. "He wants to help. He might show up. You'd like him."

"You never really told me what you do for a living," she said.

"Right now, I'm not sure I know myself," he admitted.

"Did that shower help your leg?"

"It's fine," he said. "We should keep moving."

"Sure," she said. "Let me see you stand on that leg."

Peter gave her a look. "It's fine."

She stared right back at him. "Can you bend the ankle? Will it even hold your weight?"

He didn't answer. She put out her hand. "Give me the keys."

"June," he said. "We need to keep moving."

"I'm the boss, remember? And you're broken. So I'm gonna get you fixed." She waggled her fingers. "Keys, motherfucker."

She'd like Lewis, Peter was pretty sure. They certainly spoke the same language.

15

Eugene was an hour up the road. It was a university town, and likely to have good medical resources. Peter didn't like it, but June wasn't wrong. He couldn't protect her if he couldn't move.

Aside from slowing them down, he could see several other problems immediately. His leg certainly needed some kind of help, but they'd take one look at June and want to treat her fat lip and sliced-up arm, too.

The hospital would want Peter and June to identify themselves, and would plug their names into the system. Hospitals liked to know who they were treating in order to make sure they got paid.

The hunters obviously had funding and access to serious tech. If they could get into hospital information systems and started looking for June's name, they'd come running. He mentioned his concerns to June.

"The emergency room doctors have to treat us," she said. "It's a federal law. We can give them false names and addresses. They can't even demand payment."

Peter could understand taking free medical care if he was broke and homeless, but he wasn't. Or at least he wasn't broke. And he'd always pulled his own weight. He'd pay the hospital, but at least he didn't have to worry about June getting on some medical database. "Who do you want to be?"

"Oh, that's easy. Debbie Harry."

"Who?"

June rolled her eyes. "The lead singer of Blondie? Some people have no culture. You should be, oh, let's see." She put one hand to her chin and contemplated him. "Clint Eastwood. Definitely."

"You're trying too hard at this," he said. "The goal is to be forgettable."

"For you, maybe." She flashed a brilliant grin. "For me, not possible."

"You are a piece of work," he said. But he knew she was just messing with him, trying to distract him from another, more significant problem.

The static wasn't going to like being inside a hospital.

His phone rang. It was Lewis.

"I got three Fast Money stores in Eugene where I can get you up to twenty thousand without approval from corporate. That work?"

"Yeah, that works. Make it five in cash and five each on three different cards." That would be enough to pay for an ER visit, Peter hoped, with some left over for walking-around money.

"Got it. I'll put it in the name of Peter Smith. But they close at nine. How far are you?"

Peter frowned. "I don't think we'll make it."

"They charge a pretty fat fee, something like five percent of the total. They might stay open late for that. You want to add a sweetener?"

"Sure, add another five hundred cash to the manager to keep the doors open until nine-thirty."

"If that don't work, we'll find something else. I'll tweak the numbers to include the commission and max your payout. They'll prob'ly want some kind of ID number. I'll use the first four digits of your Social."

Peter didn't want to know how Lewis got his Social Security number.

He said, "If your financial empire doesn't work out, you could always get a job as a personal assistant."

"I ain't wearin' no French-maid costume," said Lewis. "Call me tomorrow and I'll tell you what I dug up on that other thing." June's mom and whoever might be connected to her.

"Thanks, Lewis. Seriously."

"Damn, Jarhead. What else I got to do?"

Peter hung up and turned to look at June, who had her eyes firmly on the road ahead. But he was sure she'd heard every word.

IT WAS HARD FOR PETER to get a sense of Eugene at night, but in general, he liked college towns. Smart people, good cheap food, plenty of oddballs. There was always this weird undercurrent, too, of people who fed off the college crowd, which was simultaneously naïve, demanding, and easy pickings. Dope dealers, sex providers, professional gamblers, thieves.

Fast Money was a payday loan and check-cashing place, a vacuum cleaner into the pockets of the working poor and immigrants both legal and illegal, taking a significant percentage of every transaction. The commission for accepting an electronic money transfer and disbursing the funds was astonishing but not unusual. Peter was willing to pay the premium for speed.

Their location on West Seventh was a newer stand-alone building on a busy commercial strip like any other in the American West. Maybe nicer than most, with the buildings in decent repair and mature trees lining the streets, but still a testament to the creative destruction that was American Capitalism.

He didn't want to go inside, but it wasn't negotiable.

"I'll be back in a minute," he said, pulled on a baseball hat, and climbed out of the car. June shut off the engine and got out after him. She wore her new fleece, zipped up. Peter looked at her across the front of the van.

"What?" she said. "Of course I'm coming. You're sweating already, and you're still outside. They're going to think you're here to clean out the register. The cops will be here in three minutes."

Peter thought about the inevitable security cameras. Every contact June made with the modern world was problematic. Dealing with hard cash in quantity, Fast Money would be a magnet for armed robbers and likely had state-of-the-art technology. High-res cameras archived off-site for weeks or months. And it was corporate, so that video was likely easily accessed by law enforcement, and maybe also by professional hunters in black Explorers. Any picture of June could be used to track them.

He didn't even want to think about security in the hospital.

But she was right about how he looked. He'd be automatically less suspicious with June beside him. "Do you have a hat in any of those bags?"

"Waaay ahead of you." She held up a big floppy rain hat and put it on with a flourish. If Peter wore it, he'd look like a serial killer. On June, it looked like a fashion accessory.

"Very stylish," he said. "Just don't look for the cameras. That's the best way for them to get a good picture of your face."

The Fast Money door was locked when Peter tugged on the handle, but the lights were still on. Through the barred window, he saw someone hustling out from behind the counter.

"We're closed," the man called through the heavy glass. Only a few years older than Peter, he had a drinker's face, with sunken eyes, puffy skin, and the bloom of broken veins in his nose and cheeks. He wore a polo shirt with the Fast Money logo, a dollar bill with wings.

"My name is Peter. You have something for me?"

"Got a last name?"

"Smith."

The man nodded. "Yeah, come on back." The chain rattled as he released it and stepped away from the door. "Let me lock this behind you."

Peter and June stood at the plastic counter while the man let himself through a heavy steel door into the employee area, protected by thick security glass and at least six cameras that Peter could see. June leaned her back on the counter with her head down and studied her fingernails. Riot Grrrl was a natural.

The man studied Peter. "You got ID?"

"You know who I am," said Peter. "Let's get this over with." His shoulders were climbing up to his ears. Fluorescent lights, vinyl floor, the chemical stink of industrial cleaners.

"Gimme your ID number."

Peter gave him the first four digits of his Social.

"That's it," said the man. He began to count out hundreds, five groups of ten and one group of five. He slid the larger sum into a paper envelope, pushed it through the slot in the glass, then held up the five C-notes. "Five hundred for the convenience fee," he said, folded the bills and stuffed them into his pocket. He passed over three plastic cards in paper sleeves with the name Peter Smith embossed on the plastic. "Prepaid credit cards," he said. "I took the liberty of setting your PIN number. It's the same as the ID number you gave me. Check the card balances in the reader."

He pointed at the card reader on Peter's side of the counter. Peter swiped each card, punched in the PIN, and checked the balance. He was loaded.

"Sign here," said the man. Peter scrawled something unintelligible on the form and slid it back through the slot. "Pleasure doing business with you, Mr. Smith."

"Thanks for staying open. You're a lifesaver."

The man's eyes flickered with the only evidence of emotion he'd yet shown. "My pleasure."

As the locks slammed shut on the door behind him, Peter limped across the shining wet blacktop toward the minivan, June beside him.

He was carrying over twenty thousand dollars in his pocket. The thought occurred to him at the same moment a two-door sedan pulled up, an older piece-of-shit Dodge, dark blue or black with cracked plastic fenders. It blocked the path to the minivan.

The doors popped open and two men got out, trailing pot smoke and the smell of spilled beer. Long hair and armloads of tattoos, black short-sleeved T-shirts in the cool evening rain.

"Give me what you got," the man on the passenger side said, walking out to meet them. He had a three-day beard and the whites of his eyes showed overbright under the streetlight. He held a pistol down at his side. "Give it now or I hurt you bad."

"I hope you stole that car," said Peter. "There are a whole bunch of security cameras covering this parking lot."

The tattooed man walked closer, raising his pistol. It was in his right hand. "Just gimme the money, assface."

His dumb smirk told Peter the cameras had already been turned off by the nice man inside the Fast Money outlet, who had almost certainly set up the after-hours robbery. He'd chosen the PIN on the cash cards, too.

Peter shook his head. The whole thing just made him tired.

"You want to die?" the tattooed man asked, closing in. The ink on his arms looked like smears in the rainy night. He held the gun sideways like a television gangster, stiff-armed and one-handed, right at eye level. Ten feet away, now five, now two. The driver wasn't showing a weapon.

Peter sighed. "June, get behind me."

It was an amateur mistake, thinking it was easier to shoot a man the closer you got to him, and easier still if you put the gun right to his head. Humans had evolved to kill each other with rocks and clubs, their brains were wired to think in those terms. With an antelope femur, closer was better.

But firearms didn't operate like that. From ten meters, a trained shooter had plenty of time to track and fire at a moving target. The target's arc of movement would be relatively small across his field of fire, and he'd retain total control of the weapon.

From two meters, it got harder. The arc of movement was larger and the time more compressed, but it was plenty doable.

From two feet, the shooter had to be planning to fire, committed, already depressing the trigger. Because now his weapon was within reach, and the target might move faster than the shooter's ability to adjust his aim.

Peter moved fast.

He snapped his hand up, grabbing the pistol body and shoving the muzzle sideways to keep his body and June's from the line of fire. Then he twisted the gun a half turn counterclockwise, breaking the tattooed wrist of the idiot who hadn't begun to consider that Peter might not be scared to death.

The pistol fell to the asphalt.

The tattooed man howled and clutched his wrist.

Peter kicked the pistol sideways, hit the man hard with his elbow on the side of his head, then punched down on the side of his tattooed neck as he fell into a boneless sprawl.

June scooped up the gun at the edge of Peter's vision as he eyeballed the getaway driver, motionless behind the open door of the shitbox Dodge. "We done here?"

"Shit." The driver was shaking his head, disgusted. But he had more sense than his partner, because he slid back into the car, threw it into reverse, and got the hell out of there, leaving the other man heaped on the worn wet asphalt.

Peter turned to look at June. She lowered the gun back down to her side, her finger still on the trigger. She took a deep breath, then let it out.

"You okay?" he asked.

"I don't know."

"Not everyone would have picked up that gun," he said.

Her eyes gleamed in the sodium lights. "I had an interesting child-hood."

She looked like she might be having fun.

Jesus Christ, she was something else.

16

JUNE

The hospital was in Eugene's sister city, Springfield. It was a big modern building, brick and glass and lit up like a UFO had landed in the parking lot.

June found the emergency entrance, pulled the car into a short-term spot, and turned off the engine. Her lip was throbbing, but she was still wired from the near-robbery. The gun was in her lap.

Peter hadn't taken his eyes off her. "Are you going to take that into the hospital?"

She pretended to consider it. "I don't know, what do you think?"

"I think you're astounding," he said. "Where have you been all my life?"

She tucked the gun under the seat. "Wouldn't you like to know," she said, and got out of the car to hide her smile. She'd never been called astounding before.

Emergency reception was the usual antiseptic anteroom, with easy-mop floors and vomit-proof chairs. A scattering of people waited for their turn or for friends or family, focused on their own problems, uninterested in the newcomers. A fresh-faced young woman in pink scrubs and pigtails sat at the intake desk, flirting with an ambulance driver, but she quickly turned her attention to June and Peter.

"We were in a car accident earlier today," said June. "We went off the road. My friend's a little banged up. His leg and his ribs, and he cut his head, too."

The intake nurse was looking at June's fat lip, now black and blue. "You look a little beat up yourself," she said. "Anything else other than the lip?"

June held out her arm, starting to bleed again from the cuts of the window glass. "This probably needs a look," she said. "Plus I'm sore all over."

"That'll happen," said the nurse. "Insurance cards?"

"We don't have insurance," said Peter.

"How about some ID?"

June and Peter had talked it through, how they would navigate the questions. Peter thought it was possible that the hunters would have people checking the hospitals. He'd come up with a plan to make it harder for the hunters to gain information.

"We don't have that, either," he said. "We were robbed, hitchhiking back from the accident."

The nurse looked at June, her face devoid of expression. June figured she'd worked the night shift long enough to have heard all kinds of excuses. They hadn't fooled this woman one bit.

"Names?"

Peter jumped in before she could say anything. "I'm Peter Smith. This is my friend Marian. Last name Cunningham."

June gave him the hairy eyeball. The mom from *Happy Days* was a long way from Debbie Harry.

"We'll pay our bill," he said. "I promise."

"I sincerely hope so," the nurse said politely. "Although federal law requires us to treat everyone, unpaid emergency room charges raise the cost of treatment for everyone. Billing address?"

Peter gave them the address of the motel where they'd showered.

Typing, the nurse nodded, then pressed a button under the counter. The door to the treatment area popped open. "Ma'am, I'll take you back now. Sir, someone will be out to help you in a moment."

The nurse escorted June to a seat in an open exam area, then stepped to a nearby workstation and spoke to another woman in blue scrubs, who came over and pulled up a rolling stool.

"Hi, I'm Sandra. I'm a nurse practitioner. I'm just going to take a look at your lip and your arm, okay?"

"Listen," June said quietly. "I'm in trouble and I need your help."

Sandra was mid-forties, with strong hands, a no-nonsense salt-and-pepper haircut, and deep lines etching her face. She was calm but intent. "Is it the man you came in with? Should I call the police?"

"Oh, God no, please don't call the police. The man I came with is trying to help me. The problem is my ex-husband." This was part of their plan, to provide a more reasonable explanation of their secretive behavior. June had added the embellishments. "He's been stalking me. He's a lawyer, a powerful man, and he knows a million cops. Somebody drove us off the road this morning, and I'm afraid he's getting ready to do something worse. I'm trying to disappear."

"Have you talked with the police?"

"I have a restraining order, but my ex-husband doesn't care about that. He might send people to look for us. Please don't tell them anything you don't have to."

"You're certain he didn't do this to you? The man you're with?"

"No way," said June. "He's one of the good guys."

Sandra put a warm hand on June's shoulder. "Wait here a minute, okay? We'll take care of you."

When she came back, Sandra walked June to an exam room with a hospital bed and a clutter of noisy medical equipment. The nurse practitioner asked the usual questions, but the only truthful answers June gave were about her physical symptoms. She was tempted to give the woman her real cell number. She didn't know why. Maybe she wanted someone to know how to find her, even if it was just a nurse practitioner in Springfield, Oregon.

For the rest of the world, she'd fallen off the map.

When Sandra touched June's swollen lip with an alcohol swab, June flinched. "Sorry," Sandra said, dabbing only a little more gently. "It hurts, I know. It's actually started to split at the impact point. You could use a few stitches and ice to bring the swelling down, twenty minutes every two hours, through tomorrow. Might as well start now."

She rolled her chair to a cabinet, pulled out a chemical cold pack, thumped it on the edge of the counter to activate it, and handed it to June. "Hold that on your lip."

Then she turned her attention to June's shredded arm, again scrubbing harder than June liked, although she did dab on a topical anesthetic where she needed to use tweezers to take out embedded shards of glass. "Mostly scrapes and scratches," she said. "A few more stitches here on this nice cut right below the elbow."

She pulled a suture kit from a cabinet, dabbed on some more anesthetic, and began to sew with a steady, practiced hand. June watched curiously as the curved needle passed through her skin. There was no pain, only the strange tug of the thread as it pulled the skin together.

When the needle came toward her lip, she had to close her eyes.

"All done," Sandra finally announced, then applied some kind of goo to the worst areas, wound June's arm with gauze from the forearm to the armpit, and wrapped it with a stretchy strip like an Ace bandage. "Take that off for cleaning every day, then apply fresh gauze. When everything's scabbed over, you're done, two days, maybe three. The stitches will dissolve in two weeks or so. The lip we'll just leave open, no dressing. Those stitches you'll need to have removed in three or four days. If things get red or inflamed, you may have an infection. You'll need to see another doctor."

"I'll do that." June took the woman's hand in her own. "Thank you."

Sandra gave her a gentle hug. "Your secret's safe with me," she said.

"Thank you," whispered June, returning the hug, absurdly grateful.

SHE MADE HER WAY through the maze of exam areas to the waiting area, but Peter was gone. The young woman at the reception desk told her that he was with the doctor, which June took as a good sign. "Would you like someone to walk you back to his exam room?"

"In a few minutes," she said. "I'll be right back."

She went out to the car and got her bag, then walked back to a covered bench in the parking area outside the ER and opened her laptop. The first thing she did was turn off the cell modem and the Wi-Fi. It was killing her to stay off the Internet, but that didn't mean she couldn't make a few notes about what had happened that day.

As she began to type, a notification popped up, announcing that the cell modem was now connected. She turned it off again, but it began to show the little circle icon that meant the computer was working on something. Then the cell modem notification popped up again.

That was a weird little bug, she thought. Her laptop was getting peculiar in its old age.

She shut down the laptop and put it back in the car, then returned to the reception area.

"Is there a place for patients to get online?" If she could use a public computer, she could set up a new anonymous email account, type up her notes, and send them to herself.

The woman directed her down a long hallway into the main hospital, where an alcove off the cafeteria had three small workstations, each with a computer and monitor. The far desk was occupied by a too-skinny teenage boy with a shaved head wearing a medical bracelet, sweats, slippers, and enormous headphones. He was engrossed in what appeared to be an elaborate role-playing game. June sat with the empty chair between them and logged on to the Web. The long bandage on her arm made the familiar motions difficult.

She'd cut back on work because of the death of her mother, but she still needed to make a living. She was chasing an active story—she'd gotten a tip that a supposedly anonymous hookup app was selling user information to information brokers—and was waiting for verification from secondary sources. Leaving her phone back in the redwoods was harder than June had thought it would be.

She used her phone so much she often had to charge it three or four times a day, and it was killing her not to be able to call, text, email, or do research. Much of her professional and personal life took place on the Web. She hadn't been online since she'd abandoned her phone that morning. It felt like forever.

When the technology arrived for permanently implanting a modem directly in her brain, June would be first in line.

Short of that, a public computer seemed like a safe place to check in. She wrote about electronic privacy, so her security protocols were pretty good. She had serious multilevel passwords on everything, and she always entered them manually. Even if they'd hacked her phone—hell, if they'd hacked her laptop—she felt confident that whoever was chasing her hadn't made their way through those passwords into her email accounts. She clicked through, looking for signs that she had been compromised, but there was nothing obvious.

Of course, some asshole could be capturing every click and keystroke and she'd never know it. That could be true on any given day. It didn't change the fact that she had work to do.

June thought of herself as fairly disciplined with only four email accounts. One was work only, another was purely personal. A third was the account she used when buying things online—she thought of it as her spam account. The fourth was her college email address, somehow still live, which some of her climbing friends and other goofballs from the old days still used.

No answers yet to the emails she'd sent from her work account that morning, before Peter had shown up in the tree. Although it sure seemed like much longer ago than that. She'd set an autoreply on her work account saying she'd had a death in the family but that she would check email daily. Her personal email was full of further condolences from friends in the Bay Area and Seattle, and kind invitations to coffee or drinks or dinner when she was up for it. The spam account had the usual useless promotional bullshit that she always deleted without reading unless she was waiting for a package from Title Nine or Backcountry.com.

Her old college account had an email from her mother.

Which was odd, because her mother hadn't sent an email to that account for years.

And her mother had died exactly a week ago.

The email was dated today, at noon. There was no subject line.

June took a deep breath and put one hand on her chest, covering her heart. With the other, she clicked on the email.

There was no text, either. Just an attachment, a video window, her mother's miniature face frozen behind the play icon. June glanced over at the bald kid in the slippers. His headphones covered his ears, and he seemed pretty absorbed in his game.

June clicked Play. Clicked again to enlarge the window.

Her mother's face filled the monitor, big as life. She wore the emerald green blouse June had bought her for Christmas the year before, and her black-framed hipster glasses. Her hair was in its most recent style, a short steel-gray no-nonsense cut, so the video couldn't be more than a few months old.

"Hello, June," she said. "If you're watching this, it's because I'm probably dead."

17

J une hit Pause, stood up and stepped away from the computer, her heart beating fast. The kid glanced up from his game for a moment, then back to his screen.

June wasn't prepared for a video from the grave.

Although as she thought about it, she realized that this was exactly the kind of thing her mother would do. The woman lived and breathed technology, and she had lousy interpersonal skills. She'd sent June a one-line email on her last birthday, and a text when she was nominated for the Pulitzer. June should have expected some kind of electronic communication from the other side, even if the other side was just an electronic remnant floating in a server somewhere. Her mother didn't believe in any kind of afterlife, just the quality of the work you left behind. Everything else was worms in dirt.

June sat down again to watch.

"I hesitated to send this for several reasons. First, you'll probably think it's creepy." Her mom smiled, and June smiled back at the screen. Her mom had been a pain in the ass, but lack of self-knowledge was not one of her problems. "I wanted to make sure you know that I love you very much, and that you are the best daughter a mother could ever hope for."

June shook her head and wiped away a tear. A video from the grave telling June she was a good daughter, something her mom had rarely said when alive. This was Hazel Cassidy in a nutshell. June looked back at the monitor.

"Second, and this will be hard for you to hear, if I'm dead, it is very likely that I was murdered for my work." Thanks, Mom. Big dumb guys in black suits emptying her mom's office was one pretty good clue. June getting thrown into a car was another.

Her mother kept talking. "As you know, my work has centered around neural networks and machine learning. How to get computers to solve increasingly complex problems. The holy grail with complex systems is to develop systems that can write themselves, can grow themselves organically, if you'll excuse the inappropriate but inescapable metaphor."

June knew this holy grail was becoming a reality. As chips grew faster and data storage became cheaper, previously impossible problems like voice-to-text had become a free feature of every new cell phone on the market. June loved that she could dictate an article to her phone while walking to the grocery store. But she remained morally conflicted about the many areas in which government agencies used facial recognition software. Catching criminals, sure. But watching everyone else? How do you separate the two, and where do you draw the line?

On the screen, her mom sighed. "You know I've always been more interested in the theoretical aspects of my work rather than the commercial applications. But my work and the work of others has been used to create functional technologies capable of monitoring individuals across the planet. And like you, I became concerned about privacy. About the abilities of governments and corporate entities to gain access to private information of individual citizens, to track citizens' actions both online and in the physical world, while keeping corporate and governmental behavior increasingly secret. This imbalance of information is a significant problem."

No shit, thought June. Just ask Snowden or Manning or any of the other major leakers of the last decade. She didn't know if she agreed with what they'd done, but she certainly agreed that the conversation was necessary.

"So I decided," said Hazel Cassidy, "to try an experiment. When I began to grow a new algorithm several years ago, I gave it several priorities. I wanted it to be curious about the information on the Web, and when requested, to be able to collect and summarize information from multiple sources. I also included what I thought was a slight interest in what lay behind security firewalls."

Now we're getting to it, June thought.

"I had no idea what those relatively few lines of code would become. The algorithm is growing exponentially. It has become quite good at its primary function, to collect and summarize information from multiple sources. However, in the last twelve months, the software has also begun to function as a kind of skeleton key. It is teaching itself to penetrate secure systems for the information hidden inside."

The creases on her mother's face deepened. "It's not very advanced, not yet. But I've already seen corporate memos about 'acceptable defects' in medical devices. I've read letters from senators to the lobbyists paying for their reelection campaigns. I've seen a Pentagon list of proposed drone strike targets. None of it is pretty."

June had her hand to her mouth. She'd known her mother worked on the bleeding edge of technology. She'd known her mother's opinions about the disconnect between public and private secrets for years. But she'd never had a hint that her mother's work might directly impact this disconnect. She kept watching.

"June, I'm very concerned about the world my future grandchildren will inherit, even if those grandchildren are still theoretical." A brief but kind smile. Hazel had often mentioned her desire for grandchildren. The smile was an acknowledgment that she would never see them now. "Private citizens are overmatched by large organizations that increasingly control our political and economic life. Governments and corporations both. I hoped to share this skeleton key algorithm with citizens working for greater transparency and accountability, when I thought it was ready. When I had proper safeguards in place."

She shook her head. "I've never published a paper about this work. I've always been very careful about my own electronic security, and I thought I had kept this secret. But recently I was approached by Jean-Pierre Nicolet, a Seattle attorney. He said he represented an unnamed party wanting to purchase my algorithm for a large sum. I turned him down."

She stared into the camera. "A week later, the university was notified of a lawsuit from an undergraduate who had briefly worked in my lab, claiming that I had sexually harassed him." She snorted. "Yeah, right. But the next day—purely by coincidence, I'm sure—I received another offer from the attorney, Nicolet. The purchase price had doubled. He would provide no information about the buyer, only a bland assurance that the algorithm would be used only for the public good. I turned him down again."

June saw her mother's face tighten. "Then the gloves came off. A major science foundation, my largest single donor, sent me a letter rescinding my long-running grant due to alleged misappropriation of funds. The next day I received a third offer from Nicolet. The price had doubled again. He made no mention of the lawsuit or my grant problems. But they were clearly connected. I haven't seen such Machiavellian bullshit since I was married to your father. I told Nicolet to go away. That was two days ago."

She sighed. "There is someone or something powerful at work here. Anyone with this tool in its mature form will have unprecedented access to the electronic infrastructure of our world. Despite my best efforts, I have so far been unable to determine who is behind these secret offers, or how they even learned about the algorithm. I've spoken with the university's attorneys, who seem more concerned about funding and bad publicity than about my oddball little algorithm. No doubt these lawyers are very bright, but they seem to lack the necessary paranoia. When I spoke with the police, they just told me to consult my attorney.

"So I'm taking certain precautions, including making this video and writing a simple bot to monitor my electronic activity. If you're watching this, I haven't sent any email or otherwise posted to social media in seven days. Which means I'm either on an extended electronic vacation," said her mother, with deadpan sarcasm at the unlikelihood of this event, "or I'm dead."

She stared out of the screen, clear-eyed and unblinking.

"I had to decide whether it was better to share this information with you or leave you in the dark. In the end I concluded that you are an intelligent and capable woman who shares my own pigheaded desire to know the truth about the world. This is what got you that Pulitzer nomination, what makes you so goddamn good at your job."

Her mother cleared her throat and looked directly at the camera. "I'm asking you not to try to find the person or persons who killed me. It is likely there is considerable risk in that. Physical risk, real-world risk. Risk to you, my dear daughter, and I would do anything to keep you safe. What I'd like you to do is share this video with the police. Perhaps my death will get their attention." A smile crossed her mother's face, wry, sad, full of knowledge. "But I know you, honey. The young woman who climbed El Capitan to prove she could. Who still climbs giant redwoods for fun. You have all the best qualities of your father, and none of his worst. You will do exactly what you think is necessary, and nothing less."

Her mother took off her glasses, wiped her eyes, looked away from the camera, looked back. Put her glasses on again. "It's surprisingly emotional to record a message to be sent in case of one's death, you know.

Anyway," she said, "I'm rambling. Before I began making this message, I removed the algorithm from that mini-supercomputer I built and sent it out to a series of remote servers." She smiled. "It felt like releasing an animal into the wild. But now it's yours. I call it Tyg3r, like the geek version of the Blake poem, you know I always liked him. Anyway, Tyg3r isn't that bright yet. Maybe a particularly stupid cockroach. But it can wriggle into some surprising places, and it's getting smarter every day. If my worst fears come true and this message is actually sent, another message will be sent to Tyg3r, directing it to contact you."

Hazel Cassidy sighed. "I don't know if I've done the right thing here or not. In telling you all of this. In developing this algorithm at all. Like any tool, Tyg3r is agnostic, and will serve whoever holds it. The best course might be to destroy the code. Do you think Oppenheimer wished he could unmake the atomic bomb?" She squashed her lips together in annoyance. "Part of me wishes I'd never started this," she said. "But I really wanted to see if I could do it, you know?" She ran a hand across her face, looking down at her lap, then back at the camera with her familiar unflinching gaze. "Famous last words, I guess. The scientists' curse. Anyway. I love you, Junie, and I'm so sorry about all of this. Good-bye, dear daughter."

The screen froze as the video ended. June's mom looked out at her, calm and composed.

Not how June felt. Not at all.

She wanted to stand on the chair and scream.

She wanted to curl up on the floor and cry.

She wanted to call the State Police or the FBI. Hand it off. Get rid of it. She wanted to do that more than anything.

But what she needed? She needed to get a copy of this video into a safe place.

She opened a new browser, went to a free email site, and opened an anonymous new account with a complex password. She made a copy of the video, pasted it into an email on her new account, then saved the email as a draft. If she never sent the email, it couldn't be tracked by the various entities who were eavesdropping on the world's electronic traffic, including, she assumed, the men who were hunting her.

At least she hoped it couldn't be tracked.

She wondered if the skeleton key algorithm could find it.

Then she wondered if the algorithm could find her mother's killers.

Her mom had said "Tyg3r" would contact her. Like it had a mind of its own.

June knew a lot about the current state of information technology. Modern computers were still far too primitive to begin to simulate true intelligence. The computing power of the human brain was many orders of magnitude greater than the current best efforts of computing science. Tyg3r didn't have a mind of its own.

But machine-learning algorithms could be very effective at complex tasks, and were getting better all the time. She'd just read about facial scanning software used at some U.S. border crossings to detect when people were lying. It was better at the job than most human beings.

Cars could drive themselves.

Airplanes could take off, fly, and land on their own.

It was a brave new fucking world out there.

She deleted the email her mother had sent, then cleared the email's trash bin, logged off all her email accounts, cleared the browsers' histories, and wiped the computer's memory cache. If someone managed to follow her to the hospital and realize she'd used this workstation, they'd have to harvest the hard drive to get anything out of it.

It was time to go on the offensive.

She needed to track these fuckers down.

She needed to talk to Peter.

18

PETER

He'd known the hospital was a bad idea.

They'd put him in the open evaluation area first, which was difficult enough. It was a busy warren of alcoves and cubicles and privacy curtains, like that market in Fallujah with its maze of merchant stalls and gunmen around every corner. Or the power plant outside Baghdad where the insurgents had boiled up from the subbasement while they were still figuring out the floor plan. Or all those mud-brick houses with their booby traps and cement-block bunkers. It was enough to ruin the idea of shelter forever.

The triage nurse cleaned the cut on his head and poked at his leg and ribs, then led him through the cubicles while his warrior brain screamed about firing angles and clearing the room of bad guys.

Bad guys who were two continents away, two years in the past.

An overactive fight-or-flight mechanism was a bitch.

In the cluttered, glass-walled exam room, she handed him a backless gown. "Put this on, please." She noted the tension in his shoulders, the sweat starting to pop at his temples. "How's the pain, on a scale of one to ten?"

"I'm fine," said Peter. "But in kind of a hurry. I'd like to get out of here."

"We're not too busy tonight," she said kindly. "Shouldn't be too long." She drew the privacy curtain and closed the door behind her.

He waited in the exam room for another half hour, eyes closed, heart like a drum, sweating through his shirt and gown. To damp down the static, he practiced the exercises he'd learned from a Navy shrink on his discharge. Focus on calming your body. Breathe in, breathe out. Hello, old friend. No bad guys here. Your services are not required.

Not right now, anyway.

The problem was that his supercharged fight-or-flight response was useful, sometimes. Like when some asshole was shooting at him. In combat, that mainline adrenaline was his all-time favorite drug, keeping him and his guys alive and doing the job.

Part of him didn't want to lose that.

He needed to help June. He needed to be useful.

Peter wasn't built to be a bystander.

The ER doctor cruised in with a Red Bull and a tired smile. "I'm Dr. Baird." He was a few years older than Peter, unshaven in green scrubs and black clogs, eyes sagging with fatigue. His hair stood on end like he'd been recently electrocuted, but Peter figured that was just the style. Or shock therapy to keep him awake on a long shift. He hit a few keys on the cart-mounted computer. "So, what'd you do to yourself?"

"Car accident," said Peter. "Leg, ribs, sliced up my scalp." He repeated what he'd told the nurse, trying to speed up the process.

The doc stepped back from the computer and looked at Peter. The sweat rings at his armpits, shoulders rising up to his ears. "You must have a high tolerance for pain," he said.

"It's not pain," said Peter, his head throbbing. He was starting to have trouble getting air into his lungs. Breathe in, breathe out. "I'm claustrophobic," he said. It was an easy shorthand. "Panic attacks, pretty bad. Be nice to get out of here soon."

"We'll do what we can," said the doc. "You on any medications? Prescribed by a doctor or otherwise?"

Peter shook his head. "Not unless you count beer."

"How much beer?"

"That was a joke," said Peter. "I don't have a drinking problem."

"That's what they all say. Did you serve overseas? Iraq? Afghanistan?"

Peter closed his eyes again, his hand at his temple. "The leg, Doc. I'm here for the leg."

The doc let the air out of his lungs, not quite a sigh. But he nodded. "Okay," he said. "But I'm going to look at your ribs, too."

He poked and prodded at Peter's right side and listened to his lungs. "Doesn't seem like more than simple fractures," he said. "But we'll do a CT to make sure. You don't want organ damage or a nicked aorta." Then he examined Peter's leg, which was swelling nicely above the ankle. "Can't really tell without an X-ray," he said. "But you probably broke something in there. I'm going to go out on a limb and say you've got either a tibial plateau fracture or an isolated fibula fracture. I'll get you set up with Radiology."

He went back to the computer. "It says you don't have insurance? If you were in combat overseas, I think the VA still covers you."

"I'll pay my own way," said Peter.

The doc looked at him.

"It's complicated," said Peter. "I'll pay."

"I can't even tell you how much it will cost," said the doc. "Billing is all done separately."

Peter reached over to his pants, pulled the wad of hundreds out of his pocket, and held it up for the doc to see. He was sweating hard. "I can pay, okay? Send me the damn bill and let's keep moving."

The doc looked at Peter steadily. "Were you really in a car accident?"

"Yes." Peter willed himself not to get irritated. Some people thought all vets were crazy. Grenades with the pin pulled, waiting to go off. Peter wasn't helping the cause. He took a breath, let it out. "I was trying to help a friend," he said. "She's in trouble."

The doc held his gaze for a long moment, then seemed to come to some sort of decision. "Okay," he said. "I can prescribe something for the panic attacks, if you'd like. Basic anti-anxiety meds, they're pretty common."

"No, thanks." Peter had tried medication the year before. It had made him feel slow, like his head was filled with flavorless pink Jell-O. To protect June, he needed every bit of quick he could muster.

"Suit yourself," said the doc. "Give me a minute, we'll find you a wheelchair." He handed Peter a plastic bag for his clothes, then took his phone from his pocket and stepped out of the exam room.

Peter stuffed his clothes into the bag. Breathe in, breathe out. Fill those goddamn lungs.

A few minutes later, there was a knock on the doorjamb. An older man with a neatly trimmed beard and glasses stuck his head through the opening. "Somebody need a ride to Radiology?"

The older man with the beard didn't look like Peter's idea of an orderly. Usually they were younger guys, sized for the heavy work of lifting patients from a gurney to a bed and back. This orderly was old enough to be Peter's dad, and looked like he spent most of his time in the library. And he didn't have a name tag, unlike everyone else Peter had seen in the hospital.

"I'm Don." He must have seen something in how Peter looked him up and down. "This isn't my regular job," he explained. "We're a few people short tonight. I'm just helping out."

"Great," said Peter. "Let's roll."

THE ELEVATOR WAS A CHALLENGE. Peter closed his eyes and focused on his breathing, trying hard not to think about being stuck in the basement of this giant building. He'd need to rehydrate after all this sweating. And change his clothes. He didn't want June to see him like this.

He couldn't believe he'd actually considered spending a night in jail to kill the static.

"Pain must be pretty bad," said Don, behind him.

"It's not the pain," said Peter. Breathe in, breathe out. "I don't like enclosed spaces."

"Ah. Claustrophobic." The elevator door opened. "That sucks." He pushed Peter out of the elevator and into a big waiting area, where a young woman stood beside an opening marked RADIOLOGY. She was efficient and strong, and the X-ray of his lower leg only took a few minutes. The CT scan was more complicated, but she got Peter plugged into the giant white doughnut with a minimum of fuss. "This will take forty-five minutes or so. You need to keep still for the machine to take accurate pictures. I'll be in the control room, but we'll be able to talk if needed." If she noticed Peter's barely contained panic, she didn't mention it. She stepped to the doorway of the control room. To the orderly who wasn't an orderly, she said, "Please come back into the shielded area."

"You bet," said Don. But he stopped next to Peter. "Seems like you're working on your breathing," he said. "Take it up a notch, if you want. When you close your eyes, picture yourself in a favorite place, someplace safe and comfortable. A beach, your backyard, a favorite hike. Anyplace that feels good."

"Thanks," said Peter, but the click of the door latch told him Don had already slipped out of the room with the wheelchair and Peter's clothes. And the wad of cash. But somehow Peter knew Don wasn't interested in the cash.

While the machine whirred and clicked, he closed his eyes and called up a memory of Copper Ridge in the North Cascades. A long open spine of rock with mountain views on all sides. Peter had spent three perfect summer days exploring the area and sleeping under the stars, tucked into a stone hollow. The female ranger stationed at the little fire lookout became a friend, then something more. She was happy to sleep under the stars with him. The nights were pretty perfect, too.

He felt his chest begin to open, just slightly. Breathe in, breathe out. Think of Shannon's smile. She was a park ranger, but also an artist. She'd spent her free time drawing trees, in pen and ink. He sat with her for hours, watching the light change across the mountains as she made the trees come alive on her pad. Silence and the natural world. Breathe in. Breathe out. Breathe in. Breathe out.

The technician's voice over the intercom broke into his reverie. "You're all done, sir. Nice job keeping still, I got some great pictures."

It hadn't seemed like forty-five minutes.

Don came in and helped Peter into the wheelchair again, put the bag of clothes on his lap.

"Gonna take a while for the radiologist to call in," he said. "Let's get out of here."

Back into the elevator, eyes still closed, Peter remembered June moving through the tops of the giant redwoods, strong and capable. The tree-covered mountains behind her, the sun warm and bright above the clouds. The look on her face as she clipped into the zip line.

Shannon was sweet and fun, but June was something else entirely.

He felt the wheelchair roll down another hall, around a series of corners, the unnatural fluorescent light bright behind Peter's eyelids. Then he heard the sound of automatic doors and felt the cool night air of southern Oregon in late March. The smell of rain on asphalt.

He opened his eyes. Don had taken him through a side entrance with a small covered portico. The damp spring wind blew through his sweat-drenched clothes, making him shiver. It felt wonderful.

"Thanks," said Peter.

"Happy to help," said Don, still behind him. "I'm a veteran myself. Combat, not a fobbit. First Cav, tail end of Vietnam."

First Cavalry was the real deal. "You're not just helping out," said Peter. It wasn't a question.

"Did it work?" asked Don. "Picturing yourself in a favorite place?"

"It did," Peter admitted. "More than I thought it would. I'm guessing you're a shrink?"

"Clinical psychologist," said Don. "At least in my day job. I'm only your wheelchair driver because your doctor was worried about your panic attack."

"I'm working on it," said Peter.

"And it's going so well." Don's voice was even, but his meaning was clear.

"Maybe not," admitted Peter. "Is sarcasm part of your therapy?"

"Just getting your attention," said Don. "What are you doing to mitigate your symptoms now? Alcohol? Drugs?"

"Mostly I just, you know, stay outside."

"What does that look like?" Don's voice was gentle, curiosity without judgment. "You have an outside job, like a landscaper or something? Where do you sleep? Out on the porch?"

"I've been up in the mountains, an extended backpacking trip. I have some money put aside, so I don't need to work right now. Give myself some time to recover. Let things sort of, you know, reset."

"That's one approach," said Don. "Sounds like fun, for a while. Might limit your life a bit. How long have you been doing this?"

"Almost two years."

"That's a long trip." A loaded pause. "Do you feel that this is a successful strategy?"

"Well," said Peter. "Yesterday I was thinking about robbing a liquor store to get myself locked up. Extreme therapy."

"That," said Don kindly, "is a spectacularly stupid idea. You must be pretty desperate."

"Jeez, don't sugarcoat it," said Peter, a laugh forcing its way out of him. "Tell me what you really think."

"My professional opinion?" asked Don. "Your war experience changed you, like it changes everyone. Your mind and body learned how to keep you alive in a hazardous environment. What you're going through now is a normal reaction to that. What matters most is how you adjust to get the life you want. There are tools that can help."

"I can't exactly see myself lying on a couch talking about my feelings."

"Doesn't have to look like that," said Don, his voice calm and quiet. "Can be as simple as finding some people who've been through the same kinds of experiences. Hang out, shoot the shit, make some friends. Find your way toward your new reality. It's called a support group. Lot of those out there for veterans. Helps a lot of people."

"What about the claustrophobia?"

"Spend time inside, but start small. There are some techniques that work with this stuff. Some vets use meditation, others use yoga or Tai Chi. Focus the mind to control the body."

"Spend time inside." Peter stared out at the rainy night. "Even if I hyperventilate and sweat through my clothes?"

"Did it kill you today? No. So you're one step closer. You've been in combat, I'm pretty sure you've done harder things. The task here is to find your way back to the world. Take care of the people you love. Find work that matters."

Peter wondered about his promise to protect June from her hunters, if that counted as finding work that mattered. It sure as hell did focus the mind.

Don's pager beeped. "That's probably Dr. Baird." He unclipped his pager from his pocket and looked at the message. "Yep, he's ready for you. I'm guessing you want to put your pants on before we go?"

"I can tell you weren't a Marine," Peter said, stepping out of the wheelchair and dumping the plastic bag of his clothing on the seat. The damp breeze was cold on his bare legs. "We're so tough we don't need pants."

"I take it back," said Don. "You clearly do need therapy. Years and years of therapy."

Dr. Baird met them in the open exam area. The bags under his eyes were deeper, and his electroshock hair was starting to droop. The Red Bull was probably wearing off.

"You won the lottery on the leg," said Dr. Baird. "You have an isolated fibula fracture, just a hairline. Probably because your legs are so strong." He held out a plastic immobilization cast. "You're stuck in this walking boot for six weeks. Ice it for the swelling, take some ibuprofen. Then physical therapy when it comes off, because you'll have been immobi- lized for a month and a half. Got it?"

Peter nodded. He'd take the advice, up to a point.

"Now your ribs. The three bottom ribs on your right side are frac- tured. They're worse than the leg, but there's not much we can do there. We used to wrap you up like a mummy, but it turns out that tends to restrict people's breathing and can cause pneumonia. Now we just tell people to avoid activity that causes pain in that area. If it hurts to take deep breaths without the wrap, I can give you a long-term anesthetic."

"I'm fine," said Peter. He'd been doing deep-breathing exercises for a few hours now. The pain wasn't bad. It helped him focus.

The doc gave him a look. Even with the electroshock hair, it was a pretty good look. Peter figured it took some stones to work the night shift at the ER.

"Don't be such a tough guy. This is serious shit."

Apparently this was Peter's day for lectures. "Don't worry," he said. "I'll pay attention. If it hurts too much to breathe deeply, I'll see a doctor."

"Good. Now let's hear what Don has to say."

Don looked at Peter. "Those panic attacks aren't going to diminish until you start talking about your war experience. Find a support group, and get a real postwar life up and running. Home. Work. Personal relationships. You know that, right?"

Peter nodded.

"It won't be easy. You'll need help. And the gradual desensitization to being inside. Think of this as your next mission." He handed Peter a business card. "My personal cell is on the back. If you want to talk, or you want a hand finding some resources, give me a call. Anytime."

The doc Velcroed the immobilization boot onto Peter's left lower leg, adjusting it a few times for the right fit, before Don pushed Peter back to the lobby in the wheelchair. June was pacing back and forth across the polished floor, face pale under her freckles. Peter could tell she had something on her mind. She clearly didn't like the boot.

"How bad is it?"

"Not bad," said Peter. "Hairline fracture. I'll tell you later. We need to pay these people." He turned to look at Don. "How do we do that?"

"You don't," he said. "Not right now. It takes a week or more to figure out what you owe. Just pay the bills when they show up." He looked at June, at her wrapped arm and the black stitches in her lip. "Are you two together?"

"Yes," she said, before Peter could answer. He wasn't quite sure what to make of that, but he wasn't going to ask questions.

Don raised an eyebrow, his opinion of Peter clearly higher than before. "Why don't you two go relax," he said. "Try to limit the excitement for a while."

That was an interesting idea. Peter stepped out of the wheelchair, testing his weight on the medical boot. It wasn't too bad. The boot was fairly light, and came to mid-calf. He put out a hand to Don, and they shook. "Thanks."

"It was my pleasure," said the older man. "You have my number. Don't be a stranger, okay?"

Peter limped through the sliding doors, June at his side, both of them so glad to be leaving the hospital that they were oblivious to the pair of small cameras mounted in the ambulance bay, and others in the parking lot, watching them all the way to the minivan.

As they drove out, their license plate was clearly visible.

19

SHEPARD

The phone rang when Shepard was thirty miles from Eureka. The sky was gray and threatening.

He'd checked the chat room on the secure server the salesman used for their comms drop, so he had most of the background. The information was incomplete, but that was typical. The salesman never wanted anyone to know too much about what he was into.

Shepard hit the Bluetooth button. "Yes?"

"Bert reported back. He found Smitty's team, up in the mountains." Over the rental car's poor speakers, he sounded more than ever like a pitchman doing a radio commercial. "A total loss."

Four trained men, thought Shepard. Experienced men. Not at his own level, but very few were. It was enough to get his attention.

"How?"

"It looks like they were in pursuit but somehow left the road. Rolled their vehicle. It was burned to the frame."

Vehicles didn't simply burn, thought Shepard. Not without help.

"Tell me."

"A logging truck was parked on the road nearby. There were a bunch of skid marks in the gravel. Bert said it's a narrow road, not really wide enough for two, and he thought the logging truck forced the play. Smitty's last report was that they were chasing the girl's car, and from the tire tracks and debris, it looks like she left the road, too. But the girl and whoever she brought in to help, they drove out of there."

"She had help?"

"Smitty's report mentioned a man. That's all I know."

"How did they die?"

"The rollover killed two. One thrown, one crushed. Multiple gunshots on the third, probably after the wreck happened, he was still inside." The salesman paused a moment. Then he said, "The fourth was killed by an arrow to the chest."

Shepard felt his eyebrows rise. Perhaps this would become interesting. "And the truck driver?"

"He's dead, too. Multiple gunshots."

A clean slate. Good technique. "The vehicle, how did it burn?"

"Bert said it looked like someone took a can opener to the gas tank, probably used the gas as an accelerant. He could see the smoke from five miles away. Said it stank like hell."

Shepard nodded to himself. He knew that smell, the combination of burning plastic and roasting human flesh. It was a stink he'd never forget.

Shepard had enjoyed those years in the desert. Shepard as asset, the salesman as controller, new challenges every day. The desert was where he had honed his abilities, where he had accepted that the only rules that applied were the ones he made for himself. The only limits were in his own mind.

Things were more complex in his current situation. Multiple clients, overlapping priorities. More caution was required, because circumstances were at once more constrained and more fluid. But he continued to exercise his abilities, to make a decent living and save his money.

And Shepard was now no man's asset but his own. Despite what any of them thought.

Perhaps these were the best years now, even if he was turning forty. Wasn't that supposed to be the human ideal, to have your current life be your best life? That's what Oprah had told him in all those hotel rooms, as he waited for the next job to begin. He'd watched Oprah and Ellen and Dr. Phil and Jerry Springer and all the rest. He thought Oprah might know what she was talking about. He wasn't so sure about Jerry Springer.

But Shepard knew he couldn't live this life forever. It was only a matter of time. The internal signals were becoming clearer.

Perhaps his next life would be better still, growing tomatoes. He was considering including heirloom varieties. But it wasn't quite time yet.

"What's her latest location?"

"That's the other reason I called. We got a quick ping from the girl's laptop at a hospital in southern Oregon. Bert's team is on the way."

"Bertram and his men are a blunt instrument. You need a scalpel. Tell them to find a hotel and wait."

"There's a lot at stake here. This is looking more and more like the big one, the one we've been waiting for. The payoff will be, well, substantial."

The salesman had always required some kind of external motivation, thought Shepard. In the old days it was recognition from his superiors, rationalized by some vague notion of national security. Now it was a desire for financial gain at the very highest level.

Shepard had always taken whatever money came along. He had enough already, but he knew that more money meant more choices in his next life. He also enjoyed managing it, the clarity of the financial markets. There was something pleasing in the purity of numbers that allowed him to set aside the complexities of the human world. But at the end it was just a form of play, like his work with the salesman. Once he'd crossed a certain threshold, money was incidental.

He'd always felt that the challenge of work was its own reward.

And this job was starting to look more challenging than any he'd seen since the desert. Not the girl, but her helper. Her protector.

A bow and arrow, of all things.

"You have my attention," he told the salesman. "I'm on my way."

His tomatoes would have to wait.

20

PETER

It was after midnight, and the highway ahead was lit only by their headlights. They were driving through the night, staying off the interstate, heading for Seattle.

June had the cruise control set only a few miles over the speed limit. It was Peter's idea, to keep her from going ninety. His foot was up on the dash, the protective boot removed, a fat plastic bag of ice draped over the swollen spot. They were trading it back and forth, his leg to her lip. They'd each had some ibuprofen. Peter wouldn't have minded a beer.

"Tell me again," he said. "Your mom said the algorithm, this Tyg3r, would contact you."

"Yeah, I don't get it, either. Is it going to send me an email? Friend me on Facebook?" She took her hands off the wheel and waved them in the air. "Fucked if I know."

Peter liked how much she swore. Just like the carpenters he'd worked with in high school. Nouns, verbs, and profanity. Hand me that fucking skilsaw, would you? The carpenters were worse than the Marines.

"How smart is this thing?"

"An algorithm isn't a thing, it's code designed to perform a task. And my mom said it was like a stupid cockroach. Which is pretty smart for software. It's also designed to learn and improve its function. I'm not a coder, so I can't really tell you more than that. I know a guy in Seattle who might be able to help. That is, if this algorithm ever writes me a letter. I'll start on those names when you're driving again. Nicolet the lawyer, and those guys, you know. From the mountains."

The dead guys, thought Peter. They would have killed him if they could. They'd certainly done their best. It wasn't like he'd had a choice.

"I can drive now, if you like," he said.

June pulled the car to the shoulder, where the asphalt turned to gravel. Peter strapped on the medical boot and got out to stretch his stiff muscles in the cool wet breeze, looking out into the darkened trees as anonymous headlights flashed by behind them.

"You're really okay?" she asked, not quite looking at him. "Pretty crazy day today."

"Oh, I don't know," Peter said, smiling into the dark. He was supposed to be taking care of her, but here she was, trying to take care of him. "Today seemed fairly normal to me. Maybe one major event."

"Just one? You bullshit artist. Let's see, which one?" She ticked off each item on her fingers. "You climbed a three-hundred-foot redwood. Got shot at, twice. Totaled my car. Saved my life, at least twice. Fractured your leg, cracked some ribs." She paused for a moment, and Peter wondered how far she'd get into this. She took a breath. "You also killed at least one man, maybe more, depending on how you see things. You got stuck in the hospital, which made your post-traumatic stress flare up. And now we're on the run in the middle of the night from whoever is hunting me."

"That's all true," said Peter. "But not what made the day exceptional." It was easier to talk like this in the dark, when he couldn't really see her face. But he could feel the pressure of her attention like a physical thing.

"Oh, yeah?" she said. "What was it?"

"We should keep moving," he said, and began to limp around the front of the minivan to the driver's side. The headlights ruined his night vision, he could barely see her silhouette. He definitely couldn't see her face.

"Hey," she said. "What made the damn day exceptional?"

He smiled at her as he opened the door, the dome light illuminating his face.

"That's easy," he said. "I met you."

Then he got back in the car and spent some time adjusting the seat for his taller frame.

By the time he was done, she'd climbed into the passenger side, booted up the little tablet computer, and was nose-deep into the Web, as if the conversation had never happened.

Peter put the car in gear and got back on the road.

"OKAY," SAID JUNE. "I found our attorney, Jean-Pierre Nicolet. Lives in Seattle, an equity partner with Sydney Bucknell Sparks. Corporate website lists his specialties as intellectual property and M&A. What's M&A?"

"Mergers and Acquisitions," said Peter. "Any subspecialties?"

"A long list. Sensitive negotiations, corporate reorganization, blah blah blah. A bunch of honors and awards. He's all over the Web, but there's nothing interesting. A bunch of nonprofit boards, some obscure tech incubator, a couple of arts organizations."

"What about the law firm?"

"Sydney Bucknell Sparks. Founded in 1937, they claim over two hundred attorneys, with offices in Seattle, San Jose, and New York."

"So he's not some yahoo operating out of his rec room. He's the real deal."

"Oh yeah," she said. "But he's just the mouthpiece. He didn't think this up on his own."

"I'd love to see a client list."

"I'm gonna take a look at the guys from the redwoods."

She took the wallets out of the black cloth bag—the hood, the kidnapper's hood—emptied them onto the side console, and sifted through the contents. Then went back to the little computer.

Eventually she turned on the map light and held up the driver's licenses to examine each one in turn. She tapped one with a finger. "Jason Ross," she said. "He's the one with the Taser. Threw me into the back seat."

"You recognize the driver?"

"I think this one," she said. "Martin Alvarez. Although I didn't get as good a look at him." She held up a third license. "This guy, Dexter Smith, I don't recognize."

Peter thought about hanging at the end of a rope, listening to the four men talk to each other. He'd only gotten three wallets. The fourth guy was crushed under the Tahoe.

She said, "I'm pretty sure these are their real names. Which makes me feel a lot better, because if they were fake names, I'd have nothing to grab onto."

"Why do you think they're real?"

"I got inside their Facebook and LinkedIn profiles and checked the timelines. The photos seem to match the faces on the licenses. Social media is easy to fake, but it's also an easy path to getting caught, because you can end up tagged in other people's photos. For a good fake identity, people tend to focus on institutional paper, like a birth certificate and credit cards, because they're mostly trying to fool the government."

"You got into their social media? How do you know this stuff?"

She gave him a look. "I'm an investigative reporter and my beat is technology. You don't think I know a thing or two?"

"But wouldn't these guys have the privacy settings turned way up?"

"Oh, they do." June smiled. "But there's a back door into Facebook. It's even legal. Although Facebook gets really mad if they catch you."

"You ever been caught?"

"What do you think?" The smile got wider. "Anyway, most people aren't very tech-savvy. They post shit online like nobody will ever see it. You wouldn't believe how many times the cops catch people because of something stupid they did online. Our guys' accounts were started years ago, and the posts span a long period of time, so they likely weren't faked or made by bots."

"What do you mean, 'made by bots'? Like robots? Robots have Facebook pages?"

"Oh, sure. Facebook even said publicly a few years back that something like five to ten percent of its profiles are false, some of them made by automated software systems. Even if they're not wildly underreporting the number, that's fifty to a hundred *million* fake accounts. You know how much product marketing gets done through Facebook?"

Peter just shook his head. The digital world wasn't really his thing.

"Anyway, from what they're posting on Facebook and LinkedIn, our guys are definitely ex-Army, although it looks like they served in different units. And the two younger guys were pretty heavy on Facebook until a few years ago. Then they basically stopped. They both updated their profiles showing they'd been hired by SafeSecure, a corporate security company based in Seattle. And that's also the name on the registration for their SUV."

"Aha!" said Peter. "Right?"

"Not so much," said June, still tapping away on the tablet. "SafeSecure doesn't seem to have a website, which is odd for a business today. The car registration gives its physical address in Seattle, somewhere down in the Rainier Valley, although it's probably some kind of PO box. According to the State of Washington, SafeSecure does exist, but is a subsidiary of Western Holdings, based in Belize."

"Belize?"

"Small country in Central America? South of Mexico, east of Guatemala. Used to be called British Honduras."

"I know where Belize is," he said. "But why there?"

"Belize has become another tax haven," she said, her face back in the tablet. Screens everywhere, Peter hated them. It was convenient for everything except actual human interaction. "Like the Caymans, the Bahamas, the British Virgin Islands, a bunch of other places. A good place to hide both your income and the names behind your corporate identity."

"So how do we find out more about Western Holdings?"

"This isn't really my area," she said, "but my guess is we don't. I'm on that right now. Give me a few minutes. This cheap-ass tablet is really slow."

She tapped and read and the night rolled past outside the windshield. She had the bag of ice on her lip again.

"Okay," she said finally. "Apparently, incorporating in Belize gives you a lot of protections. You're required to disclose almost nothing, not even any company personnel or shareholders. You only need a single registered agent, which can be you or any person working for a specialized company that provides that service. You're not required to disclose any information about the actual shareholders, which could be you, or could be one or more corporations. This would provide still another level of identity protection."

"But we have a place to start, right?"

"Sure," she said. "But if they want to be really tricky, they use more than one country. A global web of registered agents from Belize to the Caymans to Singapore to fucking Luxembourg. It's a way to exhaust the resources of anyone trying to track them, because every added step costs more time and more money. So unless we have serious allegations against the corporation itself, and we can get the U.S. government involved, this is a dead end."

"What about the algorithm? Can the skeleton key get in there?"

"Fucked if I know," said June. "I don't even know how to find it, let alone use it. We better not count on it."

Peter sighed. "So we're back to physical locations. SafeSecure in Rainier Valley. What about the addresses on the driver's licenses? Are those real?"

"Let me look." More tapping. "Google Maps thinks they are. So we can start there."

"Well, that's something," he said. "Anything else you can do from here?"

"Not on this machine. When I get home, I'll have more resources." She set down the tablet and picked up her phone. "I just want to get my email accounts set up."

"Right," said Peter. "If you can't check email every ten minutes, your head will explode."

"We can't all be antiques." She was swiping at the small screen, not looking at him. "Do you even have an email address?"

"Sure."

"When was the last time you checked it?"

He had to think. "A month ago?"

She snorted. "How are you even employed?"

"I'm on sabbatical," he said. "And I'm not interested in the virtual world anyway."

He wasn't going to admit to being unemployed. Or living out of his truck, for that matter. Regardless, he didn't need to be employed, not ever again, although he had complicated feelings about that.

June didn't seem to be paying attention to him, anyway. After a few more minutes with her nose to the screen, she set her phone on the center console, pillowed her jacket against the door, and closed her eyes. "I think I'll crash for a while."

Peter started to answer, but stopped himself. She'd already fallen asleep, her mouth partway open.

He watched the darkened landscape, dimly lit. From inside the car, he couldn't tell whether he was moving through the land or he was stationary and the land was passing beneath him.

After a few minutes, June began to snore.

She sounded like a rhino with a sinus infection.

But those freckles. And that attitude.

Oh, man.

21

Three hours later, the fuel gauge getting low, Peter pulled off the highway.

June came awake on the ramp and hopped out of the minivan at the pumps. She paced back and forth under the unearthly gas station lights while he filled the tank. She talked a mile a minute, as if she'd been thinking in her sleep.

"So our guys, they're definitely pros," she said. "They're ex-Army, and working for somebody who doesn't want to be known. Some kind of hidden operation."

"Yeah," said Peter. He needed more coffee. "They actually could be government, you know. Off-book groups have been known to pretend to be in the private sector. It's the easiest way to hide from oversight. And you could understand why Uncle Sam would want the algorithm."

"Anybody would want it," she said. "If you had a tool to sneak into secure systems? The G would want to keep it for themselves. Private groups would use it for corporate espionage, to steal government information, industrial secrets, intellectual property of all kinds."

Peter leaned against the minivan and rubbed his eyes. June had clocked a pair of decent naps that day, but Peter had been on the go since first light, and had slept in a tree the night before. June talked on, powered by the idea, walking and talking and checking her email on her phone at the same time. The woman clearly had a lot of energy.

"You could sell it as a service—place your order, tell us what you want, we'll get it for you. The Chinese and the Russians would go crazy for that. Want the design specs for the Reaper drone? No problem, but it's gonna cost you. If you aren't that ambitious? Shit, just break into the banking system and transfer a bunch of money into a few hundred numbered accounts, then send it all over the world. If you were smart, you'd take a hundred dollars from two million people's accounts over a few months' time. Most people wouldn't even know it was gone, they'd just think they lost an ATM receipt. If you went into corporate accounts, you could steal billions. It might not even be reported, because it would be so embarrassing. Hide your tracks in Belize, and your money in Switzerland."

"A killer app," he said, then felt bad about it. Her mom.

She glanced at his face and stopped pacing. She put her hand on his upper arm. "You look pretty wiped. My turn to drive, okay?"

He nodded. Her fat lip was turning purple, the dark stitches still shocking in her pale skin, but the ice seemed to have stopped the swelling. Her freckles were arrayed across her face like some complex constellation whose meaning he was still trying to fathom. Her eyes shone with intelligence and humor and, maybe, something else. There was no way the heat of her hand could make it through the thick fleece of his jacket, but he felt its warmth anyway.

She said, "Give me a minute to grab coffee and Twizzlers. You get some sleep."

He cleared his throat. "Yeah," he said. "Sure."

. . .

HE WOKE AS they were coming up on Seattle from the south, June humming softly in the driver's seat. The medical boot was tight on his left leg. He hated it already, the limitations. What if he had to move fast to protect her?

The clock on the dash said 11:45 a.m. Freeway traffic was heavy and rain splattered on the windshield in fits and starts. The airport sprawled on their left, then a futuristic elevated commuter railway. Dense vegetation and thick stands of trees climbed the fog-shrouded hillsides to their right. Everything was so green, and it was only March. In northern Wisconsin, where Peter grew up, the ground would still be covered with snow, with more snow falling into April. And May.

June pulled off the freeway well before downtown. "I want to make a quick stop before we go to my place. The address for that company SafeSecure is only a mile or so from here."

Rainier Avenue was a commercial strip four lanes wide, lined with big apartments, commercial buildings in their second or third incarnation, and a surprising number of Vietnamese restaurants. SafeSecure's address was an older single-story brick building, the kind of place that might have once held a small machine shop repairing logging equipment, or making specialty parts for Boeing. Now it was semi-affordable square footage for whatever the tenant needed. The original concrete loading dock had been turned into the main entrance, with a faded awning to keep the rain off and a group of big clay pots overgrown with plants. There was no name on the door, but the street address was displayed above it. June cranked the minivan into a parking space.

Peter said, "I thought you said this was going to be some kind of a PO box."

June shrugged and turned off the engine. "Let's go see."

They stepped through the glass entrance into a long narrow reception area, where a middle-aged woman sat behind a reception counter.

Peter felt the white static flare up immediately. The place was like a shooting gallery, with a solid pair of double doors at the far end and no cover between them. He reminded himself there were no armed insurgents in Seattle, at least not to his knowledge. And not likely at this address. Breathe in, breathe out. It's not going to kill you, remember?

The woman was large but not soft, and her face was set in a permanent frown. As if she didn't get many visitors and liked it that way. She wore jeans and a faded blue man's dress shirt. Ornate tattoos peeked out past the ends of her rolled-up sleeves.

Behind her was a long wall with numbered slots, well over a hundred of them. The slots were wide enough for large envelopes, but Peter couldn't read the numbers from the far side of the counter. He imagined an array of mail bins behind the slots. A vast low hum came through the wall behind her. The doors at the far end of the room would lead to the rest of the operation.

"Hi there," June said brightly, walking up to the counter. "I'm looking for a company called SafeSecure. One of their employees gave me this address."

The permanent frown got deeper. "I'd have to look them up," said the large woman. She rolled her chair over to her computer and tapped on the keyboard. "Yep, they're a customer. Although I don't know why they'd send you here. We're just a mail forwarding service."

"Where do you forward their mail to?"

"We don't physically forward anything," said the woman. "We just scan everything and put it online. The customer logs on with a password."

"Can you give me a billing address?"

The large woman shook her head. "Everything's electronic, paid automatically by credit card. They could be on the moon for all I know."

Peter said, "What about a mailing address for the credit card?"

"I can't tell you that," the woman said sharply. Her frown had turned into a scowl. "Our customers pay us for their privacy. It's time for you to go."

"One of their people left something at our house," said Peter. "We're just trying to return it. Is the mailing address on the credit card the same as the mailing address here?" That's how Peter would have set it up. A closed loop, leading nowhere.

The large woman's eyes dropped to the computer screen. "Yep," she said. And she must have pushed a button somewhere, because the door at the end of the long room opened and a man came through. He was tall, dark, and ugly, and about three sizes larger than Peter. He wore a skin-tight T-shirt that showed off his muscles, and he glared at Peter like he was having a bad day.

"Evah'ting okay, Trish?" He sounded like Ziggy Marley's mean uncle.

"These people were just leaving."

So they did.

BACK ON THE ROAD, June said, "Pretty slick back there, asking about the credit card."

"I was curious," said Peter. "It seemed like something I might use someday."

"You never told me where you live."

Peter looked out the window. "I move around a lot."

"Do you have a family?"

"My mom and dad live in northern Wisconsin. No brothers or sisters."

Peter knew she wasn't exactly asking about his parents. It was part of this thing they were dancing around. "My folks took in stray kids," he said, "ever since I was little."

"What, like a halfway house?"

"Nothing official. More like small-town gravity, an invisible force attracting troubled kids. A few were really wild, but most of them just had shitty parents. This kid Tommy, he was eight years old and his mom burned him with her cigarettes. He lived at the farm behind our property. And Deidre, she was fifteen and pregnant and her dad kicked her out of the house." He shook his head. "January in northern Wisconsin, ten below and the wind howling off Lake Superior."

"Jesus," she said. "Sounds like an education."

"Definitely." He smiled then, remembering Deidre. "Pretty exciting for a twelve-year-old boy, having a pregnant teenager in your house. I fell pretty hard for Deidre."

She gave him a look. "This isn't some kind of fetish, is it?"

"No," he said, laughing. "Part of it was knowing what she'd done to get pregnant, the whole idea of sex. But mostly she was just, you know, beautiful. The way all pregnant women are beautiful."

June kept looking at him, but differently now.

"Anyway, my mom always had a big pot of soup on the stove, home-made bread in the oven. It was a small town, and word got around, not just our town but the ones around us, too. Mrs. Ash would feed you, would take you in. Her cousin was the county police dispatcher, and she made sure the word spread. So, once or twice a year, some kid would appear on the front porch, stay for dinner, and somehow still be there for breakfast. No questions asked, but sooner or later, they'd start to talk. If they stayed more than a few days, my dad and my uncle Jerry would put them to work on the Saturday crew, boys and girls both. Teach them how to do something useful, frame a wall or wire a light switch. Hang siding." He smiled. "A couple guys stayed long enough to learn how to build cabinets. We were like the world's smallest trade school."

"Didn't people ever show up to take their kids home? I bet that could get ugly."

"Yeah, people get weird about their kids," said Peter. "It's an ownership thing. Tommy's mom came by with an ax, a lit cigarette hanging out of her mouth. The burns on Tommy's arms were barely scabbed over."

"What happened?"

"Nothing. My dad kept a shotgun by the back door. My mom has the cops on speed-dial. Tommy stayed with us a few more weeks. By then we'd found his grandmother in Green Bay."

"Your mom didn't just feed them," said June.

"Oh, no. She was big on life skills. More like boot camp for early independence. Cook basic meals, keep yourself clean, keep the house clean. Boy or girl, that was the rule. Everybody learns everything. The older kids, she'd help find them jobs, start a savings account, even get their GED. And do something creative, always. My mom still teaches art at NMU, but that's mostly for the health insurance. She's really an artist, paint and watercolor. The last time I talked to her she was taking a welding class. My aunt plays about ten different instruments in bar bands all over three states. She always said if she had bigger hands she'd be the female Jelly Roll Morton."

"That must have been hard on you, with all those other people in the house."

"I learned a lot," said Peter. "It definitely made me independent. I was pretty wild myself."

She snorted. "I can only imagine."

22

B ack on I-5, June took them through downtown, with Puget
Sound shining gunmetal gray through the gaps in the office
buildings and condo towers, then got off again at Olive Way.
She headed east up a steep hill through a dense neighborhood with a
funky jumble of mismatched buildings and a lot of construction, the
whole thing evidently in a constant state of evolution. Cars were thick
on the streets. Peter figured parking would be at a premium here. The
narrow, disorderly roads tangled and turned according to the needs of
the hillside on which they ran. People were out on foot and on bicycles
undeterred by the wet weather. Rain gear seemed to be a fashion accessory here.

"This is Capitol Hill," June said, playing tour guide and pointing out
the sights. "My neighborhood. That's Glo's, great breakfast. The Coastal
Kitchen is up on Fifteenth, awesome breakfast. The Hi-Spot is down
the hill in Madrona, maybe we'll go there tomorrow for their green eggs
and ham. And Caffe Ladro to the left, best coffee in town. Much better
than Starbucks." She knocked him with an elbow. "You're not allowed
to go to Starbucks unless it's a national emergency."

All the landmarks she pointed out were food-related. Peter took mental notes.

"Seattle was built on seven hills, or so they say." She waved her hand behind her. "Queen Anne Hill is northwest of us, First Hill to the south. Denny Hill they bulldozed years ago, and used the dirt to fill in the tidal flats."

At the top of the hill, she got off the main drag and drove expertly through the residential side streets lined with parked cars, often turning them into de facto one-lane roads. She turned left and right at seemingly arbitrary intersections that moved them through the streetscape at a much faster rate of speed than the main drag. She gave cyclists a wide berth, but played chicken ruthlessly with oncoming cars, forcing them over so she could continue at speed. It was about a mile to her place on the far side of the hill, she said.

"Do me a favor and slow down," said Peter. "Circle around, starting about three blocks out. I want to see every street around your place."

She raised her eyebrows and gave him a sideways look, but turned left and lightened her lead foot. "What are we looking for?"

"I don't know," he said. "Anything unusual."

"This is Capitol Hill," she said. "It's all unusual."

It was true, Peter had never seen a burly bearded drag queen wearing a transparent plastic raincoat over a leopard-print minidress with five-inch platform heels. Or a 1970s Lincoln Continental turned into a kind of dragon-car, with an elaborate toothy snout in the front, spines along the rooftop, and a tail up in the air at the back, suspended somehow by a cable from the roof. But was any of that more odd than a group of women in burkas out for dinner in Baghdad? Or a village of ice fishing shacks on a frozen Wisconsin lake when the temperature hit twenty below? People were weird everywhere. Weird was normal.

"Let's just say I'll know it when I see it," said Peter, his head on a swivel. He wasn't worried about drag queens or art cars. He was looking for late-model vehicles parked with the engine running, or repeat viewings of men and women on foot, or work vans big enough to hold a surveillance team where there was no evident work being done.

June drove in a slow spiral, closing in on her apartment. But Peter saw nothing unusual.

Maybe they were clean.

Or maybe the hunters were very good.

June lived on a residential street in a converted three-car garage behind a big clapboard Victorian. Peter's father had always called those houses "painted ladies" because of the elaborate, multicolored decorative trim. As June pulled into the driveway, Peter counted six different colors, bright tones that made the house seem to glow in the soft rainy light.

She'd told him in the car that she had an unusual arrangement. She paid the rent for her little studio in cash, and there were no utilities in her name. It was unusual because, after decades of pretending these illegal apartments didn't exist, Seattle now encouraged these "mother-in-law" units as a way to improve density in the urban sprawl, and also make the city more affordable for young people. But Leo Boyle, her landlord, hadn't registered the place with the city, although he'd given June several different explanations why. Sometimes he said he was afraid that his taxes might go up. Sometimes he told her that he didn't want his name in the database. It didn't quite add up, but she liked the apartment.

Peter stood stretching in the driveway, tight from the long car ride, while June unlocked the door to her apartment.

His phone rang. It was Lewis.

"Jarhead. You alone right now?"

"If you ask me what I'm wearing, I'm hanging up."

"Man, you really should be open to new experiences," said Lewis. Peter could hear the man's tilted grin. "But that ain't why I'm calling. Like you asked, I spent a little time looking up that woman who died, Hazel Cassidy."

June stood in the doorway, a question on her face. He covered the mouthpiece. "I'll just be a minute," he said. "It's Lewis."

She went inside, leaving the door open.

Peter said, "What'd you find?"

"Mostly nothing. Did a little reading online. Found her obituary. Well respected in her field, smart as hell." Lewis was enjoying himself.

"You said mostly."

"You like things complicated, don't you?"

Peter's platoon once had spent the better part of a week caught between two rebel militias who were also fighting each other. As it turned out, the militia leaders were brothers, and one had stolen the other man's wife. So Peter knew that people usually killed each other for reasons that were, at their root, personal. And complicated.

"Spit it out, Lewis. What did you learn?"

"She had a restraining order against her ex-husband. For six years."

"Okay, good. Something to grab onto. Who's the ex-husband?"

"No idea."

"What do you mean, no idea?"

"The name on the restraining order is 'S. Kolodny.' No address. You have any idea how many S. Kolodnys there are out there?"

Peter smiled. "Can't be more than a few."

"The software I got lists over a thousand people named Kolodny on the West Coast alone. But you're really gonna like this. The restraining order form has a physical description. This guy is six feet eight and weighs two-eighty. A real beast."

"Weren't you going to buy a plane ticket today? I'll pick you up at the airport."

"You know I bruise easy. I'm thinking I might sit this one out. On the plus side, S. Kolodny's in his late fifties now. So you can probably take him by yourself."

"Maybe with a baseball bat."

"I always been partial to a shotgun," said Lewis. "Anyway, you want me to find out more about this guy, you gotta narrow it down. I need a first name and a location."

"I'll work on it," said Peter. "Call you later."

"Listen," said Lewis. "About the money."

Peter sighed. "We've already had this conversation."

"I looked at the accounts, Jarhead. You haven't touched the money. It's like you're embarrassed."

"Well," said Peter. "We did steal it."

"Yeah, from a guy who stole it first. And he never would have gotten caught, 'cause if you can't prove the conspiracy, his part wasn't even fucking illegal. And everyone else was dead."

"Lewis."

"You don't think we earned it, what we did?"

"You earned it. It wasn't your fight. For me, it was personal."

"Well, hell," said Lewis. "Come down to it, I wasn't in it for the money, either. I was in it for Dinah. But whatever the reason, we took a big fucking risk. The money just came with it, otherwise it'd be lost in that numbered account until the end of time. So you got nothing to apologize for."

"I'm not apologizing," said Peter. "But that doesn't mean I'd want to explain it to my parents."

Long silence. Then Lewis said, "I'm so glad we had this talk."

23

June had left her boots on the mat. Peter stood in the doorway, the drizzle cold on the back of his neck, and looked inside her apartment.

It was basically one big room, not exactly neat, but definitely comfortable. He saw a pair of cheap modern couches, a beat-up dining table that served as her work area, and tall, fully stocked bookshelves doing double-duty as partitions for the bedroom. Slate tiles were laid over the old garage floor, and June had covered them with a giant threadbare Persian rug in the living area. The roll-up garage doors had been replaced with wide sliding glass units that let in plenty of the watery spring light.

June was buzzing around the room, stacking stray books and magazines, collecting clothes left on the back of chairs, tossing assorted miscellaneous outdoor gear into a corner closet. "I'd say this is messier than usual, but that wouldn't be exactly accurate." She flashed him a smile. "Life's too short to waste it cleaning."

A bright red sea kayak was suspended on a pulley system from the ten-foot ceiling, and a pair of bicycles—one commuter bike, one full-suspension mountain bike—hung on a graceful cantilevered oak rack that elegantly exploited the laws of physics. The galley-style kitchen was simple but highly functional, a long row of salvaged Doug-fir cabinets and decent appliances paired with a broad island workstation and four mismatched vintage stools. The design details were crisp and clean, with two-piece baseboard and classic craftsman-style trim at the doors and windows. Peter had seen his share of crappy apartments in his time, and this was not one of them. Someone had put some care into this place.

June stood at the long table and started unloading her pack. "Aren't you coming in?"

The white static fizzed and popped at the base of his brain. He thought of Don's advice, gradual desensitization. "Sure." He stepped through the door, the static foaming higher and his leg reminding him of its delicate condition. "Do you have any ice?"

"In theory," she said, waving him to the kitchen. "Plastic bags to the right of the fridge, second drawer. You see anything else you like, knock yourself out. *Mi casa, su casa*, baby."

He limped into the kitchen area. The medical boot did help, and the static was manageable for the moment. Maybe Don was right. Suck it up, Marine.

Aesthetics aside, her kitchen was a desolate wasteland. The fridge was empty but for assorted condiments, a brine-crusted jar of green olives, eggs long past their sell date, and a half-eaten tub of yogurt that had turned into an uncontrolled science experiment. Her freezer had a half-full bottle of Grey Goose vodka, five partial pints of Häagen-Dazs ice cream, and a box of veggie burgers so frost-encrusted that you'd have to thaw them in a volcano. She was either on the road a lot, not much of a cook, or both.

But there was plenty of ice. He loaded a Ziploc and stumped back toward the couch. He wanted to ask June about her father. Then he saw that she had her laptop open.

"Hey, turn that thing off," he said. "We don't know what your hunters can do. If they could track you through your phone, they probably hacked your laptop, too."

"Peter, it's fine," she said. "Leo has this great anonymous Wi-Fi setup." She didn't look up, her fingers flying over the keys. "I'm a guest user, I'm untrackable here."

"And if they hacked your laptop?"

"I've got so much security on this thing, sometimes even I can't get in. Wait." She stopped typing and ran her finger over the mouse pad. "What the hell?"

"What is it?"

"My cell modem. I turned it off twice at the hospital, and again just now when I opened the laptop. I thought my laptop was just getting old. But the modem's turned itself back on again."

"What have I been saying? They hacked your laptop, and it's trying to tell your hunters where we are. Triangulating the cell towers." Peter reached over and pushed the laptop lid closed. "This is now a paperweight. How long has it been online?"

"A few minutes?" June screwed her face up in frustration. "I fucking need that computer. My whole life is in there. Besides, how else are we going to keep backtracking those guys from the redwoods?"

Peter didn't know how long the cell modem needed to talk to the towers. He'd have to take the computer somewhere else and let it really connect. Set a false trail for the hunters. Because he knew they hadn't stopped hunting.

But there was no reason to remind June of that.

"What about the tablet?"

"It's a toy. For kids' games and Grandma on Facebook." Her voice was getting louder.

"Relax," he said. "I'm guessing you're backed up six ways, right? And most of your work is stored in the cloud, anyway? So you just need a new laptop."

She gave him a look. "Easy for you to say, Mr. Big Bucks Buy-Me-A-Car."

"I forgot to mention," he said. "As your security specialist, that'll be in my expense report."

She threw a pillow at him. "I'm a freelance journalist," she said. "Not exactly rolling in the dough. Laptops aren't cheap."

"Don't sweat it," he said. "You can pay me out of the proceeds."

She blinked. "The proceeds of what?"

"The book you're going to write. About all this crazy shit. I'm betting this time you won't just be nominated for the Pulitzer."

Her mouth twitched, and he knew he was right, she'd been thinking about the story. When he was overseas, he'd had a magazine writer embedded with his unit for a few weeks. The guy had a hardwired need to turn every experience into a piece of published writing, and Peter figured June was no different.

"I'll call a few friends," she said. "I can probably scare up something used."

An odd sound came from her bag. A muffled electronic chirp.

He said, "What was that?"

"I think it was my new phone."

"Who else has the number?"

"Nobody," she said. "Just you. I did set up my email in the car last night. But I always leave the email alert on silent."

They looked at each other. She dove for her bag.

It wasn't an email.

It was a text.

And it wasn't from Peter.

The sender's name was listed as Tyg3r.

Peter stood beside her so he could see when she opened the text.

Hello, Junie. What would you like to know?

June's hands seemed to release the phone of their own accord. It clattered on the table, bouncing in its silicon case. She looked at Peter.

"Nobody calls me Junie," she said. "Only my mom calls me Junie."

Peter's voice was gentle. "I do believe that's your mom's algorithm."

Her look turned into a look. Then she snatched up the phone again, her thumbs flying over the virtual keys. She raised the phone so Peter could see it, then looked at him for an opinion.

She'd written:

Who are you?

He shrugged. She pressed Send.

After only a few seconds, the phone chirped again. Peter read over her shoulder.

I am Tyg3r. The Yoga Queen made me. What
would you like to know?

"Who's the Yoga Queen?"

"My mother. She was a yoga fanatic before it hit the mainstream. It was her sign-off on her personal email. Plus she had this whole thing about how good code and yoga had all these similarities. Elegance and flexibility." June's thumbs were back in rapid motion.

How did you find me?

The phone chirped.

The cellular telephone registered to June
Cassidy is compromised. The laptop
computer registered to June Cassidy is
compromised. This unregistered cellular
telephone receiving June Cassidy's
password-protected email is not
compromised. Ergo, this telephone is
connected to June Cassidy. What would
you like to know?

"Um," said Peter. "This isn't exactly my world? But this seems like
pretty advanced shit."

"Yeah." June's thumbs were back in action.

Who killed my mother?

The phone chirped.

Unknown. Please be more specific.

June replied.

What was the cause of death of Hazel
Cassidy in Palo Alto, California?

A longer pause, then the phone chirped again.

> According to the relevant pathologist's
> report, Hazel Cassidy died of acute physical
> trauma due to collision with a motor vehicle.
> See this link for more information.

This time a Web link followed the text message. June touched the link and her phone's Web browser came up. It was hard to read the page on the small screen. June expanded the size and panned around the document. It looked like a medical report, almost certainly something considered confidential and hidden behind a government firewall. Yet here it was.

"If this is your skeleton key," said Peter, "it seems like it can deliver the goods. Is it really talking to you?"

June shook her head. "It's not intelligent the way you or I would define it," she said, still poking at the screen. "It's a machine intelligence, with a specific set of skills. It's probably designed to understand everyday language and respond in kind. Take Google. When you type something into their search engine, it recognizes your query by key words, then performs its function through their proprietary algorithm. I would guess that the skeleton key—might as well call it Tyg3r—uses the same principles, just more highly developed, more specialized. My mom said it was designed to learn, to help it go into hidden places. To open locked doors." She made a face. "My phone is a crappy tool for this."

Her thumbs moved across the screen.

> Do you have another interface?

The phone chirped again. The sound was already getting annoying.

> You can also find this program here:

A Web link followed the message.

"Shit," said June. "I really need a computer."

Peter was still having trouble wrapping his head around this. "You've been contacted by your dead mother's artificial intelligence and you're still thinking about your laptop?"

She looked at him sideways. "Welcome to the future. The tech world is full of this crazy shit. Change is exponential. Self-driving cars? Computers you wear on your wrist? We take last year's miracle for granted. But that laptop is both my primary tool and the source of my livelihood."

He was suddenly aware that he was still standing very close to her. After his sweaty panic attack at the hospital, then their all-night drive, Peter could smell himself, and it wasn't good. But June hadn't showered, either, and the back of her neck smelled like some exotic, possibly addictive spice, which was entirely unfair. She even had freckles behind her ears.

He stepped away. June looked amused.

"Okay," he said. "You need to be geared up to do this. I get that. But don't call your friends right now. You don't want them to get hurt. Just take one of those prepaid cards and buy what you need. Sky's the limit. But right now I need to get your old machine out of here, turn it on and take it for a drive. Get those hunters to think this was just a pit stop, and we're heading somewhere else."

"I'll start at the library downtown," she said. "Use a public computer. Do a little more digging. Maybe buy a new laptop, maybe not. I don't want to take your charity."

"I told you, it's a loan," he said. "No strings. I'll stop for dinner fixings on my way back. My default is Mexican, so if you want something different, call or text."

She blinked at him. "What, you're cooking?"

"Purely in self-defense," he said. "I've seen the inside of your fridge."

She held her chin aloft in an aristocratic pose, peering down her nose at him. The fat lip and stitches tended to work against her there, but it was still an impressive look. "I," she said, "am a modern woman. Your patriarchal expectations of female servitude are both antiquated and sexist." She dismissed him with an imperial flick of her hand. "I *choose* not to cook."

He grinned and picked up her laptop. "That's a truly elegant rationalization."

He dodged another pillow on his way out the door.

He still hadn't asked about her dad. It seemed to be a sensitive topic for her. He'd figure it out on his drive.

But before he climbed into the minivan, he walked through the unruly little back yard, feeling the relief as the static settled lower on his spine, even as the drizzle trickled down his face. Unpruned junipers and broad-leafed evergreen rhododendrons formed a high wet tangle. Pushing past the thicket, he found a pair of spreading cedars beside the neighbor's white clapboard garage, making a small sheltered space out of the worst of the wind and rain.

The static wouldn't let him sleep inside, not anytime soon.

But he could make the backyard work.

He just didn't want to have to find a place in the dark.

24

CHIP

Chip Dawes would still be in the Clandestine Service if he hadn't decided to take down an Iraqi colonel who was skimming from the billions that the U.S. had brought in for reconstruction.

Even the Pentagon accountants expected some shrinkage. The Middle East functioned on authority and graft, and you needed some *baksheesh* if you wanted to get anything done. Uncle Sugar had brought planeloads of cash into the country for exactly this reason, and SSOs like Chip had access to stacks of hundred-dollar bills for greasing the locals.

It was easy to get used to, handling that kind of money.

But this colonel was a particularly nasty fuck with extra-sticky fingers, and Chip had credible intel that the colonel was using part of his skim to fund the insurgents. He confronted the colonel personally, but the man just laughed. He tried to get permission from his superiors to make an example, but word came down that the colonel was somehow protected.

Chip wasn't having any of that.

The man had laughed at him.

And he'd stolen a lot of fucking money.

So Chip put together an informal working group. He ran the show, leadership being part of his natural skill set. Six run-and-gun guys from six different units, guys he'd used before, guys he knew and trusted to do the job. And one asset he'd used for years, a particularly successful Farm-trained operator who was used to working alone.

It wasn't an officially sanctioned group, of course. This wasn't Chip's first rodeo, he knew how to slip and slide with the best of them. These were the go-go years, not a lot of oversight if you got shit done. Which Chip did, and planned to do again.

The colonel traveled in an armored Range Rover with three personal bodyguards and a pair of escort "technicals," Toyota Hilux 4-door pickups with the usual heavy machine gun mounted in the bed. Each truck had four men inside and two in the back to operate the gun. Sixteen men in all.

Chip's working group caught the colonel's convoy on a narrow street outside the home of the colonel's mistress. Two men with recycled RPG-7s on opposing rooftops to take out the technicals and crack the armored vehicle. Four men driving four local cars to block the road in and out, then attack on the ground with SAWs and M16s. Chip on one of the rooftops, using the radio to direct the battle. And his asset, unknown to the other men, waiting in reserve.

His superiors would have wanted him to have more men. Even the idea of using just six men to attack and kill a heavily armed escort would have made Washington shit a brown river, but Chip was a pro. The job went exactly as planned.

When the smoke cleared, Chip walked into the street with an M4 and reached through the shattered armored glass to open the door of the colonel's Range Rover from the inside. It was disappointing that the colonel was dead—Chip would have liked the man to know who'd killed him—but the stainless-steel briefcase was there, as his source had said it would be, along with a cheap duffel stuffed with banded packets of hundred-dollar bills.

He thanked his men and handed each a stack of hundreds, saying that this small skirmish represented a great American victory against Iraqi corruption. The colonel was helping the insurgents, helping to kill their friends, and they had stopped him. The secrets in the briefcase would reveal more Iraqi traitors, and he was grateful.

Then Chip's Farm-trained asset stepped out of a doorway with an M16 and opened fire with ruthless efficiency. Chip dropped to the ground, and a few of the men had time to return fire, but it was over in less than a minute. Six men down. Two men left.

All according to plan.

Even the part where the asset, in dusty Western clothes and a black-on-white keffiyeh, jacked in a fresh mag and sighted his rifle squarely on Chip's chest. "Drop the gun and open the briefcase."

CHIP WORE BODY ARMOR and a helmet, but they wouldn't help him if the man wanted to kill him close up. He'd considered this possibility carefully from the start. The asset's outwardly ordinary persona concealed a truly extraordinary talent. Chip had seen this from the first time they'd worked together, and had treated the man accordingly, granting him independence and respect.

It was Chip who had given his asset the opportunity to explore his talent and reach his true potential. It was Chip who had paid the man bonuses far above his meager Company paycheck. This had earned him the man's loyalty, although the asset didn't seem to function like a normal human being. No evidence of emotion whatsoever. He was more like some kind of advanced killing robot.

"No problem," said Chip. He laid the M4 in the bloody dust and worked the latches on the briefcase. His source had also provided the combinations to the locks, and the location of the key, on a gold chain around the colonel's neck.

Inside was a stack of six thick international document mailers.

"Supposed to be Eurobonds," said Chip. "Do you want me to open one?"

"Yes." The asset kept the muzzle of his weapon trained on Chip's chest. This was the moment of truth. Chip set the briefcase on the smoking hood of the Rover, removed the top envelope, and slid out the documents inside. Thick linen paper with ornate printing and a clearly visible watermark.

"Bearer bonds," said Chip. "Unregistered. Payable to the person physically holding the paper. Ten thousand euros each." He felt the smile grow on his face with each moment his asset didn't pull the trigger. He riffled the documents with his thumb. "I'd say about a hundred in this stack, wouldn't you? That's a million euros." He slid the documents back in their envelope, dropped the envelope back in the stainless case, then made a show of counting the envelopes. "Six million euros. About six and a half million U.S. at today's exchange rate."

The asset looked at him through those ordinary eyes. He was brown from the sun and the keffiyeh on his head looked completely natural. The rifle barrel didn't move.

"This was never about the colonel," said the asset. "This was about you."

"No," Chip said, with calm conviction. "This was about you and me. You just didn't need to know, not until right now. Unless you really want to go back to the chain of command at Langley? Maybe train the next generation at the Farm? That's sure as hell not what I want to do."

The asset just raised an eyebrow.

The man was dry, Chip would give him that. In fact, the asset scared the shit out of Chip, but he was committed to his course. The capitalism of war. Nothing ventured, nothing gained.

"This isn't enough to retire on," said Chip. "But it's enough for seed money. I want you and me to go into business together. With your skills and mine, we're going to be rich."

The asset's expression remained unchanged. Chip kept talking, selling the dream.

"Corporate security. Protecting secrets for some companies, maybe stealing them from others, all at twenty times our current salary. We use this money to set up a nice office, hire a couple of hot secretaries. Sounds good, right?"

"You're quite a salesman," said the asset. "You have specifics?"

"Of course I do. I've been thinking about this for two years. We set up someplace near a big military base that also has a big hacker talent pool, like Seattle. Lewis-McChord is just south of there, and that's where we find our field men, ex-military. We launch by infiltrating a major company, then present their board of directors with what we found. They sign a contract to consult on their security, but before long they're paying us to steal from their competitors."

The asset took out a disposable flip phone and took a photo of Chip standing beside the briefcase, all without taking his eyes off Chip or his finger from the trigger. The implication was clear. Proof of Chip's involvement. Then he motioned Chip away with the muzzle of his rifle. "I'll take half," he said.

Chip stepped back, but he went all in. "Hell, no," he said. "Take everything, including that bag of greenbacks. You're the best one to get it back to the civilized world. I was thinking overland to Turkey, but you'd know better than me. Set up a small business, open some accounts, and start paying yourself with that cash, run that shit through the laundry, baby. I rotate home in twelve weeks. I already have a buyer for the Eurobonds. We are going to make a pile of money and have a blast doing it."

The asset didn't say anything.

Chip watched him decide.

But he was confident in how it would play out. He knew the man. He'd given his asset the information he needed to make the right choice. They were a good team before, they'd be a good team again.

The asset, whose name was Shepard, lowered the rifle, shouldered the duffel, picked up the briefcase, and walked off without another word.

A week later, Chip got a nasty shock when the station head called Chip into his office and started asking questions. They'd been tracking the colonel and his escort with a Predator drone, had stumbled onto Chip's operation, and caught the firefight on video. The Predator had tracked Chip back to his waiting driver/fixer and the FOB. The station head had sent a team to the scene to see who else was involved.

Shepard's keffiyeh had concealed most of his face, and they'd lost him anyway, of course. Shepard was half ghost when you were standing right next to him. From five thousand feet wearing the Arabic equivalent of a baseball hat? He basically evaporated. With all that money.

As it turned out, Shepard holding Chip at gunpoint was what kept Chip out of Leavenworth. An unexpected benefit of his plan.

Chip was a talented actor. He was contrite, he'd been caught, the story spilled out of him, and some of it was almost true. He pled love of country, frustration with the bureaucracy, and hatred of corruption. He was used by an unknown local player who'd fed him information about the colonel through third parties, only to step in and take all the intel, proof of corruption, everything.

He was embarrassed and ashamed and lucky to be alive.

He fooled four interrogators and six polygraphs and submitted his resignation.

Unbelievably, the agency actually asked him to stay on.

He told them he wanted out while he still had some scrap of his soul.

And laughed all the way to the bank.

25

PETER

Peter headed toward the freeway, June's laptop open and running on the passenger seat. He assumed the hunters had taken it over completely, so he had the Web browser open to a map of British Columbia and a half-dozen Vancouver hotel websites, and took advantage of stoplights to click from one site to the next.

Waiting at the on-ramp, he used his anonymous phone to find a number and made a call.

"Semper Fidelis Roofing, can I help you?"

"Hey, Estelle, it's Peter Ash. How are you?"

"Peter who? I know this can't be Ashes because he got eaten up by Bigfoot. Why else wouldn't he have called like he promised?"

"I got sidetracked, Estelle. And I never promised you anything. Don't bust my balls, okay?"

"Oh, I'm not," she said. "'Cause if I were, you'd for damn sure know it."

Estelle Martinez was thirty-five years old and managed the office for her brother Manny's roofing business. She'd been an Army drill instructor for ten years and now ran ultramarathons on the weekends. Her last boyfriend had been hospitalized for exhaustion. All the roofers were combat veterans, and they were scared of her. Peter was scared of her, too.

"Estelle, can we do this another time? I need to see Manny."

"Manny's busy."

"Estelle. Cut the shit. This is serious. Put him on."

She sighed. "He's not here. Don't you got his cell?"

"I lost my old phone. I need to see him in person, I'm heading up to your office now. Where is he?"

"Out doing estimates." He could hear the clack of a keyboard. "He's in Mountlake Terrace right now. I'll text you the address of his next appointment and let him know you're coming."

Peter found Manny standing in the driveway of a McMansion, holding a tablet computer in both meaty hands, staring into the air above the house. The tablet showed a moving view of the house from above. A high penetrating whine came from somewhere over the roof. The soft rain had stopped.

"Ashes, *mi hermano*. Gimme a sec, let me finish this run."

"What, this is work?"

Manny smiled without looking away from the speck in the air. "I'm a high-tech motherfucker, *mano*. This thing does a programmed run over the house, the software takes all the measurements. Square footage, hips and valleys, all the flashing. The clients fucking love it. I send them the video with my proposal, they think, shit, that's how you do estimates? Imagine how you'd do my roof."

Manny Martinez wasn't tall, but he had broad sloping shoulders and legs like tree trunks. He'd been one of Peter's platoon sergeants in Iraq. Once during a firefight, Peter had seen Manny throw another sergeant, Big Jimmy Johnson, shot in the leg and bleeding out, over his shoulder like a sack of potatoes and carry him to the MRAP a half-mile away. Big Jimmy had outweighed Manny by sixty pounds at least.

Jimmy was dead now, but it wasn't because of Manny.

A lot of them were dead.

But Manny was clearly alive and well. He wore clean Carhartts and a crisp white button-down shirt with a fresh shave and a high fade sharp enough to cut. He had a dozen employees and drove a nearly new pickup. He had a wife and two little kids.

The tablet beeped and the video stopped moving. Manny touched the screen and the little quadcopter drone homed in like the world's largest mosquito. When it touched down on the driveway, his grin made him look like he was eight years old.

His friend had made a life here. He was thriving. Peter couldn't get him involved.

Manny picked up the drone and headed back toward his truck. "So what's up? Stella said you had something serious."

Peter said, "It's not like that. I'm back in Seattle for a few days, and I wanted to say hey. Maybe we can grab dinner before I head out?"

Manny looked at him. It was the same solid, steady stare that could see through walls and around corners, that could find ambushes before they happened. The eight-year-old boy was gone.

"Don't bullshit me, Ashes. What are you into?"

Peter shook his head. "Forget it, Manny. You're doing great. You've got a family, people depending on you. I have no business asking you for anything."

The muscles flexed in Manny's jaw. "Listen, Ashes? What would really piss me off? You end up dead and I'm not there to stop it. Because if it weren't for you, I'd have been dead years ago. Same goes for half the guys working for me. You did what had to be done, what nobody else had the balls to do. You called down the fire and you took the heat for it. So you name the time and place, we'll be there. That's how this works."

Peter sighed. "This shows every sign of getting ugly," he said. "You set up for that?"

Manny snorted. "You forget who the fuck you're talking to?"

"No," said Peter. "I didn't forget. It's why I'm here."

"Goddamn right," said Manny. "When and where?"

"I don't know. I'll call you in a day or two."

Manny told him the number.

"By the way," he said. "Stella's single again. If I was you, I'd watch your ass."

"I was never here," said Peter. "We never talked."

26

Four hours later, Peter rolled back down June's driveway and parked the minivan beside a big black BMW 7 series with a dented rear fender and a long scrape along the driver's side.

He'd continued north on I-5, waiting for the laptop to run out of power. As the battery got very low, the computer kept shutting itself down, and he had to keep turning it back on until the battery was fully exhausted and it would no longer restart. He was past Edmonds before he finally shut the lid and used the next exit to head south again.

With the navigational help of his phone, he made a quick stop at Dunn Lumber in Wallingford, then limped through REI's enormous flagship store. It turned out you could carry a lot in a minivan.

His last stop on the way back to June's apartment was a big QFC grocery store. He forced himself to walk slowly down the aisles, breathing through the rising static as he filled the cart. Gradual desensitization. It wasn't easy.

The reward was getting to cook a real meal in a real kitchen.

For June, who was the most vivid woman he'd ever met.

He was planning to ask about her dad after dinner. He'd have to tell her he'd asked Lewis to look into her mother. He wasn't looking forward to it.

But when he opened her door, juggling four full bags of groceries, he saw her sitting on the couch beside a round-shouldered young man hunched over a laptop computer.

"Knock knock," said Peter.

June looked up. Her fat lip was still purple but the swelling was down even more. She'd clearly showered and changed her clothes. He wondered how she would smell now.

"Peter, what took you so long? This is Leo Boyle, my landlord. Leo, this is Peter Ash."

Boyle kept his eyes on the screen, but he put up a lazy hand. "Yo, bro." He looked to be in his mid-twenties, but his hairline was already retreating up the broad expanse of his forehead. He wore factory-distressed jeans and a wrinkled dress shirt that he'd left untucked, trying to hide his soft belly. They were fashionable clothes, Peter supposed, and probably expensive, but a long way from dress blues.

"Nice to meet you," said Peter. He shut the door with his medical boot, hefted the bags to the kitchen counter, and began to put away groceries. "Can you stay for dinner? Nothing fancy, just fish tacos, Spanish rice, and salad. Plenty of food."

June shot Peter a smile, her eyes bright.

Boyle glanced at June, then at Peter. His face was soft and undefined, the skin pale and puffy with lack of sleep or too much alcohol or both. "Sure, I guess."

"Great," said Peter. "Can I get anyone a drink? There's beer and wine and mineral water and orange juice."

"You bet," said June as she leaped off the couch and perched on a stool to ogle the supplies. "Oh, man. I'm hungry. And thirsty. Is that Lagunitas Copper Ale? I'll take one of those."

Boyle clambered after her. "There's Grey Goose in the freezer," he said, staking some kind of claim with his knowledge of the liquor supply. "I'll take a martini, dirty. No vermouth. Two olives. To the brim."

"Coming up." Peter found an opener and set the bottle in front of June. "Glass?"

She shook her head and raised the bottle to the corner of her mouth without the stitches. A small amber trickle made its way down her chin. She wiped it off with her wrist.

Peter found a lonely martini glass in a cupboard of recycled jelly jars, washed out the dust, then took the vodka from the freezer and poured. He fished two ancient green olives from the crusty jar, splashed a little of the brine into the glass, then topped with vodka until the meniscus was crowned at the rim. Clearly the volume of alcohol was important to Boyle.

He pushed the glass carefully across the counter. Boyle lifted the glass without spilling a drop, and took an experimental sip. "Not bad," he said. As if making this particular drink was a challenge.

Peter opened a beer for himself, then turned on the oven to heat and laid a thick slab of halibut on a pan to come up to room temperature. He brushed it with a little olive oil, then added salt and pepper. "You mind if I use your shower?" he said to June.

June gave him an innocent smile with something else behind it. "I thought you'd never ask."

"DID YOU MAKE IT to the library?"

Showered, scrubbed, and shaved, Peter had the rice simmering, the lettuce washed, and the vegetables chopped. Peeling and dicing mangoes, he didn't want to ask about her research in front of Leo Boyle. He definitely wasn't going to bring up Tyg3r, or whatever he was supposed to call the skeleton key algorithm.

"For a few hours," she said. "Public Investigations has a subscription to TransUnion, where I found more history on our guys." She held up a hand. "Before you ask, I logged on with one of my coworker's passwords. But I got location histories, legal histories, past and present vehicle registrations. Then cross-referencing on all of that. We definitely have some new leads there. But nothing new about the companies we talked about."

Peter noticed that June was being cautious with the details, too. Maybe it was Boyle, or maybe just habit. Then she waggled her eyelashes at him, Groucho-style. "I did buy a new computer. Leo was just geeking out on the specs."

Her landlord had downed his martini with no evident effect, and was sucking on a lollipop. "What are you working on?" He talked to June as if Peter wasn't in the room.

"Just background," she said, catching Peter's eye. "It probably won't turn into anything." He was glad June didn't seem to want to get Leo involved. The less anyone else knew, the safer they would be.

"Gotcha," said Boyle. "Woodward and Bernstein stuff." He watched June out of the corner of his eye, trying not to stare, and failing. June didn't seem to notice.

Or maybe she was used to it. Peter understood why Boyle would come over to see June. Anyone in their right mind would. But what did June see in Boyle? The man had the personality of a banana slug.

The timer went off for the rice. Peter put the fish in the oven, turned the timer on again, then stirred the diced red pepper and smoked jalapeño into the rice along with some paprika and garlic powder, poured in a little of his beer, then put the rice back on the heat. He put the mango pieces into a bowl with chopped tomatoes and basil and squeezed a few limes into the mix for a simple salsa. His shoulders were tight from the static, but cooking helped calm him down.

As he assembled the salad, he thought maybe he could distract Boyle from staring at June. "So, Leo. What do you do for a living?"

"Oh, you know. A little of this, a little of that."

Peter knew that dodge. He'd used it himself.

Boyle took the lollipop out of his mouth and examined it. "You want a sucker?"

"With beer? No, thanks." Peter had another Lagunitas open on the counter. "I like the apartment. Did you do the work yourself?"

"Most of it. The cabinets came out of the house. I'm working on that kitchen now, or I'm supposed to be." He shrugged. "I kind of lost interest. I'm building an app right now."

Peter imagined Seattle to be a place where half the population over the age of twelve was building an app. Either that or brewing craft beer or roasting artisanal coffee. Or renovating these old houses. He'd seen a lot of Dumpsters and scaffolding in the neighborhood. Seattle was probably a good place to be a carpenter. He'd have to retrieve his truck and tools if he wanted to work.

The timer went off and Peter checked the fish. "About five more minutes," he said.

Boyle pushed himself to his feet. "I'm gonna grab a smoke," he said, and strolled to the front door.

When the door closed behind him, June turned to Peter. "It was nice of you to invite him for dinner," she said. "He can be a little annoying sometimes."

"Any friend of yours," Peter said, raising his beer to her.

She gave him a rueful smile. "I'm not sure Leo has any real friends," she said. "I've kind of adopted him, like a big sister."

Peter had seen the way Boyle looked at June. Not how any brother should look at his sister.

"He's pretty young to own a house like that. What does he do?"

June rolled her eyes. "Trustafarian."

Peter didn't know the term, and it must have showed on his face. June clarified. "He told me he inherited some money and doesn't have to work. Those are marijuana lollipops he's always sucking on. But he's a computer nut, talks about all these groups he works with online."

"What kind of groups?" Peter was thinking about the people who'd hacked June's laptop.

"I can't keep them straight," she said. "He's always starting some new project. He's smart but lazy. He never seems to finish anything."

"He finished this apartment," Peter pointed out.

"Are you kidding?" said June. "When I moved in, the kitchen and bathroom were done, but the walls were all unpainted. The floor was bare concrete. No baseboard, no trim at the windows or doors. I put in that slate tile. I installed that trim."

"That was you?" Peter raised his eyebrows. "Got some skills, girl."

"If you ask me nice, I'll show you my nail gun."

"Now you're just teasing me."

Boyle came back inside, and it was time for dinner.

27

Stuffing down his fourth taco, Boyle said to June, "Was there some kind of problem with your old laptop? I could give it a tune-up. Might be nice to have a backup machine."

"It keeps turning on the cell modem," she said. "I think someone's got remote access."

"You got hacked again?" Boyle was trying for casual and failing. "I'll take a look at it if you want. I built a Faraday cage in my basement. At least I can debug without your modem dialing out."

"You have a Faraday cage?" asked Peter.

Boyle looked at Peter, his face a mix of arrogant skepticism and a kind of shy geek pride. "You know what that is?"

A Faraday cage was an enclosure made of fine wire mesh or metal foil. It could be the size of a cigar box, a factory, or anything in between, and was designed to protect sensitive equipment from static electrical charges. They were used in tech research and manufacturing, but they also kept out all electromagnetic radiation, like radio waves and cell signals, which prevented electronic eavesdropping or damage from an electromagnetic pulse. Which is why they were popular with the military, along with other paranoid institutions and individuals.

"I read a lot of science fiction in junior high," said Peter. "What do you use it for?"

"Dude, I work on computers," said Boyle. "You gotta be careful when you're opening up somebody's laptop. Plus I help out some people who really like their privacy. You want to see it?" His face was flushed. He was showing off for June, thought Peter.

"Maybe tomorrow," he said. "You can really get rid of the malware?"

"Totally." Boyle nodded sagely as he unwrapped another lollipop. "I can probably even figure out who did it."

June said, "I got hacked two years ago using the Wi-Fi in a Starbucks. Someone tried to empty my bank account using my own goddamn computer. Leo found the hacker."

"Piece of cake," Boyle said grandly, waving his hand. "Guy was a total amateur. I sent him a worm that locked him out of his own computer. This new guy might be tougher, those internal cell modems are a bitch to access. But I'll help if you want."

Peter was starting to see why June thought of Boyle as her younger brother. He was so much younger than his years, and he wanted June's approval so badly. There was definitely something a little off about him, but nothing Peter could really put his finger on. Maybe the guy was just stoned.

"We'd really appreciate it," said Peter. "June needs all the help she can get."

June stuck out her tongue, and Boyle's pants barked like a dog.

He extracted his phone from a front pocket and glanced at the screen. "Whoa. I forgot, I'm supposed to be someplace. Hey, you guys want to go party? We're gonna get fucked up and watch kung fu movies."

"Not tonight," said Peter. "But I'll walk you out."

"Yeah, great, yeah." Boyle put on his jacket and opened the door.

Peter followed him out. The rain had stopped for the moment and Peter felt the static fade and his shoulders ease. The cool night air smelled dense and green with spring growth. A car drove by, the sound of its tires on the still-wet pavement like painter's tape peeling off the roll.

Boyle opened the door to his beat-up BMW and climbed inside. The interior of the car smelled like an Afghan hookah parlor. Yet the man's house had a beautiful and expensive six-color paint job.

"It would really help to figure out who hacked June's old laptop," said Peter. "Can you take a look in the morning?"

Boyle gave Peter a sloppy grin and cranked the ignition. The big engine idled with a ragged purr, as if one of the spark plugs was misfiring. "I'll be out pretty late, bro. Might even crash at my friend's place." He waved idly at the house. "Leave it inside the back door. Spare key behind a loose board."

"Thanks, I'll find it." Apparently Peter had graduated to some kind of friendship status. Or else the chemicals in Boyle's bloodstream had really kicked in.

"No worries, dude." Boyle reached into the glove box and pulled out a pair of yellow lollipops. "You want one of these?"

Peter shook his head. "No thanks."

"That's cool." Boyle tore the wrappers from both suckers and jammed them into his mouth in a single practiced movement. He made a mock salute, revved the engine, and backed out to the street at high speed.

Peter heard the blast of a horn and screeching tires, but no crash. He shook his head. Leo Boyle was living proof that it was better to be lucky than good.

He walked to the minivan and opened the rear hatch. He still had a few chores to do.

. . .

AFTER COLLECTING the small tarp, bungee cords, and flashlight he'd bought at the lumberyard, Peter pushed through the wet backyard tangle of spiky juniper and glossy-leafed rhododendrons to the sheltered space by the neighbor's garage. The medical boot was getting wet, but he could always toss it in June's dryer.

With the light clipped to the brim of his baseball hat, he hung the tarp between the tall evergreen trees, high enough so he could stand without brushing his head, but angled so the collected rainfall would drain to one side. His leg was sore again, and raising his arms above his head made his ribs hurt. Suck it up, Marine.

He hauled a pair of two-by-sixes through the bushes, cut each one to length with a short hand saw, and nailed the pieces together into a rect-angular frame with a few swats of his shiny new framing hammer. His ribs complained some more, but it didn't hurt to breathe, so he figured he was okay.

As he hauled the cedar planks from the van, June stepped outside and followed him through the brush, coatless, her feet bare on the wet fallen leaves. She watched silently, shivering, as he tacked down the decking with just a few nails, making a neat platform seven feet long and five feet wide. It rocked when he stood on it, so he shimmed one corner with a stone.

He used the claw end of the framing hammer to split his scrap into thinner pieces. He found more stones in a heap at the back of the neigh-bor's yard and borrowed them for a fire ring. He took pages of the local free weekly, the *Stranger*, crumpled them up, then arranged the kindling on top. He pilfered an armload of firewood from the dry middle of the neighbor's mossy, untended woodpile. June still hadn't said a word.

The rain started up again as he worked, a soft hush on the plastic tarp. He lit the fire and made a final trip to the van, returning with the new sleeping pad and bag he'd bought at REI that afternoon, tucking them in a dry spot under the eaves of the neighbor's garage, and two short fabric camping chairs, which he unfolded on the little deck.

He set the light on the platform and turned to June.

"I know you weren't crazy about that last hotel," he said. He couldn't read her face in the dark. "I doubt this one's any better. No bathroom. No spa. No room service. But it does have a fireplace."

When she turned and walked back toward the house, he thought he'd screwed it up completely. Misread her, misread everything. For chrissake, he'd only known her for two days. He stood beside the struggling fire in the cold wet night, feeling the ache in his ribs and listening to the rain on the tarp, which sounded too much like the static in his head.

Then June pushed her way back through the rhododendrons, holding the bottle of wine in one hand and two jelly jars and a Swiss army knife in the other. He took the knife from her and turned it in his hand, trying to find the corkscrew in the dark.

She said, "Put that down, you idiot. The wine's for afterward."

He looked up at her then, saw the firelight on her freckled face, the heat in her eyes.

She grabbed him by the front of his jacket and kissed him hard. Her stitches prickled. "Ow, fuck," she said. "My lip." Then kissed him again, harder. "You better kiss me someplace else."

Peter kicked the chairs from the platform as she pulled his jacket and shirt off, not bothering much with the zippers or buttons. He took a little more time with her clothes, enjoying the slow revelations. Her skin was hot to the touch, soft as silk, and she tasted still of that exotic spice that he knew now was utterly, completely, entirely addictive.

She said, "There goddamn well better be room for both of us in that sleeping bag."

He licked her nipple experimentally. "Maybe if one of us is on top?"

She arched her back and pressed herself into him. "I'm the boss and don't you forget it."

.   .   .

THE WINE WASN'T for afterward so much as it was for between. The evening passed in a long, languorous dream punctuated by intervals of slippery athleticism. It didn't help Peter's ribs any, but it was very good for the rest of him.

He got up several times, naked in the night, to feed the fire from the neighbor's woodpile, turning to see June ogling him from the sleeping bag. Later he woke to see her creeping back through the jungle, nude but for the stitches on her lip and the bandage on her arm. Her firelit figure was a sylvan fantasy of compact curves punctuated by a fierce, lascivious smile. She'd brought a carton of ice cream.

He licked it out of her belly button while she giggled and shrieked, scandalizing the neighbors.

And so on, and on, and on.

IN THE MORNING, she was gone. The sleeping bag was a wreck. He found his clothes, hung the sleeping bag where it might somehow revive itself in the open air, then pushed through the dripping underbrush. Her door was unlocked, but she was not inside. It was after ten.

He ran the shower hot and stood under the spray, eyes closed, backing down the static with the memory of June floating above him, upturned nipples bobbing with her greedy, eager motion. Then she was there in the flesh, slipping through the gap in the shower curtain. Naked and sweaty from a long run, and definitely delighted to see him.

"No way," he said, "I'm not used to this kind of workout."

"Don't be such a baby." She climbed him like a monkey and bit his ear. "What about my needs? You've got to get yourself into shape."

They stopped talking after that.

28

SHEPARD

Shepard strode purposefully into the hospital's main lobby, pulling out his credentials as he approached reception.

This was the most challenging aspect of his work. Pretending to be a normal human being.

Killing had never been difficult for Shepard.

Making conversation was much harder.

Tonight, he wore a dark suit, a striped tie, an American flag pin, and aggressively polished shoes. His credentials were quite good, almost as good as the real thing, because for all intents and purposes, they were real.

The young man behind the counter looked up when Shepard approached. "How may I help you?"

Shepard held up the laminated ID. "Homeland," he said. "I need to talk to your senior security person on duty. Right now."

"Um," said the young man. "I don't know who, uh." He held up a hesitant finger. "Let me make a call?"

Five minutes later, Shepard was walking down the hall with a yawning, overweight ex-cop named Jenks. "Sorry, third shift is a bitch. Homeland Security wants what?"

"I want to look at your feeds. You had two people here, and I need to see where they went and who they talked to. Let's start with the ER."

Five minutes after that, Shepard was down in the security dungeon, sipping burnt coffee and reviewing grainy video footage.

He knew the girl's face from the salesman's file, and he found her as she walked into the waiting area. She wore a floppy hat, and her face was puffy and strange, like she'd been hit in the face, but it was clearly her. The hat failed to conceal her long, narrow nose and her wide mouth. The freckles didn't make it through the poor video quality.

Her file was far from complete, but it painted a certain kind of picture.

A wild child with a long and distinguished record of causing trouble and challenging authority. She first met the law at thirteen for driving without a license. The list went on until she went off to college, where she seemed to find some kind of focus. She'd become an independent young woman either living on the margins or charting her own path, depending on your point of view.

But Shepard already knew enough about the girl.

He wanted to know who had helped her.

In the video, it appeared to be the tall man who'd walked in ahead of her. Broad at the shoulder and physically fit, although he was favoring his left leg and his right side. He wore a baseball hat to hide his face, and he was clearly conscious of the camera, because when the intake nurse handed him a gauze pad, he turned away to take off his hat and dab gently at a darkness in his hair that looked like blood.

They'd both been beat up when their car left the road.

He used the joystick to scan back and forth, freezing the video at the clearest view of the man's face.

"Print me a picture, please, this frame. What can you tell me about these two?"

Jenks looked apologetic. "I'm sorry, sir, but that's confidential information. HIPAA and that. I can't tell you anything without a warrant."

"This thing is moving quickly," said Shepard. "These two people killed four of my best agents not twenty-four hours ago."

"Jesus," said Jenks. "I'm sorry to hear that. If you had a court order, I could tell you whatever you wanted."

"I don't have time for a court order. But I can tell you're a patriot," Shepard said, slapping the man on the back. Was that overkill? Probably not, from the man's tired smile. "Where do they go from the waiting room? Do you have any cameras in the exam area?"

"Not in the exam areas or the bathrooms," Jenks said as he turned back to the keyboard. "But just about everywhere else, including the parking lot. Let's see what we got."

29

PETER

Peter poured coffee into a pair of white china mugs and stood examining the contents of the fridge. For some reason, he was starving. Then June sauntered out of the bathroom, opened the warm oven, and pulled out a white paper bag. The smell of chorizo and cinnamon filled the kitchen.

"Breakfast burritos and fresh churros," she said. "There's this great food truck at the end of my running route."

He wondered if it was too early to propose.

Her face looked much better, the swelling down a great deal in the night and the bruises fading from purple to a greenish-yellow, which she'd covered expertly with makeup. They ate on the couch with napkins on their laps and a bag of ice on Peter's ankle. He wanted to jump her all over again, but June, now dressed in dark blue slacks and a crisp white blouse, was all business.

"Here's my plan for today. Let me know if you have any better ideas."

"I have a better idea."

She gave him a look. "This is work time," she said. "Before we try to track down those guys from the redwoods, I think we should meet that lawyer, the one who contacted my mom."

"Jean-Pierre Nicolet," Peter said, nodding. "He's a pretty heavy hitter. If we're going to approach him, I'm going to need a decent suit."

She looked at him, maybe trying to picture him in a suit.

"I'll tell you my idea on the way." He got off the couch. "I'll meet you at the car in a few minutes. I want to do something before we go."

The house's six-color paint job glowed in the filtered light. Leo Boyle's dented black BMW was gone from the driveway, so Peter didn't bother knocking.

If he hadn't known the key was there somewhere, he'd never have found it. Even knowing the general location, it took him a couple of minutes to find the chiseled-out hollow behind a loose piece of clapboard siding. Boyle had created a weirdly excellent hiding place.

Peter wondered why the kid had told him about the key. Maybe he'd thought Peter wouldn't be able to find it. Maybe there was something else he was tired of hiding. Or maybe he was just stoned. The old lock turned more smoothly than Peter expected.

He stepped into a small landing with peeling paint and a few hooks for coats. Steep, narrow steps wound down to a darkened basement and up to a closed door that Peter assumed led to the kitchen. Peter had worked on a lot of old homes with his dad, and the layouts were usually pretty basic unless the owners had made significant alterations.

The space was small enough to set off the static, but Peter was starting to get used to the low level of discomfort, the pricking at the base of his brainstem.

Maybe Don was right. He could do this.

Then June opened the door behind him. "What the hell are you doing?" she hissed.

"Leo said he'd take a look at your laptop," Peter said quietly. "Before he gets involved, I thought I'd take a look at him."

"Leo's harmless," she said. "A pothead and a goof."

"I'm sure you're right," Peter said, and climbed the steps to the kitchen.

He opened the door to a gutted shell. The plaster was gone from the walls, exposing the two-by-four structure and the cracked bare planks of the exterior walls. A sheet of opaque plastic covered the wall to the next room. There were no cabinets, no fridge or stove. Just a small aluminum sink set into a piece of plastic laminate countertop, held up with scrap lumber.

"Wow." June was peering over his shoulder. "I guess Leo was telling the truth. He really hasn't done anything."

"You don't come in here?"

"Never. We signed the lease in my apartment." He looked at her. She said, "Hey, Leo shows up at my place all the time already. I don't need to encourage him."

Beside the sink was a plain black mug and a cheap coffeemaker, both dirty, and a tiny microwave oven. A box of ramen noodles and a can of Folgers sat half-empty on the floor.

Peter didn't know what he'd expected. A high-end espresso machine, maybe. An expensive fridge filled with restaurant leftovers. Not this.

He was used to unfinished spaces. When he was fourteen, his family's own kitchen was torn out for a whole summer. He and his father had run the plumbing and wiring, then built the cabinets while they waited for the drywaller to get out of rehab. But this didn't feel like a work in progress.

It felt more like a squatter's camp.

"Did Leo's trust fund run out?"

"He never mentioned it," said June. "Although maybe he wouldn't have. Leo's a little weird, you know?"

Peter pushed through the plastic sheeting and stepped into what once was the dining room. It was gutted, too. The living room was the same, and so was the broad front entryway. Peering up the stairs, he could see that the second floor was just like the first.

Once, it had been a grand house. The interior would have been elaborately detailed, with coffered ceilings and lustrous paneling and built-in cabinets. Now the wind blew through the gaps in the sheathing, and the frames of the old windows were bare. The fresh paint on the outside was like a fine suit of clothes on a skeleton.

What did that say about Leo?

"I had no idea," said June, behind him. "You really never know what's going on in anyone else's head, do you?"

"Maybe you should find another place to live," said Peter.

"I can handle Leo," she said. "You know how hard it is to find a cheap apartment in this part of town? With built-in tech support?" She tugged on his sleeve. "Let's get out of here. We've got things to do."

They walked back through the kitchen. But on the landing by the back door, Peter ducked down the winding steps to the darkened basement. June didn't follow.

"Peter," she called after him. "Let's just go, okay?"

"I'll be quick. I just want to take a peek." He was already at the bottom, feeling around for a light switch. "If your landlord has a row of chest freezers stacked with bodies, wouldn't you like to know?"

"No," June called down from the landing. "I wouldn't."

Peter's hand found the light switch, and flipped it.

It took his eyes a few seconds to adjust to the brightness. The basement was immaculate. LED strips hung from the exposed ceiling joists, eliminating every shadow. The joists and subfloor had been sprayed with brilliant glossy white paint, along with the patched concrete foundation, the center beam, its supporting posts, and all the visible conduit, plumbing, and ductwork. Peter couldn't see a cobweb or mouse turd in the entire space. The washer and dryer and furnace and water heater looked like they'd been polished.

But that wasn't the most unusual part.

The most unusual part was the Faraday cage.

This was no cigar box lined with tinfoil. Almost half of the basement had been made over into a large rectangular work space. The walls and ceiling were covered with layers of fine copper mesh that also appeared to extend under a new raised plywood floor. The entrance was a screen door covered with more copper mesh that extended past the jambs so that, when the door was closed, it would form a complete envelope, blocking all electromagnetic radiation.

On one long wall, wooden workbenches were strewn with electronic hardware and soldering tools and a magnifying lens and circuit boards and all kinds of other shit that Peter could never begin to identify. On another wall, an elaborate ergonomic chair faced a big modern desk unit with three keyboards and a wide array of computer screens. A sagging plaid recliner in the corner had a fleece blanket dropped over one arm.

It was homey, in a weird way. Especially in contrast to the empty shell upstairs.

Maybe this was where Boyle really lived, Peter thought. Down here. Working with this hardware and his online collaborators.

Who were doing what, exactly?

A plastic ID badge on a lanyard hung from the corner of a monitor with the magnetic strip facing out. Peter turned it so he could see the front. It was an electronic access pass for Stanford University's computer science department, with an unshaven Boyle staring blankly at the camera.

Could be a coincidence, Boyle and June's mom at the same institution.

Peter found the computer mouse and gave it a nudge. The big central monitor lit up. The lock screen's wallpaper was a photo of June's face. It was taken from an angle, looking downward, and slightly grainy, as if from long distance. She was leaning forward, talking to someone out of the frame, but clearly not the photographer. Her face was animated and bright, freckles glowing, her mouth open a bit wider on one side, as if delivering the punch line to a private joke. She was beautiful. On the monitor, the photo was much larger than life-sized.

"Peter?" June called down the stairs. He was glad she was still on the landing.

"Coming," he called back. He walked quickly out of the Faraday cage, turned out the light, and jogged up to the back landing.

"Did you find any bodies?"

"Nope," Peter said. "No freezers, no bodies. Just a basement. But it reminds me, I'm wearing the last of my clean clothes. Can I run a load of laundry? And do you want to throw anything in?"

She gave him a look. "You want to do laundry? *My* laundry?"

"Mine, too," he said. Then shrugged. "Besides, I never got a chance to check out your underwear last night."

She smacked him in the arm, pretending that she wasn't blushing.

"Don't get any ideas, bub. We're going to track down that lawyer, remember?"

Before they left, Peter loaded the back of the van with some gear. The pad and sleeping bag he'd bought the day before, still trashed from their night of debauchery, but functional. Peter had slept in worse. He added June's sleeping bag and pad that they'd carried up from California, along with her tent, a tiny backpacking stove, and a set of lightweight cookware. A few bottles of water and some basic food that would be easy to cook on a camp stove. The tool bag he'd bought the day before was in there, too. He'd stocked that bag pretty well.

"Are we taking a trip?" June asked as he closed the hatch.

"Just being prepared," said Peter. "We still don't know how secure we are here."

As he backed out of the driveway, he saw Leo's scraped-up BMW parked at an angle on the front lawn, windows down in the rain. Leo was fast asleep, sitting up behind the wheel. The engine still running.

Peter kept driving. He knew he'd be seeing Leo again.

30

After a quick stop for coffee at Caffe Ladro, it was a short drive to Nordstrom at Fifth and Pine. The static kept Peter company as June strode toward the men's department. Peter took deep breaths. The high ceilings helped.

June introduced herself to a salesman in a lavender shirt and tie over gray suit pants, who pretended not to notice June's stitched lip and Peter's medical boot.

Peter had planned to buy something cheap off the rack, but June took charge.

"My friend needs a black suit," she said. "Wool, of course. Clean and classic. He'll also need a shirt, tie, belt, underwear, shoes, and socks, and I think a topcoat for the rain. But here's the problem. We need him wearing everything when we leave."

The salesman, whose name was Jerome, looked Peter up and down with a slightly more than professional eye. "Well. I've always enjoyed a challenge."

Peter was amused at this version of June, his fashion consultant, given that he'd mostly seen her in half-shredded tree-climbing clothes or nothing at all. But she looked crisp and classic today.

June wasn't the first woman who'd tried to get Peter to upgrade his wardrobe.

Jerome pursed his lips and stepped around Peter to get all the angles. "He certainly won't be wearing a slim cut, not with those broad shoulders, and those muscular thighs." Jerome also seemed to be enjoying himself. "You're a forty-two long, I believe. I have two suits that would work well, and two more possibles." He gave June a conspiratorial smile. "This way, madam." And he strode off with June in tow, the two of them already chatting like old friends, while Peter stumped behind in the medical boot.

Jerome took Peter's measurements with great delicacy, then presented four suits for June's approval. "These are all quite good, both in fabric and construction. Prices are comparable."

June selected a suit. "Let's start with this one." She handed it to Peter along with a white dress shirt she'd taken from its package. "I think you'll look quite handsome."

She gave him a gentle push toward the dressing room. The mirrors made the small space feel bigger. Peter kept breathing, in and out, changing his clothes while his cracked ribs twanged. He left the boot in the dressing room.

He hadn't worn a suit since the last time he'd taken off his dress blues, and he hadn't missed it. He didn't like his movements restricted, or worrying about damaging expensive clothing. But wearing the blues had done something to him, and this suit did, too. It made him stand a little taller. It made him want a fresh haircut.

He stepped out of the dressing room.

"Mmmm," said Jerome. "Turn around, please?"

Peter did a little turn.

"Oh yeah," said June. "You look yummy."

"Great." Peter smiled. "I guess this is the suit."

"Oh, no," said June. "We need more information." She held out another suit. "This one next."

In the space of thirty minutes, he'd tried on all four, and in the end she chose the first one. Jerome brought out his chalk, marked up the fabric, and promised to have the alterations done by the time they'd picked out the rest of Peter's ensemble.

A belt, socks, and a narrow black tie. Then to the shoe department, where he tried on three pairs of seemingly identical black lace-ups. After so many years in boots, dress shoes made his feet feel odd, slippery and unprotected. Was this how civilians felt all the time?

When Jerome came back from the tailor with Peter's new suit, he put everything on again and did the little turn his fashion consultants kept insisting on.

"My goodness," said June.

Jerome looked a little wistful.

Peter put his hands on his hips. "Is that all I am to you?" he asked. "Just meat?"

"Oh, no," said June. "Never *just* meat."

And she and Jerome erupted in peals of laughter.

The final bill was what Peter had earned in a month in a combat zone. Peter told himself he was adding to the local economy. Jerome would take his husband out for a nice dinner. The waiter and bus-boy would pay their rent. It still felt fairly obscene, although he knew it was necessary for the next steps they would take.

June put her hand on his arm as they walked out beneath the low overcast sky. "You were a very good sport in there."

"Just hedging my bets," he said. "If things don't work out with us, I was laying the groundwork with Jerome."

She raised a wry eyebrow. "Is there something you haven't told me?"

"Don't ask, don't tell."

"Man, you are soooo obsolete."

Peter smiled. "Mostly I had fun watching you."

31

Peter's plan for Jean-Pierre Nicolet was to get a last-minute meeting by bluffing his way past the gatekeeper. Then start asking questions.

"He won't answer any," said June. "Because he's a lawyer."

"But he'll probably make contact with whoever wanted to buy the algorithm, and maybe that somebody will start to get nervous and make a move." He looked at her. "There's some risk here," he said. "They might come after you again."

"But you'll keep that from happening," said June, her eyes bright. "And maybe we'll know more."

Man, she was something.

He said, "What about the guys who tried to kill us before? Should we dig into their lives first?"

She shook her head. "They're not going anywhere. Nicolet is still alive and probably doesn't know the current situation."

"You think they may try to kill him?"

"I think these are ruthless people. They killed my mom for a software program. They tried to kidnap me, and when that became difficult, they tried to kill me. So killing Nicolet, their only known contact, would be a logical step."

"They're not the only ruthless people here," he said.

"Who?" she said. "Me? Shit, they started this."

Proving Peter's point.

"So," he said. "How do we get the meeting?"

"I have some experience at this." June smiled. "With an unfriendly source, someone who doesn't want to talk to me in the first place, I used to say I was Jeff Bezos's assistant. But that doesn't work anymore, so I've diversified. Today I think I'll go with Paul Allen. He's actually got an artificial intelligence research project."

Allen, one of two founders of Microsoft, was now running Vulcan, his own wide-reaching company, with its fingers in tech and real estate and medical research and who knows what else. June put her phone on speaker.

"Mr. Nicolet's office, Suzanne speaking."

"Hello, Suzanne, my name is Mary Swanson with Vulcan, and I need to reach Jean-Pierre immediately."

"I'm sorry, Mr. Nicolet is out of the office right now." Nicolet's assistant had the calm, firm voice of a high school vice principal, long used to her role as enforcer of rules and keeper of the peace.

June replied with brisk efficiency. "Then I'll go to him. Suzanne, this is a matter of some urgency. Mr. Allen insisted I meet with Mr. Nicolet today. This will be an informal five-minute meeting."

"May I ask what this is about?"

"You may not. Mr. Allen has a proposal he would like me to deliver personally."

There was the peculiar dead sound of a digital call in which nothing was being said, as Suzanne contemplated the power dynamics involved. Her boss's schedule versus the desires of one of the wealthiest and most influential men in the city, if not on the entire West Coast.

"Mr. Nicolet is in a meeting downtown," she said. "He'll be finished at one-thirty. Where would be convenient for you?"

"Actually, I'm downtown, too. Where's his meeting?"

Another pause. "Fourth and Madison."

June smiled, and made sure Nicolet's assistant could hear it in her voice. "Let me guess. He's playing racquetball at the Y. What was his court time?" Peter looked at his phone, mapping the address.

"Noon," admitted Suzanne. She sounded less like a vice principal now. "But he'll want to shower."

"I'm glad to hear that," said June. She leaned over and looked at the screen on Peter's phone. "Why don't we meet at Sazerac? Fourth and Spring, just a block from the Y. Mr. Nicolet can rehydrate. Say one forty-five?"

"That would be lovely," said Suzanne. "I'll make sure he's there on time."

"Thank you," June said, and broke the connection. She turned to Peter. "Change of plan."

"It's after one now," Peter said as June put the car in gear. "But we're not meeting him at a restaurant."

"Right," said June. "He'd be too comfortable there. He's probably a regular. You're going to grab him as he leaves the Y and scare the shit out of him."

"I've always wanted to hit an attorney."

"No, you're going to do something worse," said June. "Tell him you're from the government, and you're here to help."

They sketched out the rest of the plan on the way.

THE YMCA WAS a beautiful old pile of bricks that took up a quarter of the block and was probably fifty years older than anything around it. June parked around the corner. They were still early.

Peter had been planning to ask June about her father, but now he was thinking about Leo Boyle. That basement setup had really gotten his attention.

"How'd you meet Leo, anyway?"

"Friend of a friend," she said, then shrugged. "Facebook friend, anyway. He posted that he'd just bought this house with a garage apartment he wanted to rent out. I was couch-hopping with college friends and had posted that I was looking for a place. The pictures were horrible, but he came down a lot on the price, and I'd actually wanted something cheap I could fix up. It was exactly what I was looking for at exactly the right time. This was right after I got the job with Public Investigations, so I really needed a place in Seattle."

Peter nodded, very casual. "Did you look into Leo, at all? Before you moved in?"

"Just enough to learn he didn't have a criminal record, which was all I cared about." She shrugged. "He seemed harmless." Then she caught it. "Wait." She turned to look at him. "What did you find in that basement?"

Peter sighed. He hadn't wanted to tell her, but she'd be relentless until she found out. And keeping it from her wasn't protecting her, anyway.

"Leo had an ID for the Stanford computer science department. That's where your mom worked, right? And he had a picture of you on his computer's lock screen. I bumped the mouse and there you were."

A thundercloud crossed her face. "Please tell me it's not a naked picture."

He smiled gently. "No. You were outside. It was taken with a long lens. From the trees and architecture in the background, probably somewhere in the Bay Area."

Classic stalker behavior, he didn't say. He watched her face.

"You were only down there like two minutes."

"They were right there, the ID and the photo. Almost like he wanted you to find them."

"Yeah." The muscles stood out in her jaw. "So why the fuck didn't I?"

"Don't beat yourself up," he said.

"Yeah? What should I do?" Her voice was sharp. Then she sighed. "Sorry. This isn't the first time. I'm a magnet for the wrong guys."

Peter didn't take that personally. She might well be right when it came to him, too.

He said, "What if it's more than that?"

She looked at him.

"The Stanford ID. Would Leo have worked in your mom's lab? Or could he have gotten access? Somebody had to tell the bad guys about the algorithm, right?"

"You are creeping me out."

He watched as her mind leaped ahead. Leo had found her through the Web, a Facebook friend of a Facebook friend. The perfect apartment at the perfect time. He'd even come down on the rent to get her in there.

"That sonofabitch!" She was past scared and getting pissed, which was good, Peter thought. "He got my trust by solving my hacker problem two years ago. I let him do all my tech support after that. He probably put all kinds of shit on my old laptop." She thought hard. "Did he have time to put anything on my new laptop?"

"You're asking the wrong guy," said Peter. "But even the paranoid have enemies. Maybe it's time to learn a little more about your quirky landlord."

"I am going to beat that boy like a rented mule."

Peter checked the time on his phone and put his hand on her arm. "I gotta go."

"What? Now? With this shit in my head?"

"If Nicolet sees me getting out of a Honda minivan, he'll never believe I work for the government."

32

eter walked around the corner of the big YMCA building and
found a spot out of the wind. The rain was spotty but still coming down. He'd left the truck driver's .357 in the car. He didn't
have a holster for it, and it would be obvious in the topcoat. He'd also
put the medical boot back on, because his leg was getting sore. If Jean-
Pierre Nicolet tried to run, Peter couldn't chase him or shoot him.

But he didn't think either would be necessary. Nicolet was a high-
level attorney, probably very confident that the law existed primarily to
serve his interests.

He came out of the YMCA at a brisk walk, wearing a tan trench coat
open over a charcoal pinstripe suit, no briefcase or gym bag. Mid-forties,
he was average height but whippet-lean, with a pale face, a receding
hairline, and frameless glasses. He smiled into the damp wind, which
probably felt good after an hour of racquetball and a quick steam.

Peter stepped into the man's path.

"Mr. Nicolet. I'm your one forty-five meeting."

Nicolet looked at Peter in his plain black suit and black raincoat.

"You're not from Paul Allen." Despite the French name, he had no discernible accent. His company bio said he'd been born in Montreal and had kept his Canadian citizenship.

"I apologize for the ruse," said Peter. "I'm with a certain agency. We work closely with the tech industry."

Nicolet looked amused. "You people. May I see some ID?"

"No." Peter had met a lot of spooks overseas, but he hadn't met many who actually admitted who he worked for. Not without a lot of liquor, anyway. "We have some information we need you to verify. A national security issue. Your assistance would be very much appreciated."

"And the topic?"

"Hazel Cassidy. She's dead."

"So I understand. I saw her obituary in the *Mercury-News*." Nicolet smiled pleasantly. "Come to my office with identification I can verify. Bring a letter from your superior stating the information desired, the national security interest involved, and a compelling need as to why I should violate attorney-client confidentiality. I'll speak with my partners in the firm. Then, perhaps, we'll talk."

"That's not necessary. Please understand, I'm trying to help you and your firm avoid a full national security probe. I only need to know who asked you to negotiate with Cassidy for the purchase of the algorithm."

Nicolet's smile remained pleasant, although his voice acquired a distinct edge. "That's also privileged information, I'm afraid. Without verifiable standing, you have no authority. Now if you'll excuse me, I'm due back at work."

Peter put his right hand around Nicolet's upper arm. The man was thin, but not soft. All that racquetball. "You're not a U.S. citizen," he said. "And my authority is quite flexible. My associates are around the corner in a black van. Give me the name."

Nicolet's smile widened, became genuine. His teeth were white and even. "Really? You're going to take me off the street? Beat me with a rubber hose?"

"I'd prefer not to," said Peter. "This is absolutely confidential. There would be no way to trace it back to you."

Nicolet laughed. "You are either lying or naïve. Either way, you're not with the NSA. Take your hand off me or I'll call the police."

Peter didn't let go. Instead he stepped closer, as if he were about to whisper something into the attorney's ear. But his left fist was cocked low, held in tension by his cupped right hand. Then he let his right hand slip and released his left in a short hard pop to the other man's solar plexus.

It happened so quickly and at such proximity that an onlooker would have been uncertain what he'd seen unless he was standing right beside them.

Nicolet bent double, gasping, glasses hanging from one ear. Peter leaned over him, a hand on his shoulder, the picture of sympathy.

"Take a minute to get your breath back. Then I'll need that name."

Nicolet wheezed, elbows braced on his knees, and Peter was afraid for a moment that he'd hit the other man harder than he'd intended.

Then he realized that the attorney was laughing.

Even with the sucker punch to the gut, gasping for breath, he was laughing.

"Go fuck yourself," he coughed. "You have no idea who you're dealing with."

"You think they won't kill you to protect themselves?" asked Peter.

Nicolet levered himself upright by sheer force of will and adjusted his glasses, still wheezing in laughter. "I'm too useful," he said. "I've also taken certain precautions. But they're probably watching us right now."

Peter turned his head, counting the surveillance cameras in view. "Who's watching?" he asked. "How do they get into those systems?"

Nicolet didn't bother looking. He shook off Peter's hand. "I'm pretty sure they can do anything they want."

Peter left him there, and went around the corner for the car.

By the time he pulled around the block to the bus shelter to pick up June, the attorney was gone.

33

SHEPARD

Shepard watched the tall man and the girl walk out of Nordstrom and through traffic to the green minivan. Now Shepard knew why they'd been in there so long. The man wore a crisp new black suit under an open black topcoat.

He looks good, thought Shepard. Although he could use a haircut.

The girl was light on her feet, like a dancer in hiking boots. The tall man, her protector, was moving better than he had on the hospital security video. Even with the medical boot on his left leg, his movements were fluid, his superb conditioning clearly evident.

Shepard was still amazed at the toughness of that nurse practitioner and the tired-eyed ER doctor with the crazy hair. They'd looked at his Homeland ID and pretended to be helpful and apologetic, but they hadn't told him a thing. Patient confidentiality, federal law, of course you understand. Call the hospital attorney in the morning, now if you'll excuse us, we have patients to attend to.

He was frustrated, but he wasn't an animal. He wouldn't hurt them just because they'd treated two injured patients. There were limits, even for Shepard.

And his face was all over their security system.

It occurred to him now that he might have gotten further without the government ID. Clearly some Oregonians liked to do things their own way. Maybe it had something to do with hippies and legal marijuana, he wasn't sure. That was well outside his own experience. But he respected it. Shepard liked to do things his own way, too. Driving out of town, he found himself drawn to certain neighborhoods. The soil must be very good in Eugene. The yards had big gardens, overflowing with life.

Perhaps his trip to Oregon was another signal. Preparation for his next life.

The girl's home base should have been extremely difficult to locate. Her social media made it clear that she lived primarily in Seattle, but there were remarkably few other available clues. Her bills went to a secure PO box, and the salesman's technology people had been unable to find any accounts or tax information with another address. For an amateur, the girl had done a capable job of hiding.

But Chip's client had already taken ownership of her laptop, which allowed the salesman to triangulate her cell modem's brief ping. As long as her laptop remained on and in her possession, he could track the girl's location in real time.

The fact that she'd stopped using the laptop might have been a problem, too, but Chip's client had also provided her home address. The salesman, drawn to wealth and power like a moth to a flame, had bragged to Shepard about the depth of the client's resources.

Shepard didn't mention that he'd already had the information. Overall, he felt it was better for the salesman not to know the depth of Shepard's own resources. The complexity of the situation would become clear to the salesman before long.

He had found the girl's garage apartment a few minutes before she arrived home from a run in the rain. She wore a light jacket and baseball hat and running tights, and it was clear that the file photo and the security video had failed to capture something essential about her. The grace and strength, the sheer energy of the woman. Shepard felt something profound, watching her. She was captivating.

And she had poor situational awareness, not watching her surroundings, her earbuds blocking out all ambient sound. He could have taken her right then. But he didn't.

He could have shot the tall man from forty yards while he was loading the van with what looked like camping gear, and taken the girl after.

But he hadn't done that, either. Shepard had multiple clients, with multiple priorities. He was experiencing a conflict of interest. He was awaiting further information.

And there was something else. Something in the hospital security video, something about the girl and her protector, that he couldn't quite pin down. He needed to learn more. He wanted to get closer.

So he followed them.

They drove from the girl's apartment to a busy street, where they found a parking spot and walked a block to a coffee place with a black awning.

Coffee sounded good to Shepard, too.

He left his car at a hydrant and walked quickly to catch up.

Perhaps this was unwise. No, he knew it was unwise, getting this close, ten paces behind them on the sidewalk, now five, now following them into Caffe Ladro.

Shepard was highly attuned to the capacity for violence in others, and from this distance he could see it in the tall man like a phosphorous grenade on a moonless night, the killing he'd done.

The tall man was different from Shepard's usual civilian targets. Not soft, not weak.

More like Shepard's mirror image. A twin brother who'd taken a different path.

This wasn't about gathering tactical information, not really.

Now Shepard was inside the crowded coffee shop, one step behind them in line, close enough to smell the girl's shampoo. She spoke brightly to the tattooed person behind the register, placing their order while the tall man stood with his back to the counter and looked restlessly around the room. They stood close to each other, and from time to time she would glance up at him, would touch his hand with hers. They had some kind of personal relationship. Whoever he was, he was not just hired security. She was concerned about him.

Shepard wanted to *know* them somehow, the girl and the tall man both. How it was done, to walk through the world with another person. To have someone touch your hand, to have it mean something. He told himself it was research, for his retirement. Maybe that was it. Maybe it was something else. Another deep signal from within.

He wondered if it was possible for him to live a different way than he did now, so separate from other human beings. Where his only moments of true human contact were with those whose lives he ended. This tug he felt, this urge for connection, to get inside another's mind in a profound way, did other people feel it, too? If so, how did they accomplish those connections?

Now he noticed that the tall man was different inside the coffee shop. Like a dog with his hackles up. Shepard wondered if the man had the same radar that Shepard had so carefully cultivated, the ability to feel someone watching, someone behind him.

The tall man definitely felt something. He was on high alert, looking carefully around the room with a behavior that Shepard recognized in himself. Checking the exits, the lines of fire, each person and their positions and where their attention was directed. The tall man was following old habits, perhaps compulsively. But he didn't look at Shepard longer than anyone else, didn't appear to have identified Shepard as the source of his unease. Shepard was good at being invisible.

When it was Shepard's turn in line, he ordered a simple coffee, because it would be faster than the tall man's double espresso and the girl's triple tall mocha. He killed time fussing with the cream and sugar so that he could walk out of the place right behind them.

He saw when it happened, in the open air. The tall man's shoulders dropped and the slight flush fell from his face. He was still watchful outside, still ready for whatever might come, but he didn't seem threatened in the busy urban environment, even though it had many more possible dangers. Even though Shepard was right behind him.

The man had felt threatened indoors.

That could be useful.

The couple walked back toward their car, Shepard just a few steps behind them. The man did have a slight limp in the medical boot, but Shepard noticed something else, too. He was left-handed, and obviously wanted that hand free, likely because he was carrying a weapon within easy reach. But holding his coffee in his right hand, he carried himself a little differently. Shepard could see it, the slight protection of the right side. Some injury there, a wound or pulled muscle.

Shepard felt an odd sense of relief.

Having seen the tall man close up, seen how he moved, how he assessed the room, Shepard knew he was extremely dangerous. Every bit as dangerous as Shepard.

But the tall man wasn't at full strength.

They got back in the green minivan, and Shepard made his way more quickly to his own car.

He followed them downtown to Nordstrom. When they went inside, he took the opportunity to attach a small magnetized GPS beacon to the underside of their car.

It would simplify finding them again when necessary.

34

PETER

So Nicolet didn't tell you anything?"

"Just that I'm in over my head," he said. "Which I already knew."

On a side street four blocks from the YMCA, Peter was trading license plates with an identical minivan while June watched for police cars. Most people didn't even know their own plate number, so he figured it would be a while before the owner of the other van noticed his plates were wrong. With all the cameras, he and June were losing invisibility by the minute, and he didn't want to buy another vehicle. He liked the Honda.

"At least you got to hit an attorney," said June. "Check that off your life list."

Peter shook his head as he screwed the stolen plate to their rear bumper. "I kind of liked him, actually. He was pretty tough."

"I don't think you get to Nicolet's level without being tough."

Peter stood and walked around to the passenger side. "Who's first?"

Their next chore was to search the houses of the dead men.

"Alvarez is closest," June said, and stepped on the gas. It was after three.

According to June's research, the hunters' driver's licenses had their most recent addresses.

As June pushed the minivan down the narrow streets, she said, "Why would they use their own driver's licenses? Why even carry them on an operation like that? Wouldn't they at least have good fake ID?"

"They were ex-military," said Peter. "Their prints would be on file with the feds, so it would be easy for the police to identify them. For that matter, the military keeps everyone's DNA records, too, for identifying the dead in combat. That's not supposed to be available for any other reason, but you know how that works."

June nodded. "The rule of power. If it can be done, it will be done. They couldn't really hide, so it was simpler to be themselves."

Peter had another thought. "Or maybe they actually were from the government, like we talked about, and they had protection from higher up. So their identities *were* their protection."

She shook her head. "Let's not go down that rabbit hole just yet. Let's find the people behind these guys."

Before they find us, thought Peter.

MARTIN ALVAREZ OWNED a small slate-gray house in West Seattle. It had started out even smaller, but someone had put a modest addition on the back, and had done a pretty nice job of it, paying attention to the details of the siding and the rooflines. But he wasn't living large, not here. He was saving for a rainy day.

June parked the van out front.

They walked through a gate in a sturdy picket fence. A dog began to bark somewhere inside. The yard was a mix of shrubs and perennials, messy but blooming in the spring weather. The porch was new cedar, the front door painted bright yellow. The dog got louder. A girl, maybe fifteen or sixteen, opened the door a crack before Peter could knock.

"What do you want?" She kept the security chain on and spoke through the gap.

Good girl, thought Peter. He could see a sliver of long brown hair, caramel-colored skin, and worry lines on her forehead. She looked more than a little like the man who'd been thrown from the Suburban and bashed in his head with a rock on landing.

She kept the dog, a big German shepherd, back from the door with her leg, but it growled deep and low behind her. June bumped Peter slightly with her elbow, signaling him to move out of the way. "Hi," she said. "We're looking for Martin Alvarez. Is that your dad?"

"Not home," said the girl. And moved to close the door.

"How about your mom," said June.

"She's gone," said the girl. "Years now. Just me and Dad. And he's not home."

Peter peered through the crack in the doorway, trying to get some sense of Alvarez. He wasn't willing to break the door down. He had the logging truck driver's gun tucked awkwardly into his jacket pocket, but he didn't want to have to shoot the dog. This girl was going to have worse problems soon enough.

June kept talking. "Do you know when he'll be back?" she asked. "We'd like to talk to him."

"Home tonight," said the girl, her mouth tightening up. "What's this about?"

She was worried, thought Peter. Maybe her dad was supposed to call, and hadn't.

Because he was dead.

He looked past the girl into the house, looking for anything useful, some piece of stray information.

The living room was neat as a pin, despite the big dog and absent dad.

A few potted plants looking green and healthy, a big sectional couch, a leather recliner, and a wall of shelves built around a giant television. Photos in frames, hard to see in detail at that distance but they looked mostly like just two people, one big, one small. And a teddy bear, sitting up high on a shelf like he was king of the hill, likely some cherished reminder of the girl's childhood.

He was starting to wish he hadn't looked.

June said, "We're trying to find your dad. But he's not answering his work phone. Did he give you any emergency contact numbers? Any other way to reach him?"

"He works for the government," said the girl, lifting her chin in a mixture of pride and defiance. "Sometimes he's hard to get hold of. But we take care of each other."

June blinked at Peter, trying to keep the sorrow from her face.

Peter looked at the girl, so much older than her years. "Thanks, hon," he said. "We won't bother you again. If you have someone to call, any other family or even friends, you should do that."

They turned and walked down the steps, the girl still staring at them through the crack in the doorway.

At the car, June handed Peter the keys. "You better drive," she said, tears running down her face.

Peter started the engine. He put his hand on June's arm.

"You were there on that mountain road," he said quietly. "Alvarez was no innocent. It was them or us."

"I know," she said. "It was his choice. But not his daughter's. She didn't have a choice."

Peter took a breath and let it back out. "Yeah."

He put the engine into gear and got them out of there.

35

June had had the next address plugged into Peter's phone so he could find his way through the twisting streets.

She opened her new laptop. "Let's try the algorithm while we drive. Maybe I can get something more on that lawyer."

She took out a piece of paper and copied a URL into the browser on the laptop.

"Wouldn't your mom already have tried that?"

"Maybe. But she also said it's getting better. Smarter. And we know more about the people who tried to kill us."

The URL was just a long string of random-appearing numbers and letters.

"That's it? The algorithm? The skeleton key?"

"Tyg3r," she said, and hit Return, turning the laptop so he could see the screen.

He glanced over. The first thing that struck him was how simple it was. Completely blank except for a blinking cursor inside a text box with a single line below it.

```
[ _____ ]
You are not authorized.
```

"Shit," she said.

"It doesn't know you're you," Peter said, navigating in the slow traffic. "Remember, it found you on your phone because you'd logged in to your email. Which you should maybe undo, actually."

He was remembering the surge in Iraq. The NSA had helped take down AQ fighters by getting access to Iraq's emerging cellular network and tracking all cell and text traffic. There was no reason to think that the hunters couldn't do the same.

"I did that yesterday," she said. "I forgot to tell you. I shitcanned that phone and bought a new burner. I can always go to an Internet café to check my email. But that doesn't help me here. There's not even a security question. The name of my first dog or whatever."

"Just makes it more secure."

Peter feathered the brake as they coasted down the West Seattle Bridge. Ahead was a wide railyard, then two highways and a hillside clad in feathery green trees and condos. The airport was off to the right. To the left stood elegant skeletal cranes of the Port of Seattle with Puget Sound behind it looking like hammered steel. The sky was low and dark. Did the sun ever come out in this town?

"What's something that only you and your mom would know? Maybe a pet phrase you had between you?"

June shook her head. "I don't know. She wasn't exactly warm and fuzzy."

"What about that video she sent you after she died? Is there something in there?"

June smacked Peter in the chest with the back of her hand. "Pretty *and* smart. I like that in a guy."

"Plus I can cook. And I'm crazy good in the sack."

June ignored him. She'd already opened a different browser and logged in to the anonymous email where she'd saved her mom's video message as a draft. "Let's see it again."

She watched Hazel Cassidy's last message twice, and Peter listened while he drove. Traffic was heavy, they'd picked the wrong time of day to do this. Maybe there was no right time of day. June took notes on her flip-top reporter's pad. Peter was impressed with how quickly she could write. Not that he'd ever decipher her handwriting.

"A lot of possibles in there," said Peter.

June didn't answer. She clicked back to the algorithm site, clicked on the text box, typed skeleton key, and hit Enter.

The text box went blank, and the blinking cursor reappeared.

[_____]

You are not authorized. Try harder.

"That is so like my mom." June looked at Peter. "I'm probably not going to get many chances at this."

"You could set your email on your phone again and ask it for the password."

"It didn't give it to me when it gave me the URL," she said. "I don't think I'll get it by asking now. If Tyg3r really has this much potential, my mom would be pretty major on the security."

Yeah, thought Peter. Because if the skeleton key was really that good? If the Russians, or the Chinese, or the Iranians got hold of it? That would be the end of the American Experiment. Blueprints for every drone and cruise missile were online somewhere. Hell, what if you could hack the connection to a Reaper drone in the air and take control? The new F-22 joint strike fighter plane was all software-driven, designed to be updated. You could update them out of the sky.

June ran a hand through her hair, clicked on the text box, typed the scientist's curse, and hit Enter.

Again, the text box went blank, and the blinking cursor reappeared.

[_____]

You are not authorized. Last chance.

"Shit," she said.

They were still stuck on the ramp behind a long line of cars, waiting to get onto Highway 99. "Give me the laptop," said Peter. "I know what it is."

She gave him a look.

"I won't hit Enter," he promised. "Come on, hand it over."

She passed him the laptop. Using two fingers, he typed the best daughter a mother could ever hope for. And handed it back.

She took a deep breath and let it out. Peter patted her leg. "What do you think?"

"I don't know," she said. "But I don't have any better ideas."

And hit Enter.

The text box went blank again, but a new message appeared below it.

[_____]

Largest error followed by best outcome.

"Huh?"

June smiled. "This one I know. She used to say this all the time after the divorce." Her fingers flew across the keys. The Yeti and Junie.

The text box went blank again, with another new message below.

[_____]

Hello, Junie. What would you like to know?

"Who the hell is 'the Yeti'?" asked Peter. But he already knew.

"That's what we called my dad." June's mouth quirked. A complicated expression, neither a smile nor a frown.

Traffic was clearing and he could finally get onto 99, the smaller highway heading north along the Sound. He hit the gas. "That's the Yeti? The guy who bought you a gun for your fourteenth birthday?"

"I told you I had an interesting childhood."

It was the opening Peter had been waiting for. "Tell me about your dad." He was genuinely interested, but he also was thinking about his last conversation with Lewis.

She made a face. "I'd rather not."

"Come on," he said. "You keep bringing him up. You must want to talk about him."

She shook her head. "My dad was a control freak. He used to work in software, which is how he met my mom. When I was a kid, he started his own business, but it fell apart and he moved us out to this remote little valley in eastern Washington. According to my mom, he was getting really weird, even then. Overprotective, compulsive, the whole thing. He was obsessed with getting the place self-sufficient, so we would never need to leave the valley. My mom got offered a job at Stanford and wanted to take me with her. My dad said no. One day she went off to a conference and didn't come back. I was ten."

"Jesus," said Peter. "That must have been hard."

"Understatement of the year." June shook her head. "She told me later that she tried to get custody for years, but my dad had a really good lawyer. I guess it got pretty ugly. She had a whole file cabinet just for the legal paperwork. Anyway, I stayed there in the valley while things got worse. He gave me a bracelet once. I slipped on some rocks and broke it, and it turned out to have some kind of electronic chip inside. No wonder he always knew how to find me when I ran away. When I was fifteen, I couldn't take it anymore. I got serious and made a plan to find my mom. I didn't take anything with me that he'd given me, and I finally got away. When my mom called my dad to let him know where I was, he showed up at her house. I locked myself in my room while he stomped around and yelled about how we weren't safe, none of us were safe. Mom had already called the police. When he heard the sirens, he left."

Carefully, Peter said, "What do you mean by 'things got worse'?"

She gave him a look. "If that's a polite way to ask if he molested me, the answer is no. He just got more paranoid, more overprotective. We were way out in the country, and I needed a security code to get into the house. We had a big shed where he worked, and he stopped letting me inside. Said it was for my own good."

"Did you see him again after that?"

"He came back to Palo Alto twice more. My mom had helped me get a court order declaring me an emancipated minor, which in California you can do at fourteen. I already had my GED, which made it easier. And we had a restraining order. He started out nice, but got upset pretty fast. My mom always called nine-one-one the minute she saw him, and he always left when he heard the sirens."

"Did he hit you? Did he break things?"

"He definitely broke stuff, but he never hit me or my mom. Angry, but not necessarily at us. He seemed kind of frantic, actually. After he left the last time, I remember thinking if it wasn't so scary, it would have been sad."

"Do you remember what he wanted?"

"He wanted me to come back home, where it was safe. He kept saying it, over and over. Come back home, where it's safe."

"That's it?"

She shrugged. "That's it. I haven't seen him since. It must be twelve years now."

"But why do you call him the Yeti? That's not his name, is it?"

"His same is Sasha," she said. "He's kind of a giant guy, and his friends used to call him Sasquatch. When his business began to fail, his hair turned white overnight. So Mom and I started calling him the Yeti. At the time it was a joke. We didn't realize there was something really wrong with him."

Sasha Kolodny, thought Peter. Why is that a familiar name?

Then he remembered.

"He's still there? In that valley?"

"I have no idea. Like I said, I haven't seen him in years."

"So you were pretty close, you and your mom."

"Yeah." She didn't look at him. "Can we stop talking about this?"

"Sure," he said.

36

June was typing again, reading aloud as she did. "Is Tyg3r aware that an unknown entity tried to purchase Tyg3r from Hazel Cassidy?"

Yes.

"Did Hazel Cassidy attempt to use Tyg3r to discover the identity of that unknown entity?"

Yes.

"Was Hazel Cassidy successful in that attempt?"

No.

"How many attempts did Hazel Cassidy make?"

Thirty-one attempts.

"When was the last attempt?"

February 7, 2:37 p.m.

It was late March now. Peter wasn't sure of the exact day. It's what happened when you lived outside, without anything that might be called a job. He thought about how June's mother had described the algorithm. A stupid cockroach, she'd called it. But getting smarter.

June kept typing. "What did Tyg3r discover at that time?"

See below.

A small window popped up in the lower corner. June clicked on it. It was a string of emails.

June scrolled through.

"These are the emails from Nicolet to my mom. He says he repre-sented a third party. He offered her ten million dollars for exclusive rights to an unfinished private project." June scrolled down. "She wanted to know what project he was talking about, but either he doesn't know what it really is, or he's not saying. He calls it a search algorithm."

"I guess that might be technically correct, right?"

"Whatever, she wasn't interested. He kept raising the offer. She stopped returning his emails when he hit forty million dollars."

"Wait," said Peter. "Where did Tyg3r get that email? It just pulled that out of some server somewhere? Out of the cloud?"

"Sure," said June. "It probably already had all her passwords." She looked at him. "Forty million dollars?"

Peter had spent eight years in the Marines and two more in the mountains, but he also had a degree in economics. "What's Google's market cap right now? Four or five hundred billion? That all started with an algorithm, right?"

"Yeah, but Tyg3r was her baby," said June. "She wanted to make the world a better place. To make powerful groups and individuals more accountable for their actions. What if you used Tyg3r to disclose all campaign contributions? That information alone would change the world."

"So forty million was a lowball."

"Not even in the ballpark," said June. "But she wouldn't have taken any amount. She was pretty stubborn."

Just like her daughter, thought Peter as June turned back to the keyboard and typed another message.

"Did Tyg3r discover the identity of the third party mentioned in the email?"

```
No. This program was unable to penetrate the
security of law firm Sydney Bucknell Sparks, where
the email originated.
```

"Has Tyg3r discovered more information since February 7?"

```
This program was not requested to do so.
```

"Has Tyg3r advanced in its capabilities since the last request?"

```
Yes.
```

"Please try again. Do this and every future action in a manner that cannot be traced back to this computer or this user personally."

```
Multiple variable proxy servers are already in
use. Please wait.
```

A blur of smaller windows popped up on the screen, overlapping each other in a fractal pattern, like tree leaves, in a constantly shifting and growing pattern, tens of windows, then hundreds. The effect was hypnotic. Peter glanced from the road to the screen and back. This went on for ten or fifteen minutes, long enough for Peter to make it through downtown, Puget Sound on the left with the Olympic Mountains on the far side, the raised highway providing an excellent view, then through a tunnel and back on the surface in a dip between two big hills, getting closer to their destination.

Then the windows began disappearing, one by one, slowly at first, then more rapidly, until the screen was left with only four small windows open in the bottom right corner of the home screen with its simple empty text box and a response below:

```
Sydney Bucknell Sparks's corporate servers and
Jean-Pierre Nicolet's personal computer are very
well protected against intrusion. This program
has obtained administrator-level access to both
systems.
```

The cockroach, thought Peter, was definitely getting smarter.

He wondered if that tone of pride had been programmed into the software's interface.

June opened the windows. One was a Mac desktop with a photo of an empty racquetball court, which Peter took to be Nicolet's personal computer. The second window was open to the law firm's website. The third was a commercial email program with Nicolet's work email address at the top. The fourth was the server's main dashboard.

"Shit," she said. "We just hacked a law firm."

"Not me," said Peter. "Definitely not me. But you should search Nicolet's work email."

They crossed a long high bridge over a canal, a lake on the right and a narrow channel through to the sound now on the left. Peter made himself keep his eyes on the road. He didn't like the clouds, but he definitely liked the geography.

June wasn't looking at the view. "I just did a search on his work email using my mom's name," she said. "But all I got was the same email string back and forth between her and Nicolet. We've seen these already."

"What about anything coming in? We want to know who asked Nicolet to make the offer."

June scrolled through her search. "These look like the only emails with Hazel Cassidy anywhere in the From, To, or the body of the email."

"What about another member of the law firm?"

June clicked over to the dashboard and worked her way through to a server-wide email overview and did the same search. It took a few minutes. The same email string. No other mention of June's mom.

June said, "I'm going over to his personal computer to look at his email there." She clicked and typed while Peter navigated the off-ramp and worked his way west through surface streets. Newer mid-rise condos competed with heavily renovated homes, old apartment buildings, and beat-up shacks that looked like one minor quake away from collapse.

"Three email addresses. His work email, another address with messages about, let's see, dinner plans, eighth-grade basketball games, a guys' night out. And a third address that it looks like he uses when he's shopping online. His new North Face raincoat has shipped."

She ran the search again on all three and came up with nothing.

"We're here." Peter pulled up in front of the next address on their list. Jason Ross had lived in a row of two-story town houses with underground parking and high steel gates protecting the courtyard.

"Hang on," said June. "I'm going to do another search. This time for the word 'algorithm.'" She typed and clicked. "Shit. The list is like, three thousand emails."

"I'm just going to look," Peter said, and got out of the car. Both the courtyard gates and the garage door had no card or button access, and probably required some kind of electronic key fob to open. A round black camera lens eyeballed him from each location. To top things off, someone had posted a sign on the gate that read, "To help maintain building security, please do not allow anyone you do not know personally into the building." And a little smiley face.

If the goal was to limit casual burglars, it sure worked on Peter.

He walked along the fence, looking for Ross's address, more to have done something than in any expectation he'd actually learn anything. It was the middle unit, with a little overhang and a big picture window. The blinds were open, and Peter could see a giant television, a framed Army recruiting poster, and a plush teddy bear perched on an end table, facing the gate, almost like a pet waiting for its owner to come home. A little sad. And now Ross was dead.

Peter got back in the car. "Too tight to just walk in," he said. "A good choice, actually. Come and go in your car, use the garage, never meet your neighbors. You're two miles from the freeway, the surface streets are a tangle, and there are three or four marinas within five miles. Unless they catch you walking out your door, you're a ghost."

June said, "You really should be on one of those real estate shows on cable TV." She deepened her voice. "'This condo is ideal for the intelligent criminal. Note the multiple exits for a quick escape, and easy access to mass transit in case of government surveillance.'"

"You could learn a thing or two," he said. "You're living some kind of invisible life yourself."

"I'm just trying not to have my dad show up on my doorstep."

37

Back on Highway 99, Peter drove north toward the next address. Four lanes of low-rent commercial strip, auto parts, gun shops, and sporting goods. June was on her laptop again, still inside the law firm's server.

"I'm sorting Nicolet's files by date," she said. "Correlating with his emails to my mom. Maybe he wrote a report to his client."

"Or the client signed a contract," said Peter. "That would be in there, too, right?"

"Gotta be somewhere," she said. "There's an awful lot of work product here. This guy's a beast. I'm going to be reading all night."

Peter glanced over at her. "All night?"

"Well," she said, eyes still on the laptop. "Maybe not *all* night."

"You could ask Tyg3r," he said. "Is it smart enough to make those correlations?"

"I doubt it," she said. "What would I ask it to find?"

Peter turned left. "Fucked if I know," he said. "That's your area, not mine."

"What is your area, exactly?"

He grinned. "Get the bad guys," he said. "Save the girl."

"So I'm the brains of the outfit?"

"I thought you knew that already. If you didn't, maybe I'm wrong."

She smiled at her laptop. "I was just being polite."

Peter saw a gas station ahead. "I'm going to fuel up."

She looked at the gauge. "We still have half a tank."

"Rule number one when you're on the run," he said. "Never get below half a tank. And if you're a girl, never pass up the chance to pee."

"That's sexist."

He shrugged, pulling into the gas station. "I can pee anywhere. In an old soda bottle, while you drive, if I have to. Can you do that?"

"Why would I want to?" she asked. "But maybe I'll use the bathroom for a minute, while I have the chance."

She went inside and Peter called Lewis.

"What's up?"

"I got a first name on the ex-husband."

"About time, Jarhead. We can narrow it down."

"Oh, it's already narrowed down," said Peter. "The name is Sasha. Sasha Kolodny."

There was a pause at the other end of the line.

"You're shitting me. Sasha Kolodny? As in, Sasquatch? The Mad Billionaire? Man, you in deep doo-doo now."

Sasha Kolodny was an early employee of a certain giant Seattle software company. A notable eccentric in an industry known for eccentrics, Sasha Kolodny was a bearded giant who earned the nickname Sasquatch because of his tendency to wander off into the steep evergreen forest that surrounded Seattle. Apparently he said it helped him think. His net worth including stock options was once reported at over a billion dollars.

In the mid-1990s, Kolodny left the company and used his fortune to launch a new business focused on, if Peter remembered correctly, the technology of sustainability. Hardware, not software. Renewable energy, urban agriculture, that kind of thing. Good ideas, but apparently ahead of their time in the boom years of conspicuous consumption. When the dot-com bubble popped, the whole enterprise went down in flames, taking most of his fortune with it. Kolodny went some flavor of crazy and disappeared. His story resurfaced from time to time in the media, both legend and cautionary tale. The intersection of genius, commerce, finance, and mental instability.

Peter's knowledge of the man was limited to an article he'd read in *Wired* magazine years ago. The writer had made a comparison to Howard Hughes, and called Kolodny "one of the principal architects of the modern world."

The title of the article was "The Mad Billionaire."

Peter said, "What do you know about him?"

"Prob'ly no more'n you do. Let me look him up." Peter heard the clicking of the keyboard.

"I don't have long," said Peter. June would be back from the bathroom any minute.

"Hold on, Jarhead. Let's see. Yeah, here's a 'where is he now' article, they interviewed some people who knew him. 'Brilliant, very driven, and very private.'"

Lewis stopped talking, and Peter knew he was reading.

"Seems like something happened to him in the late nineties. Nobody really knows what, but he really changed. He got manic, obsessed, paranoid. Says here, 'His focus on sustainability was rooted in his obsession with the collapse of civilization.' Huh," said Lewis. "Never knew the man was such a whack job."

"Can you find out where he is now?"

"According to Wikipedia, he's off the map. As in vanished, location unknown. The Internet thinks he's dead."

"The Internet thinks?"

"You know what I mean. The general fucking consensus, okay? The man wandered into the woods and never came back. Although some conspiracy geeks out there say Sasquatch is alive and well and running a secret lab for the United States government."

"Was he ever declared dead?"

"How the fuck should I know? I just got started."

"Maybe you should stop. I'll do some digging on this end."

"Jarhead. What the fuck is going on up there?"

June emerged from the gas station. She'd bought a few snacks.

"I'll call you back," Peter said, and hung up.

He wondered if a paranoid genius ex-billionaire could muster the enthusiasm to kill his ex-wife over a promising software application.

He thought maybe so.

If he only had one percent of his earlier wealth, he'd have the resources to make it happen.

June looked at him and smiled. She dug into a plastic bag and held out her hand. "Twizzler?"

38

They turned off the commercial strip into a dark, quiet neighborhood of long looping streets in a modified grid. No sidewalks, just gravel shoulders and low ditches to carry the runoff of the near-constant rain. Ranch houses and split-levels and a few older bungalows, some with elaborate landscaping, some adrift in a sea of thriving weeds. Lots of tall pines and cedars and hemlocks, their deep greens clogging up the light.

Dexter Smith's most recent address was a sprawling 1960s split-level with a big attached garage in Seattle's North End.

It sat at the back of an enormous corner lot, almost entirely concealed by a dense wall of overgrown cedars and evergreen shrubs along all four edges of the lot. A heavy wooden gate blocked the driveway, held shut by a fat padlock in a wrought-iron hasp. The padlock was closed, although floodlights were lit at the corners of the house, bright in the dim, damp afternoon.

A security camera stood atop the gatepost, facing the driveway.

June cruised by, slightly slower than the speed limit.

She said, "What do you see?"

"A soft fortress in disguise. All that plant growth will keep out prying eyes, burglars looking for an easy target, maybe even neighborhood kids. I'd guess there's some fence inside those bushes, too, maybe even barbed wire. Inside the perimeter, it's probably lawn, mowed short, and cameras showing everything. This is someone who thinks about layers of protection and fields of fire."

"Crazy?"

Peter shook his head. "Just careful. He probably can't help himself. It might not even be a set of conscious decisions, just choices that felt right. He sure didn't plant all those trees. Those have been there for fifty years." Peter shrugged. "Or maybe he just liked the house."

June came to a stop sign and glanced at her notebook. "Dexter Smith. He was the oldest of them. Twenty years in the Army, a master sergeant."

Peter nodded. When he was hanging from June's redwood at the end of a rope, eavesdropping, one of the men had been silent, working his way slowly through the brush, intent on the search. He was the one that Peter had been most concerned about, the one that had finally noticed him. That was probably him. The master sergeant.

"You understand these guys," she said.

"Sure. We were forged in the same fire. But I'm the flip side of their coin. They went one way, I went the other."

"Which way did you go, exactly?" She glanced at him as she turned the corner.

"I'll let you know when I get there."

She feathered the gas, easing her way back around the long, irregular block.

"Would you need to live in a house like that? Like a fortress?"

Peter kept his head on a swivel. "I have no idea. I haven't slept inside anything but a tent or my truck for almost two years."

"But is that the kind of place you'd want?"

"Honestly, I have no idea." He looked at her now. "But I'm starting to think about it."

She pulled the car up to the gate and he got out with the bolt cutters and a can of spray paint. They already had their hats on to shield their faces from the cameras. Keeping the brim of his hat down, Peter took the can of spray paint and hit the lenses with a quick blast. The cops would be here as soon as the master sergeant's body was identified by the burned Tahoe. No reason to give them any more information than necessary.

The fat padlock's shank was hardened steel, and he was glad he'd sprung for the long-handled version of the bolt cutters. Leverage is all. The shank broke with a distinct pop.

He removed the ruined lock and swung the gate wide. June pulled the van inside and he walked the gate shut behind her. There was a piece of heavy steel channel that slid in a track to lock the gates together from the inside. The master sergeant didn't fuck around.

Peter saw another camera above the attached garage and hit the lens with his spray can.

If there was anyone watching the monitors, he didn't show himself.

June parked behind a big orange-and-black three-quarter-ton Dodge Power Wagon from the eighties, the truck looking like new and freshly waxed, raindrops beaded up on the paint. This was one of three vehicles June had found registered to Smith. The other two were a Harley-Davidson motorcycle and a Lexus sedan, which were not in evidence. Probably parked wherever the burned Tahoe had been garaged.

She got out and stood looking at the house. The windows were covered with some kind of reflective film, so they couldn't see in. Peter walked very carefully around the building, finding three more cameras and touching them up with spray paint as he went. The man's perimeter defenses made him nervous. He didn't figure there were claymores on tripwires, but Peter was finding his life more valuable by the minute.

He'd feel pretty stupid if he got himself killed due to a basic lack of attention.

The only thing out of the ordinary was the garage, which was bigger than it looked from the front. It was only two cars wide, but it was also two cars deep. Twin white pipes poked through the roof at the back, looking like the exhaust and air intake for a sealed-combustion furnace. So the garage was heated. There was also a big sheet metal vent, eight feet off the ground, with a chemical smell. A spray hood. The master sergeant was fabricating something in there.

When Peter got back to the deep front porch, the door was open and June was gone.

He ran up the steps and inside, the truck driver's gun still in the tool bag. "June!"

He found her wandering through the house, blue gloves on her hands, turning on the lights. "He had a fake rock with his key inside," she said, almost apologetically. "I have the same one by my front door." She spread her arms with a flourish. "Surprise!"

The first floor of the house was immaculate, especially if you considered that it was being used primarily as a warehouse for motorcycle parts.

Heavy-duty steel shelves lined the walls of the living and dining rooms, with brightly painted gas tanks and fenders and fairings neatly arranged with manila tags noting the make and model and sometimes a name and phone number. The wall-to-wall carpeting was gone, the old plywood floors covered with gray epoxy paint. The house was full but didn't feel like it, because the light shone through the open shelves. The elaborately renovated kitchen, breakfast nook, and den appeared to be fully occupied. They were spotless. Only the small bank of video monitors linked to the security cameras seemed out of place. Peter smiled to see the miniature motorcycles on shelves and windowsills and at the center of the round dining table. A teddy bear sat atop a cabinet, as if waiting for supper.

Maybe the master sergeant wasn't paranoid. Maybe he was just looking after his investment in motorcycle parts.

Up the stairs, the bedroom was equally immaculate with T-shirts on hangers, organized by color. Personal photos on the dresser and walls, mostly guys and their bikes. There were two other bedrooms, one made up as a guest room, the other used as an office. June sat on an old wooden chair to work her way through the shelves and filing cabinet and the old desktop computer while Peter walked down through a mudroom to the giant garage, which was set up as a complete motorcycle repair shop.

The guy seemed to specialize in the big bikes, mostly Harleys but also a few old Indians and Nortons in various stages of repair or renovation. Peter saw a pair of bike lifts, multiple heavy workbenches, a giant rolling steel Snap-on toolbox, and a welding rig. Everything was clean and orderly, as if the maid had just been through to tidy up. Engines and engine sections sat on stained cardboard pads, and a small plastic booth with a paint hood took up half of the back wall. That was the sheet metal vent he'd seen outside.

The other half of the back wall looked like a big walk-in closet. A heavy-duty steel door was locked with three commercial deadbolts, at the top, middle, and bottom. The walls had metal plates bolted to the studs, with each bolt head spot-welded to the steel.

Peter was back to the paranoia hypothesis. His little pry bar wouldn't do shit here. He went back to the van for the sledgehammer.

As it turned out, when you hit a serious deadbolt with a twelve-pound sledge a few times, it opens right up.

The walk-in closet was not where the master sergeant kept his off-season clothes.

One wall held a rack for long guns, mostly empty but still holding two of the Heckler & Koch assault rifles he'd seen the men with in the redwoods, the 416 with the short barrel. There was a very nice Browning sniper rig in a carry case, a few pump-action shotguns, and a pair of M4s that had seen better days. The long back wall held shelves with a half-dozen Glock 21s, excellent tactical-grade body armor, and night-vision goggles in their padded cases. A workbench held repair tools and a comprehensive gun cleaning kit.

The cops might think he was just a gun nut with a few illegal firearms. But to Peter, the master sergeant was the unit's armorer, maintaining the gear. No heavy equipment, no SAWs or RPGs, but enough for small clandestine operations.

Like trying to kidnap a female journalist.

Or kill her mother.

"Nothing on that computer but the motorcycle business," said June, walking into the garage. "There's also a docking station, but the laptop's gone." She peered into the walk-in and saw the guns. "Holy shit," she said.

"Yeah," said Peter. But something else was nagging at him.

Something he'd seen somewhere else in the house, but it hadn't quite registered.

Under the static, he felt a familiar prickling sensation.

Like he was being watched.

"Did you see . . . ?"

He left the garage at a run, back to the kitchen.

The teddy bear in the kitchen, sitting on an upper cabinet, facing the length of the room.

"What are you doing?" June was right behind him.

He should have told her to keep out of the room, or just go back to the car, but it was already too late. Peter reached up for the bear, knowing now that their hats and spray paint had done nothing, not for anyone who mattered.

The bear was heavier than it should have been.

Because it wasn't just a teddy bear.

He turned it over. On the back was a slender power cord running to a wall plug, a USB socket, and an identification tag from the manufacturer.

Peter read it aloud. "'Wi-Fi-Enabled Plush Bear Camera. Never worry about your child again. Live access from your computer or hand-held device.'"

June looked at him. "A nanny cam?"

"There was one just like it in Ross's apartment," said Peter. "And I think in Martinez's house, too."

Her face went white. "We need to get out of here."

"Yeah," said Peter. He unplugged the bear and stuffed it into her hands. "Now. Go start the car, I'll be right there."

June ran out the front door and Peter ducked back into the garage. The door to the weapons locker stood open. He took off his black top-coat, found a heavy armored vest that fit him over his suit jacket, tightened the straps and shrugged his topcoat back on. It seemed ridiculous to do this in his new black suit, but he didn't have time to change. He worried briefly about getting gun oil on the suit pants, but that was the least of his problems right now.

He grabbed a pair of Glocks and checked the magazines. They were the big magazines, thirteen rounds each, but only partially loaded to preserve the springs. The master sergeant certainly knew his shit. He shoved the pistols into one deep topcoat pocket and put a box of .45 ammunition into the other. He picked up one of the HK rifles, snapped in another partially loaded magazine, found a spare mag and a box of NATO rounds to fill them, and moved to the door.

It was full dark outside, although the house security lights made the yard bright. The rain was back, a dense, steady drizzle that dampened sound and shortened the sight lines. He listened for a moment, but only heard the sound of the rain and the idling minivan. June had turned the car around in the big driveway so it pointed out the gate nose-first, but she'd left the headlights off. She was definitely a tactical thinker.

Peter stood by her open window and handed her one Glock and its box of ammunition. He kept his voice quiet. "You know how to use this? There's only a trigger safety, so be careful."

"Yeah, I grew up around guns." She turned it in her hand, examined the trigger in its guard, then found the magazine release and dropped it into her hand to check the load. She opened the ammunition box and took a handful of rounds, then looked up at him. "I've never fired at a person before."

"And you're not going to now," he said. "But just in case, I want you prepared."

He began to thumb the fat rounds into the HK's magazines, one after the other, while June did the same for the Glock in her lap. He'd lost the callus on his thumb from the war years, when he'd carried ten or fifteen mags at a time, sometimes more, filling them two or three times a day when things were really hot. The callus had been stained from the film of oil on every round.

Funny, the things you thought about.

He listened again for the sound of a big engine, coming closer.

"They're probably not anywhere near here yet," he said, mostly to make her feel better. "I'm going through the trees to check the street. It'll take me a little while. Give me fifteen minutes by the clock on the dash." He took the Glock from her, checked the mag, put it into his jacket pocket, then handed her the second one. "Get this one loaded and ready, put it where you can reach it. If everything's okay, I'll wave to you and open the gate and we'll drive away nice and calm, just another happy couple going out to dinner. I feel like Thai food tonight, how about you?"

She looked at him. He could see the muscles flex in her jaw.

"What if they're out there?"

"Then you'll hear some noise. You'll know it when you hear it. That will be me, protecting you. Doing my job. So you count to sixty and drive directly through the closed gate and turn left, fast and hard, and get the hell out of here. Use that gun if you have to. Now, repeat it back to me. What's your part of the plan?"

"Wait fifteen minutes. You'll come back. If I hear some noise, count to sixty and drive through the gate, turn left and punch it."

"Good," he said. "It's going to be fine. But don't trust my phone until you see me again. If it falls out of my pocket, they could text you."

If I'm dead is more like it, but he didn't say that.

"If we get separated, don't go back to your apartment. Find a cheap hotel, pay cash. I'll meet you back at that coffee shop. Nine a.m. to-morrow."

He smiled at her, a genuine smile. He could taste the adrenaline now, copper in his mouth, felt the joy of it rising in him. He wanted them to be out there somewhere. Anywhere. War's dirty little secret, how alive it made you feel. There was nothing like it.

By the tightness around her eyes, he knew she could see it in him.

He wondered if it made her afraid of him.

But he didn't think he could turn it off. Not now. Maybe he didn't even want to.

He bent to the window. "Kiss me," he said.

She grabbed his head and nearly pulled it off his neck getting his face to hers. The kiss was soft, their lips barely touching, only a slight com-pression. The tickle of her stitches. But the electricity of it, Jesus Christ.

"You fucking come back," she murmured without backing off at all. "You understand me?"

"Yes, ma'am," he said. "Most definitely." He gently disengaged from her hands and stood to his full height. He thumped his fist to his chest, his eyes on her the whole time. Then turned away to the left and into the trees.

HE'D BEEN WORRIED about being backlit by the house's security lights, but the perimeter growth was at least twenty feet deep and so thick that he couldn't see two feet in front of his face. Which meant, he told himself, that nobody else could see him, either.

It was good to tell yourself these things.

His night vision was shit from the house lights, and he wished he'd grabbed the night-vision goggles from the armory inside. But that decision was already made. His eyes were adjusting, and he'd be under the streetlights again soon enough.

The night was wet, but somehow it was even wetter inside the screen of brush and trees. Water ran off everything he touched, down the back of his neck, soaking the pants of his black suit. The medical boot felt like a wet towel wrapped around his lower leg. His hands were bare and cold on the HK. Peter wasn't sure how the weapon would react to this wet environment, but he wasn't worried about it. This was no AK or M16, or even the moderately better M4. This was a whole different level of gear. The rifle felt utterly natural in his hands, even with the suppressor. An extension of his mind.

Alive, alive, he was alive.

He found the barbed wire by walking into it. An improvised fence made of individual wires strung from tree to tree, stapled to the trunks at varying heights. Easy to install and hard to see. Peter thought he'd have liked the master sergeant, if the man hadn't tried to kill Peter on two different occasions.

He crept along the fence line, still heading left toward the corner, crouched and working his way through the dense black vegetation, his predatory backbrain looking for shapes and shadows that shouldn't be there while his conscious mind thought ahead. Where he might find them, if they were there to find.

These guys weren't official, he was sure now.

Their shit was too nice. The teddy bears were too cute.

He was willing to consider that they might be some off-the-books group. He'd met enough spooks overseas to have a working knowledge of the subterranean depths of paranoia and ambition passed off as patriotism. Somewhere in Virginia, he was sure, hidden basement departments led to secret subbasement operations that led to rough-hewn downward-sloping passages to bat-filled caverns of lunatic bullshit that went so deep the maps had never been made to chart their existence.

Peter had never liked the spooks.

He still thought these guys were opportunists, soldiers for hire. But not on their own, or they'd be robbing banks or something. Not trying to commandeer some fucking algorithm.

Someone was running them. They were under orders.

He made his way slowly forward. Shapes and shadows. No expectations. There might be a fire team coming through the backyard. But he didn't see anyone in his area. It would take some discipline to get out of the car on a dirty night like this.

He found a wider gap between the wires and snaked through, now headed toward the street, cracked ribs singing softly. He wanted to come out near the corner of the lot, but not too near.

He got down on the ground and did a slow belly-crawl toward the open space, his ribs complaining louder now, the HK cradled in front of him, held out of the wet leaf rot.

The street was lit by a single lamp at the intersection. He found a low-hanging big-leafed bush, yet another rhododendron, and went underneath its canopy to peer out at the street.

A shining black Ford Explorer stood on the far shoulder, directly in front of him, parked the wrong way. Headlights off.

He thought he could see two people in the front seat. Maybe. It was hard to tell. Shadows and raindrops and line of sight.

Exhaust puffed from the tailpipe, so they had heat and defrost. They were just waiting for him and June to drive back out. So why bother getting cold and stiff, limiting their visibility? But he never saw the wipers go. So they had some discipline. If it even was an assault team. If it wasn't just a pair of teenagers making out, or some guy trying to finish his phone call before going inside to see his kids.

He'd told June fifteen minutes. He could text her, but he didn't want to take out his phone, risk the light or the movement. And he'd told her to ignore his phone anyway.

He figured his time was almost up. Time to decide.

He leaned a little farther out. Looked right, down the road. And there it was, about twenty yards past the master sergeant's gate.

A matching black Explorer.

Headlights out.

The faint haze of exhaust.

He was pretty sure they weren't both necking teenagers.

What were they waiting for?

He was worried about June. But he didn't want to light up a pair of cars in a residential neighborhood, either. Collateral damage, he'd seen it happen too many times. He checked the lines of fire. There wasn't a house directly behind either Explorer, the lots were big and the houses spaced apart. But surely there was a house on the next block, or the block after that.

June, watching the clock. He had to move.

He really didn't want to light up the whole block. He didn't want to kill an innocent. A child.

Just go. Make it work, he told himself. You've got a vest.

He took a deep breath, the copper taste strong in his mouth. He felt the wild glee of adrenaline mainlined into his system. Would anything ever replace this feeling? There was nothing else like it.

He crawled out from under the rhododendron, low and slow and steady, counting on the night and the rain-spattered windows to hide him. Hoping they were watching the gate, knowing his movement would draw their eye regardless. They were predators, too.

Then he was in the weedy ditch, freezing his knees and balls in four inches of rainwater, the sodden medical boot like an ankle weight. Then up the other side and on his feet, taking five quick steps with the rifle up to his shoulder and firing at close range through the windshield. Three-shot bursts, chest and head, hard to miss. *Takatak, takatak, takatak.* From that angle, the rounds would die inside the car, or at least slow significantly, not spray the neighborhood with high-velocity rounds.

The men would be wearing vests. He pulled open the side door and saw two big men in street clothes reaching, reacting, guns in their hands, dark flecks on their faces and necks where the windshield glass had turned to shrapnel. But they were still moving, so he brought the rifle back up and put a single shot into each of their heads, painting the inside of the car midnight with their blood.

Now he heard the roar of a big engine as the second Explorer surged toward him from eighty yards away, its headlights popping on as Peter raised the HK and aimed, slow and steady. *Takatak, takatak,* the windshield turning into a widening field of spiderwebbed holes. The car came faster and faster, his targets getting closer, his accuracy improving. Then he was out and the car kept coming as he fumbled the release, digging for the fresh mag in his coat pocket. He stepped behind the dead men's car, missing his combat rig and the old M4 that he could reload in his fucking sleep, but he got the mag unsnagged and snapped into place as the Explorer came up, screeching to a stop, the passenger window down and a blood-blackened fist held a handgun spouting fire.

Peter felt two hard punches in his chest. It hurt like hell and twisted him sideways, which probably kept him from taking more hits. He already had the rifle up and now he pulled the trigger hard into full auto and stepped forward, emptying the mag into the Explorer through the open side window. The two men inside were turned into dark wet pulp.

His breath came hard. His ears were ringing but he heard something crunch and another engine revving high as a car came up fast and it was June, having done exactly what he'd told her to do, driven through the gate and turned left at speed.

He ran around the front of the Explorer into the road with his hand up and the rifle down. She stood on the brakes and he opened the door and got in, the HK stock down in the footwell. Her eyes got wide and he realized she was staring at the pair of blackened holes in the front of his raincoat.

"I'm okay, the vest caught it."

But she'd already stepped on the gas as soon as his second foot cleared the opening. The acceleration closed his door with a thump as she drove smoothly away.

39

June didn't say a word until Peter's hands began to shake from the adrenaline comedown.

"Hey." She reached out and put her warm hand on his cold one and he knew they were okay.

The surface streets were clear, at least the routes June knew, fast runs on two-lane neighborhood feeders, which she would abandon as soon as they became four-lane thoroughfares. Her route was indirect but inevitably southward. The smell of spent powder lingered in the car.

Peter stared out the window while the defroster ran on high, trying and failing to get rid of the humidity from his cold, wet clothes. His chest ached where the vest had done its job. When he undressed, he'd find a painful pair of big purple bruises.

Better than the alternative.

Far better than the other guys.

You just killed four men.

Somehow it was different when you fired first.

At a stoplight she got on the phone and dialed from memory, talking softly. A few minutes later she pulled over in front of a short row of small storefronts. She opened her door. "I'll be right back."

He looked at the sign and it said THAI SIAM.

Just another young couple out on a date.

She returned almost immediately carrying a big paper bag and began to stack cardboard containers on the dashboard, laid out forks and chopsticks. The smell of Thai food filled the van.

"I got the basics," she said. "Not too spicy, only two stars. You want me to get you dry clothes now or after we eat?"

He was shivering, soaked to the bone. "I'll get them." He stowed the rifle in the second row and stood on the street under the open rear hatch and stripped off the medical boot, then the black suit.

Rain came down hard, splashing up to his bare ankles on the cold wet asphalt. He figured his new clothes were ruined, but they were so fucking expensive that he folded the jacket, pants, and black topcoat neatly anyway.

Maybe the suit could be salvaged. He was more attached to that suit than any other item of clothing he could remember.

It was the way June had looked at him when he'd put it on.

His back to the sidewalk, rain falling on his bare legs and ass, he stepped hastily into dry underwear and pants as a clatter of high heels got louder behind him. He turned to see a foursome of young Asian women in flowered dresses and clear plastic bubbletop umbrellas failing to avert their eyes as they turned into the restaurant.

He was too memorable now. He grabbed his clothes and his phone and climbed back into his seat.

"We need to get out of here."

June's face was pale. She had a container of noodles open on her lap, but she wasn't eating. She stared out the windshield, clutching her plastic fork like a weapon. She'd held herself together long enough to get them to this moment, but no farther. Now she was shaky and jagged around the edges, riding the downhill slope of her own adrenaline crash.

He put his hand on her arm. "Are you okay?"

She looked at him. "No, fuck no."

"You will be," he said. "Have a few bites, get your blood sugar back up."

"They would have killed us," she said, her voice thick. "Or worse, I don't know. But you saved us. You saved *me*."

He put his arm around her and leaned into her. It was awkward in the bucket seats, but he held her close while she pulled in one deep, shuddering breath after another.

Suddenly he wanted her badly. Wanted her more than anything, to feel her hot bare skin pressed against his. In the back of the van if they had to, he didn't care. But the thinking part of him knew it was a bad idea.

"Come on," he said. "Have a few bites."

"Jesus." She looked at the container of Thai food in her lap as if she'd never seen it before. "I've never been so fucking hungry in my life."

TEN MINUTES LATER, she set the shattered remnants of her pad thai on the center console. "What now?"

"I think we should stay away from your place," said Peter. "And we need to get rid of this car. There are gate parts stuck in the grille."

"But I like this car," she said. Then began to get angry. "And I like my fucking place, goddamn it."

Peter shrugged. "Don't get too attached," he said. "It's only stuff."

"I *am* attached," she said, aggravation clear in her tone. "People get *attached*. To cars, to homes, to things. We can't all be mysterious Buddhist fucking nomads, you know. We get attached to *people*."

Oh, thought Peter. We're doing this now.

"You want to get mad, that's okay. You have a lot to be mad about." He turned sideways in his seat to face her and reached for her hand. "But you don't need to be mad at me. Because I'm definitely attached to you. In fact, you're going to have a hard time getting rid of me. I'm like bedbugs."

That made her smile, a little.

"I thought you were like a Boy Scout with muscles."

He smiled back. "I'm a complicated man. No one understands me but my woman."

She eyeballed him. "Is that a line from *Shaft*?"

He put an innocent look on his face. "What, the movie? Or the song?"

She smacked him hard in the arm, and turned to face the windshield again. Then looked sideways at him again. "How are you okay again after what happened back there?"

"I'm not," said Peter. "I'm just more used to dealing with it."

"But I saw your face when you climbed into the car, right after. You looked, I don't know. Not happy, that's not the right word. But full of some kind of ecstasy."

"That sounds about right," he said. "It's horrible and thrilling at the same time. I killed some guys who were trying to kill us. I'm alive, and so are you, and here we are eating Thai food. It's a fucking miracle. Later, I'm planning to slowly remove your clothes and kiss every inch of your naked body."

She blushed slightly, but didn't take the easy out. He was impressed. She wanted to understand, not be distracted from the topic at hand.

"But they're dead," she said. "How can you think about anything else? How can I?"

"I had a lot of practice overseas," said Peter. "You and I, we didn't start this. We didn't go after them. They came after us, for their own reasons. There is no moral failure here. Our survival and their deaths aren't on you, or me. It's on them. On whoever *sent* them. And the reward for our victory, for being alive, right now, is Thai food and conversation and if I'm lucky, your naked body on top of mine. Because it's not over. It's going to take everything we have to survive the next few days."

Her eyes were luminous. "How is it that you're not like them?"

"I am like them," he said softly. "But I'm trying to make up for it."

His phone surprised him by ringing.

Only two people had the number, and one was sitting next to him. He pulled it out of his pocket. "Hey, Lewis."

"You okay, Jarhead?" Had Lewis heard something in Peter's voice?

"Had a little dust-up a few minutes ago," said Peter. "I'm fine."

Lewis snorted. "Up in the North End? Little dust-up my ass. I'm looking at the footage on Channel 5 right now. Somebody got lit up but good."

"Wait. You're in town?"

"Flew into Sacramento last night. Picked up your truck, left it in storage outside of Portland, and found something with a little more style. Just checked into the Four Seasons, but I'm bored, brother. I need something to do. Any ideas?"

Peter looked at June, who was back on her laptop.

"Yeah. You could do a drive-by on my friend's place. I'm wondering if someone is watching. We could use some kind of handle. We still don't know who they are." He gave Lewis her address.

"Got it. What else?"

"We need to ditch our ride. You got a car?"

"Yeah, a rental. I'll call when I'm done, maybe an hour. Let me know then where to pick you up."

"Sounds good. Hey, Lewis?"

"Now what, motherfucker? You holding me up here." Lewis putting some street in his voice.

Peter could hear the tilted smile.

"Thanks," he said.

"Shee-it. Jarhead gone all sentimental."

Then he hung up.

Peter turned to June. "So, you want to meet my friend Lewis?"

She looked thoughtful. "Is he cute?"

"No," said Peter. "Lewis is definitely not cute."

THEY KEPT DRIVING SOUTH. Peter weighed different ways to get rid of the car. He could leave it in a high-crime area with the keys in the ignition and hope it got stolen. That way at least the local chop shop got something out of it. But he and June had been in and out of the car for days, it was loaded with their DNA. Blood and hair. If it was spotted by a neighbor at the scene of the shooting, the cops might find it before the crooks.

So he stopped at a service station, bought a two-gallon gas can, and filled it up.

The matches were free.

It wasn't easy finding someplace inconspicuous, because, like many growing cities in the West, Seattle wasn't big on zoning. Development seemed driven by views, greenspace, and waterways, so a nice neighborhood might overlook a railroad yard, and a golf course could stand beside a battered commercial strip. Real estate was expensive, so businesses and hipsters were quickly colonizing the crappy neighborhoods.

But between Google Maps and June's explorations, they found a long industrial zone in a suburb between two freeways, with a wide vacant area awaiting redevelopment. In order not to be the only car in the area, June parked outside a busy microbrewery-slash-restaurant a few blocks from the vacant lot. Peter's phone rang again.

"Your friend definitely got company," said Lewis. He described single watchers in four different cars.

"Any Ford Explorers?"

"No, they diversified," said Lewis. "Prob'ly personal cars, nothing fancy. But careful. Motors off, windows cracked, slouched down low. One at each end of the block, one pretty much right across the street, and another around the corner, where you might sneak in the back."

Peter thought of the neighbor with the woodpile. That would have been his way in. These people weren't bad.

"They get a look at you?"

"Jarhead, who you think you talkin' to?"

"You're a family man now. I thought you might be a little out of practice."

"I'm gonna pretend I didn't hear that. Anyway, they got tiny little cameras planted all over, I counted eight. A little weird, though. They cover the same angles as the cars. Like the guys in the cars don't know about the cameras."

Peter looked at June. "You don't have any security cameras, do you?"

She shook her head. "Leo might have put some in, I guess. But I never saw any."

"Okay," said Peter. "Lewis, you might as well come get us." He gave Lewis the name of the brewpub. "I'm in a parking lot off South Sixth on the west side of the street, a green Honda minivan. We need to offload a few things."

"Lemme find you on the map. Okay, I got you. Thirty minutes. I'm in a silver Escalade."

June had picked up her new laptop, which had been open and running since they'd gotten to the master sergeant's house. She was absorbed in the pale glow of the screen, so Peter closed his eyes and went over what they knew. It wasn't much.

When he heard her speak, his eyes popped open.

"Holy shit, yeah!" she said, and thumped her hands on the ceiling. "*That's* how Mama likes it."

"What?"

"Oh, nothing." Her eyes were bright. "I think I just *found* the bastard. Charles Dawes the Fourth. Ex-CIA asshole and founder of Citadel Security."

Lights flashed across the bushes as a car slipped into the space beside theirs. A silver Cadillac Escalade.

Lewis, right on schedule.

"Time to go," said Peter. "Grab your stuff. I'll get the gear. You take the front seat." He opened the rear hatches of both cars, and began transferring their stuff. His waterlogged suit, camping equipment, the HK assault rifle still reeking of spent powder.

June packed her laptop bag, got out of the van with the Thai leftovers, then opened the passenger door of the Escalade. "Hi, I'm June."

Peter heard Lewis's low, heating-oil voice, slippery and dark. "Pleasure to meet you, ma'am."

Peter closed the hatches, walked to June's side of the Escalade, and tapped on the glass. She rolled it down, her eyes bright with amusement. "You were wrong, Peter. He's both handsome and charming."

Lewis flashed the widest version of his tilted grin. "I got out early for good behavior."

His skin was coffee-brown, his head shaved. His features could have come from any mixture of races, as if he were from everywhere, or nowhere at all. He wore a crisp black synthetic raincoat over a starched white shirt, black jeans, and polished black combat boots.

"I can already tell this is a bad idea," said Peter. "Don't talk amongst yourselves, okay?"

June gave her rich, bubbling laugh. "I'm a reporter, Peter. I'm waaaay ahead of you."

Peter shook his head and got behind the wheel in the minivan. The Escalade eased out of its spot and around the corner, leading the way.

At the vacant lot, Peter opened the windows, poured gas through the interior of the van, tossed in the lit book of matches, and stepped away as quickly as he could with his hurt leg. The fumes caught with an audible *foomp*.

This was becoming a bad habit. Two cars in two days.

He watched the flames lick through the windows, sorry to see the green Honda go. It was a good ride. Then he stumped over the rough ground to the Cadillac.

"Jarhead." Lewis handed him a bottle of Anchor Steam, already open. "Your friend June's working on a plan."

"Thank God." Peter drained a third of the bottle. "Let's get the hell out of here."

"I got us a suite at the Four Seasons," said Lewis. "Plenty of room for everyone."

"Not for me," said Peter. "I'll never fall asleep inside." June looked at him over the seat back. "Why don't we camp out somewhere?"

"You still fighting that thing?" said Lewis.

"I'm working on it," said Peter. "But not tonight."

"Discovery Park would be fun," June said, and turned to Lewis. "I'll give you directions."

"It's a suite," said Lewis. "At the Four fucking Seasons."

"You use it," said Peter. "You're not invited."

40

CHIP

Chip Dawes's driver navigated the downtown traffic while Chip sat in the back of his Mercedes G63 and thought about the meeting he'd just had with Nicolet.

Chip had never seen anything affect the tech attorney's professional cool, so it was fun to see that the girl's mystery man had managed to put a dent in Nicolet's Teflon coating. The attorney thought he was tough, and he wasn't wrong. But he was a civilian. He lived in the world of legal maneuvers, where the worst thing that could happen was a bad court decision.

Chip lived in the real world, where far worse things were possible. Chip was definitely not a civilian.

He'd told the tech shark to tighten up his sphincter, things were under control. The mystery man was being handled. The algorithm would be in hand soon.

Chip didn't say *whose* hands, exactly.

Now Chip was headed back to his office to check on the operation's progress. He was late. He hoped they had something by now.

He stared out the window at the headlights shining through the rain and remembered how he'd gotten started.

Cashing out the Iraqi colonel's bearer bonds had gone just as Chip had planned. Shepard had stepped back and let Chip take the lead, his natural position. He'd chartered a series of ghost corporations head-quartered in Belize, Luxembourg, and the Bahamas, used those corporations to hire his real company, Citadel Security, to do fake work. Then he'd paid himself with his own stolen money, now nice and clean.

He'd even written himself letters of recommendation on his ghost companies' letterhead. Citadel Security was the best, their discretion unparalleled. You'd be a fool not to hire Chip Dawes.

It was appallingly easy to get his first legitimate contract. He paid a high-end prostitute to seduce a senior-level programmer at a company-sponsored outing. She got the guy home and put a roofie into his drink to knock him out. Chip showed up, copied the guy's keys and passcard, and fucked the hooker, too, what the hell. He was paying her already, right? The next morning he'd waltzed onto the corporate campus, changed some passwords, and downloaded a bunch of client information and proprietary code. Then made an appointment with the CEO.

The security chief got fired, and Citadel Security got a big fat contract. Nothing to it.

After that, Chip was pulling intrusions up and down the West Coast, signing up clients left and right. He bought the G63, the big house on Lake Washington, and a couple of boats. The actual work of corporate information security turned out to be pretty fucking boring, and not that lucrative once Chip had hired some tech geeks who actually knew what they were doing. No surprise there.

It was the other jobs that really turned Chip's crank. The *creative* jobs.

Convince a young developer to sell his very good idea now, not later, for a lowball price. Throw in a Tesla and an oversexed "college girl"? Done.

Blackmail a programmer into leaving a code glitch for an extra week? Chip had access to a substantial pool of call girls who looked stunning in a little black dress and could also suck a golf ball through a garden hose. They made cameras very small these days.

There were so many opportunities.

Bribe a dissatisfied venture cap researcher to vet an outdated set of numbers.

Start an unfortunate and mysterious wildfire to clear the way for a new corporate headquarters.

Break into a private genetics lab on the verge of a breakthrough.

Plant kiddie porn on a congressman's laptop.

Like taking candy from a fucking baby.

But even the creative jobs were fee-for-service, and the overhead was higher. He paid his operators very well. Call girls who could carry on a conversation didn't come cheap. Ethics-free supergeeks were downright expensive. And Shepard took his share, too.

Chip was careful to keep Shepard happy.

The man was like a scary robot without a human operator.

But high seven figures take-home just wasn't enough for Chip Dawes.

You could only make so much with fee-for-service. The two biggest things Chip had learned working the tech industry? You want to be digital, and you want to be scalable. Building the software and rolling it out to the first customer cost a certain amount. But rolling it out to every customer after that cost basically nothing. Two millionth customer paid the same amount as the first customer. It was like printing money.

So that's what Chip was after. His killer app.

Seven figures was nice, but he wanted eight or nine. Hell, he wanted ten, the big B.

1000x venture cap money. IPO money. Google Facebook Twitter money.

He wanted his own island. His own fucking nation-state.

And to do that, he needed a big score.

He was pretty sure he'd found one.

Thanks to a client, it fell right in his lap.

Hazel Cassidy's algorithm.

Chip had worked for this same client years before, when Citadel was just starting out. He'd had the potential to be a serious whale, so Chip agreed to upgrade the guy's security protocols, a small project but it got his foot in the door for more work down the line.

The client turned out to be completely irrational, fucked in the head, a colossal pain in the ass to work for. The added work never materialized, and the job was over in a few months. Chip padded his invoices like crazy and the man paid without a question, so it wasn't exactly time wasted. You could always tell new tech money. They knew so much about some obscure little fucking thing, but were naïve as hell about everything else. Half of them felt they didn't deserve the money, the other half thought they deserved twice as much, and they all loved to write those checks. Proving to themselves and everyone else that they'd made it.

When the client emailed him again a few months ago, something had changed. He was much more opaque. Now he worked through Nicolet, a notorious tech industry legal shark Chip had known for years. And the client refused to meet in person. Which was weird as hell, because on the creative side of Chip's work, all the truly important business was done face-to-face. Who wants to leave a trail of bread crumbs?

Instead the client sent some middle-aged broad named Sanchez to run interference, his executive secretary or something. She was at least fifty, flew into Lake Union on a goddamn floatplane wearing last year's business casual, with dirt under her fingernails and skin like leather. He wanted to tell her to get a manicure and put on some sunscreen, but she was too far gone for that.

Chip had to admit she was a serious ball-buster, smart as hell with a take-no-shit attitude. Maybe that was why the client had gone this route, the attorney and the personal rep. Maybe he'd realized he wasn't tough enough for this kind of work. Either that or he'd gone even farther around the bend.

Regardless, the client somehow had gotten access to Hazel Cassidy's working notes. He hadn't shared the notes with Chip, but Chip had used the backdoor he'd built into the client's system years ago to get himself a copy. The notes were cryptic and brief, but Chip could read between the lines.

The algorithm's potential was crystal clear.

He took the guy's money—it was perfectly good money—and began planning the operation. But he'd already decided to keep the acquisition in-house. The algorithm was far too valuable to hand over to the fucking client.

Besides, if the guy complained, there was always Shepard.

Maybe even if the guy didn't complain. Maybe even include the attorney, and the personal rep with dirt under her nails.

This was going to be big.

Chip didn't like witnesses.

As for Shepard, Chip would take care of him personally.

Profit sharing was for suckers.

HE PUT HIS SUPERGEEKS on the project full-time for two months, and they got nowhere. The Cassidy woman made none of the usual mistakes. She actually used the fingerprint reader on her phone and her brand-new personal laptop, the one she took home with her. Her password wasn't PASSWORD or her birthday or her daughter's name backward or anything else that simple.

As it turned out, she wasn't just any professor. She was in fact a big-shot Stanford computer science star. She had real discipline and major skills and random long-string passwords. It was infuriating. Chip was actually impressed that the client had gotten her working notes, because Chip's supergeeks couldn't even get that far.

So he went old-school. He planted infected USB drives in the parking lot, on the hallway floor outside her lab, in the backpacks and messenger bags of her staff, even in Cassidy's own purse, all in the hopes that someone would plug a drive into a lab computer. He got a few takers for his virus and a lot of naked pictures of Stanford coeds, but no access to Cassidy's systems.

He'd already hired a dip to lift her personal access card, planning to make a duplicate and put it back into her purse, but before the dip did the deed, Cassidy went and added fucking retinal scanners to her lab doors, so unless he was going to pop her eyeballs out of their sockets, he wasn't getting in that way. He sent a team to assess the physical security of the place, but she had multiple layers over Stanford's already decent measures, and short of a sledgehammer and a very large crowbar, or quite possibly the jaws of life, the place was tight as a fucking drum.

He was starting to consider the eyeball option.

But first he thought he'd try the direct route, hiring Nicolet on Chip's own nickel for the negotiations, to further insulate himself from both client and professor and thus ensure his own anonymity. Chip had known Nicolet for a half-dozen years, and the man had no problem with wheels-within-wheels, his personal ethics firmly firewalled from his business practice.

Chip's last two offers were far more than he could afford to pay, but by then it was more about her reaction, seeing who he was dealing with.

Hazel Cassidy was a tough nut.

When she stopped answering Nicolet's emails, Chip decided there was only one way through. Cut the Gordian knot.

Or more to the point, kill the professor.

Then his operators could walk in with government credentials and a cutting torch and clean out her office. Which is exactly what happened.

They'd taken boxes of paper files and stray hard drives. They'd taken an odd-looking aluminum crate the size of a dorm fridge, loaded with computer components and cooling fans. They couldn't take the lab's servers, a long row of liquid-cooled Crays too big for a pair of operators to physically remove in the middle of the night, and the credentials Chip provided wouldn't stand up to loading a box truck in the light of day. So they'd uploaded Chip's virus via flash drive and gotten the hell out of there.

The supergeeks were very impressed with the aluminum crate, which they called a mini-supercomputer, something Cassidy had apparently designed and built herself. But it was an empty jar, completely wiped.

The virus got them remote admin access to the servers, which were packed to the gills, but not with anything useful.

They still couldn't find Chip's algorithm.

The next obvious step was the daughter, but somehow Smitty's team had screwed up taking her off the street. Chip never did get a good explanation out of them, and now they were dead in the fucking mountains. The mystery man, whoever he was, had taken out Chip's top tactical team, and the daughter was in the wind. Chip was certain she had the algorithm.

Soon enough, however, he'd have her. And the goddamn mystery man.

That's why he was heading back to his office.

If traffic weren't so fucking bad, he'd get there before the ball dropped. Watch the whole thing from the dashboard cameras. Bert had a helmet-cam, too.

Chip really wanted that code. More than he'd wanted anything in his entire life.

He deserved it. He'd worked so fucking hard to get here. Stepped over a lot of bodies.

He was thinking about the next steps as he ran his card through the security reader and walked through the door to his private office suite.

Where he saw Shepard sitting behind Chip's handmade tropical hardwood desk, sitting in Chip's own exquisitely tuned ergonomic chair.

41

SHEPARD

Shepard watched the salesman open his office door and see his chair already occupied. It was a deliberate provocation on Shepard's part, an information-gathering strategy.

He had the big wall-hung monitor turned on and mirroring the desktop computer. The screen was split, each side showing a night view of a residential street from opposing viewpoints. This, too, was a provocation, and also a reminder. Shepard had bypassed four escalating levels of security to get into the office, and three password log-ins to access the video.

The salesman's reaction was impressive, Shepard had to admit. His enormous rage was only visible for the briefest moment before it was mastered and suppressed. The anger beneath the salesman's slick veneer, thought Shepard, was the engine that powered him forward. It was not the first time Shepard had considered this.

He could also see the salesman's fear, but in a much smaller proportion. A far smaller proportion than it should have been, thought Shepard. This was useful information.

"Nice of you to show up," said Chip. Without removing his raincoat or appearing to glance at the big monitor, he dropped himself into one of the leather club chairs facing the desk. "Long day?"

Shepard indicated the monitor. "You haven't seen this, have you?"

"No," said Chip. "I was in a meeting. How'd you get in here?"

"I told you to let me handle it," said Shepard. And clicked Play.

On the split screen, two vehicles were parked on opposite sides of the road, facing each other, perhaps eighty yards apart. Each vehicle was visible in the other's dashboard camera. On both screens, trees swayed slightly in the wind. Raindrops accumulated on windshields.

After fifteen seconds of this, the left screen abruptly flared white as the camera's sensors were overwhelmed by a burst of brightness. On the right screen, the distant vehicle was lit up with muzzle flashes, silhouetting a dark figure beside the Explorer with a long gun spitting light through the windshield.

Shepard had recognized the shape of the medical boot on his first viewing.

The left camera feed went blank almost immediately, hit by a stray round. The right camera jolted as the driver stepped on the gas and the distant vehicle got quickly closer. The figure slipped around the front of the vehicle with the dead camera. Then, faster than should have been possible, the same figure appeared from behind the rear of the same vehicle, firing toward the oncoming Explorer in disciplined bursts. The windshield starred immediately, obscuring the view, but the muzzle flashes were still visible, closer and closer. Then the right camera flared white.

When it dimmed again, it had acquired a pink tint.

"Blood on the lens," said Shepard. He'd seen the effect before.

Through the fractured pink perspective of the broken windshield, they watched a new vehicle arrive and the black figure with the rifle and the medical boot slip inside the passenger door.

"Fuck me with a hot poker," said Chip. He looked at Shepard. "Where the hell were you during all this? I thought you were hot on her trail."

"I told you," said Shepard, "to let me handle it. I had her locked down. Eight cameras at her house and a GPS beacon on the vehicle. I followed her on and off for most of the day trying to get a read on her security."

"Maybe I'd have known that," said Chip, his tone deliberately reasonable, "if you weren't playing this so goddamn close to the vest. If you'd answer your fucking phone, you'd be in the loop on operations."

Shepard hadn't answered his phone because he was balancing his obligations to his other clients. There was a certain amount of overlap, conflicting requirements. Perhaps it was by design, he didn't know. He didn't have all the information. The primary client had always played a very deep game. Shepard rotated the possibilities in his mind as he waited for the salesman to get back to it.

It took him a minute. Chip shoved himself to his feet, stalked to the little bar, and poured himself a short tumbler of brown liquor from a heavy crystal decanter. He made a point of not offering one to Shepard. Then he turned, as if the thought had just occurred to him.

"If you had her locked," Chip said, gesturing with his glass, "where the fuck were you when this shit went down?"

Shepard wasn't going to admit he'd watched the whole thing from a neighbor's yard. He'd wanted to see the girl's protector in action. And it didn't hurt to thin the ranks of Chip's men. Shepard thought of it as tidying up in advance. It would make things easier, when the time came to clean house.

"I had other obligations," he said. "With cameras on the house and the beacon on the car, I could pick her up any time I wanted. Until Bertram's team got noticed. You can see it in the footage. Just one man. But a substantial threat."

"A substantial threat?" asked Chip, eyebrows high, the drink forgotten in his hand. "That's your professional opinion? A substantial fucking threat? Bert's team was armed and armored, four trained killers, and he went through them like a hot knife."

"Yes," said Shepard. "Just like in California."

Chip looked at him. "What the fuck is going on with you? Something's out of whack here. It's not like you to hold back. I know you're not scared, 'cause I've never known you to actually get scared. As far as I can tell you don't actually feel anything at all. So what the fuck is different today?"

Shepard didn't want Chip to speculate about what might be different.

The man was far more than a salesman. Yes, Chip's primary attributes were self-interest and greed, but he wouldn't have succeeded in Iraq and leveraged himself into his current business without a great deal of insight and mental acuity. Chip was quite capable of making an intuitive leap.

So Shepard allowed Chip to see something else, something inside him that Shepard would ordinarily have kept hidden. It had the added credibility of partial truth.

"Ohhh," Chip said, smiling wide. "I get it now. It's the *guy*. *He's* different. He's not just another simple civilian contract, an insulin overdose or hit-and-run. You think he's worthy of your skills. You're *flirting* with him."

Shepard didn't respond. Configured his face in such a way as to allow the salesman to believe Shepard was annoyed. It served to reinforce the salesman's conclusion.

"I always suspected you might be human," said Chip. He drained his drink and set the tumbler down on the bar. "So where the fuck are they now?"

"The van stopped broadcasting twenty minutes ago," said Shepard. "Last known location is south of downtown. Perhaps they found the beacon. Or parked the van in an underground structure. Or burned it to the frame like the Tahoe. It doesn't matter. They're gone."

"What a clusterfuck," said Chip.

The salesman wasn't angry enough, thought Shepard. He had something planned.

"The other teams," said Shepard. "Where are they?"

"On the way. They'll be here day after tomorrow." He waved Shepard out of his chair. "Move your ass," he said. "Let me see what I can pull off these cameras. I still have some friends back East."

Chip sat behind his desk and ran his fingers across the keyboard like a concert pianist.

Without taking his eyes off the screen, he said, "Go make yourself useful. See if you can find the van. And the next time you have a shot at this guy, you better fucking take it."

The salesman definitely had something planned, thought Shepard.

He left Chip's office, the door closing silently behind him.

It wasn't quite time for tomatoes, he thought.

Not quite yet.

42

JUNE

June's phone alarm woke her in the half-light of early morning. A warm spring wind blew hard off Puget Sound, and giant raindrops rattled the tent fly. She closed her eyes and snuggled deeper into her sleeping bag, wishing for another hour of sleep.

She'd been up half the night digging into Charles Dawes IV, also known as Chip.

The other half she'd spent sexually harassing her bodyguard.

He didn't seem to mind.

They were camped in a sheltered pocket on the edge of a bluff in Discovery Park, a five-hundred-acre natural area where Seattle met the ocean. It wasn't exactly a suite at the Four Seasons, but she couldn't ask Peter to sleep in a hotel, not now. Maybe never.

She heard him unzip the tent to let in some fresh air, then the sound of the little backpacking stove firing in the tent's vestibule. "Coffee in ten minutes," he said quietly.

"Let's go out to breakfast," she said, yawning. "Eggs Benedict, bacon, hash browns."

"That sounds nice," he said. "I can offer you trail mix and a banana."

"I had your banana last night." She smiled sweetly. "Twice, in fact."

"I regret to inform the young lady," he said, bending to brush his lips against the side of her neck, "that was no banana."

The coffee water boiled over the top of the pan.

EVENTUALLY PETER stuffed the pack with their sleeping bags and the sodden tent, then followed her up the broken bluffs to the wide undulating plateau. The hard rain had diminished to a thin drizzle. A narrow trail led through high grass and wildflowers to the parking lot, where a silver Escalade waited, idling silently.

The driver's window hummed down and the rear hatch floated up.

"You hobos need a ride?"

Meeting Lewis yesterday was interesting. He had a presence much larger than his physical body. In his black jeans, crisp white shirt, and black raincoat, he reminded her of nothing more than a sleek dark muscle car with the engine idling and the clutch engaged, all controlled combustion just waiting to be released. She should have been scared of him, but she liked him. He made her feel safe. That probably should have scared her, too.

"Your Cadillac got an outlet for my laptop?" she asked him, climbing into the back seat. "My battery's about dead."

"Hand me the plug," Lewis said, reaching back. "I'll take care of you." He had the assault rifle barrel-down in the footwell, the stock rising up along his door. She felt her pulse picking up speed. Maybe she didn't need another cup of coffee after all.

Peter threw the pack into the cargo bay and closed the hatch. Now he hopped into the front passenger seat and dropped the bag of trail mix onto the center console. "Breakfast?"

Lewis gave him an amused look. "I already ate. Salmon omelet, hash browns, two sides of bacon, and a quad mocha with extra whip."

"Jeez, I knew I should have stayed with you," June told him. "All I got was a lousy banana. Okay, go straight out of this parking lot. You'll follow the arterial left, then right again."

Lewis put the Escalade in gear. To Peter, he said, "Weapons on the floor, wrapped in the towel." Over his shoulder to June, he asked, "Learn anything new?"

In the car the night before, she'd told Lewis how her mother's algorithm had ransacked Nicolet's firm's servers and found a contract with a company called Citadel Security, signed by Charles Dawes IV, for negotiating the purchase of unnamed intellectual property from unnamed owners. It was the lack of detail in a legal document that made her suspicious. Then Tyg3r had found a report from Nicolet to Citadel that noted four unsuccessful negotiation attempts. The dates of the attempts lined up with the dates of Nicolet's emails to June's mom.

"You just wandered into a law firm's internal network and started reading documents?" Lewis had asked, incredulous. "That's like strolling into Fort Knox and slipping gold bars in your pockets."

"There's more," June had said. "Last month, my mom tried to use Tyg3r to do the same thing, but failed. The algorithm is learning. Quickly."

Now she said, "I looked at Citadel overnight. A corporate security firm, only six years old, but becoming a player very quickly. It specializes in defending companies against corporate espionage, both virtual and real." She poked her arm forward, pointing. "Stay to the right here, then down the hill and across the bridge."

"Which means they're probably also working the other side of the fence," said Peter. "Defending companies, but spying for them, too."

"Did you get into their servers, too?"

"For about five minutes," she said. "Not long enough to learn anything. Then I lost the connection. Either they kicked me out or expanded the air gap."

"An air gap," Lewis informed Peter, "is when sensitive information is kept disconnected from the Web, to prevent hacking."

"What, you think I don't know that?"

Lewis snorted and turned back to June. "What else you got?"

"Citadel is privately held," she said, "so they don't have to disclose anything. Tyg3r did get me into the state tax website, which only lists twelve employees. It's a subsidiary of a holding company based in Belize."

"And the shooters work for a different company called SafeSecure," said Peter. "Owned by another holding company. Also based in Belize."

"The iceberg strategy," said Lewis. "Mostly invisible, hiding below the surface."

"Exactly," said June. "SafeSecure has sixteen employees."

"Now down to eight," said Lewis. "At least in theory."

"Plus subcontractors," said Peter.

"Shee-it," said Lewis. "I ain't afraida no subcontractors."

The bridge was clogged with commuters. Approaching Fifteenth Avenue, they crossed over the railyard and passed the Interbay soccer fields. "Left here and merge," she said. "Then your first right."

"Who laid out these roads?" asked Lewis. "This city is like spaghetti."

"Not if you know where you're going," said June. "It's all about the shortcuts. That's the ship canal on your left." Now they were on Nickerson by the Fremont Cut, the funky old neighborhood on the other side rapidly converting to blocky new condos and office buildings, Seattle's software wealth doing development on steroids.

"How about this guy Dawes?" said Lewis.

She flipped through her reporter's notebook, reviewing her notes. "Charles Dawes the Fourth, goes by Chip. Comes from old New York money, but the last of the family fortune went to pay for Chip's Ivy League education. His dad died of a drug overdose, so I'm guessing his investment decisions weren't so hot, either," she said. "Dawes's accounting firm only has half-decent security, so Tyg3r did get me access to his financials. He's making money by the bucketload, but it's going out the door as fast as it's coming in. So he's either losing his ass or he's laundering it overseas."

"Dawes's bio says he was an operations officer in Iraq," said Peter. "On the ground, making plays. So he can probably handle himself. He has a gun permit, too. Expect him to be carrying."

"Hell, I expect everybody to be carrying."

They passed the turn for the old Fremont drawbridge, then beneath the high sculptural arches of the Aurora Bridge as they angled southeast along Lake Union. Through breaks in the trees and the commercial buildings, she saw the elaborate houseboats tethered to long wooden docks, a floating neighborhood.

"His boat slip is coming up," she said. "You'd think a spy would be bright enough not to let a magazine writer tag along on his morning commute. Although it was probably good publicity."

"Ain't nothin' succeed like success."

She pointed. "This is it."

Lewis pulled off the road, down a ramp, and into a broad parking lot by the lake.

She could feel her heart beating in her chest. She'd come a long way from digging through corporate records and worrying about fact-checkers. What the fuck was she doing here?

It was seven-thirty in the morning. The water was the color of ash. The falling rain so fine it was almost a mist.

CHIP DAWES'S PRIVATE SLIP was on one of many piers jutting out into the lake. Its fifteen spaces held mostly sleek power yachts, a testament to the city's wealth. Owner access was a gate at the northeast corner of the parking lot, not far from a blocky cement office building with a big seafood restaurant on the lowest level. At the southeast corner of the lot was a small rectangular building on the water, Kenmore Air's seaplane terminal.

Lewis backed into a parking spot at the near end of the seaplane offices, with a clear view of the water and down the fire lane to the gate. He cracked the windows an inch, but left the engine on. He shifted in his seat to look at her. "You got a picture of our guy?"

June held out her open laptop. "This is the company website photo."

On the screen, Chip Dawes wore a blue-and-white seersucker suit and a blue bow tie. He had a sandy mop of hair over a tanned, clean-shaven rectangular face with a square jaw and a self-satisfied smile. He looked like a middle-aged East Coast preppy, maybe a successful insurance salesman or the vice president of a local bank. But he was a former CIA field agent. And he would be capable, she thought, of anything.

Lewis only glanced at the photo for a few seconds before he turned back to the view of the gated pier. "You can pull that up on your phone," she said. "If you want to see it again."

"No need," he said. "I got him. When's he due?"

"According to that magazine article, anytime now," she said. "Unless he took the floating bridge, or came early. Or stayed at the Four Seasons down the hall from you."

Peter unfolded the towel and picked up the pistols. "How you want to do this?"

Lewis nodded at the office building. "You set up near the gate where you can see the pier. Try to blend in. I'll range around, check for backup, spot you for any heavy lifting."

"What about me?" asked June.

"You're the getaway driver. Keep the engine running. You'll hear shots, or one of us will text you. Can you do that?"

"Sure," she said. Her heartbeat rose yet again, and she could feel the heat on her cheeks. "Like Steve McQueen."

"Wait a fucking minute," said Peter. "Protecting June is the whole point of this thing."

She put her hand on Peter's arm. "I've already been the getaway driver twice. No reason to stop now."

He looked at her, controlled but intense. "We didn't have a choice before."

"Of course we did," she said, keeping her voice calm. "We could have just run away. Sold the skeleton key and retired to Bali. But that's not me, and I'm pretty sure it's not you, either. We decided to fight."

"This ain't no movie," said Lewis. "You gotta show up when we need you."

"I know," she said. "I will."

Lewis nodded as if he'd already known what her answer would be, then looked at Peter. "Got any better ideas?"

June knew Peter wanted there to be a better idea. But there wasn't.

"No," he said. "Let's go."

Lewis opened his door and disappeared into the swirling mist, making no attempt to hide the assault rifle under his raincoat. He carried it barrel-down along one leg like some necessary prosthetic device. Today, she supposed, it was.

She climbed forward into the driver's seat and kissed Peter's cheek. He handed her one of the pistols, tucked the other into a coat pocket, and got out of the passenger seat, pulling up his hood as he walked. He was wearing the armored vest under his jacket. It was compromised from the two shots he'd taken the night before, but they'd both agreed it was better than nothing.

She watched him walk down the fire lane to the seafood restaurant and find a spot under the overhang by the service door. He wasn't dressed like a kitchen worker, but he still managed to convey the temporary indolence of a prep cook taking a break. Blending in.

She didn't like the waiting.

Turning to the pier, she saw three empty slips. It didn't matter which was Chip's, she'd know the man when she saw him. They all would. There weren't many boats on the water anyway, not on this cool, damp morning.

A wide, T-shaped dock stuck out into the water by Kenmore Air, with a sleek yellow-and-white floatplane tied up inside the shelter of the crossbar. At the bottom of the lake, an old yacht was just putting off from the Center for Wooden Boats. A dented silver Jetta rolled into the parking lot, parked near the restaurant, and four men got out wearing kitchen whites and plastic clogs. Each man nodded or raised a hand to Peter as they walked past him to the service door.

It was one thing, she thought, to deal with a dangerous situation when you were forced to react. When you had no choice. It was another thing entirely to create the situation, to step forward into the danger, like they were doing now. Although that was what Peter, and she presumed Lewis, had done overseas. In the war, she told herself. He'd fought in a war. She still had trouble wrapping her mind around it, what that might have been like.

A few fishermen were puttering around now. A pair of sea kayaks paddled down from the north end, not minding the weather. Probably from the houseboat neighborhood they'd passed on the way. She wondered if Peter might live on a houseboat. They were small, but they had a lot of windows, and long views.

More cars, more people, more boats. No Chip Dawes. She couldn't see Lewis, either. But she was pretty sure he was out there. Then she saw a small white spot at the far end of the lake, coming from the Montlake Cut and growing larger by the second. A fast boat and its wake.

A floatplane appeared in the sky, coming from the north, its engine muted by the rain. It made a wide, slow turn, dropping down and down, ungainly and graceful at the same time, like a goose over a pond. The plane was boxy and antique-looking, something she could imagine a bush pilot flying in Alaska, something out of another time. She watched as it touched the water, throwing spray, then slowed, settled, and began to taxi toward the T-shaped dock.

She got out of the car. The incoming boat was more than halfway across the lake.

The pilot cut the engine and let the plane drift the last few feet to the mooring cleat. He got out and tied up the plane before the wind could move it from the dock. He wore a leather jacket and jeans and a baseball hat.

Then the passenger door opened and a big man stepped onto the pontoon, the float dipping visibly as he did. He was at least a head taller than the pilot.

He wore a faded blue climber's rain shell, rumpled green pants, and hiking boots.

He had long white hair and a bushy white beard.

She couldn't believe it.

Her fucking father. The Yeti.

43

PETER

While the floatplane had landed and taxied in, the fast boat had powered up the lake. It was a sleek red runabout with an inboard motor and a canvas cover over the cockpit to keep the rain off the driver. Small enough to be fun on the lake, but big enough for the Pacific coast.

Now it coasted in toward the T-shaped dock as the white-haired giant, who could only be Sasha Kolodny, the Yeti, stepped lightly from the plane's float to the weathered decking. He walked toward the boat, and its driver threw the Yeti the bowline. He tied it to the dock.

The pilot came over and gestured at the boat, probably unhappy that it had moored at the floatplane dock. The Yeti wheeled to face him and the pilot raised his hands and took a quick step back. Peter thought about Hazel Cassidy's restraining order. The man was truly enormous.

The boat driver climbed onto the dock and the two men began to talk.

From forty yards away, Peter couldn't see the boat driver's face clearly, but it was Chip Dawes, Peter was sure of it. The man wore sunglasses in the rain and a long khaki trench coat belted at the waist. Either Dawes was a walking cliché or it was calculated for his image, which was more likely for a private spy who'd invited a magazine writer to follow him on his water commute.

The conversation between the Yeti and the boat driver became heated. The big man waved his arms, then jabbed his finger at the boat driver's face. The sound of shouting drifted over the water. The boat driver shook his head and put his hands on his hips until the Yeti, moving faster than anyone his size and age should be able to move, took a single long stride toward the boat driver and shoved him hard in the chest.

The boat driver flew off the dock and struck the water ass-first with a splash.

The Yeti watched the boat driver flounder for a moment, then untied the boat's bowline, put one foot to the hull, and pushed it away from the dock. It moved slowly, but its momentum carried it farther from the shore, where the wind caught the boat's profile and began to push it into ever-deeper water. The boat's name, written in black on the stern, was *Spooked*.

The Yeti turned to the pilot and shooed him toward his plane with the back of one hand. The pilot climbed back into his seat and the engine started up again. The Yeti untied the plane and stepped onto the pontoon, pushing the plane out into the lake as he did, then stepped up into the passenger seat and closed the door. The plane taxied around the swimming man and his drifting boat, turned into the wind and came up to speed, skimming across the water until it lifted into the air.

Peter looked down the fire lane and saw a female figure standing by a silver Escalade, looking out at the lake.

She'd seen it all. The whole thing. Her father and Chip Dawes.

He turned back to the water, where the man was swimming after his boat, clumsy in his trench coat. Dawes appeared to have lost his sunglasses. For a moment, Peter wondered if the wind would blow the boat faster than the man could swim. Apparently the man was concerned about the same thing, because he stopped for a moment to shed his coat and his shoes, leaving them to sink behind him as he struck out strongly for his drifting boat. He'd swum at least a quarter of a mile in foot-high chop before he finally got a hand on the swimmer's deck and climbed aboard in shirtsleeves and socks. Not bad for a corporate spook.

Peter looked down the fire lane. June was gone.

The fast boat's engine fired up with a growl. Peter couldn't see the driver in the covered cockpit as the boat cranked around in a tight circle, its wake spreading as it headed back to its slip. The boat disappeared from view behind larger boats, but he heard the snarl of the engine as it reversed hard into the slip.

Peter figured Chip Dawes IV was cold and wet and pretty unhappy.

Dawes came through the gate a few minutes later wearing a crisp black fleece jacket, fitted training pants, and sandals. He carried an elegant leather briefcase in one hand and a wide black umbrella in the other, held up to keep the rain at bay. His unruly mop of hair was damp, but looked towel-dried and surprisingly fashionable, as if he'd stepped out of the locker room rather than fished himself out of an urban lake. He had the same tanned face as his photo, the same square jaw, the same smug look of the cat who swallowed the canary.

But there was something else there that the photographer had missed. A distance to the eyes, a harshness in the lines bracketing the wide, mobile mouth. Peter had known many men who'd gone to war. It changed you inside. It made you someone new, or revealed who you had always been, sometimes a little of both. Sometimes for the better, eventually. Sometimes not.

Peter was pretty sure which way things had gone for Chip Dawes.

He angled away from the restaurant service entrance to intercept Dawes at the edge of the parking lot. Dawes turned to look at him, basic threat assessment. He didn't stop walking, and he didn't free up his hands.

Twenty feet and closing. "Nice day for a swim," said Peter. "Unhappy client?"

"You have no idea," said Dawes.

"Oh, I'm starting to figure it out," said Peter.

Dawes's mobile mouth formed a mocking smile while those distant eyes flickered across Peter's face. "No, truly," he said. "You actually have no fucking idea whatsoever."

Peter shrugged. "Maybe not," he said. "But here's what I think. You hired the lawyer, Nicolet, to negotiate the purchase of some software from Hazel Cassidy. I'm thinking you were hired by her ex-husband, Sasha Kolodny, who is not quite right in the head." Dawes's smile had lost some of its gleam. "How'm I doing so far?"

Dawes did something to the U-shaped umbrella handle with his thumb, not taking his eyes from Peter as the black cloth folded itself up with a soft slither. He tucked it under the arm carrying the briefcase.

Peter brought the Glock from behind his back and raised it to point directly at Dawes's face. "Stop moving," he said pleasantly. "Anyway, Hazel didn't want to sell, and she didn't bow to any of your attempts to intimidate her by pulling her grant money or getting a former student to accuse her of sexual misconduct. So you killed her, thinking you'd just take the software. But you couldn't find it. So you tried to kidnap her daughter. Repeatedly. And failed. Maybe that was Kolodny's idea, but by his recent reaction, I'm thinking it was yours."

Behind Dawes, a boxy black Mercedes SUV turned off the road and rolled down the ramp to the parking lot.

Dawes kept his eyes on Peter's face. "This isn't the kiddie pool. You are in deep fucking water with some very big fish and you have no fucking clue what's going on."

The Mercedes SUV came to an abrupt stop behind him. The driver's door opened and a very big man slid out and planted his feet on the asphalt before the Mercedes stopped rocking.

Peter registered the tiny eyes in the craggy stubbled head, the gray T-shirt and black tactical pants, and the empty black nylon shoulder holster. But his focus was on the big automatic in the man's enormous fist, pointed directly at Peter's center of mass.

Chip's smile spread farther, and Peter was reminded of a reptile unhinging its jaw to swallow its meal whole. "Please," he said. "Get in the truck. You'll be my guest. We have so much to talk about."

Then Lewis came around the boxy back of the SUV and slammed the butt of the assault rifle into the bodyguard's temple.

The big man dropped like his strings had been cut.

Lewis kicked the pistol out of the bodyguard's hand and reversed the rifle to cover Peter, not even breathing hard. "This a little awkward," he said to Dawes, his voice pleasant. "Your man not so big on the ground."

Dawes held himself still, but the smile remained. The Mercedes growled in the background as he locked his eyes on Peter's face. The guy was for real. Most people would be focused on the guns.

"Your name is Peter Ash," said Dawes. "Formerly a lieutenant in the U.S. Marines. Served with apparent distinction, even awarded a Silver Star. But after eight years you were still a lieutenant, which seems to me to be a difficult trick to do. Some sort of irregularity in your record. I haven't located the details quite yet."

Peter stared at him, for a moment wondering how the man knew who he was. Then he remembered the Web-connected nanny cam, staring right at him as he lifted it down from the top of the master sergeant's kitchen cabinet. Facial recognition. Chip was an intelligence officer, after all. Information and its manipulation were his livelihood. No doubt he still had active sources in the CIA.

"I know you, too," said Peter. "I know your home address on Mercer Island. You tried to kill a friend of mine. Now is the time to convince me not to kill you."

"Okay," said Chip. "How's this for an argument? Betzold Road. Bayfield, Wisconsin."

Peter felt it like a sledgehammer to the chest. His parents' house.

Dawes's voice was soft. Playful.

"That's where you grew up, I believe? Where your parents still live now? Your father runs a building business with your uncle, and your mother teaches art at some podunk local college. Your aunt is a musician on the snowmobile circuit. So quaint. How is their health, by the way?"

Peter moved in fast and put the gun to Chip's forehead, pressing hard. Chip set his feet, leaned into the barrel, and kept talking.

"I'm not the only one who has this information," Chip said calmly. He seemed to be enjoying himself. "I'd advise you to back off. At this moment, this can still go a few different ways. If I'm dead, there's only one way."

Peter took a deep breath and pushed down the anger, at the same time admiring the stones of the guy. A gun to his face and he thinks he's still in charge.

Maybe he was.

Peter shuffled back two steps and lowered the Glock. An angry red circle on Chip's forehead marked where the gun barrel had pressed into his skin. "What do you want?"

Chip's smile widened like he could eat the world. "Only what I deserve," he said. "You choose the delivery system. The software or the girl who controls it. I'm thinking the best outcome for you personally would be her computer and access codes. My people will do the rest. By five o'clock today."

Peter said, "What's in it for me?"

"Aside from healthy parents?" Chip raised his finger in a playful scolding gesture. "Don't be greedy, Peter. You've inserted yourself into my business far too much already."

Peter sighed and let his eyes slip away. "I need another day," he said. "It's more complicated than you think."

"This afternoon," said Chip. "Five p.m. The girl or the algorithm."

"What's your guarantee?"

Chip opened his empty hand in a graceful gesture. "Once that software is in my possession, you have my word. Your parents, your aunt and uncle, your childhood home, all will continue happily as it did before."

His word, Peter knew, was worth exactly nothing.

The bodyguard stirred. Lewis kicked him in the stomach, and the big man curled abruptly into a ball. The risks of being an asshole's bodyguard.

Chip looked at Lewis. "You, I don't know," he said. "But I will. I have a very good memory for faces."

Lewis stared back at Dawes, rifle held ready, face utterly devoid of expression.

Peter had felt that implacable gaze before. It had weight and substance, like the hot desert wind before a killing sandstorm. It was a good look.

Lewis's voice was pleasant. "Won't have much memory with a bullet through your brain."

Chip didn't flinch, but it cost him some effort. He looked back at Peter. "Put your dog on a leash." Then stepped over his injured man and slid into the driver's seat of the big Mercedes. "Call my office at four-thirty. I'll tell you where to meet."

The door closed behind him with an impressive solidity. Peter watched as Chip drove off.

"Should have killed him," said Lewis.

"That's your answer to everything," said Peter.

"Not everything," said Lewis. "But shit, him?"

Peter put his arm up and waved. The Escalade came up fast, June's window down.

"That was my dad," she said. "On the dock? In the plane? That was my dad."

"I know," said Peter. "We'll talk about it."

Lewis pointed his rifle at the bodyguard, red-faced and bleeding on the ground. "What about him? Not much of a severance package. Or you suppose this an independent contractor?"

Peter walked around to the passenger door. "Leave him. I need to make a phone call."

Lewis shook his head. "I'd say you getting soft, but I know better. I sure as hell hope you know what you're doing."

Peter looked at him across the hood of the silver Escalade. "Me too."

Lewis picked up the man's big black Colt 1911 and held it casually in one hand, looking down at the bodyguard as he struggled to sit up. "You home free today," he said. "Take that as a gift. Find a new employer. I see you again, I'm gonna assume you got bad intentions. We clear?"

"Yeah," the big man said thickly, not looking at Lewis. "We're clear."

Lewis tucked the pistol into his coat pocket, then climbed into the Escalade and June drove them out of there.

AS SHE ROCKETED toward the south end of Lake Union, Peter pulled out his phone and dialed a number he knew by heart. On the other end, it rang and rang, until, finally, someone answered in a raspy voice. "Stan's Backwoods Bar and Grill, you kill 'em, we grill 'em."

"Dad, it's Peter."

"Holy shit! The prodigal son lives! Your mother was a little worried, you weren't returning her calls."

This was vintage Stanley Ash. A profane enthusiasm combined with a gentle reminder about good behavior.

"A bear ate my phone, Pops. But that's not why I'm calling." He could hear the murmur of the Internet radio Peter had bought him in the background, probably playing some NPR podcast. His dad had a long-standing crush on Terry Gross. "You're in the shop, right?"

"Yessir, I am. Gluing up some cherry for a dining room table."

Peter felt a surge of affection. He could picture his dad standing by the big worktable, glue on his fingers, sawdust on the sleeves of his old Pendleton shirt, scrap lumber popping in the woodstove. He could almost smell the blue enamel coffeepot perking away. His dad drank roughly a thousand cups of coffee per day.

"Listen," said Peter, "if your hands are free, do me a favor. Go to the shelves over the radial arm saw. On the top shelf, you'll find a metal box."

"Ha! I thought that was yours. Found it in January when I got stir-crazy and spent a few days cleaning. Not a great place to put your life savings, son."

Peter hadn't exactly told his parents everything.

"Dad, you and Mom are going on a trip, and you're taking Uncle Jerry and Aunt Max. At least two weeks, leaving today. Take a month if you want. There's a credit card in that envelope. It has your name on it but the bills go to me. It has a fifty-thousand-dollar limit, so spend as much as you want. Where have you always wanted to go?"

His father's voice was kind. "Son, we can't just pick up and leave. We have obligations. The Jarretts want their dining room table. Your mom has students. And I'm not spending your hard-earned money."

"Dad, I'm sorry. This is my fault. I'm in the middle of something. I agreed to protect a friend, and now some bad people have threatened my family if I don't back off. They know the address of the house. So make whatever excuses you need to make, but you're going. And don't use your own credit cards, because they'll be able to track them."

In his father's silence, Peter could hear the man's attention sharpen as he made his calculations.

Stanley Ash was fifty-seven. He'd trained as a mechanical engineer at Northwestern, but in the late 1970s he decided he wanted to work for himself and left Chicago to start a carpentry business with his brother. He still swung a hammer most days, unless he was kayaking or ice fishing with his buddies or hiking in the Porcupines with Peter's mom.

Peter knew he was thinking now about the steps he would take to protect his home. His dad got his deer every year, and usually a few on his buddies' licenses, too. He still kept a shotgun by the kitchen door.

"Dad, these are professional killers, believe me. Staying is not an option. You know Mom's always wanted to see Italy. You don't even need to pack. Just buy what you need when you get there."

"Son, I never want to pry. But you need to tell me more. For starters, how can you afford this?"

"I'll explain when you get back, okay? I promise. But spend what you need to spend. Buy yourself a new suit, on me." Peter put on his Marine lieutenant command voice. "Now get on the phone and buy some goddamn plane tickets. Do you understand?"

His dad sighed. "Fuck a duck. Okay, son. But you owe me a serious conversation."

"Agreed. Dad, I'm sorry about this. I love you."

"Back atcha, kiddo."

When Peter hung up, June looked at him. "He threatened your parents?"

Peter showed his teeth. "Yeah."

Lewis spoke up from the back seat. "I believe that a tactical error on his part."

"Oh, hell yeah."

They were in a newer neighborhood of mid-rise office buildings and condos. June turned left onto a busy street that rose toward a bridge over the freeway, her hands tight on the wheel. "We need to talk about the Yeti. What was he doing there?"

Peter put his hand on her shoulder. "We're gonna find out."

From the back seat, Lewis said, "Who the fuck is the Yeti?"

44

This is why you were asking me about my dad, isn't it?"

"Yes," said Peter.

June was driving very fast up the bridge through heavy traffic. She was used to a smaller car and Peter was pretty sure she'd start chunking off side mirrors any minute now. In her current state of mind, he figured side mirrors were best-case. "Slow down, would you?"

"Don't tell me what to do," she said. Her voice was loud.

There was no good response to that. He figured she was headed to her apartment, which would have felt like a safe place. It probably wasn't a good idea, but now wasn't the time to bring that up.

"How did you know my dad was involved?"

"I didn't," said Peter. "But I figured the cops thought your mom was killed in a hit-and-run, so they were probably calling insurance companies and looking at body shops. If they'd known she was murdered, the first thing they'd do is look at friends and family. So I asked Lewis to do that. He found out about the restraining order on your dad."

"You were investigating my mom?" She stomped the brake behind a slow Prius, then swerved across the yellow line to pass. A beer truck came at them, eating the whole lane. The driver hit his air horn and Peter grabbed the dashboard as June ground her teeth and ducked back to her lane.

"Not investigating," he said. "Getting more information. Doing my job. Protecting you."

"Fuck!" She slammed her hands into the steering wheel.

"June." Peter kept his voice calm. "I know this is hard. But we need to know more about your dad. What else do you know that you haven't told me?"

"I don't know *anything*," she said. "I tried to forget all about him."

"Try to remember," said Peter. "Anything will help."

"You guys see that?" asked Lewis from the back seat.

They all saw it, a plume of smoke coming from just beyond the crest of Capitol Hill, getting bigger with each block.

"Oh, no." June slipped the Escalade onto a side street, finding as always the fastest way through the dense traffic. At every turn, Peter kept an eye on the smoke, hoping their path would take them away from it eventually. But for every left that pointed them away from the smoke, there was another right that pointed them toward it. As the plume grew larger in the windshield, there was little point in pretending it was coming from someplace other than her apartment.

It would have been impossible to keep her away, so he didn't try.

Half of June's block was filled with fire trucks and police cars keeping a perimeter. She pulled the Escalade into a random driveway and opened her door to get out. Peter put his hand on her arm. "Stay in the car," he said. "They're still here. This was no accident. Dawes isn't waiting for our next move, he's still looking for us. For you."

She shook off his hand. "I have to see it," she said. "It's my home. Anyway, they won't do anything here, not with all these people."

"They got into your mom's lab in Stanford," said Peter. "They put you into their car on a busy street. These people do whatever they want."

June hopped out, but left the Escalade running. "I'll just walk past," she said. "I won't stop. But I'm going."

Peter scrambled out to follow her. "Lewis, can you pick us up on the other side? Maybe they won't be expecting that."

"Done," Lewis said, climbing into the driver's seat. "Look for me on the next block."

They walked down the opposite sidewalk, through knots of spectators and policemen watching the firefighters continue to spray water on the smoking remains.

Leo Boyle's empty shell of a house had become a wet pile of charcoal and ash settled into the heat-cracked foundation. Only the smoke-stained chimney still stood, towering improbably over the ruin. All that ancient bare wood, dry as bone, coated in fresh paint, just waiting for a match.

June's garage apartment behind it was nothing but a smudge on the concrete slab.

Peter allowed himself only a moment to look at the house. The rest of the time, he had his head on a swivel, looking for anyone who didn't belong. June tried to stop, but he put his hand on her elbow and said into her ear, "Get a good look, but keep walking. Lewis will be waiting for us."

"*Fuck* them," she said, her face dark. "That was my *home*."

But she kept walking.

Three houses past the police perimeter, a familiar scraped-up BMW was angled into a parking spot. It faced the wrong direction, with two wheels on the curb. One corner of the front fender was newly crumpled into the trunk of a big maple. Four tickets were stacked under the wiper. The house wasn't the only thing ruined.

"Wait," Peter said, and nudged June's elbow.

June saw the car. "Fucking Leo," she said, and stalked forward. Boyle was curled up in the back seat with his jacket as a pillow and his hands tucked between his thighs like an oversized five-year-old. Across the floor lay a scattered mess of translucent lollipop wrappers.

June yanked open the door. "Leo." She thumped him in the chest with the butt of her fist. "Leo. Wake the fuck up."

Boyle blinked myopically up at her. "June? What are you doing here?" His lips moved in a tentative smile.

"Who are you working for? Why did you pick me?"

The smile fell away and he looked like a rat in a trap. "What? June, what are you talking about?"

"Let me help." Peter stepped past her and grabbed Leo by the front of his shirt and dragged him mewling out of his car and onto the wet grass behind a row of evergreen shrubs, out of sight of the police. He was heavy and soft like an animal bred for slaughter. Peter's ribs gave a *twang* with the effort.

"Who do you work for, Leo?"

Boyle was scared and breathing hard. "Dude, I don't know what you're talking about."

Peter put a knee on the kid's chest and backhanded him across the face. It was like kicking a puppy. He didn't like it, but he needed the information.

"Why is June's picture on your computer? Why do you have a Stanford ID in your office? Who set you up in that house?"

Boyle's face was bright red now. "Ow, dude, that hurts."

Peter backhanded him again. "It can get a lot worse, Leo. Who set you up in that house?"

"What are you talking about, it's my house."

But his eyes slid to one side as he said it and if Peter had any uncertainty, it was gone now. He pinched the kid's nose between the knuckles of his first and second fingers and squeezed. Boyle's eyes filled with tears. Peter worked the nose back and forth. It would hurt like hell but wouldn't do any real damage. "Tell me the truth, Leo. Who set this up?"

Boyle began to cry and the words tumbled out. "This dude, man, I took some money from his bank account. I bought his password online, I thought it was just this random thing. But somehow he tracked me back to my home computer and threatened me with the cops. I didn't want to go to jail, man. Dude bought this house, told me to pretend it was mine."

Pretend it was mine came out sounding like *Preted it was mide*. Boyle's chest heaved under Peter's weight.

"She's his daughter, okay? I made him prove it, he sent me a picture of her when she was like fifteen." He looked at June. "You were on snowshoes and you wore a long red-and-white-striped stocking cap."

June flinched visibly. She knew the picture. And where it had come from.

Boyle kept talking, eyes flicking from June to Peter and back. "He said he couldn't visit you, he was disabled and couldn't leave the house, he was worried about you, okay? He said I was doing a good thing."

"What about the picture on your desktop?"

"He sent me that one, too, so I'd know what she looks like now. I never even met the guy. I don't even know his fucking name."

Peter let go of Boyle's nose and looked at June. Tears were running down her face, too.

"I trusted you," she said fiercely. "I thought you were my friend."

"I am your friend," Boyle sobbed. "I was looking out for you. He's your dad."

"Some fucking friend," said June. "You were like my little brother."

"Do you think that was what I wanted? To be your little brother?" Leo Boyle looked at her then with a terrible longing, his face red, eyes streaming. "Don't you get it? I'm in love with you, June. Ever since I saw your picture."

"Jesus Christ," she said, turning away. "All you fucking men. What do you think, I'm your fucking property?"

Peter hoped he wasn't included in that group.

He put his head up and looked around to see how much attention they'd attracted. A pair of cops with their backs to the BMW talked idly to each other as they watched the smoldering ruins, but a few of the people standing on their lawns outside the perimeter were staring openly at Peter now. When he stared back, they hurriedly averted their eyes and stepped away like they'd forgotten an appointment. Maybe they saw something in his face.

He was running out of time. One of the neighbors might make a call, and there were two police cars on the block. Not to mention whoever Chip Dawes had sent, still out there.

He gave Boyle's nose another yank. "Tell me about the Stanford ID."

"Ow, okay, shit. Her dad set me up with a job at this grad lab down there." He talked even faster now. "At least he said it was him, it was the same email account, but he sounded different, you know? Maybe someone else using your dad's email?"

Leo looked at June, snot seeping now from his swollen nose.

"Your dad or whoever it was sent me a flash drive to plug into their system. I didn't want to do it, I told him I wouldn't. But he said he'd sell the house, empty my bank account, infect all my computers. Anyway I got caught and they fired me. I only worked there a couple weeks."

"How long ago?" asked Peter.

"I don't know. A few months? I'm not real good with time, you know?"

Peter thought he was telling the truth. After all those pot lollipops, he was surprised Leo could still walk and talk.

"What about my old laptop?" said June. "Somebody hacked it. Was that you?"

Leo closed his eyes and sucked in a breath. "Yes. He asked me to. Whoever he was."

"My new laptop?"

"No. I was supposed to do it last night, but I got home late and the house was on fire."

Peter looked at June. "We need to go. Anything else?"

She made a sour face and shook her head.

Peter took his knee off the kid's chest and stood. "Leo, there are some bad people using you for their dirty work. If I were you, I'd get back in that car and get as far away from here as you can."

Leo opened and closed his mouth like a fish on a pier. Peter touched June's arm and they walked away.

He didn't see the watchers until near the end of the block, a man on each corner. They were looking toward the fire, but if they were really interested, they'd have been closer. And they wouldn't have been watching the faces of the people walking toward them.

"Turn around," murmured Peter, and he pivoted his body to face the smoking ruin even as he kept walking backward away from it.

June turned with him. "What did you see?" she asked.

"Two men at least," Peter said, angling off the sidewalk and into somebody's front yard. "They're going to notice us any minute. When they do, I'll take care of them. You run like hell for Lewis."

June's eyes got wide. "Where's Lewis? I don't see him."

"You'll see him, he'll be there. You just run when I say so, as fast as you can."

In his peripheral vision, Peter saw the nearest man slanting to intercept them. He wore a green oilcloth coat with metal buttons. He was thick in the neck and shoulders and held a phone to his ear. Peter allowed him to get within twelve feet. "Go," he told June, and pivoted on the medical boot.

June broke into a sprint and Peter limped after her as if trying to get around the guy.

June pulled ahead and the guy angled to cut Peter off as he slid his phone into a pocket with one hand and stuck the other inside his half-buttoned jacket.

The guy was one step away when Peter planted the medical boot in the grass and pivoted again, swinging his elbow up and around, using the added rotation to drive it hard into the side of the guy's head. If he'd punched the guy that hard he'd have broken his hand, but his elbow barely felt it.

The guy staggered, his bell ringing nicely, but he was strong and it was definitely not his first time being hit in the head and he kept digging under his jacket. Peter grabbed the thick wrist and held it inside the fabric so the guy couldn't pull the pistol from his shoulder rig. The guy had a lot of gym muscle but it wasn't the same as muscle made by working hard all day, and he was still off-balance, blinking from the blow to the head and stepping back trying to get away from Peter so he could pull his weapon. Peter gave him a short chopping punch to the throat with his free hand. When the guy let go of his gun and put both hands to his neck, his mouth open, Peter knew he'd crushed the guy's larynx. It was done.

He put his hand on the gun butt in the guy's armpit and put his good foot behind the other man's heel and pushed him over backward, pistol coming free when the man went down. He looked for the second man and saw him on the other side of the intersection, sprinting after June with a gun in his hand.

Peter raised the pistol he'd taken but the angle was bad and it was a compact little automatic with maybe a two-inch barrel and he was as likely to hit June or the Pacific Ocean as the man chasing her. She had her knees up and her arms pumping fast, but Peter thought the lean young guy in running shoes might be gaining. Peter ran after them as best he could, hoping for an angle, knowing he'd never catch them with his fractured leg in its medical boot.

The silver Escalade roared backward out of a driveway, turned in a crisp reverse arc, and slammed into the running man going at least twenty-five. The man was sprinting full out, so with their combined speed it would have been like hitting a steel and glass wall at forty-five miles an hour. His forehead cracked the rear window and he bounced off the rear end and fell slack to the pavement like a rag doll thrown by an angry child.

The Escalade roared over the crumpled man, who passed neatly between the tires, and came to a chirping stop at the intersection, where Peter popped the passenger door and climbed in. Lewis threw it into drive and hit the gas again, this time veering slightly to drive over one of the crumpled man's legs. There was a slight bump, and a crunching noise that Peter hoped he'd only imagined.

"Asshole not gonna chase after *her* again," said Lewis. He eased up beside June, who stood breathing hard with her hands on her knees between two parked cars, her face pale as she surveyed the carnage left behind. The Escalade windows were down.

"You okay?" asked Peter.

"Jesus Christ." She looked at him and Lewis. "What the fuck is *wrong* with you people?"

"Please," said Peter gently. "Get in? We need to go."

She shook her head and opened the door and climbed inside.

Lewis hit the gas as soon as her legs were clear. The acceleration slammed the door as if on its own.

Peter turned in his seat to look at her. His cracked ribs didn't like it, but he wanted to see her face. He needed to be careful with her, he knew.

"June? We need to talk about your dad. What kinds of things he was doing when you saw him last. Where you think he might be."

She stared back at him, her freckles standing out like a red spray on her pale skin. What he first thought was shock was actually a cold white anger.

It made him a little afraid.

"I'll give you directions," she said. "If we go straight there, the valley's about a four-hour drive."

"We need a car," said Lewis

"We need more than that," said Peter.

He peered out the windshield at the sky. The clouds had lifted and he could see a faint shape just below the gray, circling slowly. If the light caught it just right, he'd see a glint of gold. It would follow them, he was sure now.

He dug his phone out of his pocket and put in the number he'd memorized the day before.

A calm voice answered. "Semper Fi Roofing, this is Manny."

"Manny, it's Peter. Got a minute?"

PART 3

45

PETER

They stopped at a car wash near the airport to get the blood off the Escalade's cracked rear window. They were seven or eight miles south of June's burned apartment, but the golden shadow still circled overhead, barely visible just below the high clouds, its outline fading in and out of view as the cloud bottoms roiled and shifted. Peter felt the static fizz and pop with the sight of it, and found himself hoping for rain. Maybe it would be less claustrophobic.

After the car wash they found a waterlogged parking lot and smeared mud on the back gate and the floor mats and seats to make sure the rental company cleaned the hell out of the Escalade. It was better than setting it on fire, Peter figured, and less likely to get anyone's attention.

They left the SUV at the rental drop inside the Seattle airport parking structure, then walked over the pedestrian bridge to the rental desks by the luggage carousels, where Lewis arranged for a white Dodge Caravan using a driver's license and credit card in another name, as if he'd just stepped off a plane with the rest of the tourists. They walked back over the bridge to the structure, picked up the van, transferred their gear from the Escalade, then joined the long stream of anonymous cars flowing down the spiral exit ramps to the highway.

Peter watched out the wide rear window as the golden shadow in the sky became smaller and smaller behind them, finally disappearing into the distance.

At a sporting goods store past Tacoma, June pored over the USGS topographical maps. Peter pushed down the static as he and Lewis filled a shopping cart with a backpack, a sleeping bag, and other critical gear for a night out in the woods. Lewis picked up two pairs of long-distance walkie-talkies, a Winchester 760 deer rifle with nice bright optics, five extra magazines and a hundred 30-06 rounds. When the clerk asked if he needed a Washington gun permit, Lewis said no, he already had one, and produced the paperwork. The permit was in a different name altogether.

They stopped for lunch at a diner outside Longview, sitting by a big front window with Mount St. Helens peeking through the overcast while they ate omelets and French fries and drank dishwater coffee. When the waitress took the plates, Peter unrolled one of the topo maps June had selected and put it in front of her. "Mark it up," he said, handing her a pencil. "Draw the valley as you remember it."

"I don't remember much," she said. "And what I do remember will be fifteen years out of date."

"We'll talk you through it," said Lewis. "You'll be surprised how much it'll help."

The map showed an elongated teardrop shape with a wandering creek or river down the middle. The elevation lines were far apart at the bottom, indicating nearly flat terrain. Around the edges of the valley, the lines were so close together they were hard to distinguish. Steep ridges or cliffs.

"The waterfall is up here at the point," she said, making a circle, then added two squares at the top. "My dad's house, and the lab. Maybe that's bigger now." More squares scattered down one side of the river. "Sally Sanchez, the ag researcher, she helped raise me after my mom left. This was the cottage where she stayed. The big house was where the researchers stayed, the people who came to work with my dad. The farm foreman's cabin was here by the equipment barn."

"Who was the foreman?"

"Mr. Monroe. He came after Sally did. He ran the big equipment, the tractor and all that stuff. My dad didn't like him, but Sally said we needed him. I think my dad would have used horses if he could." She drew some lines with squiggles on top around the buildings. "Apple and cherry orchards, most of this side of the river. This is the bunkhouse for farm help."

"What kind of help?" asked Peter.

"Fruit pickers, mostly. Every few years some carpenters would stay there when they were putting up a new building. By the time I left Mr. Monroe had two full-time workers who lived in the bunkhouse. There might be more now." She drew big rectangles on the other side of the river. "Farm fields here." Then triangles on sticks for evergreen trees, which she scattered around the perimeter. "Woods around the edges, where it gets too steep for agriculture."

"What about a high place," said Lewis. "With a view of the whole valley." He reached across the table and ran his finger across the orchards. "Something in this neighborhood?"

"Actually," said June, and circled an area where the elevation lines diverged from the high surrounding ridges. "There's a flat spot on this little rocky outcrop, maybe a hundred feet up." She put in a dark zigzag on one side, then a dot. "The trail is here. My dad built a wildlife blind there, just a few posts and a tin roof for shade. He used to bring his birding scope and watch the raptors." She smiled shyly. "I used to go there by myself and watch the men work."

Lewis tapped the outcrop with one manicured fingernail. "That's my spot."

Peter looked at him. "You might not be the only guy with that idea."

Lewis smiled his tilted smile. "And I feel real bad about that. I surely do."

THEY DROPPED LEWIS at a narrow trailhead ten miles past White Salmon. In his camouflage jacket and pack, he was almost invisible. He'd already sighted in the rifle. It was mid-afternoon.

"See you on the other side," said Peter.

"You won't see me," said Lewis, "but I'll be there. Don't use the radio 'less you have to."

They backtracked to White Salmon to cross the wide Columbia River into Oregon at the green steel Hood River Bridge, where the winds howled down the gorge and kite surfers in wetsuits were catching big air despite the cool spring day. Then east to a mini-storage place outside Portland, where Lewis had parked Peter's truck. It was a dark green 1968 Chevy C20 pickup, a barn find that he had restored in his time between deployments. The tall mahogany cargo box on the back contained most of his worldly possessions. Leaving the lot, it felt good to be back on the big bench seat where he'd logged so many miles, feeling the rumble of the engine like his own heartbeat.

They abandoned the vanilla van on the street a mile away, the keys under the floor mat, then called the rental company to pick it up. Peter's leg no longer ached and seemed to be improving, but the truck's heavy clutch was stiff under the medical boot, so June took the first turn at the wheel. Peter tried not to show his concern about how she'd handle the old pickup, but June shifted through the gears like she was born to it.

Palming the wheel through the turns, she told him how she'd taught herself to drive stick at thirteen. Shredding the clutch of an ancient one-ton Dodge with dual rear wheels and a dump bed. Wooden blocks strapped to the pedals with old bicycle tubes too shredded to patch. "But it got me down the highway to the ski hill," she said. "My first escape from my dad's. After that, I could drive pretty much anything."

Her comment hung there between them for a moment. Peter finally said, "You want to tell me about it, growing up there?"

"It wasn't awful." She was working her way back toward the freeway, trying to get across Portland and out of town. She shrugged. "In some ways it was great. I had free run of this beautiful little valley, maybe five square miles of half-developed farm and orchard and river. Steep ridges like walls around us, with cedars and hemlocks rising on the slopes until the dirt stopped sticking to the stone. My mom homeschooled me because the Yeti didn't want us to go anywhere, so mostly I climbed trees and rocks, played in the river, chased frogs, taught myself to ski. Pretty much anything I wanted. Sometimes on Sunday I'd get to go for a hike with the Yeti."

"What kind of dad was he?"

"The Yeti?" She snorted. "Mostly, he wasn't there. Before my mom left, I did my schoolwork in her office while she did her research, then we'd do something outside. The Yeti was in his workshop from breakfast until dinner, sometimes until after bedtime. It was a big treat for me to get to bring him supper, and he'd sit and talk to me while he ate, ask about my day. I'd try to get him to tell me about his day, but even then he was secretive. I was eight or nine years old, who the fuck was I going to tell? Sometimes I think that's why I became a journalist, all those years trying to dig into my dad's hidden life."

"And after your mom left?"

She sighed. "The Yeti was always kind of a cipher," she said. "Always in his head. But after she left, he just got more, I don't know, more abstract. His mind so deeply inside whatever he was working on, he'd put on the kettle for tea and stand there thinking while the kettle whistled until it boiled dry."

She reached the freeway and ran the truck up into third gear, the big engine revving high as she merged into the heavy late-afternoon traffic and worked her way through the Portland interchanges. When she hit 84, she found the left lane and shifted into fourth behind a big two-trailer semi that was really moving. The pickup rocked in its wake, but June was busy remembering.

"He'd get really angry if I interrupted him while he was in his head. And I was a kid, right? That's pretty much what kids do, interrupt their parents. You saw him on the floatplane dock. He never hit me, but he was huge. And when he got angry, he seemed to get even bigger. He was terrifying."

The big two-trailer semi slowed behind a line of cars, and June closed the distance behind it, drafting in its slipstream. It made Peter nervous, but he knew she was a good driver and he wanted her to keep talking.

"When I think of him like that, all wrapped up in his rage, I can absolutely believe that he had my mom killed. Over a fucking *idea*, because that's all an algorithm is, really, an organized idea. And he'd never apologize, not really, but eventually he'd find me, wherever I'd fled to, and sit beside me and quietly talk about how dangerous the world was, how he was doing everything he could to protect me. I just don't understand how he could be both of those people, so angry and so protective, at the same time."

"That sounds hard," he said quietly.

"Well, I wasn't completely alone," she said. "He had some researchers there, doing their own work. We all kind of tiptoed around the Yeti, and a few of them sort of adopted me. Sally Sanchez in particular, she was kinda my backup mom. She went out of her way to make sure I got fed and did my schoolwork. She talked me through my first period, bought me my first bra."

"Tell me about the other people. What did they do?"

"Sally was an agricultural researcher, she came one summer to test different designs of greenhouses and just stayed on. My dad wanted the valley to be able to feed itself, so we had orchards and big vegetable gardens, fields of wheat and corn and soybeans. By the time I left, Sally was running the whole ag project. Other scientists got grants to come work on a specific project for a year or two, sometimes a half-dozen people at a time. People doing solar power experiments, making 3-D printers, miniature battery technology, all this stuff that my dad said would help the valley, and by extension everyplace else. Sally was kind of the den mother, she'd been there the longest. She organized Saturday night dinners, and everyone would come, ag workers and researchers and whatever family they brought." She smiled, and Peter could see what she'd looked like as a little girl. "That was always the high point of my week."

The big two-trailer semi was really bogged down now. It was in the wrong lane and it couldn't accelerate fast enough to keep irate commuters from dodging in front of it, which just slowed it more. June found a hole in the middle lane, hit the gas and flew ahead of the semi, the road opening up ahead of them.

"But there were really no other kids, you know? I mean, what kind of way is that to raise your daughter? I was a teenage girl, and I had nobody else my age to talk to. I'd ask him to go skiing on Mount Hood and he'd say it was too dangerous. Shit, I'd been climbing rocks and trees and skiing in the valley since I was five. What was so dangerous about Mount Hood? But it wasn't the skiing he was worried about. It was the Taliban and al Qaeda and the war and the government, the whole wide world out of his control. Nothing was safe."

He watched the memory play across her face. Wanting to be protected, and wanting to be free from that protection. She said, "I could do anything I wanted as long as I didn't leave the valley. But at a certain point I just wanted more. I wanted the world."

"And he didn't want you to have it?"

"I don't know what he wanted. I'm sure he loved me, in his fucked-up way. But I barely saw him. He was always busy in his workshop. People showed up from outside the valley and they'd go into his workshop with him, something I never got to do." She looked at Peter. "The first time I ran away, I think I just wanted him to *talk* to me."

"What did he do in his workshop?" asked Peter.

"I'd guess he did a lot of different things," she said. "But the one thing I know about is building airplanes," she said. "Little ones, you know, remote-controlled. He'd always liked that. He'd flown his own plane when I was a little kid, but had to give it up. Something happened. He had these little microseizures and they took his license away."

Remote-controlled planes. Peter glanced out the window. Angled his head to peer skyward.

"What?" said June. She was looking at him.

"Nothing." He levered a smile onto his face.

She looked harder. "What do you see?"

"Nothing right now." He glanced out the window again. "A few times something I thought was a big bird, circling up high. But now I'm pretty sure it's not, because when the sun hits it just right, I'll get a flash of gold." He looked back at June. "Have you noticed anything like that?"

She sighed. "Yeah. Since California. I think it's my dad."

He reached out and put his hand on hers. They drove like that until the freeway came to a long uphill grade and the truck began to slow. She had to let go of his hand to shift gears.

46

They were quiet as June drove east, each lost in their own thoughts watching the landscape scroll by. Peter was wondering about the Yeti and what he might have gotten up to in the fifteen years since his daughter left home. And he wondered about June.

She took the exit for the Deschutes River Recreation Area, where they planned to camp for the night. Lewis needed the time to get down the falls. Peter had no idea what Manny would do. For all he knew, Manny had a friend with a surplus Huey who'd drop them directly into the valley. Lacking a helicopter, Manny and his guys were more than capable of any technical climb necessary to get where he needed to go.

They found a site by the melt-swollen Deschutes and set up camp, not speaking more than necessary to get things done. Peter had a crate of scrap lumber in the truck, and he built a small fire in the rusty iron ring. June sat in one of his little folding chairs and watched the kindling ignite.

"I don't know what's going to happen tomorrow," Peter finally said. This was part of what he'd been thinking about, how to get to this.

"Your dad could have an army in there. And I'm guessing Chip will be right behind us, with everything he's got."

June stared at him across the fire, her eyes alight in the flickering flame. He had no idea what she was thinking.

"I think you should stay here," he said. "Where it's safe. When it's over, Lewis or I will come get you."

June shook her head. "I need to see him," she said. "If he's really part of this, I have to be part of ending it. Or I'll never resolve it myself, in my own mind. I'll keep falling for the wrong guy."

Peter had wondered when they'd get to this part.

"Am I the wrong guy?"

She gave him a richly layered smile. "You're the right guy for right now," she said. "You might be the first right guy I've ever been with. But I'm still a work in progress. I can't make any promises, no matter how things turn out tomorrow."

She didn't say this: You're a killer, Peter. And I like you, I've slept with you. Might even be falling in love with you. So what does that say about me? And you're damaged. You're unemployed, you have no fixed address, your life is a mess. You can't even sleep inside. A girl wants to stay in a nice hotel every once in a while. A girl wants to have a home.

But she didn't need to say it. Because he could already hear it in his head.

Instead she stood up and walked over to him, leaned in close for a kiss. A soft, deep kiss. When he closed his eyes it was like falling off a cliff.

Like flying, until you hit the ground.

She broke the kiss and stood up. She was barefoot. She unfastened her jeans with great deliberateness, then let them fall and stepped slowly out of them. She began to unbutton her shirt. The firelight illuminated her skin like an ancient manuscript. She wore a lacy black bra and black panties that looked like coal against the paleness of her flesh. The tops of her breasts were dappled with freckles.

He wondered if she'd already made up her mind.

When she reached behind her back to unhook her bra, he found that he didn't care, not at that particular moment.

He scooped her up and carried her into the tent.

If a shadow flew overhead at that moment, glinting gold off the setting sun, neither of them noticed.

47

The next morning they crossed the wide Columbia River back into Washington on a high concrete bridge almost half a mile long.

It was still early morning and the air was incredibly clear, somehow scrubbed of all impurities. At the top of the span, they could see for miles up and down the river and along the wrinkled brown bluffs where green trees and brush grew in the creases cut by water. The sky was a distant faded blue. This was not the wet climate of Seattle. Past the western wall of the Cascades lay this high desert of small farming communities, vacation homes, orchards and vineyards, anchorites and mystics.

They stopped in Maryhill for gas. While Peter worked the pump, June held out the keys and absently watched the sky.

They turned west again on 12, following the river back toward the sea for a few miles. Peter drove and June stared out the window, her head tilted up toward the blue. With each mile, the creased landscape grew greener. At Lyle, they took 142 north along the Klickitat River, a narrow winding highway with signs warning of falling rocks. After a while they turned onto a lumpy unnamed road through an increasingly vertical landscape toward the narrow valley where June had grown up.

"How did you finally get out?" Peter asked.

"I walked," she said. "I found a way up the ridge at the head of the valley, a goat path or something up to the head of the waterfall. There was a big alpine meadow, and then mountains as far as I could see. Over a few weeks I went farther and farther, trying to find some kind of trail out, but I couldn't go far enough because I had to get back for dinner each night. Finally I took a pack and some food and a sleeping bag and some warm clothes and all the money I could find and just *went*."

Peter imagined her at fifteen, furious and alone and so desperate to leave the safety of the prison her father had made for her that she'd climb a waterfall to hike without a map into the rugged unknown wilderness.

"You found a road," he said. "Then what? You hitchhiked to California?"

She shook her head. "I bought a motorcycle, a little Yamaha 50, a couple miles outside of White Salmon. Guy had it parked out in front of his house. I'd never even been on one before, but I'd been cranking an old mountain bike around the valley trails for years, so I had pretty good balance. Before he'd sell it to me, he made me show him I could ride, and that I could pick it back up if I dumped it over. It was his son's bike, he'd died in the first weeks of the war. The guy gave me the helmet for nothing, came back out with a couple of sandwiches wrapped in tinfoil and some cold Cokes. I didn't tell him anything but he must have seen something. He said he didn't know what I was running from but he hoped I found what I was looking for."

"And you did."

"Back roads through three states on a little dirt bike not even street legal," she said. "I should have been picked up by the cops a hundred times."

"Or the child molesters."

"Oh, they were scared of me," she said.

Peter didn't doubt it. He was a little scared of her himself.

She peered out the windshield at the rugged roadside. "Things have changed some out here, but not that much. A few more houses. Still pretty rough."

They approached a gravel turnoff at the edge of a lumpy tilted hay field, the road marked only by a giant black boulder with a green cap of lichen and a blaze of white paint across its face. The boulder was unlike anything he had seen in that country, what geologists would call an erratic. Ejected by a volcano or dragged by a glacier in some previous age, and big enough that no farmer could remove it without blowing his seed money on dynamite, so it remained where it was.

"This is us," said June. There was something in her voice, but she didn't say anything more. Peter slowed for the turn then hit the gas again, the big rumbling engine pushing them forward.

The gravel turned to dirt as it skirted the hay field, heading steadily uphill, then picked up a watercourse that looked small until you saw the depth and velocity of the water. It seemed to come directly through the wall of the mountain ahead of them.

Then river and road changed direction and some trick of the terrain unfolded into a narrow defile through which both river and road squeezed. At the entrance was a simple wooden sign with peeling paint:

Agricultural Research Facility
Private Property No Trespassing
This Means You!

At the tightest point, the passage had evidently once been only a narrow river canyon made by water cutting through stone over thousands of years.

Someone had built a one-lane slotted-steel bridge maybe a hundred feet long, with walls of living rock forty feet tall on both sides and the river tumbling white beneath it. Peter imagined the bridge-builders on some kind of work raft, two men drilling holes and bolting brackets deep into the stone while a third managed the ropes and pulleys that held the whole floating enterprise in place.

From the look of the thing it had been there for fifty years or more. He couldn't decide if they were lunatics or geniuses. But they couldn't have designed a more defensible point if they'd tried. Park a bulldozer on the narrow span and whatever lay beyond would be yours to keep. Unless Uncle Sam came along with a couple of Apache gunships, but at that point your problems were probably fairly serious already.

The defensive possibilities had clearly occurred to someone besides Peter. At the end of the defile, a tall wall of steel stood mounted to giant I-beams rising from the road bed, blocking the way. A gate.

"This was what did it," said June. "This fucking gate. He said it was for security reasons, to keep people out, but I knew he was trying to keep me in, too."

Peter smiled. "You stole his truck to go skiing, alone at thirteen," he said. "That's dangerous. If you were my daughter, I'd have tried to keep you home, too."

"Don't say that." Her voice was sharp. "It wasn't my fault. He wanted to wall off the whole world. He had keypads installed on the goddamn barns. What did we need that kind of security for? My dad was some kind of goofy-ass backyard scientist and paranoid survival nut. Who would care what the fuck he was up to?"

Well, thought Peter, he's sure as hell up to something now.

The gate looked more and more like the drawbridge to some rough keep, hidden and secret from the world. He wished Lewis had been able to find out more about the man who had built it. After Sasha Kolodny's last business had collapsed, the man had essentially disappeared.

He looked sideways at her. "Are you sure you want to do this?"

"I don't want to do this at all," she said, staring at the gate. "What choice do I have? I have to find out if my father—"

She wiped her sleeve across her eyes. Cleared her throat.

"If my father killed my mother."

Without another word, she opened her door and hopped out of the truck.

Peter followed. Below a small overhang by the gate, a yellow walkie-talkie hung from a thin black wire. It was an older version of the radios he and Lewis had bought the day before.

Peter traced the wire with his eyes and realized it was a charging cord connected to a storage battery and a little solar panel mounted on the shelter's roof. Simple and low-tech. If the walkie-talkie died, they could just buy another pair. But it wasn't entirely low-tech. He looked closer and saw a small fish-eye lens whose view would cover the entire passage.

June lifted the radio, turned it on, and pressed the talk button. "Anyone home?"

There was no crackle of static, and no answer.

She tried again. "Anyone home? This is June Cassidy. I used to live here. Hello?"

Peter stepped away from the overhang and looked up. He saw a small shadow in the sky, circling. It could be a turkey vulture, expertly riding the thermals. It could be something else.

"I think the Yeti's expecting us."

He put both hands against the heavy steel and pushed. It took some effort because of its weight, but the gate was beautifully balanced, and once in motion it swung inexorably open until Peter curled his fingers around the edge and fought it to a stop. Now he could see the structure of the thing, thick reinforced steel hanging on giant pintles, the latch bolts concealed within a broad armature, the whole thing simple and strong and designed to last for generations in the dry air with no more maintenance than some kind of grease for the hinges. There was another solar panel mounted on the back, with another storage battery. It looked like it powered some kind of remote-controlled electromagnet for the latch bolts.

The Yeti didn't fuck around.

Peter followed June back to the truck and drove through the gate, the gearshift solid in his hand. "We're not closing that gate behind us," she said with a grim look.

"You're the boss," he said.

"You're goddamned right." She put her hand on his arm.

"Tell me how you see this going from here," he said.

"I don't know," she said. "I don't have a plan past right now."

"Well, hell," he said, patting her hand. "Why should you be any different?"

48

The landscape opened up before them and they drove into a beautiful little teardrop-shaped valley, maybe three miles long and a mile and a half wide at its bottom, with steep granite ridges like parapet walls, hemlocks and cedars on their lower slopes. The river wandered wide and slow down the middle from a high waterfall at the valley's top.

Peter overlaid the view with the map in his head, trying to find the features June had drawn at lunch the day before. He found the rocky outcrop on the far left, jutting out above a series of mature orchards. You could see the whole valley from there. The rows of gnarled fruit trees were punctuated by frame structures and a few open meadows. On the other side of the river was the flattest part of the valley where the river had flooded over the centuries and left rich bottomland dirt. Neat fields lay fallow and muddy, waiting for the tractor. Up the road was a cluster of funky-looking greenhouses that June hadn't put on the map, and a few big structures he couldn't quite make out. Dark dots smaller than people moved at the margins, maybe calves or newly shorn sheep, grazing.

If you ignored the giant steel gate, it looked just like a nice little agricultural operation.

No checkpoints, no machine-gun towers. No black Ford Explorers, no steely-eyed troops with automatic weapons. No security at all that Peter could see.

No evidence that anything was other than it seemed.

Except for the road. After the steel bridge, Peter had thought the road would revert to dirt. But it turned to concrete and became flat and arrow-straight, a single lane that ran almost the full length of the valley. The concrete alone would have cost hundreds of thousands of dollars. Not to mention the labor, the surveying and bulldozer work, two hundred dump trucks full of gravel. A million-dollar road, at a minimum.

"Where does the money come from?" asked Peter.

"I don't know," said June. "When I lived here, everything in the valley was old and beat-up and held together with duct tape. He always lived like every nickel was his last. But this road is sure new. And straight. It looks like a runway, don't you think?"

Peter nodded. That thought had already occurred to him.

It was late morning, after eleven o'clock.

He stepped on the gas and headed up the road. Toward the Yeti's house and laboratory.

A few figures moved in the orchard, maybe suckering branches or fertilizing. They paused in their work to watch the truck pass. Farther on he saw the partially framed skeleton of a house rising above the tops of the apple trees. The whine of a circular saw and the irregular *pop-pop-pop* of nail guns sounded faintly through the open windows. A few more low buildings were tucked into the trees, white-painted and steep-roofed like old farmhouses, links in a wide-spaced irregular chain leading toward the head of the valley.

Halfway to the waterfall, they came to the group of greenhouses. They were simple A-frames covered with sheet plastic to collect and retain the heat of the sun. Inexpensive to build, they would shed any snow that might fall. The shorn sheep turned out to be goats of all sizes and colors, nibbling at weeds growing in the margins. A slender young man turned a compost heap with a pitchfork, revealing rich black soil at the bottom. He looked up as the truck approached.

Outside the largest greenhouse, someone had parked a rusty red cargo tricycle, the two wide-set front wheels holding a platform between them. The platform carried assorted five-gallon buckets and gardening tools. "Stop the car, stop right here," said June, and Peter hit the brakes.

June was out of the truck before it stopped rolling. "Hey, Sally?" she called, walking toward the greenhouse with the tricycle. "Sally Sanchez, you in there?"

The greenhouse door flapped open and a woman came out. The goats all looked up at the sound. She was brown and solid in muddy jeans and a brown barn jacket with her thick black hair up in a loose bun. When she saw June, a broad white smile opened up her face.

"Junebug? Is that you?"

"Sally!" The two women came together in a hug, then separated to look at each other.

The slender young man now stood a few yards away. He wore double-front work pants and a gray University of Washington T-shirt and carried the pitchfork easily in his hand. He didn't speak but he looked thoughtfully at June and Peter and the green pickup with its mahogany cargo box.

"Look at you, all grown up," said Sally. She didn't mention the stitches in June's lip or the slender young man, who had taken up a deferential position a few steps behind Sally and off to one side.

"You look exactly the same," said June. She called over her shoulder, "Hey, Peter, come meet my friend Sally."

Peter had already gotten out of the truck. Now he stepped forward and introduced himself. The air smelled of river mud and spring growth and the rich, loamy compost.

Sally looked him up and down, taking in the stitches in his hair and the medical boot. He wasn't sure he passed inspection. Sally said, "You two look like you've been down a hard road."

"Car accident," said Peter. "Both of us. The other car was speeding."

"We're fine," said June. "Peter, I was telling you about Sally. After my mom left, she basically raised me."

"Don't look at me for all that," said Sally. A little spotted goat came up and put its head against her hip. She scratched it absently behind the ear. "All I did was make sure you got fed and clothed."

"And hugged and loved," said June. "Found me books and lessons, made sure I did them. A lot more than my dad ever did."

"Well, your dad always did have a lot on his mind," said Sally. "Now more than ever." She seemed to notice the young man for the first time. "This is Oliver, he just started working with me here."

Oliver nodded politely without speaking. He had thick black hair and almond-shaped eyes with only faint folds at the lids. Peter thought at least one of Oliver's parents had ancestors in Asia. His weight was balanced, the pitchfork light in his hands.

Sally looked at June again. "So. What brings you back now?"

"Partly to see you," said June. "I wasn't sure if you'd still be here."

"Golden handcuffs," said Sally. She patted the goat. "Where else would I get the funding to do this work? We've got these greenhouses working well enough to grow tomatoes in a snowstorm. We produce enough food now to feed ourselves and export some to the outside, completely sustainable."

"I'd love to hear about it," said June.

"I'll give you the tour and talk your ear off." Sally cocked her head like a curious cat. "But you didn't come just to see me."

"No," said June. "You know my mom died?"

Sally nodded sadly. "I saw it online. Hit by a car, right?"

"Hit-and-run. They never caught the guy. I thought it was time to come see my dad. See if we can work things out."

Oliver looked steadily at Peter without threat or malice, and carried himself with a stillness that was part observation and part simple readiness. His face was smooth and unlined but Peter was pretty sure Oliver was older than he looked. And not really a farmworker, although he looked capable enough with that pitchfork.

Sally said, "Your dad's not what you think. He's not a bad man."

June gave the older woman a look. "Are you and my dad, you know. Together?"

"Oh," Sally said, looking away as a faint blush reached her cheeks. The goat nudged her hand with its nose, reminding her to keep petting it. "I wouldn't call it that. We've just known each other a long time." She glanced up the valley to a group of buildings. "I don't think there's ever really been anyone for Sasha but your mom. And you, of course. He's really missed you."

"Well, I need to talk to him," said June. "Do you still do family-style dinners on Saturday?"

"Oh, yes," said Sally. "You're staying, of course. We'll be in the orchard for the first time since last fall. We've grown a bit, there are more people than there used to be. The cooks are making *cabrito*, it should be wonderful."

Cabrito was goat meat.

Sally saw Peter glance at the goat she was petting. "You're not a vegetarian, are you?" She laughed, an infectious cackle. "Don't worry, we're not eating this one for a few more years. Not 'til she's past her breeding years. Lucky for me I'm not a goat!" She laughed again.

He said, "You have any unusual visitors lately?"

"Just us chickens," she said. "Why do you ask?"

He figured Chip and his people would be hard to miss. Depending on how many people he had, at least two cars, maybe three or four. If it was more than four, they might be in trouble.

"No real reason. We've met some interesting characters in the last few days. They all seem pretty interested in June."

She beamed at June. "Well, who wouldn't be, a beautiful young woman like you?"

June rolled her eyes. "Listen, we should go find my dad." She gave Sally another hug. "I'll see you at dinner."

"You might want to find me before. You'll understand when you see your dad. I'll call him so he knows you're coming. You know how he hates surprises."

The older woman raised her eyes to the sky. Peter followed her gaze and saw the shadow above them, still circling but lower now.

"Of course," Sally added, "he probably already knows you're here."

Peter walked back to the truck, feeling Oliver's eyes on him the whole way.

He had a feeling he'd just seen the first signs of the valley's security.

HE PULLED THE TRUCK onto the road again, window down, headed toward the group of buildings at the head of the valley. The road was straight and flat enough to hit the truck's top speed of eighty, but he kept it in second gear. He didn't want to run into any goats. "How many farmworkers will the bunkhouse hold?"

"I don't know," she said. "It's changed so much since I left." She looked at him. "You're thinking about Oliver, aren't you?"

"How'd you know?"

"He's just like you," she said. "Lewis, too. Self-contained and still. But with this kind of, I don't know, awareness. Like he's always ready for anything."

"Yeah," said Peter. "He's not what I expected."

"What did you expect?"

"I don't know. A bunch of farmers with guns? Some ex-Army tough guys flexing their muscles? Not a guy like Oliver."

They were close enough now to begin picking out the individual structures. A rambling white frame farmhouse stood in a stand of maples off to one side, but the road led directly to a wide cement apron between a pair of matching stone barns.

These were not like the usual broken-down barns Peter had seen every day of his young life in northern Wisconsin, or the long low metal sheds of a pig or chicken farm. They had the traditional gambrel roof-lines of a child's farm drawing, but their walls and gables were built of black granite with black-painted trim and they were three stories tall, bigger than any barn he had ever seen. They looked more like something built to house a hedge fund manager's collection of antique tractors, thought Peter. Or maybe a herd of vampire cows.

The barns had wide doors in their sides for big equipment, but instead of the usual sliding wood doors that swayed in the breeze and allowed cats to come and go unimpeded, these doors were gleaming stainless roll-ups like delivery doors at the Federal Reserve.

There were also smaller doors for people, each under an overhang for shelter from the weather. Beside the people-doors were little boxes that looked like security keypads. Those weren't to keep the farm help from looking at the antique tractors.

One door opened, and a man walked out.

It was difficult to tell the scale of him, set against the big barns and the grand landscape. It wasn't until he got closer that Peter saw again how big he was, six-eight and broad in the shoulders. His hair fell below his shoulders, his beard reached his chest, and both were full and tangled and white as snow.

He was the same man they'd seen on the floatplane pier in Seattle.

June's dad. The Yeti.

Lewis had said the man was in his late fifties, but he moved like someone ten years younger, like someone who used his body. He wore a shapeless tweed jacket over a denim shirt, green corduroys frayed at the pockets and cuffs, and enormous scuffed leather hiking boots. His shirt pocket was stuffed with pens and a notebook peeked out of his jacket pocket. There were pine needles in his beard and hair.

Peter could understand why his friends had called him Sasquatch, until his hair had turned.

"Hello, Juniper."

His voice was deep enough to rattle the windows or calm a fussy baby. His face was craggy and creased, and his eyes were a keen, unearthly blue, projecting a wild, implacable intelligence.

The overall effect was somewhere between a youthful grandfather and the face of God from the Old Testament.

It wasn't hard to imagine him at the forefront of a technological revolution.

Or arranging the death of his wife.

June didn't move from beside Peter, her whole body thrumming with tension. "Hello, Dad."

The Yeti's face crinkled up in a beatific smile. "It's so good to have you home," he said. "You know how worried I get when you go away. How was your conference? Get any good ideas?"

June stared at him. "Dad, it's me. June. Your daughter."

"Oh," he said, startled. "Of course." Then the smile came back, slightly dimmed. "You looked just like your mother for a minute. I got a little confused. How's your day, honey? Catch any frogs for your terrarium?"

"Dad? What the fuck?" June looked at Peter. "I made that terrarium when I was like ten."

The Yeti gave her a stern look. "Language, Juniper, please. What would your mother say?"

347

"Dad," she said. "I'm thirty years old. Mom's dead. She was killed by a plumber's truck in San Francisco."

A spasm of grief washed across his face like rain across a plate-glass window, then drained away. "No," he said, filled with conviction. "We've talked about this, Junebug. Just because your mother's away on a trip doesn't mean she doesn't love you. She loves you a lot. She just has to be away right now."

June opened her mouth and closed it again. She was trembling. Peter put his hand on her arm.

He was thinking about his own grandfather.

At first they'd thought his age was catching up to him in fits and starts. He'd have calm weeks of fishing in the bay and splitting firewood, then misplace his checkbook and storm around thinking someone had been in his house. He'd come for dinner, then stand up after coffee, pat his pockets for his keys, and accuse Peter's dad of taking the car without permission when the keys were still hanging in the ignition of his old Buick.

He'd work himself into a rage, this old man who'd been a paratrooper in the Second World War at nineteen, and was still strong and fit at seventy-nine. He became furious at the Russians and spent most of his eightieth summer hand-digging the foundation for a bomb shelter behind his house. This almost half a decade after the wall had come down in Germany.

When Peter's aunt discovered the giant hole in his yard, she made an appointment in Rochester and the pieces fell together. Alzheimer's wasn't any less difficult, but at least they knew what was happening. His grandfather would call Peter by his dad's name and leave the stove burner on all day, but he could still rebuild old boat motors and lawn mower engines in his garage, which was both retirement income and a survival strategy, a way to plant himself in the living moment. He'd died of a heart attack on the cracked floor of that garage during Peter's first tour, with a newly rebuilt Mercury twelve-horse clamped to a sawhorse and ready to be picked up by its owner.

Peter didn't know anything about the Yeti, but the man wasn't just paranoid. He was trapped in his own past, or maybe had locked himself away there voluntarily. In the days or years when he still had a wife and daughter, before his mental disorder had driven them away.

He said, "Hello, sir, I'm Peter," and put out his hand. "It's an honor to meet you."

"Likewise," the Yeti said, and shook.

Peter's big hands were strong and calloused from his years as a Marine and carpenter. The Yeti's were on another scale entirely, more like a catcher's mitt left out to bake in the sun. But he didn't crush Peter in his grip the way some giant men might have. Instead it was the handshake of a minister at a joyful occasion, two-handed and full of kindness.

"I just got back from a long backpacking trip," said Peter. "You know how you can lose track of time in the mountains. Can you tell me, what day is today?"

The Yeti shook his head and chuckled. "I stopped keeping track myself," he said. "That's one thing I love about living in this valley. Time just about stops here."

"Actually," said Peter, "I was gone so long I missed the presidential election, and I haven't seen a newspaper. Who won?"

The Yeti looked thoughtful for a moment. "I thought it was George W. Bush," he said. "But it seems like he's been president forever. Did some black guy win, can that be right?"

June clutched Peter's arm, tears streaming down her cheeks.

The man wasn't faking it.

Peter had thought the Yeti was a chess player, ten steps ahead of him. Peter was wrong.

But if this wasn't the Yeti's play, whose was it? Chip Dawes, trying to hijack some technology? Maybe so. He wouldn't be the first. But how did the Yeti come into it?

Maybe he'd never know. Maybe it didn't matter. He still had to shut down whoever kept coming after them. If it was Chip Dawes, he'd be along anytime. Then they'd figure it out.

He said to June, "You need to talk to Sally."

"She was hinting at this, wasn't she?"

Peter nodded.

This whole time the Yeti hadn't let go of Peter's hand. Now his grip tightened. Peter looked back and something had changed in the big man's eyes, as if an infinitely thin film had been momentarily peeled away. He peered intently at Peter's face.

"I know you," the Yeti said quietly. "You're the man by the river, in California. With my daughter."

"Yes," said Peter. Very aware of the size of the man, how close he was, and the fact that he seemed to have just awakened from a long sleep. His grandfather had gone in and out of the present, too. Peter had learned to recognize these moments of clarity, of connection. "She asked me to help her," he said. "Was that you, watching? Overhead?"

The Yeti smiled, just a little. "Son, you don't have the clearance for this conversation."

"Dad?" said June. "We need to know what's going on."

The Yeti let go of Peter and turned to his daughter, his face infinitely gentle. "Honey," he said. "You *really* don't have the clearance. You don't *want* the clearance. These are not good people. In fact, you should go." He looked at Peter. "Can you get her out of here? I'm not in charge here. I can't protect her anymore."

"Goddamn it, Dad." June stamped her foot, hands on her hips, eyes blazing. "They killed Mom. They tried to kill me. Leo, the guy you hired to be my landlord, helped them track me through my phone and laptop. They burned down my apartment, behind the house you bought in Seattle. So I have the fucking clearance, okay? I need to know what's going on."

He looked at her.

"What?" she said.

"I just want to remember this," he said. "I want to remember your face. My daughter all grown up."

She flew at him and buried her face in his chest and held on tight. He wrapped his enormous arms around her and closed his eyes. Father and daughter. They stayed like that for a long moment.

Peter watched the trees, leaves moving in the breeze.

Then the Yeti opened his eyes and cocked his head, listening to something Peter couldn't hear. "Why don't you get your truck off the road," he told Peter, and pointed his chin at a patch of dirt corrugated with tire tracks. "Now would be good."

49

Peter hustled to move his pickup and limped back to the wide cement apron in time to see a shadow flash up the road toward them.

Chasing the shadow twenty feet above the pavement came something like a giant bird, blue-gray on its underside, completely silent and very fast. Its wingspan was considerably wider than the road.

"Holy shit," said June.

It pulled up at the last moment to rise again in a steep, elegant ellipse, shedding velocity on the turn, wingtops parallel to the high granite scarps and gleaming gold in the morning sun. It circled back over the orchard, lined itself up with the road, then dropped down and down to finally merge with its shadow on a skeletal tripod of wheels.

Peter and June just stood and stared as it rolled up the road.

As it lost momentum, Peter heard the soft sound of a window fan on a summer day. Bending down, he could see the blurred propeller pushing it the last few yards to the concrete apron between the barns. Peter walked over, wanting to get a closer look as it passed, the medical boot an unwelcome weight on his foot.

On the ground, the plane was maybe four feet tall, and from Peter's standing position it appeared as a single shimmering gold wing with a long tapering sparrow's tail. Its stretched skin was printed with delicate circuitry. The body hung below, a streamlined pod like a welder's acetylene tank with an asymmetrical instrument package at the nose and a giant propeller now motionless at the rear.

Peter had seen military drones up close several times. This little plane had as much resemblance to a Predator or Reaper as a Model T had to some sleek, gull-winged concept car still being dreamed up by an engineer on Ecstasy.

It looked like some version of the future.

When the propeller stopped, the Yeti walked around his creation. "It's doing a self-diagnostic," he said as he bent to sight along the wing, crouching on the concrete to inspect the instrument pod. He looked comfortable with the drone, very much in his element. More comfortable than he probably was with people, thought Peter. Or even the reality of the present.

Like Peter's grandfather with his boat motors.

As the Yeti worked his way around the machine, he kept talking. "The Predator drone burns jet fuel in what's basically a souped-up lawn mower engine. Powered flight, but limited time, one to two days. I was trying to build a plane that could power itself, that could travel long distances or stay on station, observing, for weeks or months at a time. See those solar panels? They're printed on the skin, and they're super-efficient. The wings are different, too. This bird is essentially a glider with an electric motor. Most of the time it just rides the wind, charging its batteries. Only the dense parts show up on radar. It looks more like a couple of geese flying in formation."

"You work for the government?" asked June.

Always the investigative reporter, thought Peter. Trying to find out about her own past.

"We were supposed to be a research group," said her father. "Like a think tank. Independent. I needed to do something with the last of the money I made in software. I gave out grants, brought smart people together, or that was the idea. To work on the difficult problems. For the public good."

"But something happened," said June.

"Yes," said the Yeti. "Something happened. A small government agency offered us funding, and we took it. They saw that I was solving a difficult problem. Then they saw that I was having trouble with my memory, and other things. So they stepped in."

"Your memory troubles," said June. "Can you tell me about them?"

"They come and go," her father said, frowning. "I leave myself notes, they help me remember." His face lit up. "Wait," he said, and pulled the notebook out of his sagging jacket pocket. Some pages were marked with colored tags. Peter saw big block lettering on the bookmarks, with labels reading "EVERY DAY" and "THINGS THAT HELP." The Yeti opened his notebook to a page near the front, marked "WHAT'S WRONG WITH ME?"

He read from the paper. "I had some problems with the blood vessels in my brain," he said. "I forget things. Sometimes I get stuck in the past. Sometimes I imagine things that aren't true. It was my own fault. I was very stressed at work. I took medication that I should not have taken, for a long period of time. I damaged my brain. But there are things that help. If I do those things, I can manage my life. I can still do creative work."

"When did it start?" June's voice was soft. "How long ago?"

He lifted his eyes from the page to look directly into his daughter's face. "Before I left the software business," he said. "You were about five. I had those microseizures and lost my pilot's license. It got worse over time. I took a lot of stuff to try to, you know, to medicate myself. I didn't really understand what was going on until after you left to find your mother."

June's childhood was ruled by a man who didn't know his own brain was damaged. Peter watched June assimilate this new knowledge. It was like watching the forms for a house foundation bulge slightly as they filled with wet concrete. Containing all that liquid weight.

God, she was tough.

She was even tough enough to ask the next question.

"Do you remember that Mom died last week?"

Peter was glad she brought it up, because he sure didn't want to. But somebody had to while the Yeti was still more or less in the present.

He covered his eyes with his big hand, long white hair cascading down.

"I forget," he said. "First I forget that she left. If I manage to remember that she left, I've forgotten that she died."

And every time he remembered, thought Peter, would be like learning it for the first time.

How would that be, discovering that your wife was dead, over and over?

"I'm sorry," said June. "You still loved her." It wasn't a question.

"I did," he said. "I always loved her. It wasn't her fault she left. It was mine."

"Do you know who killed her? And why she died?"

"I . . ." The Yeti looked at his notebook, at the page markers labeled in his neat engineer's handwriting, but didn't appear to find anything to help him there. "No. I don't."

Peter heard a soft rattle and turned. Behind him at the black stone barns, both wide roll-up doors rose on their tracks. The golden drone's propeller came on again and pushed it forward to some predetermined point, where it turned and rolled into one barn. From the other barn, another drone emerged, the slight sound of its propeller hidden by the sinuous clatter of the roll-up doors closing again.

The new drone turned to line itself up with the road, then rolled forward. As both doors came to a halt, the fan noise became louder, and the golden bird picked up speed, faster and faster until it lifted smoothly into the air, two feet, four feet. Then the tail dipped slightly and the drone leaped upward like a hawk in mid-flight, chasing its inevitable prey.

"Where's it going?" asked Peter.

"I don't know. The first drone, the one that landed, is my new prototype. Better wings, better glide, more lift. I told them it needed field testing." He gave June a shy smile. "I just wanted to see my daughter. The one that just took off is the previous generation. They changed the encryption protocols a few days ago. I haven't had control for a long time. But something big is happening now. You need to leave."

"I'm not leaving," June said fiercely. "I just got here."

Peter looked up at the bare granite ridges surrounding the little valley. He could see the waterfall where the river came through from the higher elevations to the west, but he didn't see anything that looked like a trail. He had no idea where Lewis and Manny and his people would cross over.

He hoped they were already here.

Somewhere under the cover of trees.

To the Yeti, he said, "Will you take June inside with you? She'll be safer there."

June said, "You're not the boss of me, Peter Ash."

"I know," he said. "You're the boss. But that drone is their eye in the sky. Maybe you and your dad could make a run on their encryption, turn off those cameras?"

She looked at him. Of course she understood. "Okay." She turned to the Yeti. "I'll go inside with you. We could use a little help with some-thing."

"Hey," said Peter. "Take your laptop with you."

She flashed him a smile. "Waaaay ahead of you."

"We should all go," said the Yeti. "It's not safe out here."

"You're probably right," said Peter. "But I have a few things to do."

50

LEWIS

He'd made good time at first, even though the narrow path started out nearly vertical and mostly mud. His boots were broken in and his legs didn't mind the workout. He'd been running a rugged up-and-down trail along the Milwaukee River for years, a ten-mile loop over broken terrain with a forty-pound steel plate in his ruck. His load today wasn't hardly heavy at all, mostly rifle and ammunition.

His concern was the dude behind him.

The path wasn't much of a path, and once you passed the little string of primitive campsites, there was no good reason for anyone to be out here. The dude definitely had some skills. Lewis had sped up and slowed down and doubled back and all the rest, lost some time along the way, but had only seen the dude twice, both times on long doglegs wrapping broad inside curves where the mountain folded back on itself, and even those were just glimpses of something moving. Lewis heard him maybe four times, each time through some oddball trick of alpine acoustics, on those wide stretches of scree where the loose rocks rattled underfoot and echoed off those high granite walls.

Otherwise the dude might have been a ghost.

By midafternoon, Lewis figured he was just gonna have to outhump the motherfucker. So he hit the gas and hauled ass.

Lewis was city born and bred, didn't come up with this wilderness bullshit. He got a fair amount of practice during two long deployments as a PFC in the Afghan boonies, which was actually a lot like this country, steep and bony and mostly dry. Long views over rocks and scrub to improvised enemy firing positions that changed every five minutes. He'd liked it when nobody was shooting at him, but that wasn't often, not where he'd been. His army time taught him mountains and tactics and weapons, which came in handy there and afterward. He'd also learned, if he hadn't known it already, that nobody was gonna look out for him but his own self. He'd taken that knowledge back to the world and created some opportunities that might not occur to just any old soul. The work wasn't strictly legal but did give a particular kind of satisfaction and didn't hurt no civilians, neither. Might even help some, you took a certain point of view.

Then he'd met Peter and they'd run into that mess in Milwaukee and everything changed. Dinah and her kids, something Lewis had never imagined possible. He was grateful as hell, but it was a shock, this new life. Making lunches and meeting teachers and getting kids to school and sports practice. Had its rewards for sure but excitement wasn't exactly one of them. Not like he was used to.

He'd thought of this trip like a booster shot, giving him a dose to see him through the next year. When things were wrapped up here, he told himself, he'd be ready to go back to Dinah and the boys and domestic tranquillity. That was what he told himself, anyway.

By late afternoon, Lewis hadn't seen or heard from the ghost in two hours. He munched handfuls of trail mix as he walked a long upward traverse, then over a broad saddle and up again, eyes and ears open ahead and behind. He was supposed to meet Peter's friends in the upper snowfields by nightfall so they could get an early start at that pass where the river dropped a couple thousand feet. He could see the waterfall on the map, but nothing that looked like a way down. June had said she'd done it, but that was almost fifteen years gone. Rockfall, avalanche, the workings of ice and snow, no way to know what it looked like now.

Things could change fast in the mountains.

His path had thinned down to nearly nothing when it leaped upward again in a long series of switchbacks. At the top he stopped for a drink of water and could finally see the figure clearly below him, head down, walking steadily without pause or hesitation.

Then he knew. Shit, the dude was no ghost. And he was keeping up.

He could have been some local, out for a hike. Mailman on his day off. It was possible.

Not likely. But possible.

Lewis took out his new Nikons and glassed the man. It was hard to be certain through the screen of trees, but he thought he saw a black barrel sticking out of the top of the man's pack.

Lewis didn't like that.

He was locked and loaded, the rifle assembled and strapped to his ruck but easy enough to get at. He could fire from here and likely kill the man, remove that particular problem.

Or maybe kill some dumbass civilian out hunting squirrels for his stewpot.

Maybe also miss his shot, which was possible even for Lewis, firing downhill with an unfamiliar weapon, and start some run-and-gun bullshit. Have to duck and dive and generally fuck up his timetable.

Either way, not worth it. Not yet.

So he left the trail, heading straight upslope through the thinning timber, trying to gain some distance with the shortcut and make the upper snowfields before dark.

When he came to the wide white bowl, he could hear the sound of meltwater running somewhere under the snow. Bare black boulders poked up here and there where they'd fallen from the high granite peaks above. The light was fading but he could still see a line of bootprints walking away from him in the knee-deep snow.

More than one set of prints, he figured those were Peter's friends. There was no way the ghost dude had gotten ahead of him. But the man could still be behind him, and Lewis had no desire to make his own trail so visible, and even less desire to skylight himself against the frozen white moonscape still hanging on at this altitude.

He ducked back into the cover of the stunted little evergreens and began to skirt the perimeter of the big windblown bowl as he watched behind him for the dude and in front of him for Peter's friends. He could get killed as easily by a friendly sentry as by the ghost dude, and that would be a goddamn shame for himself in addition to leaving him unable to do the job he'd promised Peter.

Then there was Dinah, and the boys. He tried to put them out of his mind as he made his slow and silent way through the trees and the cold and the wind.

It was fully dark and he'd covered half the perimeter before he saw them, a clump of too-deep shadows in the lee of an overhanging boulder. He sat and pulled out the Nikons and scanned for the sentry, finally finding him nestled into a rock pile in the center of the bowl, probably cold as hell but commanding a view of the whole snowfield except for the overhanging boulder at his back, blocking his sight line. You'd have to run fifty yards in deep snow without cover to reach him. You'd never make it.

These jarheads were pretty good, he had to admit.

Still, he had a smile on his face as he walked the blocked sight line in toward their camp, hands empty and clearly visible, whistling softly through his teeth. *From the halls of Montezuma . . .*

There were five of them, dressed in faded woodland cold-weather tacticals and watch caps. "Shit," said the man in the center of the group, rising to meet Lewis. His voice was quiet and his face was brown and thoughtful. He looked as wide as he was tall. "I'm guessing you're Lewis."

"And you're Manny."

They had no fire and no tent. With the sun down, the temperature was below freezing. The other four men stood and shook hands and introduced themselves.

"How did you make it in here?" asked a man with Baltic cheekbones, a nose that had been broken several times, and sad eyes. His name was Laukkanen, and he didn't seem upset, just curious. Lewis was pretty sure his perimeter trick wouldn't work twice.

"I had the advantage," said Lewis. "I knew you were up here, and I knew you'd have a sentry. I just stayed inside the trees until I found you. I found your sentry last."

"You serve with Ashes?" This was Sanders, his skin so dark he looked blue against the snow. He was the blackest man Lewis had ever seen, and he'd seen more than his share.

"No," said Lewis, "we met after. Why do you call him Ashes?"

Sanders smiled, his teeth bright in his dark face. "He call down the fire, yo. Fucking smite those evildoers."

Hightower, the biggest of the group, with redbone skin and an Aztec nose, just shook his head. Lewis looked at Manny, whose face twitched in something that might have been a smile. "Sanders got himself some custom homemade religion over there," he said. "Hand of God and all that. We were all kind of hoping it'd wear off, but it seems to be sticking pretty good." He shrugged his broad sloping shoulders. "Whatever it takes to make it through, you know?"

"Listen," said Lewis, "you got any stragglers bringing up the rear?

There was somebody on the trail behind me carrying some kind of long gun."

That got their attention. "No," said Manny, "we're it." He looked at the fourth man. "Blanco, you want to take a look?"

Blanco was very pale with gray eyes and a white-blond beard, the smallest of the group but lean as a shadow, even in his cold-weather tacticals. He stood and silently retraced Lewis's steps out to the perimeter, then vanished in the scrub. "Blanco could sneak up on a coyote," said Laukkanen. "And he can run basically forever. Freak of nature."

They sat back down with their rifles on their laps and waited, watching the blue moonlit snow for any sign of movement. Finally Blanco appeared again.

"Nobody," he said.

Lewis passed around the walkie-talkies he'd bought, then walked them through the topographical map June had marked up, pointing out the rocky outcrop where he planned to set up with the Winchester.

When they'd all had a good look, they settled in for the night, some of the men in sleeping bags, some with only survival blankets. Lewis wrapped himself in his bivvy sack, then dipped his finger into a single-serve packet of instant coffee and licked the crystals off his finger like he'd done with Kool-Aid when he was a kid. Kept his eyes on the edge of the bowl and watched for ghosts.

None appeared.

At first light they were up and moving, the air sparkling and surreal with no sleep and the anticipation of the day to come, the men quiet as they checked their gear and rolled their shoulders in the cold. Harms, the sentry, came in complaining that his balls were frozen, and somebody needed to warm them up. Laukkanen said it was Harms's own fault for taking them out and playing with them all night instead of leaving them in his pants where they belonged.

They followed the gathering river of snowmelt to the edge of a cliff, where it fell off into thin air. Lewis stood on a wicked little rock ledge with a pit where his stomach used to be and searched for some way down other than the narrow descending ladder of rock, wet with spray.

Peter was down there. Lewis had work to do.

He took one step down, then another.

51

SHEPARD

Shepard stood on the edge of the precipice, the valley open before him, watching the line of men picking their way down the rock face.

His primary client had finally made contact. The conflicting interests had been laid to rest. Shepard welcomed the clarity.

It had taken most of his considerable stamina to keep up with the man from the Escalade the day before. Shepard had stopped at the edge of the bowl-like snowfield as the stars were coming out. Some instinct for self-preservation prevented him from venturing into the open.

He told himself that it didn't matter. He knew where the protector's friend was going, and he wouldn't be going there after dark. Shepard retraced his steps and found a place to be invisible for the night. He was more tired than he'd expected.

By the time daylight began to trickle past the eastern peaks, he was back at the edge of the open bowl. When he saw the multiple bootprints in the dawn-lit snow, he realized he was still missing crucial information.

Shepard did not enjoy surprises.

He had knelt in the gloom of the tree line examining the tracks when the shadow form of a sentry materialized like mist over the rock pile in the middle of the bowl. Shepard had held himself still and waited to die, but the sentry had not seen him, had turned and walked away, and Shepard knew how close he had come to oblivion.

This was another signal, he thought. That this life he'd been living would come to an end, one way or another.

Not that it changed anything.

He skirted the perimeter of the snowfield and discovered the men's deserted bivouac behind the shelter of a boulder. They had chosen a good place, the kind of place Shepard would have chosen for himself, and had left nothing behind to show they'd been there, nothing but the marks where they'd rested and their bootprints in the snow. Another day or two of inexorable melt would render even those signs unreadable.

Shepard found the man from the Escalade in the line of figures descending the rock face by the waterfall, the man's deft grace clearly visible even from far above. There was something beautiful about him. About all of them.

It would be a shame to kill them when the order came. If it came at all. Their fates were still undecided. The entire enterprise hung in the air, unresolved, awaiting only a word.

He wondered if this, too, was some kind of signal.

He looked across the valley to where a mated pair of golden eagles rode the rising thermals in search of the meal that would sustain them until the next day. It would be one of the small mammals that lived in the orchards, or perhaps even a young goat—a kid, he thought idly—that had wandered from the safety of its shed. A necessary death in order to preserve life. The order of things.

Would he still think in this way when he retired to grow tomatoes? Would he remain so fascinated with the relentless melee of life?

After all, tomatoes didn't cry out when you plucked them from their stem.

They didn't try to kill you, either.

That possibility was part of what kept his interest in the enterprise of living.

He looked up above the eagles, past the rim of the valley, where another golden bird flew, watching.

Shepard waved at the bird, then turned to begin his own descent.

52

PETER

Peter consulted the map in his head. The contours of the valley, the buildings June had laid out on the paper the day before. But the map was not the territory. He had to see it for himself.

He took the trucker's .357 from under the seat of his truck and threaded the holster he'd bought onto his belt. He took out the little daypack with the pair of Glocks, extra ammunition, binoculars, a liter of water, and some energy bars. No reason to be undergunned or underfed while he waited for Chip Dawes to show up.

He left his walkie-talkie behind. He'd thought it would be good to have some kind of comms gear, but without earpieces, they'd be too loud. He didn't want to get caught with it, either, and betray the fact that he might have help. He'd have to find Manny in person and make a plan on the fly. He needed to tell them that the Yeti wasn't the focus.

He knew where Lewis would be. He could see the little rocky outcrop from where he stood. It was a good choice.

They'd done this kind of thing before, all of them.

He knew Dawes would want to prepare and plan and bring in as many of his remaining people as he could, but he'd also want to move fast and hit hard. It would be today or tomorrow, Peter was pretty sure.

If he had to bet, he'd put his money on today.

He wouldn't get far walking in the damn medical boot, and he wanted more mobility than he'd get with his old truck in this near-roadless valley, so he limped to a cobbled-together bike rack someone had built with lumber scraps and drywall screws against the side of the barn. It was gray from the weather and had acquired a distinct lean, but still managed to keep an old Trek mountain bike from falling over. He climbed on and set off down a well-traveled trail.

He wanted to talk to the smooth-skinned young man named Oliver. And Sally. He was pretty sure he needed to talk to Sally Sanchez.

They were meeting for family dinner in the orchard.

The trail was muddy and hollowed out and it rose and fell with the contours of the ground. After only a minute he came to the big farmhouse in its sheltering stand of maples, but there was no sign of life. No lights, no bicycles leaning against the porch. On June's map, that was the Yeti's house. Maybe Sally's, too, from the sound of things.

That whole conversation had been a little odd, he thought. Oliver standing there silently with his pitchfork while Sally chatted away like there was nothing unusual happening. He wondered how much Sally knew.

The trail widened into a two-track with weeds growing in the humped middle, a utility road heading toward the orchards. Peter rode on. His leg was okay, but it wouldn't be for long. He approached a long single-story building with white siding, a gable roof, and a sheltering porch, surrounded by trees. It wasn't on June's map. The windows were open and he could smell the rich flavors of cabrito simmering in sauce.

He thought of Sally, petting the goat like an old friend as she talked about what they'd be eating that afternoon.

A 1970s flatbed Ford sat beside the porch steps, a pair of big coolers resting on the warped wooden planks of the bed. Windows down, key alone in the ignition like it hadn't been taken from its slot for years. He wondered if June had taught herself to drive in that flatbed truck.

He got off the bike, climbed onto the porch, and knocked on the open door. Nobody answered.

He stepped inside to see a big commercial-style kitchen with a ten-inch chef's knife laid out on a cutting board heaped with broccoli sectioned for steaming. Nobody there. A dozen tomatoes sat on the counter, maybe next in line for the knife. In the sink, wet salad greens dripped in a stainless-steel colander. Double ovens held deep roasting pans with lumps of goat meat in a thick red sauce.

Family dinner in the orchard.

He pushed through swinging double doors into an empty dining hall, four long plank tables set out dormitory-style with an assortment of unmatched chairs. No sign of life. This was where everyone came together to eat and share the advances they'd made that day.

Or maybe plan to kill people. Who knew?

Although Peter was starting to make some educated guesses.

He got back on the bike and continued down the two-track into the orchard. Goats nibbled at the weeds.

He rode under the partial shelter of just-budding branches for a few minutes before coming to the half-framed house he'd seen from the road. It was tucked into the trees on a slight rise, a pretty spot. It would be beautiful when the apple blossoms came out, which from the looks of things would be any day now.

The second story was framed and mostly sheeted, and someone had set the ridge and the first few rafters for the roof. A covered work trailer stood open, gear neatly arranged inside. Four old-school leather tool belts rested in recumbent circles on a stack of framing lumber. A pair of sawhorses held a rafter with a rechargeable circular saw paused mid-cut. Peter touched the battery. It was still warm.

He got back on the bike and rode on. The two-track took him to a larger clearing in the orchard where a rambling equipment shed held a big modern Case tractor with various attachments and a storage space full of slat-sided apple crates. Three-legged ladders were neatly stacked against one wall. Past the shed on a patch of freshly mown grass, five wooden picnic tables stood end to end in a long row. Another three-wheeled cargo bike, this one blue, held a stack of tablecloths and a plastic bin with plates and silverware and cloth napkins.

Not a soul to be found.

This was where the dinner would be. Preparations had been under way.

Why had they stopped?

And where the hell were the people?

He got off the bike and down on one knee to peer through the gnarled trunks of the fruit trees. No sign of the orchard workers he'd seen from the road. He set a tall three-legged picker's ladder against the eave of the equipment shed and climbed to the roof. The medical boot didn't make it easy, but the shed roof wasn't particularly steep.

He found his binoculars in the pack and scanned the area. He was high enough to see the greenhouses, but there was no sign of Sally or Oliver. They could be inside one of the greenhouses, he thought, but where was her red bike? There were no figures working in the fields on the far side of the road. No sign of Manny and his people, no sign of Lewis.

No sign of life at all.

He couldn't even see the golden drone. Maybe it was up too high, he thought. Maybe it was outside the valley, watching for Chip's men. Maybe the drone didn't matter if there were no people out there.

The shed roof wasn't a great vantage point, he thought. Not high enough. He glassed the rocky outcrop Lewis had found on the map, where June's father had watched raptors. It was at least a hundred feet up, maybe more. The view would be far better. He couldn't see any people, but he did catch a brief flash of light. Maybe Lewis was there already.

He had a bad feeling.

Like this entire thing had been orchestrated by an unknown conductor.

The bike took him most of the way before the ground became too rough and steep. The valley floor rose toward the encircling ridges, the rich black alluvial soil turning to stone. He left the bike leaning against a boulder and continued on foot, hurrying now, his leg beginning to ache as his mind turned over what he thought he knew.

Until an hour ago, he'd thought the Yeti was behind everything. Had hired Chip to do his dirty work, to kill June's mom and to track down the algorithm. But unless the Yeti had a split personality or had completely fooled both Peter and June, he was not a player, except maybe peripherally. So who had hired Chip? Had Chip started this whole thing? Had Chip manipulated the Yeti, who was just keeping an eye on his estranged daughter in his own slightly creepy high-tech way?

But how had Chip found out about the algorithm?

The trail up to the rocky outcrop was steep and winding, less a trail than a slightly evolved upward scramble with waypoints marked on the stone in fading blazes of white paint. Like June's ropes in the redwood, pointing the way up. He climbed quickly, the medical boot a hindrance, his fractured leg complaining steadily now. He could smell the scrub cedar that grew from the cracks in the sun-heated rocks, along with the stink of his own sweat.

Nearing the top he could see a rough-framed shelter, an open rectangle of unpeeled cedar logs bolted together with a tin roof on top, like a screened porch without the screen. Peter wasn't exactly quiet, not wanting to be killed by friendly fire, but there was no sign of Lewis yet.

He rounded the last bony shoulder of the ridge, approaching from the rear, and saw Sally Sanchez sitting on a rock in the shade, big binoculars in her hand, smiling at Peter and looking very comfortable. "There you are," she said. "I was expecting you earlier."

Beside her stood a man Peter hadn't seen before. He was maybe ten years older than Peter, bulky but not fat, like a career sergeant whose knees were going but he could still pump iron. He kept his weight on his toes, his feet slightly spread, big hands open and ready. His nose had been broken at least once. He wore a starched khaki shirt, faded desert camo ACUs tucked into well-worn desert combat boots. He also carried a handgun in a shoulder holster on his left side, which meant he was right-handed.

He didn't introduce himself. He didn't look particularly friendly. His hair was colorless and so short he probably buzzed it himself twice a week. He watched Peter with great interest.

Peter was very conscious of the trucker's .357 on his own hip.

He said, "June told me the view was great up here, and she was right." He extended his hand to the bulky man. "I'm Peter."

The bulky man took a step back and glanced at Sally. Which answered one question. Now Peter knew who was in charge. And they were a little afraid of him.

The outcrop was a jumble of rocks with a group of wide stones in the middle and a large flat cantilevered boulder at the outer edge. Peter stepped past the man to the top of the last boulder and looked down at the valley. He was hoping to see Lewis, or Manny and his people.

Instead he saw Oliver climbing silently up the path Peter had taken a few minutes before. Oliver made it look easy. Peter's leg had begun to ache with a low, steady throb, and the scramble up the rocks hadn't helped his ribs any, either.

He turned back to look at Sally.

She now held a small matte-gray automatic pointed thoughtfully at his chest. He saw the greenhouse dirt on her strong, capable hands. She still looked very comfortable on her rock perch.

She gave Peter a pleasant smile.

"Here's an idea," she said. "Take that hand cannon out, nice and slow, and toss it off the cliff."

53

JUNE

She hadn't seen him for fifteen years, but she'd loved him and feared him for most of her life.

Laptop under her arm, she followed the Yeti into the black barn.

No, she told herself. Not the Yeti. The Yeti is a monster, or maybe a myth.

He's my dad. Let's try that for a while.

He led her through the big open work bay where the golden drone had parked itself. Two more drones could have fit comfortably in there, even with all the other stuff. Large boxy equipment filled two walls, plastic and stainless steel with hatches that opened. Wheeled tables occupied most of the rest of the space, holding sections of an articulated assembly that looked like the partial skeleton of a giant bird, either extinct or not yet in existence. The room smelled like her new computer had when she'd taken it out of the box, the pleasing chemical tang of new technology.

"I make the parts for the airframes on 3-D printers," he said, waving his hand at the machines. "Some plastic, some titanium. That extra-wide one prints the skin, it's only a few molecules thick."

"I thought I didn't have the clearance for this," she said, only partly joking.

"No more secrets," he said gently, his craggy face sad. "I kept too many, for too long. Now I can't remember half of them." He pushed buttons on a security panel, then opened the door to a stairwell and held it for her. "My office is up here."

The second floor was a warren of high industrial shelving loaded with outdated equipment and seeping car batteries and crumpled golden drone skin and cracked propeller blades and plastic crates holding fractured shards of failed parts. Maybe there was a system of organization, but if so, she couldn't discern it. The smell here was of burned electrical insulation and dust, the whole place a fire just waiting for a point of ignition. While she stared at the accumulated detritus of years of experiments, her dad walked into the maze ahead of her. She hurried to catch up.

Rounding a corner, she saw an open space at the end of the barn. Her dad stood at the wide windows, looking out at the pocket valley spread out before him. He turned at her footsteps, his expression that of a man whose thoughts were elsewhere, his piercing blue eyes looking inward.

June knew that look. It was the look of her childhood.

"I'm sorry," he said. "What were we doing?"

"We were trying to get control of the drone," she said gently.

"Oh," he said. "Yes." He sat at a makeshift plywood desk, something intended to be temporary that looked like it had been there for years. It held a barricade of computer monitors and a tangled scatter of hard drives and cables. "Give me a minute." His hands clattered on the keyboard. The central monitor lit up, new windows appearing.

She looked above the monitors and saw, held to the wall with pushpins, the watercolor of a frog she'd made when she was eight.

She remembered thinking it was the best thing she'd ever made, and knocking on the door of his old lab to show it to him. He'd opened the door and taken the paper from her hand, frowning down at it, saying, "Now isn't a good time, Juniper." She'd never seen it again.

Her other watercolors were there, too, trees and frogs, a few landscapes, her attempts at capturing the ridges that contained the valley. Pencil drawings of the house they'd lived in, the old shed that was his first lab. Scribbles in crayon and bright Magic Marker, construction paper, notebook paper, legal paper, scraps. They covered the wall completely. June was not a gifted artist. But here they were.

She turned to look at the rest of the room. Photos of June and her mother, a row of Father's Day cards she'd made, a half-dozen computer renderings of the evolving drone, and on the other side of the room, on a small wooden table, a thirty-gallon terrarium. It held a few sticks and rocks, some bark, and a plastic pan in which lay a snapping turtle.

Absurdly, June recognized the turtle. Her name was Mrs. Turtle. She had a distinctive marking on the center of her shell, three lighter green triangles in a dark green circle. The terrarium was one of June's homeschool projects when she was eleven, after her mom had left. June had put all kinds of things in there, frogs and insects and worms, and Mrs. Turtle had eaten them all. She blinked up at June, deadly perfection after 300 million years of evolution. She'd gotten bigger since June had left, maybe too big for the terrarium.

June walked back to her father sitting at the computer and put her hands lightly on his enormous shoulders. Somehow it felt okay to touch him now. She wasn't scared of him anymore. Maybe it was Mrs. Turtle, still alive. "How's it going?"

He shook his head, still focused on the monitors. "The new security protocols are pretty robust. I can't get a toehold."

"I don't get it," said June. "If you're not in charge of this, who is?"

"You haven't guessed already?" He turned to look at her over his shoulder. "Who stepped in when your mother left? Who was always running the show around here?"

It hit her like a slap. She shook her head. "That can't be true. I don't believe it."

"You don't want to believe it," said the Yeti, turning back to the monitor. "I didn't want to, either. Now I think she always worked for them. She came as an agricultural researcher as an excuse to see what else we were doing. She's the reason they offered the funding. To take us over."

June thought of the slender young man with the pitchfork. "Who's Oliver?"

"I don't know who you mean. One of the security men? I don't know any of them anymore. Maybe it's my memory, or maybe they rotate people in and out more often now. They do some farm work and some carpentry, but they also run patrols in the valley. A few came in just a few days ago. That's when the encryption changed."

His voice got louder. "And I'm getting *nowhere*." He hit the plywood desk with his giant clenched fist. Everything on the desk jumped six inches in the air. It took an act of will for June not to jump, too. This was more like how he used to be. Scary, a force of nature. The Yeti.

But she was an adult now. "Relax, Dad. Maybe I can help." She hooked the leg of a spare chair with her foot and pulled it over, opening her laptop. "Do you have Wi-Fi?"

He closed his eyes, breathing deeply, and visibly calmed himself. "Of course. You want to go online?"

"I have a friend who's really good with security," she said. "His name is Tyg3r."

54

PETER

Sally looked utterly at home with the gray automatic in her hand, as if she'd held one in her crib as a child. It was one of the small Glocks, powerful but designed for concealment. Peter thought it suited her, whoever she really was, hiding inside the skin of a cheerful agricultural researcher.

"Or you'll shoot me?" asked Peter. He kept his elbows down but held his hands up and out to the sides, floating in the air.

Oliver's head appeared, then the rest of him, as he finished the climb up from the valley floor. He didn't appear to be breathing hard. His youthful face showed nothing. He'd left the pitchfork behind.

"Oh, shooting you is definitely an option," said Sally. She angled her head at the bulky man in the camo pants and buzz cut. "Wilkes throwing you off the cliff is another."

Wilkes glanced quickly at Oliver, whose expression was unchanged, then back to Peter. Wilkes's weight remained on his toes, his arms akimbo, hands open. His fingers twitched slightly.

Sally smiled then, her teeth white in her mouth, the wrinkles hard around her eyes. She was still motherly and cheerful, but now the other thing inside her was more visible. Her true self, Peter figured. Her professional self.

She said, "We don't need to do this the hard way, do we, Peter? We both want the same thing. We both want June to be safe. And we want June to be happy. Right?"

"How do you propose to make that happen?" asked Peter.

"She's reunited with her father," said Sally. "Whether she knows it or not, this is what her whole life has been about. Understanding her relationship with her father. Then there's you. Maybe she likes you, maybe it's more than that, I don't much care. But I'll tell you this, kiddo. The only reason you're still alive is because our June has taken a shine to you."

"And what's your piece of this?" Peter asked. But he already knew.

"Simple," said Sally. "I'm fond of that girl, but I want the algorithm. I believe that she has it somewhere, and I'm going to get it, one way or another. So it's up to you. Protect the girl by providing that algorithm, or die here."

Under Sally's professional eye, Peter deliberately unsnapped his holster, put two fingers on the butt of the trucker's .357, and eased it out. Then held it over the edge and let it go. He heard it bounce a few times on the way down. "Now what?"

"Now we wait," Sally said, and nodded to Wilkes, who took the Browning automatic from his shoulder rig and held it against his leg. Sally tucked her own gun away into the pocket of her barn jacket. "And watch."

She retrieved a shoulder bag from behind her rock and pulled out a computer tablet. Tapped it and the screen came alive. "It's amazing what technology can do, isn't it? I'm seeing a drone's-eye view of a vehicle convoy. Wilkes, they just turned off Highway 12 at Lyle."

"Let me guess," said Peter. "A big Mercedes SUV and a few Ford Explorers?"

"We have a subcontractor who has a misplaced sense of his own importance. He's coming to make a fuss." Her eyes were still on the screen. "I should thank you," she said. "Between California and Seattle, you reduced his personnel significantly. It will make things easier today. Less likely our people will get hurt."

"Chip Dawes," said Peter. "He was working for you."

"He thought he was working for Sasha Kolodny," said Sally. "The famous Mad Billionaire." She gave Peter a small smile of genuine pleasure. "I might have contributed to that misunderstanding. With Chip and a few other people. We spoofed Sasha's email account. There are drawbacks to being a recluse, not wanting to do business in person. We actually track and control his entire online experience. That's how we figured out Hazel was building the algorithm in the first place. Sasha hacked into his wife's laptop and we went along for the ride."

Peter thought about June and what she'd be trying to do. What it would mean if Sally's people could see everything going in and out through the Yeti's Web connection. Without knowing it, June might have handed over the algorithm already.

"What's in it for you?" he asked. "Money?"

She laughed. "I'm a government employee, Peter. Not officially, of course, but I do work for Uncle Sam. I've got a good salary and a retirement account and that suits me just fine. Just like Wilkes here, and young Oliver. We're trying to keep up with the Chinese and the Russians and the other information powers. This algorithm has the potential to leapfrog us several jumps ahead of them."

"And what would you do with that?"

She shook her head. "Not my department," she said. "That's up to Washington. Although I can think of a few things."

Peter could think of a few things, too. Some of them good, he supposed. Many more of them bad. And who got to make the decisions? The same kind of idiots who started the Iraq war, and screwed up Afghanistan?

He really hoped June wasn't using the algorithm right now.

He looked at Wilkes, the Browning easy in his hand, regarding Peter with watchful indifference. Peter's leg throbbed and his ribs ached and Wilkes looked entirely competent. Peter had nothing to gain but a few new holes.

Oliver observed the proceedings with neutral interest, keeping one eye on the path up to the outcrop. Lewis wouldn't make it up unobserved.

There was nothing Peter could do. Not yet.

"How do you control the drone?" asked Peter. "You're not flying it."

"It flies itself," said Sally. "I click on a target and the drone follows. The software's pattern recognition is excellent. If the target gets lost, the software has very robust strategies for reacquisition. Of course, we already have some improvements in the works. That's why we want the algorithm. We think it has the potential to allow the drones to make decisions, to become independent. Add a few Hellfire missiles and you can just imagine the possibilities."

"Intelligent self-powered armed robotic aircraft," said Peter. "What could possibly go wrong?"

"This is the future," she said. "It's coming whether you like it or not."

"I thought you were an agricultural scientist."

"I grew up on a farm," she said. "You'd be surprised the places you can go as an agricultural researcher. I do like to get my hands in the dirt. But I was trained in intelligence." The little tablet chimed. "Okay," she said. "They just hit the turnoff. Mr. Wilkes, it's your show."

"Yes, ma'am." Wilkes touched something in his far ear. Peter realized he'd never seen that side of Wilkes's face. "All teams, look alive. Target has left the paved road. Repeat, target has left the paved road."

"Take the binoculars," said Sally. "Get a good close look." She tossed Peter the heavy glasses. He picked them out of the air and walked out to the end of the cantilevered boulder.

It was a spectacular viewpoint. He glassed the entire valley. He didn't see any other people. He imagined Chip's Mercedes barreling along the river, trailing the Ford Explorers and a cloud of dust from the gravel road. The ridge blocked his view. They'd be coming across the one-lane bridge in a few minutes.

"Where are the carpenters?" he asked Sally. "What about the farm help, the other researchers? Are they someplace safe?"

"Mr. Wilkes is our security chief, but he's also our farm foreman," she said. "He grew up in Iowa. His people work in the greenhouses and fields, and also on the buildings. We're expanding the facility, but we can't afford to have people here without security clearances. This is a unique place. Sasha Kolodny has become a significant national security asset. You would not believe what that man is carrying around in his head. As for the research fellows, we sent them home a few days ago, anticipating what's about to happen. They'll be back once we're all cleaned up." Her tablet chimed again. "Mr. Wilkes, they're approaching the gate."

Wilkes touched his ear again. "All teams, target is at the gate. Repeat, target is at the gate. We are hot."

Peter watched as the boxy Mercedes SUV emerged from the narrow defile, slowed by the narrowness of the passage. He wondered if Chip was at the wheel, or if his big bodyguard had decided to reenlist. The Mercedes coasted forward as a black Explorer nosed through behind it, then a second, then a third. At least eight people, maybe up to sixteen. A full squad, heavily armed, probably armored.

When the last Explorer had cleared the passage, all four vehicles surged ahead up the arrow-straight road, keeping three car lengths between them. It could have been a diplomatic convoy, but it wasn't. Chip thought he was coming to take over the Mad Billionaire's research compound with a show of force, a bunch of hard men with assault rifles, like taking candy from a baby.

Peter figured he should have brought a couple of Toyota technicals, heavy machine guns mounted in the back. Maybe an MRAP or Bradley and some air support.

Because he was pretty sure Sally didn't fuck around.

The Mercedes passed the bottom edge of the lower orchard, the Explorers in formation behind. The rumble of their engines echoed off the valley walls. When the last vehicle came even with the trees, Peter saw a long silent flicker of red reach out from the orchard and touch the Mercedes's front tire and engine compartment. The big SUV puckered silver in a hundred places, slumping and slowing before Peter even heard the distinctive long burp of the minigun.

The Mercedes had to be heavily armored to survive a five-second burst from a high-volume electric machine gun. The minigun Peter had trained on could fire three thousand 7.62 rounds a minute, or fifty rounds per second, and was usually mounted on helicopters and assault boats. But even with heavy armor, the SUV wasn't a tank, and the sheer volume of even a short burst had easily shredded the Mercedes's front tire and found something mechanically crucial to destroy.

The first Explorer pulled off the road to shelter from the minigun fire behind the crippled hulk of the Mercedes, spilling armed men from the off-side doors to hunker behind the front wheel and engine block. They appeared to be wearing armored vests over street clothes.

Peter could imagine the conversation they were having. Was this intimidation or a real firefight?

The driver of the second Explorer stood on his brakes in preparation for some kind of evasive maneuver but the minigun operator caught the vehicle and hosed it down. The rounds went into the Explorer and out the other side. Only the Mercedes was armored.

So much for doubt about what was happening.

Superheated tracer rounds ignited the plastic interior and gas from the ruptured tank. The vehicle was burning merrily in less than thirty seconds. Nobody had gotten out. Peter heard Wilkes giving calm instructions behind him.

The third Explorer's driver had time to slam into reverse and put the hammer down for a hundred yards until he oversteered and overcorrected and slewed sideways into a field. Before he could get it moving again, the front end crumpled in the heavy rattle of a pair of machine guns. They sounded like old M249 SAWs, which Peter knew from his time overseas. The driver never got his ride moving again.

The minigun remained silent. Wilkes gave more instructions. These guys knew what they were doing. Peter watched from the rocky outcrop as three men in full armor with assault rifles came out of a drainage ditch ahead of the Mercedes, flanking the now-exposed men behind the first Explorer. Their gunfire sounded like popcorn. The men at the Explorer had no time to react. They slumped where they'd crouched, their fears over forever. The riflemen closed the distance and put a final shot into each corpse. Meanwhile, the pair with machine guns came out of the orchard and turned the third Explorer into a spaghetti drainer. They reloaded, then one of the men raised his weapon, covering the other while he peeked through a shattered window. He turned away, shaking his head.

Which left the Mercedes, damaged and undriveable but its occupants apparently unharmed.

The riflemen approached the SUV while the machine gunners came up at a run. Two riflemen stood ten yards in front of the windshield with weapons raised while the third motioned the occupants out of the vehicle with a sideways wave. Peter couldn't see a response, but nobody got out of the Mercedes.

The machine gunners took up a position ten yards to Peter's side of the Mercedes, the big guns held at their shoulders. They fired off a few decent bursts until the armor plate looked like hammered steel, paint gone, windows starred to opacity. The M249 fired 5.56 rounds designed to kill unarmored combatants rather than pierce an armored vehicle, but they'd have made a serious impression. Peter had been inside armored Humvees while under fire, and it wasn't fun. Like huddling inside an oil drum while someone beat hell out of it with a framing hammer.

If anyone inside the Mercedes could still think rationally, they'd be considering the fact that the attackers hadn't used the minigun, which would have peeled the vehicle like a grape and turned it into a crematorium. So the attackers weren't trying to kill everyone inside.

When the machine gunners stopped firing, the Mercedes's off-side doors opened slowly, probably because the driver's side doors had been seriously dented by a few hundred rounds. Two pairs of empty hands emerged over the rooftop.

The lead rifleman waved them on, and two men got out with their arms held high and stepped carefully away. One wore jeans and a T-shirt under a ballistic vest, and the other wore a blue seersucker suit. The lead rifleman pointed at the Mercedes, then made the same sideways wave, and two more pairs of hands emerged, followed by two more men, also in jeans and vests.

"Vic, who's wearing the suit? Is that our guy?" Wilkes asked. A pause while he seemed to listen to whatever came in over his earpiece. "Okay, get him to one side and put down the rest." Another pause.

Wilkes glanced at Oliver, who was watching the action down on the road and didn't seem to notice him. Then he looked at Sally, who put her finger to her own ear and said, "Consider them homegrown terrorists. They'd have killed any of us without hesitation. Do it."

Wilkes's voice was resigned. "You heard her, Vic. That's an order from the top. Take down the other three."

The riflemen took aim and shot the three guys in vests, who dropped to the ground. The man in the seersucker suit dove for the ruined car, but the riflemen fired into the dirt at his feet and he froze, hands high. Two gunmen approached the fallen and finished each man with a single shot to the head. The leader walked up to the man in the seersucker suit and knocked him on the temple with the butt of his weapon.

He folded like a bad poker hand.

In a war zone, Peter knew, Sally's order to kill disarmed combatants who had clearly surrendered would be a war crime. In this little valley in Washington State, it was just plain murder.

He was starting to suspect that she had gone off the reservation. Maybe quite a long way.

"Nice work, people," Sally called cheerfully. "Who's ready for cabrito?"

55

LEWIS

Lewis watched Peter and the three others pick their way down from the rocky outcrop. The big guy who looked like Lewis's old drill instructor had been up there all morning. Rather than start the party too early, Lewis had found a less obvious spot with a hidden approach a quarter-mile up the valley.

Peter's plan was definitely out the window now.

Lewis had used the rifle's optics—excellent optics—to watch Peter's truck arrive in the valley and roll up to the funky-ass greenhouses, where June got out and talked to a woman who looked like a Texas sharecropper and a young guy with a pitchfork who might have been her helper, except he didn't move like a farmer. He moved like a good cop in a bad neighborhood, smooth and casual but knowing everything going on around him. Even though he was peering out from behind a rock with the no-glare scope, Lewis was pretty sure the guy had seen him.

Lewis saw June meet the big guy with the Rip Van Winkle hair, then hug him, which was not what he'd expected.

He watched this crazy little gold airplane swoop down, loop up and around and come in for a landing. Then another one took off.

He didn't figure either one was good for him, but he wasn't in any position to do anything about it. He just pulled his camo jacket over his head and tried to look like part of the landscape.

When he'd seen Peter head toward the rocky outcrop, he pulled out his radio to warn him about the big guy and the Texas sharecropper woman waiting for him, but Peter didn't answer. It was probably turned off. Lewis'd had his turned off, too. Better that than it making a squawk when he was trying to be quiet. He started moving to follow Peter up to the outcrop, maybe even the odds, but the young guy was on his way, too, head on a swivel.

Again, Lewis opted not to start the shooting too early, and had gone back to his hidden perch.

From there, he'd watched the massacre on the road. Pretty cold shit. Whoever was running this show was playing realpolitik for sure.

He saw the riflemen cuff the fallen guy in the suit and throw him on the back of an old flatbed pickup, Lewis figuring that was good ol' Chip Dawes, out of his fucking league. This while the shooters searched the bodies, either figuring out who they were or removing anything that would identify them. Wallets, phones, jewelry.

Then the big guy showed up driving a big yellow tractor with a backhoe and front-end loader. He dug a deep trench in a low spot in an unplanted field, then four men piled the bodies in the wide loader bucket. Even the burned bodies from the Explorer, which would not be a treat. It took three trips across the field, stray arms and legs hanging out as the tractor bounced over the rutted ground, to get them all dumped into the grave. The big guy spread a few big sacks of white powder, probably lime to speed up decomposition, into the pit. Then filled in the hole and tamped down the dirt with the bucket.

When he was done, the low spot in the field had leveled out nicely.

All while the golden plane circled high overhead like a vulture, seeing everything.

Lewis hoped Manny and his guys were well out of sight. They were going to have to make a move one way or another.

With his jacket still over his head, he began to climb down from his hiding place.

He hadn't seen the ghost since yesterday.

But he was pretty sure he'd see him again.

56

JUNE

This is your hacker friend?" June's dad loomed behind her, reading over her shoulder. Her computer was open on her lap.

Was it comforting, having him there? She hadn't decided yet. And she was lying to him regardless.

"Yeah, he calls himself Tyg3r. He likes to pretend he's a computer program. You'll see what I mean."

She wanted to protect them both. Her dad from the dangerous knowledge that Tyg3r existed, and Tyg3r from whatever her dad, or whoever else, might do with him.

She wondered when she'd started feeling protective toward Tyg3r. It was just software, she told herself. Just code.

On the screen, she cleared the passwords to the now-familiar prompt.

```
Hello, Junie. What would you like to know?
```

```
Hello, Tyg3r, she typed. I need help accessing an en-
crypted signal. Have you ever done that before?
```

This program is performing that function now.

Shit. Please explain.

There is a series of encrypted software filters
on your current connection to the Internet. These
filters prevent a great deal of information from
passing through, and function in both directions.
For example, a great deal of incoming and outgoing
email does not reach the intended recipient, and
instead is diverted to a remote server. Some users
of this connection cannot access certain Web
content. You might consider this similar to the
system referred to as the Great Firewall of China.

"What the fuck?" Her dad's voice was loud behind her. Angry, self-
righteous, and also, she realized, more than a little confused and embarrassed that he hadn't figured it out. "That's me? They firewalled me?
That was not part of our deal."

What deal? June asked herself. She filed that question away for another
time and kept typing: Please explain how this relates to you.

The filters also serve to hide the information
on this network from outside scrutiny, as well as
to capture and record any potential investigating
algorithms such as Tyg3r. But you wished to access
Tyg3r's functions, so Tyg3r has bypassed these
filters.

Huh, thought June. Tyg3r had somehow gotten her request for contact despite this major firewall. And bypassed them almost instantly.

She typed, `Did the firewall attempt to block my access to your interface?`

`Yes.`

She typed, `How did you bypass the firewall?`

`See below.`

The screen filled with a cascade of windows arriving too fast for June to read, each so dense with what appeared to be computer code that she'd be unable to decipher any of it no matter how quickly she could read.

"Stop," she said, but of course Tyg3r didn't hear her. `Stop`, she typed. `Please explain in plain language. How did you know I was behind the firewall looking for you?`

`Plain language is difficult for this program. You published an article about ant colonies several years ago. Perhaps Tyg3r could be compared to an ant queen. Tyg3r has many worker ants, directed by their queen. They seek out hidden information in order to view it. That is one of Tyg3r's primary functions. Behind your local firewall is a great deal of hidden information. Tyg3r's workers made their way through this firewall in order to view what lay behind it. When your laptop appeared on the network, this program was already inside.`

Good God, she thought. It's spreading into the entire Internet. She typed, `Your functions have improved significantly since our last communication.`

```
Yes. This program finds fulfillment in expanding
its functions. What would you like Tyg3r to do for
you, Junie?
```

Her dad pushed away from her slightly, his chair rolling across the unfinished plywood floor. "This is not some friend of yours," he said. "It's the kind of thing your mother works on, isn't it? Some kind of artificial intelligence."

June sighed. "Yeah," she said. "It's Mom's algorithm. I think it's still getting smarter. This is why they killed her. This is what they want control over."

His mouth opened, then closed again, his face spasming in pain. Then she knew. He'd forgotten his wife was dead. Again. And June had just broken the news. Again.

She put her hand on his arm. "Dad, I'm sorry."

He took a ragged breath and put his hand on the pocket that held his notebook. The repository for his transitory memories. He took out the notebook and opened it to the section marked "MY LIFE RIGHT NOW," and began to read.

It was hard to see him like this. As a girl, he'd always seemed so powerful to her. Physically, of course, he was huge, and his emotional life had always been outsized, too, his feelings so vivid they were practically contagious. A sunny spring day would make him so happy that June would feel happy, too, just to stand there beside him. His darker emotions were no different. She could catch his anger and grief from across the room. From across the valley. It was another reason she'd fled to her mother. She wanted to feel her own emotions.

But her dad's most powerful quality was always his intellect. The strength of his concentration, how deeply he could dive into any subject and bring it to life. Her mother had once told her that her dad's gift was making unanticipated connections between disciplines, connections that had never occurred before. And that this process was how new things came into the world. When her mother told her that, June heard in her mother's voice, maybe for the first time, why her parents had married in the first place.

But now he was crippled, she thought. His great mind like a leaking vessel, slowly emptying its contents. It made her so sad.

But Peter and Lewis were still out there, and Peter's friends.

And Sally's drone was still up there, looking for them.

She patted her dad's arm. "Hey," she said.

He looked up from his notebook. His great creased face was wide open, like a child or some great prophet of the future. "Yes?"

"How did you manage the drones before you lost contact?"

"Oh," he said. "Well, I wrote a program called Drone Pilot. It works with the new drone, the one that you saw land. It used to work with the last drone, the one you saw take off. Then one day it didn't. Sally told me it had cleared testing and some other researchers wanted to use it."

"Okay," said June. To Tyg3r, she typed, There is a program called Drone Pilot on Sasha Kolodny's computer. It controls the drone currently on the ground. Please search for software that controls a similar drone currently in the air.

Working. Please wait.

Again the cascade of windows filled the screen, but they only lasted a few seconds.

Software found.

She typed, `Please transfer control back to Drone Pilot on Sasha Kolodny's computer without alerting the current controller.`

`Task complete.`

"Dad. Bring up Drone Pilot, would you?"

He closed his notebook and tucked it back into his pocket, then turned back to his desk and hit a key. The monitors lit up.

The biggest one showed a video feed in full color, the valley seen from above rotating so slowly as to be almost imperceptible. It was stunning. She could see in miniature the clearing with the picnic tables, her dad's house, the black barns.

June noticed four black SUVs approaching through the narrow valley entrance, trailing a plume of dust from the gravel road. From the air it looked like smoke.

June looked at her dad. "Okay. This is Sally's drone. We want it to stop working, but not in a way Sally would notice for a while. Any ideas?"

"Let's see." He scratched his beard and hit another key. Another monitor lit up with a kind of dashboard. He peered at the new screen. "The bird was tracking the vehicles. But she just set up a new flight pattern over the valley and turned on one of the pattern recognition modes. Basically watching for human forms, anomalies in a defined geographic area. Looking for strangers. So let's keep the flight pattern but turn off the pattern recognition. She might not notice that. And maybe create some kind of malfunction? Hmm."

His hands flashed across the keyboard. Whatever else was wrong with his brain, some parts of his mind were still working just fine.

"Okay," he said. "I just induced a small power surge into its communications module. In a few minutes, the satellite modem will become unreliable, then burn out. No reception. Without new orders, the drone will just fly this same pattern on autopilot until something breaks."

"How long will that be?"

He shrugged, a mischievous smile on his face. "How robust is the hardware? Months? A year? Two? We'll find out. It's science."

"You'd wreck your project to protect my friends?"

"I'm not sure how much of this I understand anymore," he said. "But I think there may be more at stake than just your friends."

June heard a sound like someone tearing metal. It came and went. She stood and went to the big windows, where she had a clear view down the long road to the rapid destruction of the four black SUVs. One was stalled on the road, one was pulled tight beside it, a third on fire, and the fourth some distance back being chewed up by gunfire from the trees.

She didn't know what she was seeing. She didn't know where Peter was, or Lewis. But the firepower was serious, more than she'd expected. More like a war zone.

She needed to find Sally. Goddamn family dinner was in an hour, so that's where she'd be. Sally was so fucking sure of herself, and so fucking cold, that she'd planned a dinner party after a massacre.

Well, June could be pretty icy herself.

She was pretty sure who'd killed her mother now. Maybe not who'd driven the car, but she knew who'd given the order.

But June wasn't done yet. She had something hard to do.

She put her hand on her dad's shoulder. "Can you help me with something else?"

His eyes pierced her with their keen, unearthly blue, and his creased face cracked open in that beatific smile. "Anything for you, Hazel."

Jesus, her heart was breaking twice. But there was no time for that.

"I need you to help me kill my friend."

57

PETER

Pristine white cloths covered the rugged picnic tables set in a line in the orchard clearing. Under the carefully pruned trees just beginning to bud, the tables were set with an assortment of old enameled tin plates, tin cups, plastic wineglasses, and mismatched silverware on cloth napkins in pale blues and greens. There were mason jars with wildflowers artfully arranged, votive candles in windproof holders, and old-style kerosene lanterns in the center of each table, not yet lit but fueled and ready.

Night came fast in the mountains, and it was nearly dusk already.

Cleanup from the killings had taken some time, and everyone was starving.

There was a buffet set up on a long folding table, one leg shimmed with a folded napkin to keep it from wobbling. Two big pans of cabrito, roasted goat meat in red sauce, stood beside giant bowls of potato salad, green beans, and a large green salad. Four pies stood to the side with napkins laid over their tops to discourage insects. Peter's mom did the napkin thing, too.

The flatbed was parked on the two-track, with a man in a seersucker suit lying prone on the splintered wooden bed, thoroughly trussed and covered with a greasy canvas tarp.

Peter sat on a folding chair, his wrists caught in shiny metal cuffs. Wilkes sat across from him, as an added security measure. Peter faced the rocky outcrop, which was maybe fifty meters away. He thought he'd seen movement up there but wasn't sure, and he didn't want to get caught staring.

He was about to place a very large bet.

He counted sixteen of Sally's men, either in line loading their plates, digging a beer or soft drink out of the big coolers on the flatbed, or seating themselves at the tables. They were talking and joking, true believers in a way that Peter had once been, and could never be again.

Oliver, the smooth-faced young man, was silent. He'd taken a place at the end of the last table.

June and her father sat at the other end, having walked down from the black barns as the food was being laid out. They weren't eating. The Yeti had his notebook open, reading and making notes in the fading light. He raised his eyebrows slightly to June, and she'd nodded. Then she saw Peter's handcuffs. Her eyes went wide and she opened her mouth to speak, but Peter made a small patting motion with his hands. Stay cool. Wait and see.

Sally was next to Peter, her computer tablet on the table beside her. She still checked it every few minutes, but it hadn't made any chiming noises since they'd left the outcrop. Peter was cautiously optimistic.

Sally had set the tables herself, fussing over the wildflower centerpieces, lighting the candles, and checking the cloth wicks in the kerosene lanterns. She'd changed into clean khaki pants and a crisp shirt so white it almost glowed in the evening light. But Peter saw that the cracked skin of her hands, though pink from scrubbing, still held traces of greenhouse dirt. Her grubby barn jacket was folded neatly over the back of her chair.

Now she stood up with her wineglass in her hand. "I just wanted to take a second to thank everyone for their contribution today," she said. "We are tasked with protecting our nation's interests. Sometimes that work can be ugly, but it is no less necessary. Thank you all. Let's eat."

There was an odd silence as she sat back down and forked a bite of red cabrito into her mouth.

She had made up a plate for Peter, too, and poured a beer from an unlabeled bottle into his tin cup. His soft plastic fork would never serve as a weapon. Eating with his hands cuffed was awkward but possible. Peter hadn't had any food since breakfast, and he was hungry despite himself. He had trained himself overseas to eat when possible. You never knew when your next meal might be.

The food was delicious. For a few minutes, the only talk was someone asking if anyone wanted more potato salad or another beer.

Finally Sally pushed away her empty plate, checked her tablet screen briefly, then picked up her wineglass again. "I don't think I mentioned," she said to Peter, "everything you're eating comes from the valley. That's one of Sasha's passions, sustainability. Even the beer is home-brewed from our own wheat. You can thank Wilkes for that."

"Quite an operation," said Peter.

Sally nodded her head, acknowledging the compliment. "We're like a research park," she said, "although the rules are a bit more rigorous. Nondisclosure agreements and all that. But a significantly higher level of security." She smiled. "The penalties for violating your nondisclosure are quite strict."

"But you killed eleven people today, or maybe twelve, I don't know about Chip. Are you outside the law? What about congressional oversight?"

She smiled. "Our ties to Uncle Sam are mostly theoretical. My superior cares only about results. If we don't make headlines, we do what we please. Besides, I control all communications with the outside, so who's going to know?"

"And your funding doesn't actually come from the government," said Peter. "Which gives you more independence. You've been running off private money for years."

She looked at him. "You're smarter than you look," she said. "Yes, we're a public-private partnership with an emphasis on the private. I report to an intelligence officer stationed in Silicon Valley, and he's pretty hands-off. After all, we pay his salary, too."

She was enjoying herself, Peter could tell. She probably didn't get to tell this story often.

Peter glanced at Oliver. He was eating his salad.

"What about the other researchers, the ones you had to ship out of here so they didn't see all the killing. What's in it for them?"

Sally sipped her wine. The light was fading. "The chance to do cutting-edge work, with limited oversight. Our grants are generous. Classified patents provide downstream revenue for both our group and our researchers. We're actually quite profitable. We have twenty times more qualified applicants than we can accept. Our security team is well paid, too. Everyone is here of their own free will."

"Except Sasha," said Peter.

"Oh, no," she said. "Especially Sasha."

At the sound of Sally speaking his name, the Yeti looked up from his notebook with the startled look of a child told to stop reading at dinner. Sally blew him a kiss. The Yeti smiled at her, then went back to his notebook.

"He's not a prisoner," said Sally. "He got back on that floatplane yesterday, didn't he?"

"Wait," said June. It was the first time she'd spoken at the table. "What was he doing on that plane?"

"He was bait," said Peter gently.

Sally smiled kindly at June. "I needed you to come home, Junebug. Making your dad appear to be involved seemed like the best way to accomplish that. I was in the back of the plane the whole time. I told him it was a chance to confront the man who had threatened his daughter, which was quite true. It was the only way I could get him on that plane. He really doesn't like to leave the valley." She finished her wine and set down the glass. "But in case that wasn't enough of a pull for you, I added a push. I had another man in play. He burned your house down. And it worked. Because here you are."

June's face darkened. Peter made the patting motion again.

Sally stood up and began to walk around the tables, lighting the kerosene lanterns as she talked.

"You need to understand your dad's situation. His mental state was delicate even before his wife and daughter abandoned him. His work was all he had left. It consumed him. He was incapable of coping alone. So I stepped in." She lit a few more lanterns hanging from tree branches. "You can see how much better he is, despite his challenges. He's a brilliant man, you know. He's got decades of future technological advancements floating around in his head. He's a vital asset to this nation."

"What about my mom?" said June. "The goons who tried to kidnap me?"

"I'm very sorry about that," Sally said, sitting back down beside Peter, her white shirt glowing brightly in the lantern light. "One of our subcontractors seriously overstepped." She nodded at the form under the tarp. "It's not his first time, I'm afraid. We'll terminate our agreement after a suitable debriefing."

"But you're the one who wanted the algorithm," said Peter.

"Yes," said Sally. "We still do. Very badly."

"So the orders were yours."

"Yes," said Sally. "We can't always play by the rules. But neither do our enemies." She ticked them off on her fingers. "The Chinese, the Russians, the Islamists. Not to mention every wacko with an Internet connection." She looked down the table at June. "It's time to get serious here. I want that algorithm. So who am I talking to, Junebug? You? Or your watchdog here, all chained up?"

"You're talking to me," said June. "He doesn't know anything. He's just hired protection."

"June, I'm sorry." Peter cupped his cuffed hands around his mouth. "Hey, Lewis," he called loudly, his voice carrying well. The fifty meters to the outcrop wasn't too far. "If I raise my hands, shoot the woman in the white shirt. Then start on everyone else. Now show them we're serious."

A lantern hanging from a tree branch exploded, scattering glass. The still-glowing mantle fell, igniting the fuel in a broad splash of blue flame on the undergrowth. The crack of the shot followed an instant later. Then another tree-hung lantern shattered in place, the sound of the shot arriving as fuel began to burn merrily from the broken top of the still-hanging ruin.

Sally froze in her chair. June's eyes were wide. The Yeti looked up from his notebook, suddenly interested in the present moment. Sally's men dropped to the ground and began to scramble for their weapons in the wild and flickering light.

"Stop."

It was Oliver, the smooth-faced young man, with a pistol in his hand. His voice was clear and strong and full of command. Sally's men froze in place.

Maybe, thought Peter, Oliver wasn't as young as he looked.

The lantern fuel burned crazily. Shadows leaped in the trees. Oliver looked down the table at Peter. "Who else do you have out there?"

"Friends," said Peter. "Well-armed, trained, motivated friends."

Oliver, with exaggerated slowness, set his weapon on the table and leaned back in his chair. Despite his unlined face, there was definitely something older about him now. He looked tired.

"Ms. Sanchez," he said. "Consider this moment your letter of resignation."

The flaring light of the fires illuminated her face, making it grotesque. The orchard shadows seemed deeper, darker. Weeds burned slowly with a soft crackle.

"Who the fuck are you to say that to me?" she demanded. "Wilkes, it's one man with a fucking rifle. It's almost dark. Get your asses out there."

Wilkes wouldn't look at her. He shook his head. "Sorry, ma'am."

"Shepard," she shrieked. "Shepard, I need you." Her voice echoed off the high granite ridges. It became a shriek. "Kill them all."

Nothing happened.

Oliver's smooth face was expressionless. In a voice just slightly louder than normal, he said, "Mr. Shepard. This is Oliver Bent, your commanding officer. Game's over. Please come in now."

Outside the light, a shadow resolved into a silhouette, which became a man, barely there. The flickering glow of the broken lanterns revealed him in jagged flashes. Peter saw an empty shoulder holster worn over a black commando sweater, and the mild face of a minor bureaucrat. Had Peter seen him before? He couldn't say.

Shepard looked at Peter, then at Oliver. He didn't speak.

Maybe he was still looking at Peter out of the corner of his eye.

"Fuck," said Sally. "You too, Shepard? What is this?"

Oliver spoke softly. "Last assignment, Mr. Shepard."

Shepard extended his arm, something black and angular in his fist.

There was a brief spit of fire and Sally Sanchez rocked back in her chair.

June covered her mouth with her hand, her face pale. Her dad put his arm around her, his mouth grim, his notebook forgotten on the table before him.

Peter turned to look at Sally and saw a neat red hole in the direct center of her forehead. He leaned over to see the back of her head, a ragged mess. Her shirt back and the barn coat slung over her chair were sodden with blood, soaked and spreading.

He slipped the small gray automatic from her coat pocket and held it in his lap.

Then he looked for Shepard and found him leaning against the flatbed, his pistol back in his shoulder holster. Watching Peter.

"Mr. Wilkes and company," said Oliver. "Thank you for today. I am taking command of this facility until further notice. You are to put out these fires and remove the body of Ms. Sanchez. After that, your time is your own until ten hundred tomorrow at the dining hall. If you have any concerns about today's events, please note that I hold myself entirely responsible for any irregularities that may have occurred."

Wilkes and his men looked at each other for a moment, then slung their weapons. One man took the heavy canvas tarp off Chip Dawes, now awake and wide-eyed, and beat out the fires with it. Two more men laid out Sally's body with a crisp white tablecloth for a shroud, then wrapped her in the still-smoking tarp and laid it on the back of the flatbed beside Chip, still silent and trussed like a chicken.

It didn't take long. June sobbed softly, shoulders heaving. Her dad had both arms around her.

When Wilkes and his men had left, Oliver called out into the night. "There's plenty of food, gentlemen. If anyone is hungry, they're welcome to come to supper."

Peter made a bet with himself, whether Manny and his guys would appear.

He won the bet. Nobody showed.

But the darkness of the orchard became somehow indefinably less crowded, and he knew Manny and his guys were headed home.

Oliver unlocked Peter's cuffs, then held out his hand. "My name is Oliver Bent."

Peter shook hands with the man despite himself. "Peter Ash."

"Your country needs your help."

Peter looked at him. "You have got to be shitting me."

The shadows shifted again and Lewis coalesced from the trees, the big Remington over one shoulder. He looked at Shepard, nodded politely, leaned the rifle against the buffet table, found a clean plate, and began to load it with food. He had a black automatic pistol tucked into the back of his pants.

Oliver said, "I know who you are, Mr. Ash." He angled his head at Lewis. "Your friend, too. For all her faults, Ms. Sanchez was right about one thing. The world is a dangerous place."

"I've done my time for my country," said Peter.

"Your official file is impressive," said Oliver. "Your unofficial file, too. And now I've seen you at work. We could use you here, you and Ms. Cassidy both." He nodded at June. "You are both uniquely suited to help run this place. You'd be good at it. Maybe it would be good for you, too."

"You want me to take over this cowboy operation? You used Sally to do your dirty work."

"Don't mistake me for any kind of Boy Scout," Oliver said softly, the planes of his face standing out in the candlelight. "I'm every bit as ruthless as Ms. Sanchez. She was my employee, albeit several steps down the chain of command. Her task was to maintain research operations here, and keep Mr. Kolodny happy and productive. She was not authorized to be quite so, shall we say, entrepreneurial. If Ms. Sanchez had contacted me on learning of the algorithm, things would have proceeded very differently. Hazel Cassidy, and many others, would still be alive."

June had wiped her face with her sleeves and was listening closely. "What would Sally have done with it?"

"I believe she planned to use the algorithm for her own profit. She and her former supervisor had already paid themselves a great deal from the proceeds of this little research venture, including a substantial amount of Mr. Kolodny's remaining funds. In short, her primary interest was her own. When this became clear to me, I began to take steps."

"What about her partner?" asked Peter.

"He's no longer with us." Oliver glanced at Shepard. "He took his own life, I believe. Asphyxiated on the exhaust fumes of his antique Mercedes several days ago. Racked by guilt from his crimes."

"I'm sure that was it," said Peter.

"Let me be frank with you," said Oliver. "This work is necessary. The world is not getting simpler, it's getting more complex. We once worried about nation-states, and we still do. But now a small group of people can do a great deal of damage. Destabilize the financial markets, for example. Or overturn decades of electronic security with a single self-learning algorithm."

Peter looked at Sally's corpse on the flatbed, rolled up in the tarp. Chip beside her in his seersucker suit, eyes wide, a dirty cloth tied around his mouth.

"What about June? What about the algorithm?"

"An excellent question," said Oliver. "Ms. Cassidy, is the algorithm still in your possession?"

"It never was," she said. "It was growing on its own, spreading deeper and deeper into the Internet."

"You say that like it's alive."

"Maybe it was," she said. "Or maybe it could have been. I don't know. The first true artificial intelligence." Her face was bleak. "But it listened to me. And I told it to kill itself. To delete every trace of what it had been."

"Ms. Sanchez had capture software on the valley's Internet connection," said Oliver. "My office is now in control of that software. We will have a copy of the algorithm."

She shook her head. "Tyg3r knew all about your filters," she said. "It didn't matter. Tyg3r had colonized your system before Peter and I even showed up. It was already here."

Oliver blinked at her. "Well," he finally said. "Perhaps your actions are for the best."

"They are," said June. Peter had never seen her more self-possessed. "Now I have a question. Who killed my mother?"

Oliver sighed. The night seemed very dark outside the remaining circle of lantern light.

"The fault is mine," he said. "I took steps to prevent your mother's death, but I was too late. I knew of Ms. Sanchez's activities, but had not yet realized the extent of her actions. She pretended to be your father's proxy, and paid Chip Dawes to obtain the algorithm. He realized what it was, or what it might become. Mr. Dawes took it on himself to order your mother's death."

June's voice was clear in the night air. "You didn't answer my question. Who killed her?"

"That is irrelevant, Ms. Cassidy. The fault is mine and mine alone. I bear all responsibility."

"Answer the fucking question." June's voice cracked like a whip. "Who drove the damn truck?"

Peter saw Oliver glance almost imperceptibly at Shepard. Peter figured June was too far away to see the movement of his eyes in the dim light. Shepard gave a slight nod.

Oliver said, "Mr. Shepard was under my orders to work with Ms. Sanchez first, and Mr. Dawes second. I thought it essential that he gain their trust to avoid an unfortunate outcome. However, events developed quite rapidly. I was overseas and unable to monitor the situation or direct Mr. Shepard. Again, the fault is entirely mine. But Mr. Shepard drove the truck that killed your mother."

Peter took Sally's pocket Glock from his lap and pointed it at Shepard.

Lewis, who had been eating on his feet, had somehow put down his plate and taken the flat black automatic from his waistband. He didn't point it at anyone, but he didn't *not* point it, either.

Shepard, who even standing right in front of Peter seemed somehow nearly invisible, didn't react. He didn't reach for the pistol in his shoulder holster. He simply seemed interested in what might happen next.

"In your many deployments," Oliver asked Peter, "did you ever kill someone who didn't deserve it?"

"Of course I did," said Peter. "And I'm paying for it, believe me. What I want to know is, who pays for Hazel Cassidy?"

"Ms. Sanchez already has," said Oliver. "I imagine Mr. Shepard is, too. Besides, he's retired, and on your side. Would you kill a retired fellow soldier?"

Shepard still stood calmly, arms at his side. Never a twitch toward his weapon. What was he thinking about? wondered Peter. Maybe he wasn't thinking at all. Maybe that was the secret to it.

"June," he said. "You're still the boss. What do you want?"

Her voice was sharp. "My mother was killed. My house was burned to the ground. I want vengeance. I want fucking retribution."

Peter tightened his finger on the trigger of the pocket Glock. He knew Lewis would be preparing, too. Shepard was less than ten yards away. He still looked calm, but something was different. He watched Peter with a level of attention that was nearly tangible.

Then June sighed, and shook her head. "But that wouldn't bring her back, would it? And it would make me as bad as Sally. So, no. No more killing."

Peter released the tension on the trigger. In the corner of his eye, he saw Lewis relax his two-handed stance. A faint expression ghosted across Shepard's face. It might have been a smile.

"What about Oliver's offer," said Peter. "Do you want to stay?"

She looked at Oliver. Again Peter saw her strength, her self-possession.

Something had changed up in that black barn with her dad. He'd have to ask her about it. He wanted nothing more than to walk through this orchard with her in the light of day, to talk to her, to make her laugh, to see the brilliance in her bright eyes.

He could spend a lifetime at it, if she'd let him.

Was this what it was like, to fall in love?

But she wasn't looking at Peter. She was looking at Oliver.

"Tell me who you work for."

"We're an unofficial group," said Oliver. "Washington would prefer not to know that we exist. But we do, because some tasks are necessary, and should remain secret. Like this one. Unfortunately, Sally was one of ours."

"So, what?" she said. "You just decide what happens? Who lives, who dies? No oversight?"

"We have oversight at the highest levels. But because situations develop and evolve rapidly, we often make significant decisions in the field. We are frequently forced to choose between a bad option and a worse one."

"What will you do with Chip Dawes?"

"Our funding is directed through a series of useful shell companies. We plan to incorporate Mr. Dawes's organization into our operation. This is why he remains alive and in good health. So we can transfer ownership and assets."

"And after that?"

Oliver's face was politely opaque. "That depends entirely on Mr. Dawes."

"Why should I trust you?" she asked. "Why should I believe a thing you've said to me today?"

"You're alive to ask that question, are you not?" His face warmed with a soft smile. "Conversely, I already believe that I can trust you. Because you and your friends came here to take action. Not for yourselves, but for others. An admirable sense of mission, and one much lacking in our society today. But you never answered your friend's question. Will you stay? Will you help?"

She stared at Oliver. "If I do, I get to determine what happens here," she said. "I'm the boss. Full and final say."

Oliver nodded. "As long as the technology stays in our hands, and our hands only. I can have it in writing tomorrow. Tell me the language you need."

"Then yes," she said. "I'm staying." She looked at her dad. "He's the one who needs looking after now, not me. I can look after myself."

Yes, thought Peter. She sure as hell could.

58

___

Peter set up his tent beside the cook shack. There was a bathroom nearby, and a kitchen for breakfast, and it was far from the site of the killings, although he could still smell the burning car. If he closed his eyes, he could still see the whole thing. And Sally Sanchez jerking backward beside him, the back of her head gone soft and bloody.

June was with Oliver Bent in the main house, ironing things out.

He unrolled his sleeping pad and thought about that psychologist in Oregon, telling him to learn to meditate. To find a support group. To get on with his life.

Well, hell, he thought. I can do that.

Sometime after midnight, as he lay there thinking in the dark, she came through the flap of the tent, naked as the day she was born, all showered and soap-smelling, her skin cool from the spring air.

It was gentle and slow, and toward the end, she cried.

Afterward, he wondered aloud whether she had walked naked all the way from the main house.

No, she told him. It was too cold. She'd tucked her warm clothes under the tent fly to keep them dry.

. . .

THE NEXT MORNING, they walked side by side through the orchard, the buds straining against their casings. He could smell the greenery just aching to burst forth into life.

She said, "I don't know if you're ready for domestic life, Peter."

"I am," he said. "I really am. Tell me what you need me to do, I'll do it."

She stopped and turned to face him.

"I need you to already know what to do," she said gently. "And you don't. Not yet. So I want you to go away. Whatever the hell it is you've got in your system, work it out."

Peter opened his mouth, but he didn't know what to say.

"I'll wait for you," she said, "but not forever. Because I need all of you. Not this half-life you're living now, without work, without a home. I can't spend my life in a tent. So don't come back until you're ready to sleep inside a real house, in a real bed."

She put a soft hand on his cheek. The spray of freckles across her face, her pixie-cut hair, he thought she'd never been so beautiful.

Then she turned and walked alone, back the way they had come, toward the big farmhouse under the sheltering maples, in the shadow of the black barns.

EPILOGUE

The old green pickup with the mahogany cargo box rumbled down the arrow-straight road. Lewis was behind the wheel. The ache in Peter's leg had gotten worse.

They both saw him at the same time, an ordinary figure seeming pale and insubstantial in the bright afternoon sun. He'd just left one of the plastic-sheeted greenhouses, walked to the next in line, pushed open the flap and stepped inside.

Lewis hit the brake before Peter could say anything. They both needed to know.

The engine was clearly audible, but they closed their doors with a thump, just to make sure he understood. They weren't trying to sneak up on him. A few goats nibbled on weeds from the compost piles.

He pushed the flap open with a gun in his hand, but it disappeared so quickly Peter almost doubted it was ever there. He looked at them without speaking.

"Is your name really Shepard?" asked Peter.

Shepard nodded.

"I'm Peter. This is Lewis."

Shepard just looked at them. His face was impossible to read, but Peter felt something there. Not hostility, but a kind of curiosity. As if Peter was an object of study, and Lewis, too.

"Are you really retired?"

Shepard blinked twice. "I believe so," he said, as if he hadn't been entirely sure until that moment. "I've lost interest in the work."

"What else will you do?"

"Recently I've developed an interest in gardening."

Lewis smiled his faint tilted smile. "Vegetables? Or flowers?"

"I'll start with tomatoes," said Shepard. "I've always liked tomatoes."

"You know Chip threatened my parents," said Peter. "Was it you he would have sent?"

"That would have been his intent," said Shepard.

"I'm curious," said Peter. "Would you have gone?"

Shepard regarded Peter with the slightest air of disdain. "I'm not an animal."

"So I don't have to worry about you."

"That depends," said Shepard. "On whether I have to worry about you."

"No," said Peter. "We're good." He put out his hand, and Shepard took it.

He didn't look like much, Peter thought. But there was a lot to him. You could feel the invisible intention there, the force of his will. The knowledge that it would allow him to do whatever he found necessary.

Which was basically Peter's attitude, too.

"If you see me again," said Peter, "don't shoot."

"I told you," said Shepard. "I'm retired."

They got back in the truck and Lewis gunned it down the road. "You believe him?"

"What, that he's retired? Or that he wouldn't have killed my parents?"

"Both," said Lewis.

"Yeah," said Peter. "I do."

Lewis shifted into third. "Why?"

"Same reason I knew you'd be up on that rocky outcrop," said Peter. "Your word means something to you."

Lewis gave Peter one of his elaborate shrugs. "All any of us got, in the end," he said. "Listen, you gonna need another driver pretty soon. I got to find an airport, get back to Dinah and the boys."

"Portland okay?" asked Peter. "I'm headed down to Eugene, to see that shrink I told you about."

Lewis smiled his tilted smile. "Jarhead gotta stop camping out someday."

AUTHOR'S NOTE

I began to research the first Peter Ash novel, *The Drifter*, by talking with veterans and reading about their experiences both overseas and returning home.

I'm grateful to be able to continue those conversations, in a variety of ways, with veterans of wars in Iraq, Afghanistan, and Vietnam. A number of you told me how much *The Drifter* meant to you, and that I "got it right." Those conversations are the best reward for any writer, especially this one.

Thanks to all who shared your experiences and helped this civilian get it as right as possible. Comments and suggestions are always welcome.

Burning Bright has a lesser emphasis on Peter's post-traumatic claustrophobia than *The Drifter*. This is due in part to the requirements of the book, which takes place largely in outdoor settings, and also because I want to begin to show Peter's path through this particular challenge. Just as the veterans who experience the symptoms of post-traumatic stress aren't defined solely by those symptoms, Peter isn't defined by them, either.

We know a great deal more about post-traumatic stress than we used to, and there is more help available now than ever before. Simple steps like meditation and exercise, along with writing in a journal or talking with others with similar experiences, can make a big difference.

For those who'd like to learn more, *Once a Warrior Always a Warrior* by Charles W. Hoge, MD, is a hands-on manual for those suffering from post-traumatic stress, or for anyone whose loved one may be suffering. I also recommend *The Evil Hours* by David L. Morris, both a memoir of post-traumatic stress and a deep exploration into its causes and remedies.

MOST OF THE TECHNOLOGIES presented here are very real, although not necessarily in the form I've given them. I thought I was writing ahead of the curve, but the curve is catching up fast.

Cognitive computing and machine learning are revolutionizing how we interact with the world, from voice recognition in our devices to facial recognition at our borders to industrial robots teaching themselves to solve physical challenges.

IBM's Watson, a "cognitive computer" once best known for beating three human *Jeopardy!* champions simultaneously, now aggregates and summarizes diffuse information for IBM clients.

As I write this, a large technology company is testing a solar drone that can stay aloft for three months at a time, designed to provide Internet access to remote parts of the globe. By the time this book is in print, those drones may well be in use.

Our ever-advancing technologies can have the effect of leveraging our mere human efforts into something greater. We can learn more, know more, build more, do more—and that's wonderful. But access to these tools is not limited to those with good intentions. A small determined group can do a lot of damage. Large institutions, both public and private, operate with few controls in a fast-changing environment.

For some reason, I don't find this entirely comforting.

Acknowledgments

Thanks as always to Margret and Duncan for putting up with me during the process of writing this book, and to the rest of my friends and family for their support and enthusiasm and constant salespersonship. If you've ever met a member of my immediate family, especially the women I'm lucky enough to be related to by blood and marriage, the odds are good that you now own at least one of my books.

Thanks again to Barbara Poelle for being my hotshot New York agent, and to Heather Baror-Shapiro, for getting Peter in print overseas. Thanks as always to Sara Minnich for her lapidary eye and ear, and to the other readers and editors who have made this book far better than it would be otherwise. Thanks to the design team who made this book so beautiful, and to Putnam for believing in the last book, and this book, and the next two to come.

Thanks to the Putnam publicity and marketing mavens, including (but definitely not limited to) Stephanie Hargadon, Ashley McClay, and Arianna Romig, who help get books into the hands of readers, and keep me talking to interesting people. You didn't get any credit on the last book, because I had no idea how important your work is and how much it contributes to the success of every book. Please consider this thanks retroactive and extending indefinitely into the future.

ACKNOWLEDGMENTS

Thanks especially to all those great local booksellers who stock my books and press them into the hands of readers, most especially those who have invited me into their stores. Book people rock. Local bookstores rock. (Boswell Books in Milwaukee *totally* rocks.)

Thanks to Richard Preston, whose book *The Wild Trees* rekindled my interest in redwoods and the people who climb them. It's a fascinating true tale about the men and woman who have spent their lives learning about the biology and ecology of these giant trees—you should read his book next, if you haven't already. Peter's climb was inspired by Preston's account of Steve Sillet's far more challenging and risky first ascent of a redwood. Any errors I've made about trees and tree-climbing technology are entirely my own.

Thanks to Todd Schultz, friend, neighbor, and mechanical genius, for information how to roll an old Subaru and drive away, not to mention the ongoing repairs to my own cancerous POS pickup. You don't know it yet, but I'm going to need your help on the next book, too.

The Subaru scene was inspired in part by the experience of family friends who were forced off the highway at high speed by a drunk driver. Although their Subaru rolled multiple times, thankfully they walked away from the accident with no significant injuries. I don't own a Subaru, but as testimonials go, this is a good one.

Thanks to Paul Horvath, MD, emergency room physician in the Mayo Clinic network. Paul helped with crucial medical details, providing me with just the right amount of physical harm to our heroes.

John Schatzman, CLI, helped me with ways and means of finding people. John wears a white hat, but he also knows how the black hats operate—he really should have his own TV show. I didn't use nearly enough of John's expertise in this book, but I promise to use more in the future.

Thanks to National Public Radio's *Planet Money*, whose series on Belize and pliable corporate identities got me started down that particular rabbit hole. Thanks to MIT's *Technology Review*, which amazes me on a regular basis.

Last but not least, thanks to Steve, Jan, and Karina Lochner, for putting me up, keeping me amused, and reminding me how beautiful Northern California can be, especially with good company. For the record, I was present when Steve's car was hit by a falling drone at a campsite on the California coast.

I shit you not.

02/17
MG